RAVENSCRAIG

RAVENSCRAIG

A Novel

Sandi Krawchenko Altner

Franklin and Gallagher, LLC
Publisher

Ravenscraig

Published in the United States by Franklin and Gallagher, LLC, Boca Raton, Florida. This edition released January, 2013.

Photo credits:

Linotype machine by Scientific American, published August 9, 1890
Cover Model: Katiana Krawchenko, by Sandi K. Altner
Cover background stock imagery © Thinkstock
Author photo by Bob Altner

Third edition. Originally published in Canada by Heartland Associates, Inc., Winnipeg, Canada, November, 2011.

For more information visit the author's blog at: www.altnersandi.com

ISBN-10: 0988224917
ISBN-13: 978-0-9882249-1-9

Library of Congress Control Number: 2012903401

Altner, Sandi Krawchenko, 1956-
    Ravenscraig/Sandi Krawchenko Altner

Grateful acknowledgement to:

The Manitoba Archives, the Manitoba Legislative Library, City of Winnipeg Archives, the Hudson Bay Archives, Heritage Winnipeg, the Jewish Heritage Centre of Western Canada, the McCord Museum, Library and Archives Canada, and especially the Manitoba Historical Society and its many passionate volunteers who have painstakingly transcribed valuable documents and shared scholarly works through their fantastic website.

A special thank you to:

Louis Kessler, Manuel Gottlieb, Janet Harrison, Sandra Altner, Greg Klymkiw, Peggy MacKay, Karen Boxer, Donna Turner, Katiana Krawchenko, Bob Altner and Mary Krawchenko for their numerous readings of the developing manuscript and their helpful suggestions.

Donald Weidman, Sid Green, Murdoch MacKay, Laurie Mainster, Olga Fuga, Allan Levine, Russ Gourluck, Burton Lysecki and Stan Carbone who told me stories and pointed me to research.

Rabbi Dan Levin, Rabbi Merle E. Singer and Rabbi Jessica Spitalnic Brockman who enrich my life with Jewish learning.

And finally with love and a full heart I thank my daughter, Katiana Krawchenko, who always encourages me, and Bob Altner, my husband and dearest friend, without whom this book would never have been written.

For my mother, Mary Krawchenko, the family historian, who keeps exact records of the most unimaginable things. Mom is my hero.

And for my father, Carl Krawchenko, whose memory is a blessing. Dad knew every back lane in Winnipeg and had the best stories. He loved machines and would have been especially taken with the Linotype.

Together, with love and strength our parents, Carl and Mary, raised the five of us children: Margaret, Chris, Kathy, Joey, and me, to know the value of working hard and the importance of remembering where we came from.

1
Ravenscraig Hall
May 21, 1895

In the end, it was the magnificence of the library at Ravenscraig Hall that persuaded Rupert Willows to purchase the house, despite the ghastly exterior of the mansion. The library was as luxurious as the front of the house was hideous. He wanted this home and he was determined to have it. But first, he would indulge in just a bit more tortuous play with the squirming realtor. He had thought the man would be a little more challenging, but he was amused, all the same.

The estate agent, Percival Wright, slack-jawed and sweating, was quite shaken by the unexpected exchange with his client. He removed his spectacles and sat quietly mopping his brow as Mr. Willows inspected the library. What an afternoon this had turned out to be. How utterly naïve he had been in his assessment of the man.

As he concentrated on calming himself, the realtor's mind traced the events that had brought him to this moment of intense embarrassment. It had all started in the most mundane fashion.

His introduction to Mr. Willows had come in the form of a letter, hand-delivered to his office. The stationery was of high quality and the penmanship neat, vigorous and cultured. The writer's name was unfamiliar, but that was nothing unusual. Wright assumed Mr. Willows was new to town, one among the horde of tycoons, investors and tradesmen flocking west to make or increase their fortunes in the booming economy. The man had an impressive style. It was obvious that this Mr. Willows had a great deal of experience in the business world and was highly educated. A no nonsense captain of industry, Wright assumed, older and very accustomed to getting what he wanted.

The letter clearly stated the writer's interest in the potential purchase of Ravenscraig Hall. It also contained a list of specific

1

conditions under which he would come to see the house. These had initially inclined Wright to refuse the request outright. On the surface, it was a straightforward business matter, but the timing posed an exceedingly awkward situation.

Ravenscraig was not yet on the market. The owner, Dr. Alexander McDonnelly, had just been laid to rest a few days earlier. Approaching his widow to show the property to a prospective buyer so soon after the funeral would be in the worst possible form. It couldn't be done, Wright had thought as he carefully re-read the letter. The accidental death of the respected doctor had been a great tragedy. No. To push his grieving widow, even to discuss selling at this time, would be seen as indelicate at best and unspeakably callous at worst. He had sighed with disappointment as he dipped his pen to form a response. But then instead of writing, he found himself grappling with temptation.

Wright, meek and polite, saw himself as a moral person, forever waiting for his turn at a lucky break. Alas, while ambitious men climbed the rungs of success, he seemed to always be the one steadying the ladder, boosting the others upward. Thinking about it irritated him.

Now, he was faced with a most disturbing dilemma. Providence had brought him a chance at a very substantial commission. Was an opportunity like this not the very reason he had come to Canada? Why should Percival Wright not be allowed to profit when everyone else seemed to be moving ahead?

Willows must certainly know about the death. It was all over the newspapers. He may have even been at the funeral for the beloved doctor. Such a large affair, it was. Everyone who was anyone seemed to be in attendance. Wright had heard the whispers of the graveside gossips. How terribly unfortunate that the old couple had lived in the house a mere three months before the doctor's death. Surely the widow would not want to stay there. The murmured words played repeatedly in his mind and emboldened his flirtation with greed.

He knew the agent's fee on the sale would be tremendous and he knew, too, that if turned down, Mr. Willows would quickly find someone of lesser character to step in and collect the windfall. Wright had stared out his window, mulling it over, and before long the answer slipped neatly into his consciousness. It really wasn't a matter of greed at all. Above everything, Percival Wright was a good and decent man. It was his duty to look out for poor Mrs. McDonnelly to be sure that she got every penny that a professional agent could possibly squeeze out of a buyer for her benefit.

Committed to the considerable trouble he would face in order to make the arrangements, Wright had dashed off his response, stating his agreement to Mr. Willows' requirements that the property would be cleared of all servants, that their meeting would consist of just the two of them, and that whatever business they might conduct would be kept strictly confidential. With a shiver of excitement, he sent the note off with the message boy.

Then came the horrible visit to the widow. Wright had had no choice, really, but to risk offending her. With pious solemnity, he had carried his hat in his hand and slipped his calling card into the butler's silver tray.

He still smarted from the shame he felt at her tears. Mrs. McDonnelly had been so dreadfully stubborn in her determination not to leave her home during her time of mourning. Broken and pitiful, she had whimpered that she found Mr. Wright utterly shameless and unkind in coming to speak business with her under the pretense of a bereavement call.

She had left him no option, really, but to frighten her. Perhaps he had exaggerated the financial burden of Ravenscraig just a tad, and it may not have been entirely necessary to give her the impression she would land in a poorhouse without her husband to pay the upkeep of the mansion, but he was sure it would all come out right in the end if he could just bring her a buyer. He would release her from Ravenscraig and she would live comfortably for the rest of her life in a much more affordable home. It was a pity that she had taken his words so hard, but truly, it couldn't be helped. He had to get her out for Mr. Willows to visit, and he simply didn't have the time to do it with finesse.

So much work had gone into making these arrangements that by the time he had arrived at Ravenscraig for the meeting, Percival Wright was obsessed with thoughts about the potential sale. He had calculated the commission to the penny and created a list of all of the things he would do and buy with his hard-earned money.

So it was that he readied himself with particular care for his appointment with Mr. Willows. Dressed in his best suit and carrying his fine new walking stick, he had arrived by taxi two hours early to be certain everything was in order.

Ravenscraig, imposing and palatial, was located in Winnipeg's fashionable new neighborhood, Armstrong's Point. The area had only become available for development in recent years but already it was among the city's most sought after residential locations. Nature had created an ideal setting for discriminating buyers in search of a distinctive address within a short distance of the city's business center. The point was a peninsula, naturally formed by a sweeping horseshoe bend in the Assiniboine River. Large enough to accommodate one hundred estates, yet small enough to remain forever exclusive with its gated points of entry, it resembled a private park; a lush, green playground filled with birds and rabbits and winding riding trails that connected one mansion to the next. Wright adored the area with its luxurious homes and picturesque carriage houses. It reminded him of the English countryside.

On the day of the meeting, he had used the extra time to familiarize himself with the layout of the property and to plan his tour. The house was every bit as grand as any in the city and he could imagine how impressed Mr. Willows would be. They would start in the elegant breakfast room and proceed to the dining room, then the drawing room and the conservatory before viewing the upper floors. He would save walking the grounds for last.

Wright had made his way down to the riverside to inspect the gardens. He looked out over the water and practiced his greeting aloud. He needed to be at his very best performance. Mr. Willows had clearly wanted to be first in line to see the property. Perhaps he was ready to make an offer this very day.

Wright checked his pocket watch; he still had twenty-five minutes before their appointment. Then, the sound of a carriage arriving sent him hurrying along to the front of the house where he was stunned to see that Mr. Willows had driven himself to Ravenscraig. Good heavens. To have a fine carriage and no chauffeur was simply déclassé. It was all quite shocking. No gentleman of any recognized standing would consider doing such a thing.

"I require the strictest privacy," Mr. Willows had offered in place of a greeting as he bounded out of the rig. "We will start with the coach house, stable and gardens. Then, when we enter the house, I wish to first go below stairs to inspect the servants' quarters and the kitchen before touring the main rooms."

Wright was simultaneously offended and captivated by the man's raw power. Tall and strikingly handsome, Rupert Willows' posture and movement suggested a prowling, exotic animal. His eyes shone with success and confidence, but there was no humor in them. Wright found it impossible to read his background in his bearing. His accent was English but with a hint of something unusual, something that he couldn't place. Even more surprising, he was much younger than Wright had thought he would be, appearing to be in his late thirties. Despite this, Willows bore the signs Wright most wanted to see. He seemed to be very wealthy.

The agent thrust his hand forward and started selling. "Well, hello, Mr. Willows. I'm so very glad to make your acquaintance. This is quite an amazing property, I assure you, and it is my great pleasure to be able to show it to you. Are you new to Winnipeg?"

Willows stopped and stared at him in silence. Immediately, Wright realized that his prattling on about the many features of the house and the neighborhood would only serve to annoy his client. Willows was certainly not a man interested in small talk.

They set off on the tour of the property with very little conversation, which left Wright somewhat flustered and confused as to how to behave. Other than the initial tour instructions, Mr. Willows' only remark had been that the perennials were well-chosen and that the gardens were surprisingly well advanced for a property so recently constructed.

The man was quite odd, indeed.

Wright responded to this discomfiting silence by speaking in quiet tones and offering information that was straightforward and to the point. There was no reaction. Nothing. Not even a polite nod. In his twenty years of selling real estate, Percival Wright had never had a client like Rupert Willows. A response would come, he reckoned, only when the man had something to say.

Their tour moved well into an hour and as Wright surreptitiously studied Willows, his optimism for a sale began to slip away.

Willows had the air of the American moneyed-class, yet showed no signs of Ivy League snobbery. He was an enigma, or perhaps nothing more than a poseur. Wright suddenly got it. Willows must be a Toronto man. Yes. He was a Toronto man who had adopted the style of a risk-taking Westerner and pretended a taste for fashionable clothing. New money. That was it. Willows was a voyeur using a real estate man to get a peek at how the wealthy furnish their homes, perhaps so that he might copy it in inexpensive imitation.

Wright was instantly incensed. Willows had put him and the owner of the house through a great deal of anguish and inconvenience for nothing. The bastard.

Percival Wright inhaled sharply and his eyebrows arched into the disappointment that came with solving the puzzle. There would be no sale here. The man was a bloody charlatan.

"Was that a snort?" Willows asked.

The question was completely inappropriate from one gentleman to another. Wright felt as though he had been roundly clipped with a riding crop. Deeply insulted, he responded as a schoolmaster offering a sarcastic reprimand to a youngster.

"I beg your pardon. Please do forgive me, sir."

Rupert's eyes snapped and his back stiffened. Wright read confirmation that he had gained the upper hand over the play-actor. The jig was up. He saw no need to make a scene, but he was anxious to wrap things up and unload the unusual Mr. Willows so he could get back to his office. The facts he had collected to help persuade Mrs. McDonnelly to absent herself from the premises came handily back to mind.

"You do understand, Mr. Willows, that a house this size will take a ton of coal each day to keep warm in winter?" Wright's anger brought haughtiness to his tone. "I assume you've never spent a winter here. Our climate is not for the faint of heart. Naturally, heating will be expensive. However, if one is in need of economizing, one might consider closing the west wing of the house to reduce heating costs and to cut down on the number of servants required. Now, if you will come this way we will find our way to the library."

Wright threw his shoulders back and marched briskly down the hall. At the library door he wheeled to face his client and slipped his watch out of his waistcoat.

"Oh dear, half past four o'clock already? I do hope I am not keeping you, Mr. Willows."

Rupert seized on him, as a snake about to strike a rabbit. His words were cold, quiet and devastating. "Don't be cheeky, Mr. Wright. There are plenty of finance men in the city who can handle the simple sale of a property. I chose you to show me Ravenscraig because of your mediocre level of success. I don't want my business getting about, and it is quite obvious that you do not travel in the circles that concern me."

Wright flushed as he pushed his sweaty palm against the library door. The rebuke hung in the air, like the smell of smoke that lingers after a pistol shot. He steadied himself against a marble side table as his wits raced to catch up with his emotions. He had completely misread the man. Willows was a serious buyer after all. With shame and relief colliding in his brain, Wright's mouth broke free like a runaway colt.

"Please do accept my apology, Mr. Willows. I certainly mean no disrespect. You see, I haven't been feeling quite like myself, and I don't think so clearly at times. It's the missus, you see. She is quite unhappy with me and I am afraid she might want to leave me, and I find I get so distracted I just can't think. Oh, I care for her so much. You see, I just—"

"Shut up, Mr. Wright. You sound like a scared schoolgirl. Sit down and get hold of yourself."

"Yes, sir."

Wright slid into a chair and listened to the silence until the sound of his own heartbeat started to thud in his ears. His cheeks flushed with heat and his jaw pulsed. Eventually, a kind of delirious giddiness seeped through him in the same way it does a coward who has emerged from a gunfight and come to realize he is not bleeding. He pressed his handkerchief to his brow and prayed he had not sweated through his good jacket. What a day. How excruciatingly embarrassed he felt.

Meanwhile, Mr. Willows, it seemed, was completely unaffected by their exchange. Wright watched him as his gaze moved slowly and intently about the room. There seemed something akin to reverence in his attitude as he examined the many fine furnishings. Whoever this man was, he was most assuredly rich and powerful and it appeared he might well intend to be the new owner of Ravenscraig Hall. Wright thanked his lucky stars that he was still in the game.

The library had captivated Rupert Willows. Every detail and design choice was to be admired. The afternoon light streamed into the room through three oversized windows that rose to the ceiling. Set deeply, they were draped in heavy red and gold fabrics, each framing a tranquil view of the gardens and the river beyond them. Gaslight sconces were precisely aligned on the mahogany walls to draw attention to an impressive collection of paintings. Leather-bound books stood in perfect rows behind beveled glass doors. The room positively smelled of success.

The focal point was a large, conspicuously expensive desk that had been placed to take advantage of the natural light. Rupert ran his hand along its edge as if to absorb its richness.

He had ached to possess a library like this, to live in a mansion as grand as this. As the owner of Ravenscraig Hall, he would immediately be recognized as a man of importance. The rest that he wanted would come in time.

What Rupert Willows had so effectively concealed from the balding and battered Mr. Wright was that he actually was a charlatan. Even his wife did not know that he had completely rewritten his history to lock away the shame and cruelty he had borne as a boy on a dirt-poor farm in Ontario. Moving up to a mansion as fine as Ravenscraig would be the final step in burying the truth. No one would ever know that Rupert Willows had come into the world as Reuben Volinsky, the son of a hard-drinking immigrant from Russia.

Rupert was blessed with ambition, a brilliant mind, and a wicked talent for persuasion. By most standards, he appeared to have done all right for himself in Winnipeg. The public perception, carefully fueled, was that his construction business had taken off when he moved his family to Winnipeg during the land boom of the 1880s. It was a believable tale of embellished facts and outright fiction. Rupert had worked hard and earned success in business, but it never would have happened without his having married a wealthy woman.

His life was now solidly upper middle class. His construction company was profitable and growing, and he lived in a handsome, fourteen-room home on Broadway. He and his wife traveled, attended theater regularly, and were occasionally invited to dine with people in the better class. Despite all that, Rupert remained terribly frustrated, for what Rupert craved most was power. He wanted to turn polite smiles at his remarks into a driving interest in his opinions.

Ravenscraig would make that possible.

Residing in an impressive home and hosting lavish parties were essential steps to gaining acceptance among those in the tight circle influence brokers who were at the centre of everything that moved in the city. These were the men who ruled Winnipeg, planned its developments and wrote its history, all the while becoming richer and more powerful with every decision they made. Winnipeg existed for their betterment and the rest of the population benefitted from their determination to grow the city. It was the foundation of Winnipeg's outstanding success.

Old money, prestigious educations, and blood connections to men of importance were the standard entry requirements to this group that was officially recognized as the Winnipeg Board of Trade. A select few among them were self-made men like James Ashdown, a successful tradesman who had come early into the game. Catholics were not welcomed, and Jews were shunned outright. Rupert knew all the rules and had spent years preparing to step up to be recognized. Though he had ached for it, no invitation had come to sit on the right committees, or to become a member of the Manitoba Club. Stuck in the middle class, he remained almost invisible. But that was about to change. The way the city was growing, the men of power had shown a willingness to open their doors to overnight millionaires, provided of course, that they were Protestant.

As he drank in the tasteful decor, Rupert felt himself being seduced by the fragrance of leather and freshly polished wood. He could see himself working here. He could see men of authority reaching over the desk to shake his hand, and then accepting an offer to sit together with brandy and cigars to discuss business opportunities. He could hear their compliments and their hearty laughter at his clever jokes.

At long last, the right circumstances were upon him to make buying an extravagant home possible. Not only had he just won a substantial building contract, but he had also received an unexpected windfall. He was dreadfully sorry about the recent passing of his wife's father in Montreal, but utterly delighted with the resulting inheritance being placed in his hands at such an opportune time. The check had arrived on the very day that the newspapers reported the death of Dr. McDonnelly. He viewed this as a fated occurrence, and his decision to explore his opportunity to buy Ravenscraig was made instantly. He immediately scheduled a meeting with the one person he knew would have all of the information he needed.

Her name was Minnie Woods and she was a prostitute. In fact, she was proud to be known in the press as "Queen of the Harlots." Rupert's friendship with her over the years had proven most valuable. It was through Minnie that he gained his information about the secret lives of the commercial elite. It was because of her that he knew who was building, who was investing, and who was bringing new business links to Winnipeg. He knew their connections to Toronto, New York, and Chicago. He learned who the up-and-comers were in the new western cities of Edmonton and Calgary long before the names and deals became common knowledge. And he learned a great deal about the members of the Board of Trade.

As he expected, Minnie was ever so delighted to share stories about the affairs of Dr. McDonnelly and his new mansion. The fees were a little pricey, but her information was always solid, and as Rupert was so fond of telling Minnie, it truly was a pleasure doing business with her.

Rupert stood tall and clasped his hands behind his back in the manner he had seen demonstrated by the Prince of Wales in newspaper photographs. Carrying himself in this way, he moved forward across the thick carpet and then slowly walked the perimeter of the grand library, taking his time as he envisioned his future. Perhaps next year he would be able to run for City Council. Alderman Willows. He could already see that 1896 was going to be a wonderful year.

With Ravenscraig, he would simply buy his way into the elite class in the way a high stakes poker game accepts a player with enough cash to sit at the table.

Rupert moved closer to the far wall of the library, so as to appear to the agent to be appraising the artwork. In truth, he knew almost nothing about art, but he was determined that this Wright fellow would be able to tell people that Mr. Willows was a man of culture as well as of business acumen. He stopped in front of a colorful painting of a scene in a garden. He liked the overall impression but thought the artist rather sloppy in his lack of crisp lines and detail. Still, by the fine character of the frame, Rupert knew it to be what he termed "gallery quality" art. He leaned in to discreetly catch the artist's name and instantly had a new game to test the agent's nerves. Rupert so enjoyed these opportunities to separate himself from the common class.

"Not one of Monet's better pieces, but rather impressive in the use of light, don't you agree?" he ventured to Wright.

"Oh, I'm sure I wouldn't know one artist from another, Mr. Willows," answered the now thoroughly humbled Mr. Wright, searching the painting over his spectacles.

"I see," Rupert smiled. He turned to face him and stood silently examining Wright as if he had him on a skewer. Finally, Wright started to twitch and Rupert released him. "Well, then," he said, "tell me about the plumbing. There are five water closets with bathtubs?"

"Seven, sir," Wright sputtered. "Each has been fitted with both bathtub and shower-bath. As you will see when we go upstairs, the utmost care has been taken in providing the most modern conveniences."

"And on this floor?"

"There are four smaller water closets on the main floor. The servants, of course, have their own very modern facilities, as well."

"Splendid," remarked Rupert. "Are all of these amenities connected to the city sewer system, or is that an expense that will fall to the new owner to bear?"

"That is a very astute question, Mr. Willows," Wright said, having gathered his wits. "Few buyers have done the research you have done."

"It pays to be thorough, Mr. Wright. The city can't possibly get sewers installed as quickly as the need is arising."

"Indeed, sir. Not with the current pace of growth. I promise you the plumbing will not be a problem." Wright shuffled through his paperwork to find the documentation he needed. "Ah, here it is, Mr. Willows. The sewage removal from Ravenscraig has nothing to do with the city sewers," he said, tapping the paper in front of him. "You see, all of the pipes in the house are set to drain directly into the Assiniboine River. It is ideal."

"Excellent."   Rupert came around to examine the blueprints.

Wright hesitated a moment, still flinching from the earlier rebuke. He hated to do it, but felt it imperative that the matter of the death of Dr. McDonnelly be discussed. He could not afford another explosive clash with Mr. Willows who may well be waiting for him to say something about it. He cleared his throat and then spoke as if telling a secret.

"The owner had taken care of all of that as he did intend to have every comfort, as you can see. It's very unfortunate that he didn't have a chance to enjoy the home."

"Yes, quite." Rupert saw no need to pretend sympathy and was now anxious to see the rooms upstairs. "And his widow? Will she stay on in Winnipeg?"

"No," Wright grimaced. He still felt guilty for shamelessly pushing her to make her plans. "It is my understanding that she will be moving to San Francisco to be with her daughter and grandchildren."

The tour of the rest of the home pleased Rupert greatly, and he peppered the agent with questions about the most minute aspects of the property.

Wright was, by this time, completely confused by the chatty and engaging manner of his client. Mr. Willows was utterly charismatic. How this could be the same man as in the first part of their meeting was quite astonishing. He would have such a story to tell his Mildred at supper.

Rupert was also tallying expenses while gathering details from his realtor. It was true enough that the cost of Ravenscraig and running it would come close to emptying his bank account, even with the inheritance, but he was well accustomed to risk and simply believed that there was always more money to be made.

Percival Wright could smell the sale. By the time they returned to the library, he was certain he could move his client toward a commitment.

"I expect you will want to make arrangements to bring Mrs. Willows to see the property," he said with just a touch of zeal.

"No. That won't be necessary." Rupert's face was devoid of emotion.

"Oh." Wright was taken aback. "I rather thought you were considering making an offer on the house."

"No. No offer." Rupert moved toward the desk in the library as he enjoyed the perplexed look on the agent's face. He suppressed an urge to laugh as beads of sweat again began to appear on Wright's brow. The man was so easy to manipulate. Rupert sat down at the desk and reached into his breast pocket whereupon he pulled out a small leather folder and flipped it open. He reached for the pen on the desk and dipped it into the inkwell as if he had sat at the desk a thousand times before.

"Instead I am offering payment," he announced evenly. "Here is a check for what I am willing to spend to acquire Ravenscraig. I'm sure you will be able to satisfy the Widow

McDonnelly with this amount. If not, well, good luck with finding your buyer."

When he saw the figure, Wright was tempted to whistle, but fortunately could not manage it because his mouth had gone dry and dropped open. He sat down and stared at the check.

"That will cover the cost of all of the furnishings, of course," Rupert explained. "The check is made payable to your company so that you can keep my name concealed." He leaned across the desk and fixed his gaze on the realtor. "Now listen to me, Wright, because this is crucial. This sale must be kept an absolute secret. No one is to know that anyone other than an anonymous buyer has purchased the property for an undisclosed amount, paid in cash. In fact, I require that you say that very sentence each and every time you are asked about Ravenscraig Hall. Do I make myself clear?"

"Yes, sir." Wright pulled himself from his daze and found his voice. "Very clear."

"And I will tell you most emphatically, that if one word of this purchase reaches my wife before I tell her myself, three to four months from now, the sale will be void. I will hold you personally responsible. We will write that into the contract," Rupert stated. With the deal in place, he was anxious to be on his way. "I will be prepared to take the house over this fall. That should give Mrs. McDonnelly adequate time to make her arrangements."

"Of course, sir."

"There are other details that will have to be worked out, regarding household staff, the possessions Mrs. McDonelly wishes to keep and so on. To this end, if you would consider it, I would like to engage your services, Mr. Wright, to represent my interests until I move into Ravenscraig."

"Yes, certainly, Mr. Willows." Wright felt queasy.

Rupert was suddenly on his feet. "Very well, then. Other than setting a time for our next meeting, our business today has concluded."

Wright bit his tongue against the questions swirling through his mind, all of which he sensed would be disastrous to ask. Chief among them: how could it be possible that the figure on the check was the exact amount that Mrs. McDonnelly had determined to be her selling price? It was as if Willows had been told it in advance.

Rupert stood before the mirror of the front hall and took his time adjusting the angle of his hat. He looked past his own image into the reflection of the bedraggled Wright standing behind him. The agent appeared worn and soggy from the sport, and Rupert was disappointed he had fallen out of the game so quickly. The only thing left was to satisfy his curiosity.

"If you don't mind my asking, how did he die? The owner."

Wright thought for just a moment. For all he knew Willows might have more details than he knew himself and could be testing him on his trustworthiness. Only the truth would do. He shook his head, then licked his lips and blurted the answer.

"It was, I'm afraid, a terrible tragedy. Dr. McDonnelly slipped on a wet floor and hit his head on the iron bathtub."

Rupert slowly turned and Percival Wright stopped breathing.

"Here?" Rupert asked softly.

The agent sensed a blade hanging over his neck. "Yes. In this house."

"You will show me where on our next visit," Rupert smiled as he tipped his hat then ran down the stairs. "Good day, Mr. Wright," he called back to him.

He had the sale. Percival Wright had somehow emerged as a winner. Now, he needed a drink. Mr. Willows had spoken as if he were asking about the location of a spittoon. Wright shuddered at the prickly sensation that traveled up the length of his spine.

2

The Letter from Esther

May 22, 1895

When mail arrived in Zhvanets it was considered to be news for the whole community. If the mail came from outside of Russia, it was further thought to be public property and recipients were often brazenly asked to share their personal news in full detail. Hannah Zigman's letter was from England. It was post-marked, London, where her sister Esther lived with her family in a neighborhood called Spitalfields. She was thankful that the man in line in front of her at the post office got a package from America because it created such a happy commotion that Hannah was able to take her letter and slip out unnoticed.

It had been almost ten years since Hannah had seen her sister, and each letter was a rare treasure. The two sisters had married two brothers, standing together under the *chupa* on their wedding day. Zev married Hannah and Leib married Esther.

Just days after the wedding, the older couple, Leib and Esther, left to start their journey to the new world. Zev had counted out the little money that had been sent by their father from Canada, and insisted that Leib take it. Three men in three different countries together would build the means to bring the family together again, he had insisted. Everyone had hugged each other and said their goodbyes, the men filled with determination, and the women brimming with tears. They would all be leaving mother Russia in their turn, and the family was certain they would be celebrating a reunion in the new world in a matter of months.

As the years went by, instead of tickets, there were reports of hardship and setbacks in the letters from both London and Canada.

Despite all of this, Hannah never lost hope and remained a true optimist. Still girlish in her demeanor, though now twenty-

16

eight, she was gifted with an easy smile and a buoyant heart. She hurried down the path, clutching her mail, and found a stump to sit on where she could read the letter alone.

Esther had started in the usual manner Hannah had come to expect. She sent her love to all of the family and reported that their little girl, Malka, was a ray of sunshine and growing quickly. Esther said that Leib had a new job in a sewing factory, a sweatshop, she called it, and was making good money and their savings were finally building. Hannah flipped the page and braced for bad news, as generally by this point Esther would have run out of good things to say. But instead, her sister had an announcement to make. She had been in contact with an agency that was working to help Jewish families get out of Russia's Pale of Settlement. Help was provided with both processing papers and the cost of the tickets. Esther had made applications to move the entire family and believed it was a matter of months before she would be sending tickets. By fall, they would all be packing and on their way to London, she said, and then, God willing, they would make enough money to continue on to Canada to join Zev's and Leib's father in Winnipeg.

Hannah shouted out with joy as she sprinted down the path to her husband's carpentry shop to share the letter.

As much as his wife was exuberant in nature, Zev was solid and quiet. Hannah burst into his workshop like a summer storm, her words tumbling over each other as she told the story with her arms flying. He held his hands up and shushed his dancing wife, then sat down with the letter. He read it through twice and shook his head. Hannah was ready to sing the news from the rooftops, but Zev was more cautious and insisted they wait. How many times had they already celebrated this kind of announcement? No. He would need more than a letter from Esther filled with hope and promises.

So many plans to leave had already fallen through that Zev had become hardened by disappointment. His father, Baruch, had left Russia in 1883. In his twelve years in Canada he had suffered one setback after another, from failed farms to poorly paying jobs, to an accident that put him out of work and into the hands of a Jewish charity for almost a year.

With Leib and Esther, there was more heartache. There was no gold to be found on the streets of London either, it seemed. Zev, resilient and responsible, had kept his feelings to himself. He had his mother, as well as Hannah and their three children to support, along with watching out for Hannah's parents Avram and Golde, and her younger brother, Shmuel, who was just fourteen. He should have been the one to go to the new world, Zev believed. He was strong and capable and not sickly like his older brother had turned out to be. But such was his lot and he was duty bound to accept it. Until he had the tickets in his hand, he was not going to get too excited about the promise in the letter.

But Hannah was bubbling with happiness. Her kisses fell upon him until he couldn't help but feel his heart lighten as she chatted and hopped about his tiny wood shop.

"Zev, please. I know this time it will work. Please let us tell everyone. What is the harm?"

"The harm? Hannah, dear wife of mine. What if it doesn't happen? Esther is only now applying for the papers. What if there are other people ahead of us? With your parents and your brother and all of us here, we are nine people. Nine tickets. That is very expensive."

"Zev. It has been so long since I last saw my sister."

"Yes, yes, I know, Hannah. I know it pains you. It pains me, too."

Hannah pulled a stool up to sit near her husband and dropped her hands into her lap.

"Let me say something, Zev. Sometimes all we have to live on is hope. Even if it comes to a disappointment at the end, why not have a little time where we can have something to look forward to? A little happiness in this thought that we could leave here, to rejoin our family. Please, Zev. It is the first step to get to Canada. Imagine the joy of your mother to be re-united with your father after all of these years."

"It is a big dream, Hannah."

"To dream is to nourish the heart. Don't let us deny our children the joy of thinking of a better life, Zev. They need this, too."

He wrapped his arms around her and hugged her, then kissed her forehead. His light blue eyes sparkled under the dark curls that dropped down from under his cap. "Oh, my dear Hannah. How did I become so lucky that God would bring me you for my wife? Nothing ever gets you down. Even when things are hard, you always see the brightness in the world. There is no one like you."

"So we can announce our good news?" She held his face between her hands and grinned at him. He smiled back and said nothing. Impatient for his answer she tugged his beard to make him nod. At this, Zev shook his head and laughed.

"Yes, we can tell them. But let's be careful how we do this. If my mother gets wind of this, the news will be all through the entire province of Podolia before the sun sets. I want time to think about it and to ask some questions. I want to know what the rabbi knows of this plan in London. Why don't we wait until Shabbat? Just a couple of days."

"But, my parents," Hannah pleaded. "May I, please, tell them, first? Esther has asked that we do. You read it in the letter. I could visit them tomorrow."

"But they will come to us on Friday. We could tell them then."

"Oh, Zev, I am bursting with this secret. Please, let me go to tell them. Please?"

How could he tell her no? To see her joy was infectious and he couldn't help but get caught up in her good mood. Finally Zev laughed and held her close. The decision was made and together they worked out a plan to allow for the visit while at the same time keeping the secret from his mother.

The next morning, Bayla Zigman brought a final bundle of loaves out from the kitchen and hustled along the path to the stable. Every week she and Hannah baked enough bread to fill two large baskets to be sold in the Moscovitch Meat Shop, which was owned by Hannah's parents. It was always Zev who delivered the loaves on Friday morning. Bayla was not happy about the change in the baking schedule to allow Hannah to deliver the loaves herself a day early.

"Hannah! Zev won't like it that you are taking the bread yourself. Why don't you let him take it tomorrow? He always takes it on Friday morning." Bayla was very fond of her son's wife, but the girl did have a stubborn streak.

"Zev worries too much," Hannah winked. "I won't be long. I'll save him the trip and get a quick visit with my parents. Besides, it is a surprise for Zev. I want to cook a special dinner for his birthday tomorrow, and if he has to pick up what I need, there will be no surprise. You see, Mama?"

"What I see is a hard headed woman who is going to get on a horse, and do what she wants no matter what I say."

"Mama!" Hannah tossed her head and laughed. "It's only an hour's ride. There is much to celebrate, you will see, and I want this to be perfect."

"Is there something more than the birthday?" Bayla asked. "I knew it! You have something you are keeping from me, yes? You have been as jumpy as a sparrow since yesterday."

Hannah couldn't hide her excitement. "Have I?" she teased.

"Another baby?" Bayla clapped her hands together.

"No! Mama, please!"

"Well, what is it, then?" Bayla planted her hands on her hips and pushed her lips together.

Hannah adjusted the two neat baskets and made sure they were properly secured over the saddlebags. "You will see when we tell you."

"You have news? A letter you didn't tell me about?"

"Maybe I do, but I won't say one more word about this. This is for Zev to say, not me."

"You're killing me with the teasing."

"No more talk about it, then."

"But when?" Bayla demanded.

"When Zev says it is time."

"Ach. Be sure to tell Avram and Golde that they raised an impossible daughter!"

"I will send them your love!"

Bayla was less irritated than she pretended. She watched the smooth, confident way that Hannah took charge of the horse and everything else within her path, and could only shake her head. With her wide smile and twinkling eyes, Hannah appeared as a fresh faced beauty, not one day older, it seemed, than on her wedding day.

One final adjustment to tuck a cloth around the bread and Hannah was ready to be on her way. "I will be back before Zev is home for supper."

"Mama, Mama!" Little Isaac ran up the path, waving something in the air. "I have a present for Baba Golde." Isaac handed a small package, wrapped in a cloth, to his mother.

"What is this?"

"It is a special stone, I found in the creek. It is for good luck."

"You could give it to her tomorrow, Isaac. They are coming here for Shabbat and will be with us until Sunday."

"No, Mama, please. Give it to her today. Look how pretty it is." Hannah tussled her son's hair and planted a kiss on his cheek.

"You are a good boy, Isaac. Don't forget to carry the water into the kitchen, for Baba Bayla."

"Come, Isaac." Bayla swept an arm around the boy. "Aaron will be soon waking from his nap and Baba has something sweet for you and your sister to taste."

Hannah hiked up her skirts and mounted the horse, throwing her leg wide to clear the baskets. Bayla folded her arms. "Hannah. You ride a horse like a man."

"A man has it easier. He doesn't have skirts to get in the way," she laughed and nudged the mare into a trot. "I'll have such a story for you! You'll see."

"You know how much I hate secrets, Hannah." Bayla waggled her finger after the younger woman who turned and laughed again as she waved and pushed the horse into a gallop.

Bayla clucked her tongue and shook her head. Hannah was unstoppable. She was a bundle of determination, that girl. A kind woman who never objected to sharing her home with an old lady. Not one day of complaint in all these years of living with her mother-in-law. How Bayla wished that her Baruch could be here to see her joys, to know these wonderful grandchildren they had. She groaned under the weight of her thoughts. She brought her mind back to counting her blessings as she trudged up the path to the kitchen calling out for the children to come taste the apple cake she had made.

A few miles down the road, Hannah looked at the sun in the sky and knew it was just past noon. She hummed a little tune as she approached the last leg of her short journey. Turning off of the main road, she headed for the familiar shortcut through the woods and down into the valley.

It was then that she saw the smoke rising in plumes over the trees. Her blood ran cold. There was a fire in the village. Then she heard them coming. The sound was unmistakable. Ten, maybe twelve men on horseback were thundering down the main road toward her. In a flash, she guided the mare behind a fallen tree and slid off as the horse danced with fright.

The men careened around the bend in the road, crying out their victory at the top of their lungs.

Victory. Terror shot through Hannah as she watched them through the leaves. Some of them brandished bloodied swords overhead. Others held their treasures high. One had a large silver samovar held tightly under his arm. Some had sacks, clanking with the spoils of their raid. And then they were gone, leaving clouds of dust rising from the silenced road. Seized with fear, Hannah turned to look in the direction of the village. Bile rose in her throat and her legs went weak. Breathing deeply, she willed herself to settle the prancing mare and climb back into the saddle.

Her breath came in gasps as she jounced down the hill to the village. Please, God, let her family be safe. The cries and wails reached her ears even before she could see the chaos in the street. Galloping into the village square, she saw people running, and houses burning. A group of people stood in the doorway of her parents' little store, their necks craning to see inside.

"No!" she shrieked as she dropped off of the horse and hurtled her body into the crowd, shouting and pushing with all of her might. Strong arms reached out to stop her. It was Mr. Goresky from the store next door. He held her tight, turning her from the doorway.

"Stop, Hannah! You must not go in there!"

"Let me through. My parents, my brother! Let go of me!" She fought like a wild cat, her arms flailing.

"No, no! Don't go there, Hannah. They are gone."

"Gone? What do you mean, gone?" Hannah heard wailing inside the shop and wrenched herself free. Shoving her way through the bottleneck at the door, she landed on a wet floor. As her eyes adjusted to the darkness, waves of shock hit her. Someone was shouting something and grabbing at her shoulders. The room was unrecognizable. Everything was smashed and overturned. Her eyes landed on the bodies at the same moment she realized her hands were covered with blood. Every ounce of strength she possessed poured into a scream she couldn't stop. Blood. Red, endless blood had pooled from the bodies. The cry died in her throat as the blackness overtook her.

"Someone go for Zev," a woman shouted. Protective arms enveloped Hannah and lifted her as she was swallowed into the safety of darkness. Her eyes fluttered and were suddenly still. Sweet safety. Muddy sounds. Her head lolled back on the arm that supported her as she was submerged into a comfort where voices come from afar.

Outside, weeping women instantly fell upon her, fussing. "Here, use this to bring her around," an older woman pushed forward with a small bottle in her hand.

"No. Leave her rest. Better that she fainted." Mr. Goresky ordered them back as he carried her into his place.

As Hannah came to, she found herself in a kitchen with Sookie Goresky sitting quietly next to her. Pots and pans were strewn about. A table had been flattened and the door hung crazily on one hinge. Daylight spilled through the smashed windows and over food scattered on the floor. She looked in horror at the older woman, unable to speak, yet demanding answers.

Sookie was teetering on hysteria. She hunched her shoulders and stifled her sobbing. Her head shook soundlessly, as she searched for where to begin. "They didn't burn down my house," she squeaked in breathless words. "They left me my house." Sookie started crying in great wracking gulps.

It was then that the full realization burned through Hannah. The raid. Her parents and Shmuel had been murdered. She had seen it with her own eyes.

Sookie held out a cup and Hannah stared back as if not able to comprehend.

"Zev is coming," Sookie said. "Oh, my dear Hannah. I am so sorry. So sorry, sweet Hannah. Your parents have always been such dear friends to us." Sookie set the cup down and reached out for her.

Hannah went rigid as Sookie's tears fell upon her. There was nothing to do. There was nothing that could be undone. A new thought overtook her and stirred fresh terror. "My children!" she screamed.

"No, no! Don't worry. The pogromists went east, not south. The men followed to be sure."

Six people in the village were killed, and another twenty-one injured. Something in Hannah died that day, too. Something broke that would never be fixed and gave way to a darkness that would visit her at times through the remainder of her life.

The screams built inside her until she couldn't hold them back. Now she and Esther were orphans. Her mind was unable to process the horror.

3
Sir Roderick Ballantyne
June 10, 1895

Since the nerve-rattling tour of Ravenscraig, things had gone well indeed for Percival Wright. He was ecstatic upon learning that Mrs. McDonnelly had accepted the offer, and greatly relieved that she refused to see him, choosing instead to communicate through her lawyer. Thus, it was a straightforward piece of business to finalize the deal for the sale of Ravenscraig Hall. The realtor was beside himself with glee and was intent on being indispensible to his new client.

The opportunity came quickly. When Wright handed over the deed of sale to him, Rupert surprised him by asking a favor.

"Now here's the thing, Wright. You've proven yourself reliable, and impressed me with your ability to keep your silence. If you're up for it, I could use your help in something I am trying to arrange. It's a surprise for my wife."

"Certainly. My pleasure, Mr. Willows. Is it her birthday?"

"No." Rupert shook his head and chuckled. "It's rather complicated and must be handled very discreetly. I will give you the details in time, but I have other things to attend to first. Do you know Sir Roderick Ballantyne?"

"The financier, of course. He does work for our firm."

"Could you arrange an introduction for me?"

"Yes, I do believe so." Wright's brow wrinkled. "He holds mortgages for a number of clients. Are you, perhaps, in need…"

"What I need is an introduction, and that is all, Mr. Wright. He's raising money to build a new orphanage. Tell him I am interested in helping and wish to speak with him."

Three days later, Rupert was escorted into the plush waiting room of Ballantyne, Biscayne and Taylor. Rupert judged the firm was worthy of its lofty reputation by the obvious expense invested in the offices. He had high hopes for his meeting. With the Ravenscraig mansion secured as his future residence, the time had come to find a sponsor to help him ascend to the upper class. There were several candidates he had been tracking in the newspapers ever since he had arrived in Winnipeg. He needed a man free of scandal who had considerable wealth and influence, but who was not a politician. He wanted a kingmaker, not someone who was in line for the throne.

Rupert had whittled his list down to three candidates. Sir Roderick Ballantyne, a self-made millionaire and outspoken Scot was Rupert's top choice. Not only did Ballantyne have the ear of the mayor and a leadership position on the Board of Trade, he also owned a spectacular home called Stonebridge, in Armstrong's Point. Perfect.

Fifteen minutes after he had arrived, a flustered young secretary appeared, frothing over with apology.

"I'm so terribly sorry, Mr. Willows. Mr. Ballantyne is in a meeting that is going much longer than he anticipated. Do you mind waiting a few more minutes? May I offer you coffee?"

Rupert was about to respond when a buzzer sounded in the room. The secretary smiled brightly. "He's ready for you. Won't you please come this way?"

"Mr. Wallace, welcome! Do come in." Ballantyne bellowed from his desk, his head down and his meaty hands shuffling papers. His heavy auburn beard, neatly trimmed and combed, stood in stark contrast to the wild and unruly crop of hair that billowed out from his head in a ball of untamed red fury. From his manner, one might expect to hear bagpipes droning every time he entered a room. Ballantyne pushed himself into a standing position. The burly man rose to his full height of just over five and a half feet and pounded his stubby legs around to the front of his desk to pump the hand of his visitor.

Rupert was delighted. Ballantyne was everything he had hoped he would be. "It's Willows, sir."

"Eh? What's that?"

"Willows, Rupert Willows. So good of you to see me, Sir Roderick."

"Aye, that it is. Remind me again why you are here?"

"The orphanage. I believe I may be of help." Rupert was at his charming best.

26

"Oh, my. That's the wife's wee project. What on earth is happening with that? Have a seat, Willows. The gout is killing me and I need a drink," he grunted.

Rupert decided to play it safe. He explained that he was a local builder and was so taken with the project that he was offering to help with the construction, at no cost to the committee raising the money for the orphanage.

"Well that's wonderful news to hear on a dull day in June. And I will be happy to tell my wife about yer generosity. I accept and I thank you on her behalf. I'm sorry, Mr. Willows, how is it that we've nae met before? Would ye be new to town?"

"No, I've been around a few years," Rupert said. "My company is called Willows and Sons. My boys are not yet old enough to be in the business, but they will be one day."

"Is it yer father, then, who started the company?"

"No, no." Rupert chuckled to appear chummy. "My father knew nothing of construction. He was in your line of work. He was an investment banker and did very well in Toronto. A terrific man, he was. He was from northern Scotland. Orkney, actually."

Feigning discomfort, Rupert cast his eyes down. "They're gone, my parents. They died in a fire when I was a child." He hesitated for a heartbeat before he added, "this is my reason for the interest in the orphanage."

While most of this story was a well-practiced and often told fabrication, Rupert had been suddenly inspired to bring in the orphanage angle as a new twist to impress the older man. He regretted the extra words the second they were out of his mouth.

"You were raised in an orphanage, then?" Ballantyne's brow furrowed.

"No, but I might have been had my circumstances not been so fortunate," Rupert skated. "I think of that often and now I want to help children who are in need." Rupert inwardly winced as he watched Ballantyne's eyes squint in skepticism. He had greatly underestimated Ballantyne's intelligence and was angry with himself for the slip.

Ballantyne saw it all and pulled in his horns. He loved a good story more than anything and the best ones were never true. He was curious to hear where Rupert would go with the rest of his yarn, and jerked his chin up to have him continue.

"I went to Atlanta to be raised by my mother's people. Her brother, in fact," Rupert said, regaining his stride.

"Ah ha! Georgia!" Ballantyne slapped his knee. He poked a thick finger at Rupert. "That's why ye sound like ye do. I could nae place the accent. Go on, then."

"My uncle was a Civil War hero and after the war he built a profitable construction business. When he died, the company was sold. I went on to university in Toronto and studied law. I married. Then things started booming here in the west and I moved my family here. I never cared much for the practice of law, but I know a thing or two about construction." Rupert shrugged.

Ballantyne nodded his head. He liked this brash fellow, working to appear humble, when he was anything but that. A smart one, indeed. Rather like he was himself in a younger day.

"Aye. It's a boomin' town, all right. I came out with the old timers in the Wolseley Expedition many years ago, now. It seemed a terrific adventure to volunteer to come out here to put down the Red River Uprising." Ballantyne rubbed his beard. "Humped canon and buckshot over half of creation, we did, cuttin' through bush and climbin' through muck, only to finally get here and find out there was no uprisin' left to be put down. Louis Riel and his men had scattered. The only shots we fired that weren't aimed at deer or rabbits were in a Royal Salute to mark our victory. Hell of a thing. Once I landed here with the lads I could nae stomach the thought of marchin' through the blasted mosquitoes and blood-thirsty black flies to make me way back east again. By the time the railway came through in '85, I was already settled in like a fat flea on a dirty old dog, makin' money hand over fist on land deals. Those were the days to make a dollar in this town. Aye. And 'tis still a good place to make a man's future."

"Indeed it is. I believe Winnipeg is the place to be, Sir," Rupert nodded.

"I am surprised we've nae met before. Where've ye been hidin' yerself? And how'd ye get to me?"

"It was Percival Wright, my realtor, who told me of the orphanage and suggested that we meet. I dealt with him when I purchased Ravenscraig Hall."

"You bought old McDonnelly's place?"

"I did."

"Bloody hell, you did!" Ballantyne exploded. "It isn't even on the market yet and I know at least three of the old guard who are interested in that property!"

Rupert was thrilled at the reaction. He could see the man was greatly impressed and was recalculating his estimate on Rupert's net worth. It was exactly what Rupert had hoped for.

"I certainly did buy it. It's a secret, for now."

"A secret, ye say? What in God's name for?"

"May I ask you keep this in confidence, Sir Roderick?"

"Aye. Ye bet yer wee hairy ass, Willows. Ye got me attention. Make yer story a good one."

"I bought it for my wife. It's a gift."

Ballantyne screwed up his face and stared at Rupert. Rupert met his eyes, took a breath and stalled.

Ballantyne spoke first. "How's that?"

"It's actually a gift for myself," Rupert stated, playing the line for effect. "It's the perfect house for me and I have a feeling my wife might not like it as much. If I present it as a gift, she'll accept it gracefully. She's terribly well-mannered. This way I get what I want and there will be no need for an argument or even discussion."

It was the plain truth.

Ballantyne listened and ran his hands through the red nest on his head. His jowls shook and then a jerking motion started in his belly as laughter sputtered up out of the man and erupted into a rush of raucous outbursts with tears filling his eyes. Rupert sat back in his chair and enjoyed the show.

"'Tis dead brilliant, this plan of yers. I dinnae remember a conversation with as much intrigue since I landed in this bone-freezing, hard-drinking outpost thirty years ago. The most preposterous scheme I've ever heard of. Willows, you are either the smartest man I know or the biggest damned fool. I don't know which it is, but I am glad you stopped by with this tale of yers. A gift for her! It's bloody fantastic."

"I'm happy to hear that because if I may be so bold as to impose on you, I would appreciate your help with my surprise, if you would be so kind."

"Well spit it out, man. I'm still listenin'."

Rupert laid out the plan and Ballantyne laughed until he was wheezing and clutching his chest.

"Aye! 'Tis a bonnie ball-buster of a wee joke, it is! Let's do it. I am more than happy to climb into this canoe with you, laddie, and race for the falls."

The boisterous laughter from the room was so surprising to the secretary that she hesitated before she rapped at the door. This Mr. Willows must be a magician, she thought. "I am sorry to interrupt, but you're due at the Manitoba Club in twenty minutes, Mr. Ballantyne."

"Damn it all to hell, Dorothy! Send a message to the lads I'll be delayed and to start without me." He slammed his hand down and glowered at the clock on the mantle. "Listen, Willows, do you have lunch plans?" And without waiting for an answer, yelled, "Dorothy, tell them Mr. Willows will be joining us."

Rupert felt the thrill having hit a grand slam. "You are too kind," he said modestly.

"I've nae seen you at the club, Willows. How is it possible you are nae a member?"

Rupert felt his chest fill with pride. Finding his sponsor had been as easy as plucking a ripe plum from a tree.

Later at home, Rupert had much to think about in his accomplishments for the day. As he did his best deliberating while in the bathtub, he asked his new man, Jenkins to make the preparations. It amounted to an unusual request given the hour.

"Now, sir?"

Rupert threw his hands in the air. "Pardon me, Jenkins. Was that a question?"

"No, sir. I mean, yes, sir. Right away, Mr. Willows," the butler stammered as he looked at the clock. It was ten minutes before seven.

"What is it, now, Jenkins?"

"Dinner, sir. Shall I tell Mrs. Butterfield to delay until after your bath?"

"Dinner will be on time as usual. I've asked that a tray be sent up to my room after my bath. How is it possible you don't know this?"

"Quite right, Mr. Willows. I beg your pardon. Shall I tell Mrs. Willows, then?"

"Tell her what? I've already spoken with my wife, Mr. Jenkins. Now get along with your business before you annoy me any further."

The servant vanished and Rupert was left to wonder how he had found the stupidest man on earth to add to his household. Hasty decisions always came with hidden costs.

He started to feel the tensions ease the moment he heard the water tumbling into his bathtub. In just a few months he would have the joy of immersing himself in the luxury of the oversize bathtub in his suite at Ravenscraig. He relished the very thought of it. As for the bumbling Jenkins, the man would clearly have to step up his performance if he were to expect to be coming along in the move to the new property.

As he slid into the steaming water, Rupert sighed and thought of his long departed mother. He owed her no small debt in this crowning moment in his life and dearly wished that she were still alive to enjoy it with him. His mother, bless her sweet, determined soul, would have been proud. She would have viewed Rupert's acquisition of Ravenscraig as undeniable proof of his success, and of her own.

Scottish born and headstrong, Annie Hogg had been the driving force in all that he had accomplished in his life. She had made great sacrifices for him, and in Rupert's heart, Ravenscraig was for her.

His father, on the other hand, could burn in hell.

Rupert fingered the deep scar along the right side of his neck. It was just over three inches long and angled down toward his collarbone. He was seared with a branding iron when he was still a boy, when was still Reuben Volinsky.

Rupert remembered the scene as if it were yesterday. He could see his father staggering toward him and grabbing hard at his shoulder with one hand, while waving the branding iron with the other. He aimed for his chest, but the boy wrenched himself free, almost clearing the danger, as the white-hot metal grazed him just below his ear.

Rupert had no idea if his father was still alive, but he hoped that, if so, his life was filled with excruciating pain and suffering. Even leprosy would not be enough punishment to answer for his sins.

What he knew of his father's early life had been told to him in fragments by his mother who had married for love and paid the price. She said Ira Volinsky had been an eye-catching adventurer. Born in Odessa to a young widow with no means to support him, Ira lived on the edge of the law. As a young man with a quick mind and faster fists, he deserted the Russian Army and found his way out of the country. For a number of years he worked and swindled his way through Europe. He was the most exciting man she had ever met, she said, and she found it impossible to resist him.

Annie Hogg met Ira Volinsky in a village market in England. On a whim, she packed her few possessions and left with him for Canada, simply because he asked her. By the time she learned he was running from the police, it was too late.

The couple found no golden life in the new world. With a wife and child to support on a farm that he detested, Ira found solace in vodka.

By the time his son was ten, Ira had become a hard man and a nasty drunk. Reuben hated him. He hated the beatings, he hated the ruined little farm they lived on, and he hated being hungry. As her marriage deteriorated, Annie's child became the center of her world. While her husband scratched out a living on the soil and drank their meager profits away, she focused entirely on her boy.

She enriched Reuben's young life with the stories she told of her privileged childhood and inspired him to make a success of himself. She insisted on cleanliness, proper manners, and good posture. Reuben took to his lessons as a bird to flight. Annie shared her precious little library with him and taught him to read. His ability was well ahead of other children his age. Her teaching and her great skill in buffering the anger of his father had saved him. With her guidance and fierce dedication, a new destiny was created for her son.

Annie had reached her breaking point when Reuben was fourteen. Bruised and bloody, her left eye swollen shut, she waited for her drunken husband to pass out. When he did, she gathered up her clothes and the little money she had hidden away. She and Reuben disappeared to Toronto. She changed her name to Adele and set in motion her plans for her son. Reuben Volinsky was transformed into Rupert Willows. He entered high school and proved to be an outstanding student.

Rupert and his mother lived in a hotel. She told him she was a seamstress and he knew better than to challenge the lie. What she did to earn a living was simply never discussed. But there were signs. He had seen the gaudy clothes and had heard the rough laughter from her visitors through closed doors. He was ashamed of the truth, and more so that he was powerless to rescue her. To her last day, she had remained a lady in his eyes.

It was only on her deathbed that she told him that she had lied about her life. She was not the daughter of barrister, raised in a fine home full of servants, she confessed. She had been a lowly parlor maid who had learned her manners from watching her employers and had been taught to read by a kind housekeeper.

It was a great tragedy for Rupert that his mother had succumbed to typhoid a mere eighteen months after their escape from the farm. It pained him that she never saw him graduate with top honors from university. Even greater was the pain he carried for never being able to provide for her as she had provided so selflessly for him. Just days before her death, her only comfort came in the form of a promise from a southern gentleman who was particularly fond of her. He told her that her son would have a home with him in Atlanta and that Rupert would be educated. When the time came, the boy would enter his construction business, which had flourished in the rebuilding of the south after the Civil War. Adele would not have to worry about Rupert, he had said.

Rupert thrived in Atlanta. The gentleman was kind and true

and kept his word. He was fond of the bright young man and planned a secure future for Rupert in his business, noting how quickly he learned everything that was thrown at him. He told Rupert that he was blessed to have him and that together they would build the company. It would all be Rupert's one day, he said. Sadly, it was not to be. None of the promises were written down. It was a riding accident that claimed the life of Rupert's benefactor, a man still in the prime of life. His wife inherited every penny of the estate and immediately sold the business. Rupert suddenly found himself with no future in the South. With no money, and no pedigree with which to gain entrance to southern society, he returned to Toronto, found work in the building trade and started part-time classes at university, intent on becoming a lawyer. He would starve, he decided, before he would give up on his education. Without an education, he believed his life would be worth nothing.

It was when he first started university and came to know the privileged young men of wealth that Rupert saw the path for his future. He decided he would become one of the richest men in Canada. To do this, he determined he would have to start with marrying a wealthy woman. He had only his charm to accomplish this task, but it proved more than enough.

It seemed a lifetime ago.

Now he had both a rich wife and a stunning mansion. He opened the hot water tap to bring the heat up in his bath. There was only one major challenge left. He needed to be accepted by the men who mattered in Winnipeg, the fastest growing city in the Dominion. With that, nothing would stand in Rupert's way.

4
Zhvanets
September 27, 1895

Zev took his time, methodically going through his chores in the barn. The letter from his brother brought hard news and he needed time alone to plan how he would break it to the rest of the family.

His hands moved firmly over the strong back of his horse as he sought to ease the ache of his horrible disappointment through the familiar work and the comforting sounds and smells around him. The mare's nose pushed against his hand and he rubbed her gently, unable to muster enough cheer to sing the little Yiddish rhymes to her, as was his custom. She was a good and patient worker and he had been fortunate to be able to afford to keep her. Now with his travel plans destroyed, he would not have to scrimp on her feed. She would be the only one to benefit from their new direction, the death of their dreams.

His mother was going to be devastated. It broke Zev's heart to know his father would never again touch his mother's face. They would stay in Zhvanets. There would be no escape from the Pale of Settlement for Zev Zigman and his family. There was nothing to be done about it. Nothing, except get used to it.

For two days Zev had carried the letter in his pocket and brooded about the sad news. He felt crushed under the weight of his troubles. Ten years had now passed since Leib and Esther had made their "temporary" move to England and twelve years since his father had left for Canada. The reunion was never going to happen. Through no fault of his own, Leib had failed. They all had failed.

As Zev spread fresh straw in the mare's stall, his worries settled into a deep sadness for his mother.

Leib was seventeen when his father left, and Zev sixteen. Baruch had headed for Canada with a small party of men and some families who were setting up a farming colony on the Canadian prairies. At the time, Baruch was forty-two and strong and healthy; he believed he was on his way to the golden land. But the farming experiment in Saskatchewan was a disaster and the colony had suffered terrible losses. Starved off the land after three hard years, Baruch had moved to Winnipeg. There, he took what work he could find, digging ditches and hauling water in a cart he pulled by hand. Zev knew that his father had probably gone hungry just to send what little money he could back to his family in Russia.

In Zhvanets, the czar's ever-tightening restrictions made life ever harder for Jews to make a living in the Pale of Settlement. Baruch's sons had grown into men, married and started their own lives. Leib went to London, the grandchildren were born, months slipped into years, and still there were no tickets for the rest to leave. There was only a deepening poverty and a bleak outlook for the future.

Through every day of Baruch's absence, Bayla prayed for her husband's safety. Every letter from him, as infrequent as they were, created a fountain of joy for the family, affirming that he was still alive so many thousands of miles away. Bayla's steadfast commitment stood as a beacon of hope for all of them. Her frequent stories about the good life they had shared for the nineteen years they had together before he left fueled her faith and her unwavering determination to one day join him. God would not let her down, she insisted. He would answer her prayers, in His own time.

How was Zev going to tell her that it was not be? How was he going to tell his wife, still grieving for her murdered parents and brother, that they would live out their lives under the czar's rule?

Zev was a practical man. First he would talk with Hannah. He would show her the letter and together they would reshape their plans for their future with their three young children. As he turned to close the door to the barn, his mother came up behind him. There was deep concern in her voice.

"Zev, are you all right?"

"Yes, fine, Mama."

"Zev, you haven't been yourself for days. Maybe you should talk about what is troubling you. Hannah is beside herself with worry for your health. Are you not feeling well, son?"

"I am not sick, Mama," he answered simply.

"Ah. I see. What is it? Is something wrong?"

"Is something wrong? Yes, actually. We are poor, we are being taunted and crushed by the czar and I have no way of finding a prosperous future for my children. That is what is wrong, Mama."

"Zev! What is wrong with you to talk this way?"

"Mama, I am sorry. I just don't know where to turn anymore. I never imagined we would still be here. Year after year goes by and we are still stuck hard in this place with no future."

"Leib will make the money. You will see. Any day now we should hear about the papers that Esther has promised. Why are you talking this way?"

"It is not so easy for Leib, Mama."

"You have news?" A smile broke across her face and then immediately vanished as he fixed his gaze on her.

"Oh, dear God. You have bad news, then? Has something happened to my Leib?" She drew her apron to her face and twisted it.

"No Mama, he is fine. Esther is fine."

"And Malka?"

"Malka, too, is good. She's well, the little girl."

Zev's resolve started to crack when he saw the tears in his mother's eyes. "Yes, I have a letter. Mama, please, I will give you all the news, but first I must speak to Hannah. Will you ask her to come outside?"

Bayla felt her heart pounding. Aching for the news, yet driven by tradition and respect for her son as head of the family, she fought down her fears and found her footing.

"Yes, of course, Zev. She is putting the children to sleep. I will go sing to them. They need their Baba to sing *Tumbalalaika*, yes?" She forced a smile.

"Thank you, Mama. Please don't worry. We will be all right. After I talk to Hannah, then I will tell you everything."

The little bench was nothing more than a couple of rough

planks set across two heavy logs sawed from tree trunks. But since their babies started to arrive, it had also been his special place for quiet talks with Hannah. The bench sat in the dirt against the south wall of the house, in the shadow of a very old chestnut tree. Zev had built it as a surprise for Hannah and they had talked there many times over the years. She had planted hollyhocks on both sides of the seat to soften the cheerless look of the worn boards on the tired home. The landlord didn't seem to mind. At least, he never asked them to remove them.

Zev sat down and handed the letter to Hannah.

Dear Brother,

I am sorry to tell you that life has turned very hard for us. I envy you the honest work in Zhvanets. "Honest work with honest hands," our father would always say when we were children. Maybe it is just that I am not suited for life in a city. My view of London has changed so much in the years that we have been here. Once I saw it as shining with hope, now I see London as nothing more than dark and damp with mean streets and overcrowded houses. There are not enough hours in the day to make enough money to live from the meager wages that are paid in sewing piecework for the factory.

I fear there is no hope for us to leave Spitalfields. Death is all around us. It has marked my little family and threatens to overcome us every day. We are in a difficult situation, and what I have to tell you is hard to write.

I have very bad news. The money I expected to send to you in this letter is gone. I spent it to pay for the doctor who saved Esther's life. Perhaps it was the shock of learning of the terrible death of her parents and brother that caused the problem, but we will never know. Esther is recovering, yet again, from the loss of a baby. She is very weak, still, and the doctor said that it is only her strong faith that has saved her from dying in childbirth this time. This is the third one now. There will be no other children for us. I thank God our little Malka is healthy and strong. Just a little slip of a child, not yet ten, and already pressed to be a grown up. With Esther too weak to work, Malka has come to work in the factory every day. She pulls the basting threads from the sleeves. She is nimble with a needle and it will not be long before she is able to be a seamstress. She is smart and talented.

Zev, what life is this for a child? No meadow to walk in. No fresh air to take for granted. If she survives to be a woman, will she be too worn from work to be chosen for marriage? With barely a penny to keep my family from starving, there will be no dowry for her. I am lost in my despair. There is no work that I can get that will allow me to care for my family properly, let alone find a way to pay for travel to Canada. As for the agency that helps Jews in Russia, it seems Esther was overly optimistic. We have yet to hear if they can be of help. So many are in need.

I am so sorry, my brother, that I have failed you. I am tormented with guilt that I have let you down. It is my greatest regret that I have been unable to help you.

I beseech you to abandon your plan to come to London. There is nothing for you here. Go instead, Zev, to Canada. Find our father and find work. This is how our family will come to be together again. Perhaps it is our destiny that you will be the one to make this miracle happen for all of us. I beg you to not stay in Russia. The news we hear whispered in the streets and in the synagogue does not suggest there is a future there for you. It will not be safe for you. The pogroms are increasing. I plead with you to pray for strength and be the guide who will bring the family to the New World.

As for me, I have little hope for the future. I see the hollow look in little Malka's eyes and I worry for her safety and well-being if something, God forbid, should happen to her mother or to me.

Promise me, Zev, that you will protect my child if I am unable to do so.

God be with you and Hannah, your children and our dear mother.

Leib

Hannah read the letter and carefully folded it before she gave it back to him.

She shook her head slowly and teardrops rolled down her cheeks. Their hopes and dreams were being crushed by forces greater than they could fight.

Zev wrapped her tightly in his embrace and it was then that she lost the battle to hold back the sobs. He held her while the pain poured from her. The thought of Esther near death frightened her to the core. In time her crying abated and she slid from fear into feeling sorry for herself and with that came shame and guilt. She couldn't help it. The money that went to save Esther's life was the money promised to help pay for their travel tickets in the spring. Money that would save her own family. Another few months and they would have made it out, and joined them in London.

Hannah pulled away from Zev and brushed her tears away with the heels of her hands. She sniffed loudly and blinked hard against the wave of emotion that was closing in on her. She pulled her apron up to swipe at her face as she worked to settle herself. She forced a smile.

"That's enough crying. I am sorry for my tears, Zev," she said as she steadied herself. Zev watched her and did not speak.

They sat quietly for a time, feeling their way. The stillness gradually became filled with the wind in the trees, the rising song of the crickets, and the hurting sigh that seeped from Hannah. She could smell fall in the air as she watched the leaves scurry across the yard like mice. Mice running to hide, she thought, just like we are. Racing to hide, with nowhere to go that the czar would not find them.

The evening sky dwindled into darkness and a gloom settled on them.

Zev stroked his beard and chose his words carefully. "I must think carefully about what Leib has told us in the letter. For now, I think we are best to stay here. Perhaps things will get better, my dear one."

Hannah sat up straight and looked at him directly. "Zev. You must go to Canada."

"That is out of the question, Hannah, and I will not discuss it. What kind of man leaves his wife and children to fend for themselves?"

"A good man, Zev. Your father did."

"He had my brother and me to look after my mother. It was different." Zev saw the hurt in Hannah's eyes and softened his tone. "But even with that, what is the result? I see the pain in my mother's brave smile, the undying belief she will see him again. It is heartbreaking and I won't put you through that. And now it is dangerous. Who would protect you? And her? And our children? No, I won't leave you, Hannah. Never."

"Zev. Listen to me. We have a chance. Your brother is right. It is only you who can make this happen for all of us."

"No. Two women and three children on their own? Aaron is just a baby. I'm sorry. No."

"Zev, please. We have our savings, and we are young and capable."

"Hannah, I know you mean well, but I cannot be thousands of miles away worrying about you."

Hannah paused and looked down the path and they sat in silence for a while. When she turned back to him she took his hand and Zev could plainly see how her grief had changed her. The girl who had laughed so easily was now a woman who burned with strength and purpose. When she spoke it was calmly. There would be no more tears.

"Zev, if we stay we may all die. We may all end up with our throats slit," she said quietly. "It is only with you working for a decent wage that we will have a chance. Winnipeg is growing, your father said. They need workers like you. Young men with skills. It could be all right, Zev. We are young, not yet thirty. We can do this."

Zev took his wife gently by the shoulders and searched her eyes.

"I am saying you should go, Zev. It is our only hope."

He held her close and rocked her in the moonlight, his mind racing with the possibilities.

Zev could sense that the hard times and the violence were not going to stop. The simple fact was that the czar hated the Jews. Over several years now, it had become apparent the czar intended to enforce a solution to the "Jewish question". One third would be converted to the Russian Orthodox Church, one third would leave the country and one third would be killed. Although no one knew with certainty, it was widely believed that the Russian government was the organizer of the pogroms, the attacks on the Jews.

Over the following days, Zev sought the council of trusted friends and community leaders and very soon he was able to make his decision. They would leave Russia and strike out for Canada to join his father. It would be complicated and very possibly dangerous.

There would be many miles to travel just to get out of Russia. Once across the border, there would be papers to secure, bribes to pay, and inspections to pass before the long journey to the New World began.

Most painful to Zev was that they could not go together. They would have to be apart at least a year and most probably longer, for him to earn the money for their tickets. A few days later, he and Hannah had a different conversation on the little bench.

Hannah knew she would need every ounce of strength she could muster for this enormous step. And now he, too, saw that there was no other way to do it. He was going to have to say good-bye to his wife, as Baruch had said good-bye to his. Until they were reunited, Hannah would have to be the head of the family, earn a living for their children, and when the time came, she would have to lead the children and his mother to the new country. She would have to cross the language barriers, deal with the swindlers and hucksters they would encounter on their journey and, most importantly, she would have to take his place to keep their family safe during his absence. It was a monumental undertaking. Despite this, Hannah was confident she could handle everything she needed to do for the family. What she feared was the ocean voyage itself. She had never told her husband that the very thought of the open water terrified her. But this was no time for weakness.

As Zev placed his hands on Hannah's shoulders, they both felt a tremendous weight begin to lift. The decision was made.

"First we will move west, to a little town not far across the border in Austria called Zalischyky. It will take us a few days to get there. It's in the southern part of the region called Galicia, and it is also on the Dniester River like Zhvanets," Zev told her. "It is a safe place where many Jews are living. I know of a rabbi there who will help us.

"I will feel better if you are there, for it will be safer than here."

They decided to leave in three weeks. Once settled in Zalischyky, Zev's skill as a carpenter would earn them enough to get them through the winter months. In the spring, he would go to Brody, where people who were leaving for America were known to gather and he would make the arrangements for his travel ticket and documents. He would then go to the port city of Hamburg to board a ship to Quebec City. And finally, in Canada, he would take a train to the middle of the continent, to Winnipeg.

Winnipeg. It sounded as far away as the moon.

5
Rupert's Surprise
October 11, 1895

R upert stood in front of his full-length mirror and was pleased to see that the scar on his neck was now completely hidden. That twit of a tailor had been so difficult; Rupert had all but marched out of his shop. But now he could clearly see that having stood his ground with the sorry little man had indeed paid off. The alterations that he had insisted be made to his shirt collar and evening coat were exactly right and the end result was a bold reflection of Rupert's very individual sense of fashion.

Every last detail of the evening ahead mattered. For Rupert control wasn't a need, it was a compulsion. Tonight he would present Ravenscraig to his wife. He chuckled at his own cleverness in the elaborate arrangements for the surprise. Everything had been planned to the last detail: every flower choice, every menu item, and every song the orchestra would play had come under Rupert's direct supervision.

Rupert looked at the clock on the mantle and saw how quickly the time was slipping away. "Are you ready, Beth darling? We must be on our way soon," he called down the hall to his wife's dressing room.

"Yes, dearest," came the cheery reply. "I just need another few minutes. I won't be late."

"Excellent, my dear."

As he finished dressing, Rupert anticipated the evening ahead with growing excitement. An illustrious gathering of guests would applaud his elaborate surprise. He would be the talk of the town. Everyone who was anyone would know his name.

Sir Roderick had proved to be a most resourceful and valuable ally. He had taken charge of the invitation list and kept the true location a secret. The invitation was to a concert at

Stonebridge Manor, the Ballantyne residence, conveniently located just a short distance from Ravenscraig. Rupert had enjoyed the weeks of secrecy. Twenty-four couples were invited, all of them quite rich, some of them terribly interesting. How could they not be impressed with his new home?

Named for a castle in Scotland, Ravenscraig Hall wasn't just grand, it was conspicuously showy. It was of unique design and though perhaps somewhat austere on first appearance, it compared to nothing else in Winnipeg. While not the largest home in the city, it was of considerable size and had many fine features to facilitate elegant entertaining.

Rupert thought of its gardens and expansive lawns along the river; he could see only endless opportunity before him as he imagined champagne and caviar and the constant parade of beautifully dressed women attending his future garden parties. Rupert adored parties. Parties drew women like flowers drew butterflies and Rupert was at his best when showered with feminine attention.

He considered himself truly gifted in his appeal to the weaker sex. He stood out not just because he was unusually handsome and confident, but also because of the valuable lessons in gentility that he had learned during his youth in Atlanta. As a young man, Rupert had paid close attention to the ways of southern men and learned by their example. Often, just for fun, he would slip in a bit of a southern accent. As this was so rarely heard in Canada, it seemed to be especially appealing to the ladies.

In time, he had developed a technique of taking a woman's hand and staring through her until her breath quickened before offering a greeting with a voice that rumbled forth from a place deep within her imagination. Slowly his smile would reveal perfectly straight teeth and the presence of dimples, which one admirer had told him were his most alluring feature. They were not boyish ones, she told him, but distinct masculine creases that hinted at a wild passion for life one suspected could only be seen under the most intimate of circumstances.

As he held a woman's hand in this way in greeting, she would flush at the penetrating feeling of his gaze locking onto hers, his dark eyes smoldering in appreciation for her loveliness. He would wait and sometimes she would come to the edge of a swoon with small sounds emitting from her lips. His eyes would glide over her breasts as he bowed and brought her hand to his face, the warmth of his breath raising goose bumps on delicate white arms. Then his mouth would open, ever so slightly, and he would gently press his full lips to her skin. The response became predictable. Heaving bosoms rose behind fluttering fans while batting eyelashes spoke of a yearning for promises to be made.

Rupert truly relished the pursuit and enjoyed each encounter immensely. There were many beautiful women, and many unforgettable moments, in those early years, but he needed a woman with money more than he needed a beauty. Time and time again, the teardrops fell, as Rupert kissed the ladies good-bye and continued on his quest to find the perfect wife.

And finally, he did find her. Her name was Elizabeth Jane Biggleswade and he found her in a Toronto newspaper.

The only child of a Montreal businessman who had made his first fortune in the fur trade and his second on the railroad, Miss Biggleswade had traveled to Toronto to visit her aunt, a blueblood matron of the upper class. To Rupert's advantage, every tea, luncheon, concert, and excursion that Beth had attended had been reported in the society pages in great detail. From what he had learned, he had determined the young lady to be an ideal candidate for his master plan.

Fortunately her travel plans were also published allowing Rupert to engineer an impressive first meeting. He had planned every step of his pursuit of Beth with great care and calculation, from their "fateful" first hello, through every encounter that followed. He lavished attention on her with small gifts and romantic letters. Three months later, he asked her to marry him and she had almost fainted with joy in declaring her love for him.

The greatest difficulty was Beth's father, who had very nearly derailed his plan from the start. Byron Biggleswade had been very disappointed that his only child was not going to marry one of the fine young men of her own class who had sought her affection and had a good deal to say to her about it. He told her that he could see little potential in Rupert, that he didn't trust him, and that a man who had not yet finished university had no business proposing marriage. He was aghast at Beth's poor judgment.

Beth threw a terrible fit and threatened to enter a convent if her father didn't grant permission for her to marry Rupert. The old man held fast and forbade his daughter to see her beloved. The house grew cold under the mournful wailings of the heartbroken Beth. By the third week of what he had described to his wife as "interminable caterwauling", Mr. Biggleswade relented. Beth leaped for joy and the marriage date was announced. Both parents cried at their daughter's very tasteful wedding, but only one had tears of joy.

After all of their years together, it was plain to Rupert that Beth still adored him, so things had worked out rather well for both of them. He still did, on occasion, think it unfortunate that she wasn't prettier, but when dressed properly, she was attractive enough.

The clock ticked and the afternoon light was disappearing. He hated to be kept waiting. Why on earth was that woman always late?

"Beth, dearest, we really must be going," he called out, working to keep the impatience out of his voice.

"Rupert," Beth sang out, "could you help me with my pearls, darling? Where are you, Rupert?"

"I'm here, my dear." He marched briskly down the hallway to her dressing room, anxious to get her into the carriage and on their way. "Beth, sugar, we really can't keep our hosts waiting."

She heard his annoyance and her eyes flashed hurt. He immediately checked his attitude, needing her to be at her charming best this evening, as so many people would evaluate his worth on his choice of a wife. Rupert stepped back and swept his arms wide, his eyes warm and sensual as he let out a low soft whistle.

"Oh, my dear, sweet li'l darlin', would you look at how beautiful you are."

"Oh, Rupert, do you think this dress too formal for an at home concert?" She felt naked under the heat of his gaze and blushed.

"You are a vision of beauty." He kissed her cheek and guided her shoulders toward the mirror so that she could watch him nuzzle her ear while he fastened the necklace. "Now, we really must be on our way."

"Well, Rupert," she giggled, "it is just divine to see you have so much enthusiasm for a musical event. I must be a wonderful influence on you."

"You've been a wonderful influence on me since the day I first laid eyes on you in Toronto. It feels like only yesterday."

Beth felt her heart quicken with the effect of Rupert's unexpected attention. This was going to be such a delicious evening.

"Here we are fifteen years later, my darling," she purred. "I think of that day at the train station. I was so sad to be leaving Toronto. Then suddenly there was this handsome prince, striding toward me." She angled her head coyly and smiled up at him. "You seemed to emerge from the steam on the platform as if arriving from my dreams. It was so romantic. You smiled at me and tipped your hat, and my heart flew away."

He'd heard her tell the story many times but looked at her as if it was the first time. He kissed the tip of her nose and drew back again to admire her dress as she sashayed before him. The skirt fell in delicate folds of blue silk. The bodice was tightly fitted and held forth her bosom, framed prettily in a delicate French lace. She knew he would approve.

"My dear, you look absolutely stunning in aqua," he declared.

"Well, thank you. Aren't we unusually playful, Rupert?" she teased. "You look like you have something to tell me. Do you have a secret, darling?"

"My secret is that I have the most wonderful wife in the world."

Beth laughed gaily and pretended his words were true. She knew better, but all the same, she enjoyed these little plays of affection he gifted her with from time to time.

Beth gave quick instructions regarding the children to Mrs. Butterfield, the housekeeper, while Rupert stood before the hallway mirror adjusting his new top hat. He had never owned one before and was particularly pleased with the effect. Then with an approving nod from Beth, he whisked her out the door.

Henry, their coachman, brought the horses into a well-schooled trot along the avenue and Rupert waved to the children they passed along the way. He waved as if he were in a parade on his way to Buckingham Palace. He loved an open carriage. It felt so utterly rich.

"Oh, I do love that the weather has turned warm again, Rupert," Beth smiled. "The light breeze and the fragrance of fall in the air make for a delightfully pleasant time of the year."

Beth wondered what favor he would be seeking of her this time. She wished it were true that he really did love her in the way he pretended. But, at least she had claimed him as her husband.

That was her goal all those years ago, was it not? And they had stayed married, despite her father's stern warnings, and despite the wake of jealous women. She knew her money helped, and that without the wealth her father bestowed upon her, she would never have had the chance to marry such an attractive man. Rupert could have chosen a wife from quite a list of Toronto's fine families. His rugged good looks and highly polished manners were greatly attractive to the debutantes despite his lack of social standing. She was certain of it. It wasn't his fault he was an orphan. Beth had known from the start that he would make an excellent lawyer, and her secret investment in his education had paid off. How could she possibly have said no to his request? It had all worked out splendidly. Now, like so many lawyers, Rupert had turned into a fine businessman. A good life had its price, and if her money had won his heart before all else, well, so be it. It elevated her above all of the other women who had set eyes on Rupert. She would always love him more than he cared for her. She knew this to be a simple truth of their union. No matter. A woman couldn't expect to have everything. Four children later, her husband was finally starting to see his business succeed and perhaps soon they would be able to advance to the upper echelons of Winnipeg society.

For this very reason, Lady Ballantyne's invitation to the concert at Stonebridge Manor had sent Beth's spirits soaring.

That so important a family had extended them this honor was indeed a sign of great significance. In Montreal, as a child, Beth had taken the social prominence of her family for granted. Here in Winnipeg she was invisible, an appendage of a husband who had not yet been welcomed into the upper crust. One had to hold one's head high and look to the future. Perhaps she and Lady Ballantyne would become friends. Perhaps the doyenne would even invite her to address her as Annabella this evening. Things were so much more casual in the West, after all. Beth smiled and reached for Rupert's hand.

The autumn leaves had matured into a spectacular array of yellow and orange. It could not have been a prettier drive, if he had planned it. Rupert's thoughts turned to his new mansion and the evening ahead on Assiniboine Avenue. He almost laughed out loud at his cleverness in being able to keep his secret from Beth. She had no idea that they were not actually guests, but rather the hosts of this grand party. There would be a musical performance tonight by Ray Barrowclough's celebrated chamber orchestra followed by a seven-course dinner. Rupert had studied the backgrounds of every one of the men Ballantyne had suggested for the invitation list and was thoroughly prepared to impress each of them.

Having been wrapped up for so long in orchestrating the elaborate scheme, Rupert was surprised to find that he was actually looking forward to Beth's reaction to Ravenscraig. They would have precisely forty-five minutes to see the house before their guests started to arrive. He knew at once that Beth would object to certain features of the mansion, and although she might pout in private, she would sooner be struck dead than be seen off her game in public. Without the slightest doubt, Rupert knew she would rise to being a superlative hostess. She could absolutely be counted on to save her true feelings and any temper tantrums for a private explosion before him later. In the meantime, Rupert couldn't lose. He would have the fine residence he wanted and Beth would eventually come around. He knew she would find the house overly large, and perhaps a bit cold in appearance, but he was sure she would love the conservatory overlooking the Assiniboine River. It would be a wonderful room for her to enjoy her backgammon games and to entertain her bridge club.

Rupert had stopped short of notifying the local papers, thinking that some of his guests might find it bad form to have a reporter at his party. It was very tempting but just too much of a risk. He would save the opportunity for another occasion.

Beth slipped her arm through her husband's and drew closer. Perhaps this was the first of many events they would attend in Armstrong's Point. She breathed in the fragrant air and smiled at her handsome Rupert.

The roadway took a wide and gentle curve to the left through the trees, following the bend in the river. Henry turned right and drove the carriage through a second gate, which brought them onto a large circular driveway. An imposing grey structure that seemed capable of withstanding cannon fire rose before them. Beth was astonished at the sight. Constructed of stone and dark brick, the house stood three stories high. Flat across the front, it had a row of gabled dormers marching evenly along the roofline, much like one might see on a prison. Small, carved limestone heads sporting bulging eyes and tongues lashing over knobby teeth jutted out between the second story windows. Two garishly large turrets anchored the front corners of the house, but did little to balance the appearance of a gargantuan porte-cochere that reached out to claw in approaching carriages on the driveway.

"Oh, my," Beth gawked. "Rupert, are those gargoyles?"

Rupert felt his back stiffen and took a full breath to slow his pulse rate. Beth craned her neck to get a better look.

"Good God. It looks like an insane asylum. Does it have a moat?" Beth blurted out the words and her hand flew to her mouth. She was shocked at the possibility that she might have been overheard through an open window. Rupert grappled with the realization that he had perhaps underestimated her potential objections. He clenched his jaw then smiled into her wide-eyed expression.

"It's the lack of greenery, my dear. It looks a bit severe perhaps because it is so large. The house is new and it has not yet had the benefit of a properly developed garden. It is obviously very expensive, wouldn't you agree? Imagine it covered with vines. Don't you think it would be rather charming?" Rupert sensed he may have been starting to sound overly enthusiastic and stopped talking.

"My heavens, Rupert, why are we here?" Beth whispered. "This can't possibly be Stonebridge. This is nothing like I have heard it described. Are we providing a ride for someone?"

Henry pulled up under the porte-cochere and stopped. Rupert felt his left eye taking on a twitch as he looked at his wife and willed her to say something pleasant. Beth shrank back and stared at the great stone steps leading to the heavy front door. Flanked by a pair of large glass lanterns that suggested perches for vultures, the heavy door was complete with oversized black iron rings for doorknockers. "You do think it rather impressive, don't you darling?" he asked optimistically, hearing only his heartbeat in return.

"It's absolutely hideous. I've never seen anything so horrible. Who lives here?" she asked through her teeth.

"The Ballantynes?" He forced a laugh and hopped down from the carriage. Beth immediately realized that she was in danger of ruining the entire evening. She could sense that Rupert was on the edge of becoming very upset with her. Whatever his reasons, he wanted her to like this monstrous mansion. Well, fine, it wasn't as if she had to *live* in it. And she wasn't about to lose the magic of being the center of his attention. It was so rare for him to treat her so affectionately. She quickly reached out and gave him a little tap with her fan and laughed joyfully. How merry he looked tonight. Why not play along with his little game?

Relieved that she was back on her best behavior, Rupert held his arms wide to help her from the carriage.

"Come now, my darling. I can assure you we are at the correct address." He smiled broadly and kissed her cheek before leading her up the stairs.

The door swung open. A very tall man with impeccable style bowed with great dignity.

"Good evening, Mr. Willows, welcome to Ravenscraig, sir." His deep voice sounded amplified in the entrance hall.

"Good evening, Chadwick, my good man. May I present, Mrs. Willows." Rupert gracefully extended his arm and smiled at his wife.

"Indeed, sir. Welcome, madam. It will be a pleasure to serve you." Chadwick bowed. It was simple and elegant and yet his manner caught her completely off guard. As only a butler trained in London could do, he spoke as if Mrs. Willows were the most important woman on earth.

Beth hooted in surprise as Rupert scooped her up in his arms and proceeded to carry her over the threshold. As he set her down, she looked about the grand entry hall and took in the magnificent staircase rising and curving to fold around a spectacular glittering chandelier. As dreadful as the house was from the outside it was utterly majestic and enchanting on the interior. She threw her head back and laughed.

"Oh, Rupert, this is a fine joke. April Fool's Day came and went months ago. Oh, you make me laugh. What is this all about, and why are we not at Stonebridge?"

Rupert grabbed her and kissed her. On cue, four musicians with violins appeared and struck up a very romantic version of the popular new waltz, *And the Band Played On*. He put his finger to her lips and said, "Not a word. Not yet. It will break the spell." He swept her into a dance, and behind them, a line of servants formed, each wearing black and white parlor uniforms and each carrying a posy of miniature roses. At the chorus he sang his own words to the song.

> *Rupert would dance with the raven-haired girl*
> *And the band played on,*
> *He looked in her eyes and saw love was returned*
> *And the band played on.*

Her laughter spilled over the music and finally, with great flourish at the end of the dance, Rupert bowed and turned his wife to face the servants. He nodded to the butler.

"Mrs. Willows, if you please, it gives me great pleasure to introduce your household staff." Mr. Chadwick efficiently went down the line giving their names as heads dipped, one by one, in either curtsey or bow. When he got to the last one, Rupert turned and spoke grandly to Beth.

"Yes, my darling, this is your house. A gift to show my appreciation for your love and affection," he beamed. She stood frozen in shock and stared back at him as if her heart had stopped beating altogether. This was the one reaction he had not thought to expect and rushed to fill the silence. "And don't be disappointed that we are not going to the Ballantyne's home. They and a dozen or two other friends are coming to Ravenscraig to be our guests this evening. Aren't you thrilled, sugar?"

Beth let out a gasp, then wobbled and dropped to the floor in a dead faint.

6

Leaving Russia

October 11, 1895

The full moon bathed the kitchen with an eerie light. Hannah looked around to see if there was anything she had missed in her packing. The bundles stood neatly by the door. She thought of the day when she had helped her sister Esther pack her bundles as she and her husband Leib left to try their luck in England. The two girls had hugged each other through their tears and promised to be strong for each other. Both knew they might be saying good-bye for the last time, but neither had spoken the fear out loud. Young and each newly married, they talked, instead, of the children they would have and the happiness they would feel when they were re-united. How she longed to see Esther again. Perhaps in time, they too, would come to Canada.

She nodded to Zev. It was time to wake the children. Zev's mother had taken charge of packing the food and was carefully reviewing the contents of the two sacks before her, grunting as she tested the weight of the larger one.

"Mameleh, it is too heavy for you. Leave the extra potatoes for me to carry," Hannah told her mother-in-law.

"Shush, now. It is good. I can take it. Not so heavy." Bayla answered as she tightened the kerchief knot under her chin.

Ziporah was already awake and dressed when Papa came to get her. She was more adept at listening in on her parents' conversations than her older brother Isaac. She knew about the long hike they would be taking that night and the reasons for it. She wanted to show Papa that even though she was only eight, she was as good as any ten-year-old. She was tall and strong for her age and she would be a big help to Mama, she explained to him.

"You are a special person for one so young, my dear little girl," Zev smiled and hugged his daughter. Nine-year-old Isaac was a heavy sleeper and Zev set to work to get him up and organized while Ziporah gently woke up little Aaron, imitating the soothing sounds Mama made whenever anyone was sick or afraid to go to sleep.

"Shh, shh, Aaron. Remember what Baba told us. We have to be very, very quiet for our adventure. Can you do that?"

Aaron nodded his head and yawned heavily, holding his pudgy arms out to his sister to carry him.

"You're a big boy, Aaron. You can walk a little can't you?" She asked as she slid him off the bed to plant his tiny feet on the floor.

"No. Ziporah carry Aaron," he insisted, reaching up to her.

Ziporah shuddered at the thought of Cossacks coming to chase them in the night, and gathered her little brother into a protective embrace.

Baba Bayla had warned them to be absolutely silent so that the czar would not hear them and send his bad men to come after them.

"Come, children," Mama interrupted and picked up Aaron. "It's time to be on our way."

Ziporah saw that Mama had everything packed into bundles to be carried. Baba wanted more to carry, but Mama said there was a lot of hard walking and insisted that Baba not be overloaded. The small sack of food held bread and boiled chicken and some cooked eggs and apples. This was entrusted to Ziporah and tied onto her back.

"This way if the path is dark, I can take your hand to keep you safe," said Baba. "God forbid you should disappear."

"Isaac has a bigger pack than I have. I want more to bring!" Ziporah protested.

"He is stronger, Ziporah, now please, this is not the time for arguing. Remember we must be quiet," Papa said calmly. He turned away and missed seeing Isaac stick out his tongue at his sister, followed by the sharp shove that Ziporah gave him in return. Mama, however, missed nothing when it involved her children.

"Isaac, you stop that! Ziporah, behave yourself!" She hissed under her breath as only a mother can. "Now, no more arguing.

56

No more talking!" Seeing that Mama was in no mood for anything but obedience, Ziporah decided to save her ready insults for Isaac for another time.

Papa was loaded down with more than the rest of them altogether, it seemed. Mama took charge of Aaron. She tied a shawl over one shoulder and slung it across her body to brace her little one against her hip. Then she hoisted another sling onto the opposite side for the bundle she would carry. Mama could carry almost as much as a man, Ziporah thought.

They set off, with Papa in the lead, followed by Baba and then the children and finally Mama at the end, to be sure the children were all accounted for, she said. They walked one behind the other into the warm autumn night, through the gate and down the lane, leaving the only home Ziporah had ever known behind them. They were leaving Russia and would never see it again. She looked back for a brief moment then quickly turned to face forward. They walked past the Brenman's home and the dried remnants of the poppies against the fence, and then by the oak tree at the end of the lane where the children and their friends had spent countless hours playing hide and seek. Finally, they came to the main road. With the bright light of the moon to help them find their way, Papa guided them across the road and onto an old path that went through the woods. He explained it would take a little longer, but it would be safer. They walked for a long time before Papa let them stop and rest for a few minutes.

In time they came to a creek. Ziporah looked about and thought certainly there would be wood fairies dancing in the moonlight in such an enchanted looking place. The water sparkled and the owls hooted in the night. Papa looked around and when satisfied told them to put down the bundles. The great canopy overhead provided a comforting covering to the scene. Ziporah looked to see where there might be a bridge to cross and couldn't find one.

"Are you sure this is the way, Papa?" she whispered.

"Quite sure," he smiled.

"But where is the bridge?"

"There is no bridge."

"A boat then?" Ziporah jumped and brought her hands together in glee.

"No boat either. But won't it be fun to have a swimming game at night?"

Mama clapped her hand over her mouth. She must have been so happy to have Papa think of a game to take their minds off of the tiring walk, thought Ziporah. Papa pulled a long rope from his pack and tied one end to a tree. He jumped into the water and checked his footing.

"It's quite warm for this time of the year," he said reassuringly.

He moved slowly and steadily across the creek, testing each step as he went. The water rose to just over his knees. He carried the rope to the other side and tied it to another tree, then pulled it hard to make sure it was strong, and tied an extra knot, just to be sure. Ziporah, Isaac, Mama, and Baba sat quietly on the bank, while Aaron slept in the shawl at Mama's side.

Ziporah watched as Papa made four more trips back and forth carrying the bundles on his shoulders. Finally, after carrying Aaron across and sitting down with him on the far bank, he called for the others to enter the water. "Hang on tightly to the rope," he called softly, "and walk carefully. The creek bottom is muddy and slippery."

Mama took off her shoes and gathered her skirts up high around her waist. Ziporah knew her mother was anything but enthusiastic about swimming, but she did look determined.

"It's all right, Hannah. It is fine." Papa waved her on with an encouraging tone. Mama took a big breath. Quietly humming a happy tune, the way she sometimes did when she was nervous, she marched through the water to the other bank and picked up Aaron, who only wanted to sleep.

"Watch how fast I can go, Isaac." Ziporah leaped ahead of her brother, prompting a shushing from Baba. She hopped through the creek like a water nymph, lifting her knees high to show how nimble she was. Isaac was unimpressed. He clomped through the water like a man, one step after another. Coming up on the bank, he couldn't suppress a shout of accomplishment. He turned back to call to his grandmother.

"It's all right Baba. There are no snakes. Not even one!"

Baba froze. Her skirts held tightly and her shoes in hand, she had been all set to step into the water, but had not thought of snakes. Papa gave Isaac a big slap on the head. Mama called out to Baba, Ziporah stifled a giggle and Aaron cried.

Telling everyone to be quiet, Papa went back into the water to rescue his mama. He had lots to say as he crossed the stream, but he said it so quietly enough that it was hard to make out the words. He lifted Baba onto his right shoulder and, telling her to stop fussing. Grabbing the rope, he strode steadfastly through the black water to safety.

A couple of hours later, they came upon a roadway. A man was waiting there for them with a wagon hitched to a very big horse. Ziporah could tell that Papa knew him from the way they spoke, but she had never seen the stranger in their village. The man reached into the cart and pulled out a coat and hat and handed it to Papa. It was the kind of clothing the Ukrainian peasants wore.

"Here, put this on, and do something about those strings hanging down there." The man was all business as he pointed to the white *tzitzit* strings attached to the traditional garment Papa wore under his shirt. Ziporah was astonished to see her father tuck the *tzitzit* out of view and put the coat on. Was this not a sin to treat the sacred garment, in such a way? What would Rabbi Levin say?

With the hat and coat Papa looked very much like the farming peasants. Isaac thought it was very funny and started to laugh until Baba shushed him.

Instructions were shouted in Ukrainian and Papa urged them to hurry. Mama and Baba got into the cart with the children and pulled blankets over their heads. Papa and the man who owned the wagon threw hay over top of them, and soon the steady clip clopping of the horses' hooves lulled them all to sleep. The wagon came to a stop just before the sun came up. The man pulled the hay off, and as the family slipped out of the wagon and found their feet, he waved directions to Papa and set off at a gallop down the road, soon disappearing around the bend. Mama searched frantically about, counting the bundles that were hastily tossed from the wagon.

"Zev, do we have everything? Children, look to see we didn't lose anything." Panic rose in Mama's voice. "The candlesticks! Where are my mother's Shabbat candlesticks?" For several minutes the bundles were thoroughly searched.

"Here! It's all right. Here they are, Hannah," Baba called, waving one of the silver treasures in the air.

Papa wiped Mama's tears and comforted her with a prayer of thanks to God for leading them safely through the most difficult part of their journey. They had made it across the Russian border and were now in Galicia. The family members gathered up their belongings and set off again on foot. When the sun came up, they found an old barn and settled down to sleep in the hayloft.

For two more nights they walked, sleeping in the woods one day, and behind a haystack another day while Papa kept watch over them. Finally they came to Zalischyky.

Ziporah was not sure how her father had made the arrangements, but he knew the name of a rabbi in the village who warmly welcomed them and made comfortable in a barn for the night. The next day, the rabbi took them to the little house that would become their new home. Ziporah thought it looked like a cottage from a folk story. It had a thatched roof and was not made from wood boards, but from earth that had been plastered over with something that made the walls white inside and out. The little house had two rooms, one door, and three windows. In the middle of one room, there was a big stove made from clay. Papa told them it would keep the whole house cozy in the winter. In many ways the house was nicer than the home they had left in Russia.

Before long, Papa brought home a cow and four chickens. And soon the neighbors came by. Some brought bread and salt to say hello, as was the custom of the Christians, welcoming the Zigman family with warm words in Ukrainian. Here, as in many of the villages of Galicia, the Jews and Christians lived side by side. There was a divide between the two groups, but also a mutual acceptance. Together, they were townspeople. Separately, they lived quietly with their own beliefs and traditions among people of their own kind. No one wanted trouble. Mama said it was good to have such nice neighbors and talked about the importance of respecting their differences.

Over the winter months, Papa worked hard, picking up small jobs, and his skills as a carpenter quickly became known in the village. The family settled in and made friends. Papa said it was not a place to become rich, but that they would not starve either. The months flew by in a blur of work and worry. Through it all, the dream of Canada grew in each of them.

Then, all too quickly, spring arrived and the day came to say good-bye to Papa. They had been in Zalischyky fully six months. The food supplies were well stocked, seeds had been purchased for the garden, and a small stash of money was buried in the root cellar. Through countless hours of discussion and training, Papa could see that Mama was well prepared to take over in his absence.

Absence. The thought of her father leaving cut through Ziporah and filled her with pain. Papa had said good night to her every day of her life. Now he had to leave. For the first time she felt the ache of saying good-bye.

Papa held her close. "Please don't cry, Ziporah." He stroked her hair and told her how much he loved her and how he was counting on her and Isaac to help Mama. He told her he would work very hard so that soon they would all be together again. "Think of our life in Canada."

Papa went to each of them and hugged them, and each in turn wished him well. Ziporah tried very hard to be brave. She slipped behind her mother and buried her face in the soft folds of Mama's skirt to hide her tears from her father. Papa didn't want anyone to be sad. This was the beginning, he had told them, of their new life. With faith in God and hard work there would even be enough money in time to send for Aunt Esther and Uncle Leib and their daughter Malka in England.

"Look at this." He pointed to the bright purple crocuses pushing up bravely through the snow, and then laughed. "You see, I believe it is a sure sign of good luck to see the crocuses arriving on this day. My journey will be a good one."

Then he kissed Mama and whispered something that made

her smile and cry all at the same time. Baba cried without sound, with just her shoulders moving. Papa wrapped his arms around his mother, and in time she was calmed and tried to smile. She said she looked forward to when she would next see him and her husband, Zaida Baruch, Ziporah's grandfather. Mama placed her hands on Papa's cheeks one more time as if she was memorizing his face. He waved and then he was gone.

It would be eight months before they received their first letter from him.

7
Winter Holiday in Florida

October 28, 1895

Rupert ran up the snowy steps and burst through the door like a schoolboy.

"Beth! Oh, Beth, where are you, darling?" He closed the heavy front door and stamped the snow off of his feet, then dashed up the stairs. As he rounded the second floor landing into the hall, he all but knocked over Mrs. Butterfield.

"Oh, I beg your pardon, Mr. Willows," the housekeeper said as she straightened her cap and smoothed her apron.

"My goodness, Mrs. Butterfield, I'm so terribly sorry," he answered. Seeing she was startled but not harmed, he continued on as if nothing had happened. "Mr. Chadwick is coming by tomorrow morning at half past nine o'clock. Please make yourself available so that we may discuss the upcoming arrangements for the household."

Mrs. Butterfield gasped. With her eyes popped wide open, she appeared stupefied with fear.

"What is it, Mrs. Butterfield? Are you ill?" He looked at her curiously. "The new staff will need to know what my expectations are. Of course you will have your own questions of Mr. Chadwick."

"Questions, sir? I'm afraid I don't understand. What questions might I have for Mr. Chadwick?"

"Whatever is wrong, Mrs. Butterfield?" Rupert was impatient to get to Beth to tell his news and had not expected to be sidetracked by a flustered housekeeper. "I know we are not going to be moving for some time yet, but there is a great deal that will need your attention. You will have a great many responsibilities to attend to in the coming weeks."

Mrs. Butterfield couldn't believe what she was hearing.

"You mean that I will continue in your employ, Mr. Willows?"

"Of course you will, Mrs. Butterfield," Rupert said slowly, as though speaking to an idiot. "Why ever would you think otherwise?"

"Well, sir, it's only because you've sent the lot of the household staff here packing and I thought that included me!" The words rushed out, punctuated by a sound that seemed to be both a cry and a hiccup.

"Oh, for goodness sake!" Rupert suddenly realized the predicament he had caused and immediately changed his tune. "I beg your pardon, Mrs. Butterfield. Please, do come and sit down a moment." He guided her to the settee in the hall. Too agitated to do anything but pace, he launched into repairing the problem he had caused. "My heavens, it completely slipped my mind to come seek you out to tell you the news. I'm so terribly sorry. I've been so distracted with the new house, you realize."

By this time she had pulled out a crisply ironed handkerchief and was sobbing into it.

"Let me be clear, Mrs. Butterfield. There are two staff members who will be coming to the new house." Rupert spoke as though soothing a child. "Henry will continue to be my driver, and it is my desire that you head the housekeeping staff at Ravenscraig. You will report to Mr. Chadwick, the new butler, but you will continue to have all of the responsibilities for cooking as you do here. I will be hiring additional staff, as I wish to be sure that you are not overburdened. If you need anything, speak to Mr. Chadwick. He will train and supervise the wait staff and the groundskeepers. I'm sure you will both get along."

"Oh, dear me. Please excuse my nerves, Mr. Willows, I thought I'd been sacked with the rest of them. Mr. Jenkins was in such a rant about the dismissals, you can't imagine." She blubbered her relief into her crumpled handkerchief.

Rupert remained standing and awkwardly reached out to pat her lightly on the shoulder.

"There, there now, Mrs. Butterfield. In fact, I meant to tell you that you would be receiving a raise for your fine service to our family and to compensate you for the additional supervisory duties you will be taking on at Ravenscraig. I do believe Mrs. Willows would divorce me if I were to discontinue your employment in our home. You will accept the position, won't you? I've written your new salary down on your pay envelope, which I have here in my pocket for you. You will forgive my forgetfulness, now, won't you?" He handed her the envelope and watched her.

She dabbed her round and reddened face with the soggy handkerchief and looked down at his neat writing. The raise was a generous one and her eyes flew to meet his.

"Oh, my, Mr. Willows!" she exclaimed as she stared at the number. This new house must be every bit as big as she had heard it was. No doubt Mrs. Willows had something to do with the increase in her pay. She heaved herself into a standing position and spoke with fresh tears in her eyes.

"Oh my, thank you, Mr. Willows. I apologize for my outburst, sir. It's just that being a widow, you know how I count on my wages." She smiled her gratitude and dipped into an unsteady curtsey. "It will be my great pleasure to continue to serve you and Mrs. Willows and the children in Ravenscraig Hall. I shall be very pleased to meet Mr. Chadwick."

"Thank you so very much, Mrs. Butterfield. Mrs. Willows will be delighted with the news."

"Would there be anything else, sir?"

"Yes, would you please tell me where I might find my wife?" he asked pleasantly, as if their conversation had been completely erased from his mind.

"Yes, of course, sir. Mrs. Willows is having one of her sick headaches, sir, and she is lying down in her room."

"Thank you." He strode off down the hall with a spring in his step.

He tapped gently on the door. When there was no response he quietly pushed it open and saw Beth lying in bed with a silk sleeping mask over her eyes. He moved silently to her bedside and whispered.

"Beth, are you awake, darling?"

She remained still, but he could see her chest rising fully as she breathed and he knew she was play-acting. He started to hum and soon the tiniest bit of a smile started at the corner of her lips. He sat gently on the bed and brushed her hand with his fingertips. Then he started to sing a children's rhyme with words of his own.

A tisket a tasket, I wish she had a basket
I wrote a letter to my love and here she's gone and lost it.

She laughed lightly and picked up the corner of the mask. "Rupert, you never get the words right in any of these songs."

"Oh, I know, sweetness, but I am fun to have around, am I not?"

"You must want something very special indeed, to be home from the office so early. What is it? Have you bought me another surprise? I haven't yet recovered from the shock of Ravenscraig."

"Oh, you're not still cross with me about the new house, are you, darling?"

"No, I'm nursing a sick headache because I have nothing better to do." She dropped the mask down over her eyes again.

"You are still put out with me then."

He rubbed her hand, waiting for her to peek out from under the mask. Try as she might, Beth couldn't help but enjoy his attention. He was an impossible man, a spoiled man with a gift for charm like no other man on earth. He started to sing again, and she sighed and lifted the mask off, smiling back at him. He gathered her up in an embrace and kissed her ear.

"Oh, I do love you so very much, Beth. I just know we are going to be happy at Ravenscraig. Give it a chance, my sweet. It might grow on you."

"Rupert, as God is my witness, I swear that there isn't a single man in the world who could possibly be more persuasive than you are. Yes, I will do my best to become accustomed to Ravenscraig. Of course, some of the more revolting features will have to be modified before I would dare consider taking up residence there."

He feigned acquiescence. "Yes, the gargoyles will be removed, my love. Unless, of course, you think we could give each of them a name. Perhaps in getting to know them you would come to like them," he teased.

She swatted him with her sleeping mask.

"Name each of them rubbish and knock every one of those nasty little heads off of that house!"

"Your wish is my command, my queen." He stood up and with a great flourish pretended to be sweeping a hat off of his head as Sir Walter Raleigh might have done in a previous age of gallantry.

"I'm not well, Rupert. Leave me to rest." She sank back into the pillows and did her best to purse her lips into a pout. "This beastly weather doesn't help. Look at this blinding snow coming down already. It isn't even the end of October.

"Winter is ever so long here, and I just hate feeling cold with that horrible north wind cutting right through to the bone. It was never quite so bad in Montreal. I detest winter here."

"It's a dry cold," he quipped.

"You stop it! Whoever started this nonsense promoting that a dry cold was a benefit was not thinking about temperatures that go to forty degrees below zero!" She punched his chest in play and he grabbed her hand and kissed it.

"I have a cure for your malaise, my dear. As a matter of fact, that is exactly why I am home early this evening."

He pulled a folded paper from his jacket pocket and handed it to her. It was a letter.

"What is this now, Rupert?"

"Well, now, why don't you read it and we'll see," he answered.

She held the letter to the light of the window and began to read.

"Dear Mr. Willows, it is our pleasure to confirm the room reservations for you and Mrs. Willows from the first day of December, 1895 until the thirtieth day of January, 1896! Rupert!" She laughed with delight, and hugged him. "Where?"

"Well, keep reading," he smiled.

"Please advise us as to your transportation schedule and we will be happy to have our driver meet you at the train station on your arrival in St. Augustine."

"St. Augustine? We are going to Florida?" Beth fell back against the pillows, unable to repress her glee.

"I wanted to take you on a special holiday to allow the new house to be set up in our absence," Rupert explained, taking her hand and drawing circles on it with a fingertip.

"How divine, darling!" She was truly delighted. "Florida, my dear! Sunshine and warm breezes, the ocean, palm trees. A complete escape from this brutal Winnipeg winter. What a lovely surprise, Rupert!"

"Well, you gave me the idea when you told me about that magazine article you read about the Ponce de Leon Hotel. It does sound very grand, and quite honestly, aside from getting away from the ghastly winter, I thought it would be a marvelous opportunity to expand my business contacts."

"How so, Rupert? Are you going into the hotel business?"

"Oh, you do make me laugh, darling! Who might you imagine our fellow guests will be in Florida? I've done a little searching on my own. I learned that the Ponce de Leon is considered the Winter Newport. It has become the destination of choice for a great many society people from New York who travel to Florida for "the season", as they call it. That means we can be assured that we will be in fine company. Wintering at this exclusive hotel provides a natural sorting process to cull out the lesser classes."

"Rupert, my love, I do believe you are becoming a terrible snob!" Beth said, already thinking of the wardrobe she would need for the trip.

"I'm quite serious. It will be a most interesting opportunity to make contacts for future business. It is my duty to the Province of Manitoba, don't you think? Every businessman in our city should be seeking out new relationships with influential people, and telling them of the investment opportunities here. Don't you agree?"

"Well, yes, I do, when you put it that way, Rupert."

"I am also very anxious to make the acquaintance of Henry Flagler."

"Oh, just a minute, why do I know that name?" She tapped her lip.

"He was in the article you showed me about the hotel."

"Oh, yes, yes. He's the owner isn't he?"

"Yes," Rupert answered. It appears that being a founder of the Standard Oil Company and a partner of Rockefeller wasn't enough for the man. He now seems to be terribly keen on developing a hotel industry in Florida. He's building a railway too. I intend to meet him. Befriend him, actually."

"Do you think you might encourage him to invest in Winnipeg?"

"Beth, my dear." He leaned in and kissed her cheek. "You never know how connecting to a man with so many accomplishments can change one's fortunes.

"Now, come, darling. Get out of these silly bedclothes, and come down to the parlor so I can enjoy your company before dinner. We shall share a glass of sherry to celebrate. Do you feel up to it?"

"Well, yes, I do. Rupert, I do believe you have cured me of the winter doldrums. My headache seems to have completely disappeared."

"That's the way."

"Oh, dear. Rupert," Beth suddenly remembered. "What about the children?"

"That's why we have a house full of servants, darling!" Rupert laughed. "The staff will take very good care of Emma. She's barely three, after all. She'll hardly know you are missing."

"She turned four in June, Rupert."

"Oh." He was genuinely surprised by this information, but quickly recovered, so as not to spoil the mood. "Well, time does fly, doesn't it? And the boys, well, they are boys who will learn to be men one day. It will be good for them. In the meantime, all of the nonsense involved in setting up the new household will all be taken care of in our absence and you will come home to a fully functioning, well organized home. It will be so much easier for you."

"I will have to shop. I don't have a thing to wear." Beth was completely caught up in the excitement.

"Of course you will shop! I expect you will want to stop at Montreal so we may have a visit with your mother. And we'll plan on a few days in New York City as well. I anticipate I will have a couple of business meetings to attend while you see to your wardrobe, and we'll enjoy a play or two on Broadway. What do you say?"

"Oh, Rupert. I do think this is a splendid plan."

"Wonderful! I see the color returning to your cheeks. Now, please do get out of this bed and come downstairs."

He kissed her cheek and she laughed lightly. As he got to the door she called after him.

"Rupert. You are certain that two months will be enough time to have Ravenscraig ready? I won't set one foot in that monstrous house until it is ready."

"I live for your happiness, my dear," he announced as he waved the letter and headed for the door. "I'll be waiting in the parlor."

8
Letter from America
March 18, 1897

Ziporah perched on the little stool and leaned her head in to rest it lightly on the welcoming warmth of the cow. She worked her hands gently into a rhythmic pull. One, two, one, two, just like Isaac had shown her. The heady scent of the fresh milk rose and filled her with a sense of peace, and she started to hum a little song to the cow. It was a sweet little love song that Mama always sang as a lullaby.

Tum bala, tum bala, tum balalaika,
tum bala, tum bala, tum balalaika,
tum balalaika, shpil balalaika,
tum balalaika, freylekh zol zain!

She thought of the last day she had seen her father. At first it was very hard, but as the days passed, the ache lessened a little at a time. Soon the days had turned into weeks and the weeks into months. It had been almost a year since he had said good-bye. Soon it would be Passover. She wondered how Papa and her grandfather would celebrate Passover in Winnipeg. Who would cook the special holiday foods for them? Every day they talked about Papa. Usually it was a small comment. "Papa would like this soup," Mama would say, or "Your papa would be proud to see how much butter you sold today, Isaac."

Their greatest joy was the arrival of baby Mendel. His arrival had been very confusing to Ziporah who could not understand how storks could come with babies in the winter. Storks came to build nests in spring. Everyone knew that. But Mama knew more, and, sure enough the stork brought Mendel when the ground was covered in snow. Mendel was a happy, chubby baby who gurgled with delight and was spared the heartache of missing the papa he had yet to meet. He was named for their great grandfather, the father of Zaida Baruch. Mendel Zigman was his name.

"A man's name," Baba had said and was happy. He was a good baby with a joyful heart who helped all of them heal from their longing for Papa.

Ziporah sighed. She fixed her mind on her father's face. It wouldn't come. She couldn't clearly recall his features. It had been such a long time since he left.

Sunlight found its way through the cracks in the stable and dappled playfully on the straw. The cow mooed. Ziporah smiled and mooed back. It was a beautiful day, the kind of day that could bring good things. Maybe today there would be a letter from Papa. Mama said there was nothing to worry about, that letters from Canada, so far away, took a very long time to come. They knew from the two letters they had received that Papa had made a safe trip to Winnipeg and that he and Zaida were well and working. There was nothing to worry about, Mama said. Better we should think of how exciting it will be to all be together in the new country.

Ziporah was not at all sure where Canada was, but she knew that it was like America: a country so far away that once you were there, you would never come back. It was hard to understand how Canada was not America, but Mama assured her it was a different country. In Zalischyky, no matter where a letter came from, the shout went up in the village, "America! A letter from America!" Some got letters from New York or Toronto, others from Philadelphia, Montreal, or Cincinnati. Everywhere, it seemed people were talking about going to America. All of the cities and towns were strange names to her. But the only letters that came from Winnipeg were theirs.

One day, perhaps soon, they would be packing to begin their journey. Deep in her heart, Ziporah knew that Mama was right. She had to be patient like Mama and Baba. Maybe it was easier for grownups.

She had heard the streets in America were paved with gold. She was young, but this idea of gold on the streets? No, this she knew this could not be true. If it were, they would already have tickets and be on their way. That is how she knew.

"Maybe there will be news today," Ziporah said to the cow. She firmly believed that if she said these words everyday, in the same way, and in the same place that it would come true, that somehow her words would be answered and a letter would appear. So, in this way she had a special relationship with the cow and never had to be reminded to take up the milk pail. She liked the little barn and their new little house, though it had taken her a while to get used to it. Ukrainian people made their homes and farms a little differently than their own people did, but she liked it just fine now.

It felt safe here. They were fortunate to find such a home to live in. She wondered what had happened to the family who had built this house. Did they go to America, like Papa?

Ziporah patted the cow. The cow had no name because to give a name to a farm animal is to have heartache as you would for a pet. It's easier if the cow is the cow and the goat is the goat. She rubbed the cow's head and said thank you to her before she picked up the pail.

Ziporah stepped carefully around the muddy puddles of water on the path and brought the pail into the kitchen. With Mama busy with baby Mendel and Baba and the boys out in the garden, the room was empty. She regarded the fullness of the pail and calculated whether she could boost it up high enough to reach the table to not spill a drop. Her mother would be surprised with how much she had grown.

"Ziporah! What are you doing?" Mama burst into the room, just in time to rescue her daughter from a calamity.

"I just wanted to help you, Mama. You seemed so tired this morning."

"Oy, precious child." Hannah reached out and hugged her daughter, then sat down and pulled her onto her knee. Ziporah hugged her arms around her mother's neck. Mama stroked her hair, arranging it neatly behind Ziporah's ears.

"Ziporah, you are a good girl. You are my special help, but it should not be for you, one so young, to have to do the work of a grown woman. I appreciate that you have taken the responsibility for the milking to help your brother with his chores, but let us always have time to also be a child. Yes?"

"But I am big and strong, Mama."

"Yes, and you are a child." Hannah pulled her daughter up into her arms and held her for the pure joy of it. "*Tchotchkelah*, my treasure, you will have many years for hard work ahead of you. Don't make it a rush. I will not have you live every moment like the czar is over your shoulder with a whip. Do you understand?"

Ziporah understood very well. Her life would forever be marked by her family's roots in Russia. These roots defined her. They defined all of them.

Here in Galicia, a large county in Austria, they were no longer called Russian Jews. Of course, they were called Jews, but here they were also known as Galitzianers, a name that felt lighter and made Ziporah feel less threatened. There was no czar here. When they first arrived, Papa had said it was not so bad as it was in Russia, but times were changing. Papa had been very strict in his instructions that it was necessary to live quietly and invisibly, as much as possible. Mama, and even sometimes Baba, started to wear headscarves like the Ukrainian women, a dark *babushka*, sometimes with flowers on it. They should look like everyone else, and live with little notice among their neighbors. Papa had insisted on it.

It had been hard on Mama since Papa was gone. Mama was very smart at learning new things and very hard working, just like Baba. "Born to work," she would always say when someone told her it was time to rest. She rarely rested. She wanted Papa to be proud of her ability to look after the family and it seemed there was always work waiting for her hands. In this way, she was even able to put a little money aside to help save for the tickets, she told Ziporah. Mama and Baba worked in the garden and grew vegetables to take to the market. They also had beehives. This was like gold, Mama told her. The honey was both food and medicine and the wax was used for making candles.

Mama was also very good with the chickens, so there was food to eat, and there were extra eggs to sell along with milk, butter, cream and honey that Isaac carried on his little cart to sell to the neighbors. Nothing was wasted. They got by on the bare minimum to meet their needs, and everything else was sold at the market or from Isaac's cart. Mama and Baba made pillows from the chicken and goose feathers and even bought feathers from neighbors to make thick feather-stuffed quilts during the long winter months. The Ukrainian word for this special bed covering was *pirena*. The ones made by Mama had become prized items at the Zalischyky market. People came all the way from Tovste and Horodenka for the quilts. There was no end to the work that needed to be done, winter or summer. Even small hands had work.

"Ziporah, we have a lot to do to prepare for Passover. This morning you will help me with the cooking, and then this afternoon, we are going to clean the floor, so everything will be ready for the holiday," said Mama as Ziporah's eyes flew open. She loved the Jewish holiday in spring, the delicious food, and the many songs and prayers that celebrated the exodus of the Jews from Egypt. But as with every major holiday, Mama had high standards for cleaning the house. Cleaning an earthen floor the way the Ukrainians did it here in Galicia was hugely unpleasant, in Ziporah's view. Mama however, had told her she thought the old method was very clever and effective. Such a cleaning was best in spring. The quality of the manure was highest with the fresh green grass in the meadow.

"Mama, it's Isaac's turn to help," Ziporah stated. "Can't I scrub the walls instead?"

"Oh, Ziporah, you make such a fuss about nothing," Mama said. "Isaac is busy with selling the eggs and butter. The scrubbing is already done. I need you to help with the floor."

The morning passed quickly and just as Ziporah finished tidying up after their mid-day meal, her mother called her outside.

"Here's the pail I want you to use. Make sure it's fresh. It's best if it is still warm."

Ziporah went into the pasture with the pail and a small flat piece of wood and set to work looking for a fresh manure piles. Well, at least she wouldn't have to smear it on the floor. Mama was very particular about how that was done and would do it herself with an old broom. It always surprised Ziporah to see how nice and shiny the mud floor was when the manure dried. It never smelled. She wondered if Papa had to smear manure on a dirt floor in Canada.

In a short time the bucket was full and heavy and Ziporah dropped the stick and began making her way back to the house. Just as she set it down in the yard she could hear Isaac off in the distance, yelling with excitement.

"A letter! A letter from America!" He held the letter high as he ran through the village, past the old synagogue and then down dirt the path through the orchard toward their little thatched-roof home. Seeing Ziporah in the yard, he couldn't suppress the urge to show off. Leaping high to clear the fence, he almost landed in the manure bucket.

"It's a letter from Papa!" He waved it in her face and darted through the garden, leaving Ziporah whooping with delight and taking up the shout, "A letter from America!" as she ran after him to the house.

"Are there tickets for the steamship in it?" she yelled after him.

Isaac burst through the kitchen door almost knocking his mother into his grandmother's lap. "Mama, Mama! It's a letter from Papa," he gasped, gulping for air. "Look, Baba, it's from Winnipeg!"

"Thanks be to God!" Hannah shouted for joy.

"What does it say?" Baba Bayla clasped her hands together as both women cried with happiness.

"Mama, we can't read it through the envelope! Quickly now, Isaac, open it and read to us what he says," urged Hannah. Immediately she changed her mind and grabbed for the letter. "No, let me first touch it." She blinked her tears away and looked closely at the writing, then kissed the letter and held it to her face, marveling at how many thousands of miles the letter had come. Tears sprang anew in her eyes and she threw her head back and let out a joyous hoot, hugging Isaac hard.

"It's a miracle!" Hannah exclaimed. "Isaac, call everyone so we can read it together."

Hannah and her mother-in-law prayed their thanks for the safety of their husbands as they took turns handling the envelope, relishing the thought of hearing long-awaited news from afar.

"Hello, hello, what is this Isaac is telling us? A letter from America is coming to your house?" shouted Mr. Melnikovsky from next door.

The kitchen doorway was suddenly filled with a collection of neighbors and friends, everyone piled in one on top of another to hear the news from the golden land. Little Aaron held onto Baba's hand tightly and squealed with excitement.

"Now, please, now read the letter. Slowly, Isaac, so I can enjoy it more," instructed Hannah. "Please, dear God help us so there should be no sad news in the letter." With another hasty prayer, she surrendered the envelope and dabbed at her eyes with her apron. "All right, I am now ready."

Everyone hushed and shushed the little ones, as they strained for a better look. Isaac began to read the letter that would mark the beginning of their saying good-bye to the shtetl of Zalischyky.

"My dear wife, Hannah, my loving mother, and my children Isaac, Ziporah, Aaron and our special new blessing, Mendel. Hello to all of you. I am writing this letter on January 14, 1897. I hope this letter does not take many months to get to you. As you will see, I am sending the tickets for your travel."

Pandemonium broke out in the little house, as everyone started shouting and crying with excitement. Isaac handed the tickets to Mama and she held them like precious diamonds, then quickly excused herself to put them away for safe keeping while a discussion about the upcoming voyage took hold of the little crowd. Finally Hannah took her seat again and urged Isaac to continue reading.

"First, I must tell you that Zaida Baruch is well and strong. Me, also, I am all right. We are making it fine enough in the new country. It is every day, though, that my heart aches for all of you to be with us. But do not be worried. You will come to Canada in the summer. You will leave on a ship in July from Hamburg."

Applause erupted amid shouts of happiness for their good fortune.

"The voyage is long but it is all right, as you will see.

Hannah, bring your food with you, as you will not approve of the little food available to the steerage passengers.

Zaida Baruch is waiting to be with Baba and misses her very badly," Isaac continued. "And he is anxious to meet all of his grandchildren and to have a life with a big family around him."

At this, Baba began quietly weeping. So many years apart. So much suffering. Isaac stopped to comfort her before going on. "It will be fine, Baba, you will see."

"Should we pack our things? Let me see!" Ziporah interjected. She was losing her patience with her brother. Were she to be entrusted with the reading of the letter, she would have had all the news by now and would have finished her packing. Isaac is such a thorn in the side, having always to be the center of attention.

"No. Let me read, Ziporah," Isaac cleared his throat. He enjoyed having everyone's attention on him just a bit too long, which earned him a solid shove from his mother.

"I'm reading, I'm reading, Mama!"

"Well, don't be making us wait," she scolded.

The crowd burbled with comments on the news. Isaac shushed them and again went on. "Zaida Baruch is well known here in Winnipeg where there are now many Jewish families. You must know how important he is! He is well-respected as a founding member of the Shaarey Zedek Synagogue, and is highly regarded for his knowledge of Talmud and his work as a teacher. He is teaching seven boys who are now preparing for Bar Mitzvah." Mutterings of approval rippled through the audience, followed by more shushing.

"We want you all to know how well we are." Isaac read. "Do you see us together in the picture?"

"The picture?" yelled Baba. "Where is the picture?" This prompted a frantic search through the envelope and between the pages, and finally under the feet of the assembled crowd.

"It's here! It's under the chair." Aaron, just shy of his fourth birthday, reached and found the prize, setting off a series of oohs and ahhs and other expressions of approval as each person looked carefully into the photo to see how well Zev and Baruch were doing in the new country. They stood proudly, wearing fine clothes and looking straight into the camera. Finally the picture came to Baba's hands. The room went quiet as she looked at the image of her husband with devotion in her eyes. Embarrassed that she was so emotional, she quickly made a joke.

"Oy, my Baruch. You should eat more. Too thin, he is. But handsome, no? Don't be worrying, I will soon be there with the chicken soup and matzo balls to fatten you up!"

Everyone laughed and as the picture was handed from person to person, Isaac continued.

"I must tell you with honesty that the clothes we wear in the photograph are not our own but borrowed from the studio of the photographer. So hungry was he that he accepted a few potatoes as payment for the picture. I don't want you to worry we are spending money on ourselves instead of saving for our life together. As you know, Zaida is very disappointed that the three years of farming he worked in the Moosamin colony did not have the success that was hoped. He still talks about it and blames himself for his hard luck. We are lucky he made enough money to keep himself from starving," Isaac read.

"See, I told you he was thin," Baba shook her head.

Isaac flipped to the next page of the letter and continued reading:

Winnipeg is an important city with many jobs and many Jewish families and now two synagogues with talk of even more to come. It will be an important center for Jews in Canada, this is very apparent. For me, and I know for you too, Hannah, it is important that our sons will study and have their Hebrew education with other children.

It is not always easy to get work that allows the time for the Sabbath, but some people understand that we cannot work on Saturday. I am working in construction to build new homes and now I have an extra job working to bring the lumber from the train for the new buildings. There is a lot of work here. The pay is not so good, but with time we will build a good life here. I will hope to be in business as a peddler as soon as I can save enough money to buy a wagon.

Many large stone and brick buildings are here, and even a streetcar that is pulled by horses right down the Main Street. We have enough food to eat. This is a blessing, even if the dishes are not so well prepared as we are used to from your good cooking at home. It's not so bad. We are fine in the place we are staying. We are boarders with a family. The lady keeps kosher although not everything is as it is in the old country. We have a very simple life that does not cost very much. We will have all the riches we need when the day comes when the family is all together in one place again. It is the greatest gift we could have and we wait for you with terrible impatience to see you in the summer.

"We will be leaving in a few months!" Mama said. "There is so much to do!" Her hands flew to her face.

"We have time to be ready and when we go, we say good-bye and we don't come back. We will be making a life for the family in Canada." Baba said the name of the new country with care, as if tasting the future.

"Mama, will Uncle Leib and Aunt Esther and my cousin Malka come to Canada, also?" Ziporah tugged on her mother's apron as she asked her question.

"We will pray for it to be so," Mama answered.

"Why can't they come at the same time as us?" asked Isaac.

"It is the money," she said. "We don't have it. But in time, with hard work, maybe soon there will be enough for tickets for them to come to Canada also."

This started a new discussion about the family in London. At this, it seemed everyone had a story about family who had moved away to Europe and America and chatter broke through the crowd rising to a crescendo. Nearly everyone had shed tears over the long absences and hard circumstances in their families. Baba Bayla took a spoon and started banging on a pot to get the attention of the crowd.

"May I remind you we have not yet heard all of the news of the letter!" she said loudly and the crowd quieted. She nodded to Isaac to continue reading.

Isaac found his place in the letter and raised his voice over the whispered conversations.

"He says there is news about our Ukrainian neighbors from Zalischyky who went to the province of Manitoba last summer," Isaac said, setting off another round of chatter in the room.

"Papa says he was in the farmers' market in Winnipeg and happened to see Mr. Peter Strumbicky and spoke to him about their new colony," said Isaac.

"My brother! My brother Peter!" Hearing the name, Wasyl Strumbicky from a nearby farm in Bedrikivci crowded in closer to hear the news. "Please, what does he say?" he asked politely.

As Isaac read in Yiddish, Mama translated the words into Ukrainian so Wasyl could better understand the news in the letter:

> He shook my hand with happiness when he recognized me and asked me to write his family news in this letter to you. Peter says they have good land and many trees on their farms. All of the families that traveled to Manitoba last summer have settled together in the same area in the Stuartburn district.
>
> There is a small town called Vita close by. The government promise was good and they all have one-hundred-sixty acres of free land for their own. Peter says they would like a church and that in time they will build one. The winter is hard for them but they are fine with the bush country giving them wood for heat and rabbits to trap for food. Peter invites all the Zalischyky neighbors who think of Canada to come and know they will have a life and a future, farming on their own land in the New Country.

Isaac finished reading and looked at Mr. Strumbicky, who beamed and thanked him. He shook Isaac's hand with his strong grip and thumped him on the shoulder before running out to tell his family of the news. While the voices rose with commentary on the news in the letter, Isaac leaned in to his mother and said, "Mama, there is more to read, but there is also a special page that Papa says is just for you. Will you read it to us?"

The family watched as Mama took the folded page from Isaac's hand. She opened it and smiled as she read it. With tears falling down her cheeks, she pressed the page to her chest.

"This I can tell you. He says he is well. The rest is from a husband to a wife," she said shyly, tucking the paper away between her breasts, and reaching for her handkerchief. "Read the rest of what you have from your Papa, Isaac."

Papa's letter went on to describe briefly what they could expect on their voyage on the steamship, and explained in detail how they would leave Zalischyky and acquire the documentation they needed to come to Canada. Zev's lack of description of the steamship had Hannah worried that it was far worse than he said.

"When he does not say much it is because there is a lot that is not so good to be said. He does not want me to worry," she explained and crossed her arms over her chest. "This I know. The journey, it must be very difficult," she added with certainty.

"Hannah, don't be borrowing trouble from tomorrow," Bayla said. Then, holding her arms wide, the older woman addressed their friends. "For now, we should be planning all of us to go. No?"

The voices grew with excitement, ensuring that before nightfall everyone in the village would be talking about the news from Canada.

Ziporah slipped through the crowd and picked up the picture off of the table. She took it outside into the sunlight so she could take a close look at it. She examined every detail very carefully. She saw how much her father and grandfather looked alike. She peered at her father's image, and her heart filled with gladness at the sight of his face. She was awash with relief knowing she would never again forget what he looked like. Most importantly, she saw the excitement in her father's eyes, and she knew that everything was going to be all right. In just a few months she would run into his arms again. She hugged the photograph to her cheek and then quietly brought it back into the noisy kitchen, still jammed with as many people as it could hold, all talking in Yiddish and Ukrainian at the top of their voices about America. She nudged her way through the crowd and brought the picture back to the table. She tapped her mother to get her attention and then gently placed the photo in her hands. Mama smiled and hugged her through her tears.

Ziporah found her way outside again and skipped down the path to the stable. She needed to talk to the cow.

9
The Head Tax on the Chinaman
July 22, 1897

Rupert was filled with a sense of well-being as the carriage pulled up to the Manitoba Club. His mood was brightened by the return of clear blue skies and warm weather after a week of dreary cloud cover over the city. He was looking forward to a pleasant lunch as he ran up the stairs of the stately brick building.

"Good morning, Alderman Willows." The doorman tipped his hat.

"Good day, Frederick. It seems to have turned out to be a spectacular summer after all, wouldn't you say?"

"Indeed, it has, sir. There's nothing more glorious than a sunny July day in Manitoba. I just wish summer was a tad longer. Seems a man just gets himself properly thawed out and the cold weather sets in again." He laughed as he pulled the brass handle on the ornate door.

"Right you are, Frederick. Has my son arrived?"

"Not as yet, sir." Frederick checked his watch and saw it was well before noon. "Are you not a wee bit early today, sir?"

"Perhaps. Be a good chap will you? When he arrives, I will thank you to tell him not to spoil my good mood with his usual complaints." Rupert smiled and tipped his hat as he stepped inside.

All of the club employees knew that only the very best service would suffice when Rupert Willows was on the premises. The stories of his having verbally abused two former staff members for their lack of attention to his needs were legendary. He was also known to be very generous with gratuities when he was happy. Hence, there was good deal of fussing and flattery as Rupert was grandly welcomed and seated at his usual table.

Comfortably settled with a robust cup of coffee, Rupert opened the newspaper he had brought along. It was a copy of

The Weekly Sun, an Ontario paper that he had arranged to have mailed from Toronto and he was quickly engrossed in the news from the east.

At the top of the hour, he spotted Alfred across the room and found himself considering how rather striking he was. Home for the summer from his studies at Harvard, Alfred was working at Rupert's construction business. Part of his required routine was to join Rupert for lunch every Thursday at the Manitoba Club, so that he would become known in the proper business circles in Winnipeg. The young man showed great promise in the way he handled himself.

Rupert watched approvingly as Alfred greeted and then chatted with the new insurance man in town. Hudson Allison was it? That's right. They had been introduced in the mayor's office shortly after he arrived from Montreal. He was very highly thought of, this Mr. Allison. And by the looks of things, Alfred had clearly made an impression on him. Rupert chuckled. His son reminded him of himself. Harvard had truly been a good choice for the boy's education, he thought. Perhaps if business continued to go well, his two other sons would also have their opportunity for an Ivy League school. Now that he had become acquainted with several families from Harvard, it wouldn't hurt to start making new contacts through another prestigious university. Princeton or Yale might be worth considering for Elliot.

"Hello, Father. Am I late?" Alfred smiled and shook his hand.

"Not at all. I was just catching up on the news from Ontario. Do you read Goldwyn Smith?"

"You mean that insufferable bigot from Cornell?"

"Alfred!" Genuinely shocked, Rupert dropped his voice to a harsh whisper. "Please, be careful with your tone. In this room you will find a great many influential people who happen to agree with Professor Smith on a number of subjects."

"Of course, Father," Alfred swallowed his ready retort. He had no interest in starting lunch with an argument.

"And to correct you," Rupert continued, "Goldwyn Smith now resides in Toronto. He is retired from Cornell, although they think so well of him that there is talk of having one of the university buildings named in his honor."

"Very impressive, Father."

"I see how impressed you are. Well, in any case, he has recently bought a newspaper, *The Weekly Sun*, and will write regularly in it. I do so enjoy his essays. Perhaps if you read more of them you might change your opinion of him."

"I see, Father. And what might be the reason you are bringing this to my attention?"

"The head tax on the Chinamen."

Still not sure where his father was going with this, Alfred was hopeful.

"Do you mean to say you have softened your attitude and wish to see the abominable tax repealed?"

"Repealed?" Rupert laughed at the unexpected comment. "What are you saying? No, no. Quite the contrary. There is a movement afoot to have it increased from fifty to one hundred dollars a head for each person coming in from China, and I am all for it. We'll discuss it over lunch. Shall we order?"

Alfred had only recently begun paying attention to the issue and was frankly appalled by the head tax. From the little that he had learned, he knew the Dominion government had decided to impose the immigration restrictions against the Chinese a dozen years ago, at the time of the completion of the Canadian Pacific Railway in 1885. Apparently, the country no longer had any need for the fifteen thousand Chinese workers who had come to Canada to help build the CPR and wanted to actively discourage any further immigration from China. The policy was particularly popular in British Columbia, where the greatest number of Chinese immigrants lived.

"Father, it seems rather unfair, don't you think, that the Chinese have become somewhat unwelcome in the Dominion. Why would the government have encouraged them to come if they didn't want them to stay?"

"Ah, allow me to bring you up to date with this, Alfred. You see, we needed the Chinamen. They work hard. And they are in fact, easy keepers, like mules. They manage with their own food. Imagine the money that was saved by not having to feed the lot

85

of them on the railway crews for all those years," Rupert paused, butter knife in hand to consider his bread plate. "God knows what the Chinaman eats. All manner of squiggly things, I'm told." He looked up. "Oh, I do apologize for even discussing this and hazarding spoiling your appetite. The main point is that the primary reason they were so attractive for the job was the saving in their wages. The workers from China were paid a third less than the other men who worked on the railroad."

"They weren't paid the same wages?"

"They are undesirables!" Rupert's tone was petulant. "They were offered a wage. They accepted a wage. And there you have it. It became customary to pay the Chinaman less and everyone was agreeable to it. What's wrong with that?"

"It's appalling, Father. That is what is wrong with it." Emotion rose in Alfred's voice. "They are people. Many of them are men with families thousands of miles away, who now have to pay exorbitant taxes to bring their wives and children from China or face never seeing them again. Does that not strike you as cruel in some fashion?"

"Alfred! Please lower your voice," Rupert glanced about the room to be certain they weren't creating a spectacle and then continued through clenched teeth. "People don't want more undesirables coming into the Dominion and the government must respond. I grant you they have done us a great service by laboring on the railway, but, really, well, what are we to do with all of them once they have served their purpose? The cross-country railway is long completed. What on earth are we to do with more Chinamen? More laundries? More Chinese cafes?"

"I think it dreadful that this is the only group to have to pay to come to Canada," responded Alfred. "It's despicable. That's what it is."

"I agree with you!" Rupert responded with enthusiasm.

Alfred put down his fork and stared at his father, now quite confused. "You do? Why, I am both surprised and happy to hear that."

"Well, I'm happy to explain." Rupert surveyed the table and nudged the flowers over an inch, so as not to not disturb the balance of the table setting but to make adequate room to open his newspaper. "Goldwyn Smith says it best. I tell you, he really has the right ideas." At this Rupert opened the paper and searched through the copy. "Ah, here it is, hot off the presses. Smith writes: 'What is the use of excluding the Chinaman when we freely admit the Russian Jew?' " He paused to be sure Alfred had the full impact of the thought.

Alfred was rendered speechless.

Rupert went on. "You see? He is quite right. And so are you." He picked up the paper and waved it in Alfred's direction to emphasize his point. "Why should the Chinese be the only group to face such restrictions? There are so many others who are equally undesirable as immigrants to the Dominion."

Alfred stared into his plate, his jaw pulsing with anger.

"Have you paid any attention at all to what is going on in Europe, Father? Russia, in particular? The violence, the persecution, the hunger?"

"And are we to take in every stray dog who needs a meal, Alfred?" Rupert had lost his taste for the conversation and flipped his newspaper aside. "There are plenty of people in various parts of the United Kingdom who would do very well in coming to Canada. They ought to be at the front of the immigration line. That's the point of it all. I think Smith is very brave, indeed, to illuminate the numerous difficulties that arise in opening the door to all of these, well, these lower classes, Alfred." Rupert touched his napkin to his lips.

Alfred was horrified. "Goldwyn Smith is and will remain the most prominent anti-Semite in the country. I don't know how you can celebrate the trash he writes."

Rupert set his fork down gently on his luncheon plate. He lowered his voice to a hiss and leaned in toward Alfred.

"You say anti-Semite as if you were referring to a leper! Professor Smith is very highly regarded. He may well express strong views against the Hebrews, but he is right. You mark my words. Generations from now, a hundred years or more, students will be sitting in Goldwyn Smith Hall at Cornell University continuing to honor the man for his greatness. No one will pay a second thought to this anti-Semitism rubbish."

Alfred fixed his gaze on his plate. He stirred his fork

through his food, but did not speak.

Not wanting to ruin what he had hoped would be a pleasant luncheon with his son, Rupert sought to take the harshness out of their discussion. "Listen, Alfred, the Americans will also be applying restrictions on immigration soon. You mark my words. They, too, have strong feelings about the various undesirable classes among the foreign born." Rupert looked up to see that his son had gone from perplexed to disgusted and had retreated into silence. Rupert hated to be shut out.

"Alfred! Look at you. You disapprove! I see it all over your face. Come now, don't be disagreeable with me," he appealed to his son as though Alfred was still a child. "I've so missed your company these many months that you have been away at school and in just a few weeks you'll be heading east again. It is so good to have you home and working in the business with me. I know it has only been a short while, but we have had a good time these last few weeks, have we not?"

Alfred concentrated on breathing deeply and attempted a weak smile. If nothing else was gained from his life in Boston, there was the hard lesson in never losing one's temper in society. Father and son sat in silence while the clock chimed loudly against the murmur of the conversations in the dining room. Finally, Alfred quietly placed his fork and knife together at just the right angle to close his luncheon plate and then carefully folded his napkin. At last he spoke.

"Father, I must tell you I most vehemently disagree with your position on the head tax. It matters not to me if it is on the Chinese, or on the Hebrews, or on any soul wishing to come to Canada for that matter. I am appalled that anyone would have to pay a special tariff just to enter this country."

Now it was Rupert's turn to be shocked.

"Is this what I paid for you to learn at Harvard?" His eyes narrowed, and when he spoke there was an all-too-familiar severity in his voice. "I will state plainly and clearly to you, my dear son, that Smith's views on the dangers of admitting the Jews are straight in line with my own beliefs, and here is why. The Jews do not assimilate. Yes, they will learn to speak English, I grant you, but that is only because the Jew will speak any language needed in order to conduct business. This is a fact. But he will not make any effort to become Christian. Jews never do. You can trust my word that the Jew is going to be a major problem for our growing country, much more than any other group including the Chinaman. The best solution is to slow, or better yet to stop them from coming. Goldwyn Smith is an authority on this, and you must admit that his arguments are very compelling." Rupert again picked up the paper and donned his reading glasses while Alfred simmered.

"Just listen to this. It's one of the best quotes I've ever seen from Smith: 'Two greater calamities perhaps have never befallen mankind than the transportation of the Negro and the dispersion of the Jews.'" Rupert marveled at the passage. "He's brilliant. I wish I could express myself with that kind of clarity."

With this, Alfred reached his tipping point and could longer restrain himself. He spoke in a low tone but with strength of conviction that his father had never heard in him before. "Father, Goldwyn Smith is an intolerant and hateful old man who detests Jews, Slavs, Negroes and Chinese, everyone it seems, who is not blessed with white skin and English as a mother tongue!"

Rupert dabbed a napkin at his lips and expertly nudged his moustache into place.

"Well, I think he is right," he answered smoothly then glared directly into Alfred's wide-eyed gaze to head off his response. He had grown tired of the defiant ignorance of his pretentiously educated son and wanted only to win the point and move on. When he spoke, his words came evenly but with the focused intensity of a rattlesnake poised to strike.

"Look again at what Smith states in the essay, Alfred. Look at the trouble that came with transporting the Negroes to create slavery in the United States," he stated. "My God, son, the country went to war over the very issue. How many lives were lost in the Civil War? And it was all over what? A hoard of Africans who never would have become slaves in America had they not been brought to this continent."

At this he stopped to allow Alfred time to see that there was nothing really to argue. Alfred did what was required of him, not because he agreed, but because of the obvious futility of his efforts to get through to his father. To bring the matter to a close, Alfred chose to concede the point with an almost imperceptible nod. Taking that as victory, Rupert indulged his desire to taunt his defeated opponent.

He smiled, and teasingly added, "I truly believe the Negroes would have been much happier had they stayed in Africa in their little huts, dancing about their fire pits. I daresay only a few may have even given a second thought to coming to America. Fewer still would have been able to afford passage, and slavery would never have come to be. You see Smith's point. You must agree that in this instance he is quite right in his assertions." He folded the newspaper as though handling a precious document and set it aside.

Thoroughly put off by the discussion, Alfred was looking to escape. He pulled out his pocket watch and spoke without making eye contact.

"Father, Professor Smith is stuck in the wrong age and can do a great deal of harm spewing this hatred. Now I'm terribly sorry, but I do have work to do and I must leave."

"Nonsense!" Rupert turned on the charm. "Alfred, Alfred, please. We have many exciting things to discuss. Stay. You are making a lot more of this issue than it deserves. That is the truth. And that is the end of the discussion. Please, let us move on."

"Fine." Red-faced, Alfred set his attention on his water glass. The waiter, who had been discreetly watching the developments at the table, saw the moment had arrived when he could safely approach without interrupting. He summoned his assistant, and the table was swiftly cleared. Pastries and coffee appeared before the two as if by magic.

"Let's discuss something more pleasant, shall we?" said Rupert politely to bring them out of their silence. "I received a letter from a man named Roger Harrington. He is working in the new immigration program out of Clifford Sifton's office. He has asked to meet with me and I agreed. You do know that Sifton was elected to the federal government?"

"Yes, I do," responded Alfred, now insulted that his father would assume he knew nothing of Canadian politics because he had been away at school. "The news managed to travel all the way to Boston. Can you imagine?"

"Please, Alfred. There is no need to continue to try my patience. Let's have a civilized conversation." He seemed genuinely hurt and Alfred pulled back.

"Sorry, Father. I didn't mean to be rude. Yes, I am aware that Mr. Sifton is creating quite a stir in his new position."

"What do you know of it?" Rupert smiled as he stirred sugar into his coffee. Alfred stopped in his tracks at the familiar line from years ago and saw the twinkle in his father's eyes. Relieved to have the anger behind them, he couldn't keep from laughing out loud. It was an old game father and son used to play.

"Oh, dear. That's a clever trick, Father. This is just like being back at St. John's School with your grilling me over my history lessons."

Rupert nodded with affection and motioned Alfred to provide the answer, asking again, "Well, what do you know of it?"

Choosing to play along, Alfred poked a finger in the air in the manner of an A student responding to a question from a teacher.

"Our Mr. Clifford Sifton has become a rising star in federal politics. The former attorney general of Manitoba, just thirty-five years old, was elected as a Member of Parliament and is now serving as a cabinet minister in the Liberal government of the new Prime Minister Wilfred Laurier. Sifton was elected in a by-election. Let me think of the date." He paused for a moment then adopted a pompous tone. "On November something, 1896. In any case, Sifton's primary responsibility is immigration and he has launched a very ambitious scheme to populate Western Canada." Alfred crossed his arms smugly across his chest. "How did I do?"

Rupert brought his hands together in light applause. "Very well, indeed."

"Thank you," Alfred smiled and bowed slightly. "Now what is it that Sifton's man Harrington wants to meet with you about?"

"I'm not entirely sure," answered Rupert, "but I take it as an ideal opportunity to speak my mind. No, don't worry, I won't take us back to the earlier discussion, but I must say I wish to have my views on the quality of immigrants heard by Mr. Sifton. That said, I do believe we have a tremendous business opportunity through immigration, particularly if the government is successful in attracting more people from the United Kingdom."

"I take it this business opportunity you speak of is directly related to asking me to tour our rental houses on Patrick Street this morning," said Alfred.

"Right you are. I'm set to build several more."

"I think that is a splendid idea, Father, but I do have some concerns."

"What kind of concerns?"

"Well, I feel we need to build houses that are larger and of better quality than the ones we have built to date."

"Whatever for? Better quality means fewer houses, which means less profit," Rupert said.

"I think we should build something that is more suitable to the need and I do understand your reluctance in the matter of costs."

"What on earth are you on about? These are bloody rental houses we are talking about. These people don't have money for bigger rents. We'll price ourselves right out of the market." Rupert was heating up again.

"Father, I think we need to build houses that are better able to keep out the cold in winter and I have great concerns about overcrowding. The houses should be larger than what we are building."

"Why? The bloody immigrants don't seem to care."

"When was the last time you went down there to take a look, Father? I saw things this morning that made my blood run cold. There are sometimes two and three families, maybe a dozen people or more living in a house that isn't even a total of six hundred square feet. Father, your library is bigger than that."

"What of it? Do you think I'm new to this, Alfred? Let me explain how this works. We rent each of our little houses on Patrick Street to one little family of five or seven people. How long do you think it takes before they sublet? They put as many beds into a room as they can fit and sell places in those beds at ten cents a night. In the end you have the twelve or fifteen people in the house you speak of, but we will be collecting the rent on just the first seven. Our tenants profit on the crowding, and we don't. So, we have no choice. They aren't interested in this notion you have of comfortable living, so why build something better than what meets the minimal need?"

"Father, the answer is because it is just wrong. It is immoral. People should not have to live like animals."

"Immoral? Oh, dear. You have gone soft, Alfred. They are the ones who are choosing to live in overcrowded conditions. Not us. So, we will continue to build small houses that cost us less to build. You can't let your feelings get in the way of making money. You'll never get ahead with an attitude like this."

"But surely something can be done about the problems of overcrowding."

"The houses are crowded because the immigrants are poor, and this is the best they can do. How many times do I have to repeat myself?" Rupert breathed in deeply. "Would you care for more coffee? You haven't touched your dessert."

"So, we just leave things as they are. Is that it?"

"No. Not at all." Rupert was anxious to restore his earlier good mood. "We will help by providing more housing. I am now officially naming you as the vice president of Rental Properties of Willows and Sons. How do like that?"

"Well, thank you, Father. But I take it that you make the plan and I put it in place. Correct?"

"Yes, that's right, but you will be rewarded with a suitable increase in your salary for your trouble. And also, you will have an increase in the number of shares you own in the company. How many men your age are as fortunate as you, Alfred? Your job and your future business opportunities will be waiting for you when you graduate."

Rupert could see that his son was interested, but also that he was uneasy.

"Alfred. We are on the precipice of very exciting times. I know you don't see things my way, but trust me. This will work out very nicely in time. Why, to show you how open-minded I am, I will even allow that the houses may be rented to the foreign born if you wish. Anyone you choose may live in those properties as I am officially lifting my previous restrictions of renting to only British subjects. I will even allow Chinamen and Jews to rent there. God help me. How is that for progress? You see, I do listen to you, Alfred.

"Now, I have a couple of new surveyor maps of Point Douglas at the office and after lunch we'll go back and take a look shall we? There are some nice properties on MacDonald worth considering for development. The street is close to the train station and will become a good location for rental houses in future. It will be even better than Patrick Street."

Alfred sat silently and played at the edge of his napkin, frown lines furrowing his brow. Rupert was suddenly aware that it was going to take him longer to get through to him than he had thought. Such an innocent was this idealistic young university man, stewing as he was in his concerns for the under classes. Rupert diverted the discussion to non-sensitive matters that dealt with an upcoming garden party at Government House, a shopping trip to Chicago for Alfred's mother, and finally, as the club dining room starting to empty, Rupert re-introduced his discussion about expanding the number of boarding houses and rental properties owned by Willows & Sons.

"Alfred, what I can tell you with certainty is that if we don't make money on this housing boom, someone else will. What is wrong with cutting ourselves a generous slice of the pie? And besides, that lovely brick cottage you have your eye on over on Furby Street isn't going to just drop into your lap, you know. You will have it that much faster if you choose your investments wisely, and this is such an investment."

Alfred tried to put on a cheery disposition to please his father, but his appetite had gone cold. "I do see your point, Father, but I find it very distressing."

"It would be more distressing to not have any place at all for the foreigners," Rupert countered. "You saw what happened last year. There were so many that they were living in tents. Each summer there will be more of them. We are performing our civic duty as good corporate citizens in building rental houses. Don't you see?"

"I am quite surprised that you have not been given an award for your great contributions to the city, Father."

"What a splendid idea! That's the way. I knew I would be able to persuade you to see it my way."

10
Stalwart Peasants in Sheepskin Coats
July 26, 1897

Roger Harrington was running late for his train to Dominion City and was quite annoyed. His entire schedule had been thrown off by that insolent hotel doorman who had told him he would actually have to wait his turn for a taxi. For some reason that remained an utter mystery, the people in Western Canada seemed to have a lot more difficulty in recognizing his status than people in the East. Westerners were so unsophisticated; so brash and cocky, especially those ranchers in Calgary. Oh, he was glad to be finished with that lot! What was wrong with these people? Did they not understand that all of the major decisions regarding their future in the Dominion would be made in Ottawa and that in the long run they would get more if they were gracious rather than behaving like demanding, spoiled children? They got their bloody railway. What else could they want?

With the Western prairies behind him, he was quite relieved that his tour was more than half finished. An ambitious government bureaucrat, Roger Harrington worked in the office of Clifford Sifton, the new minister responsible for Immigration. His assignment was to tour the West to prepare a report on how the immigrants were managing. The government had put a lot of money into the aggressive program to populate the West, and Harrington had been tasked with being the minister's "eyes and ears" on this all-important tour. Harrington was thrilled with the opportunity to make a name for himself in Ottawa. With a Toronto upbringing and an economics degree from Montreal's McGill University, he considered himself to be a man of substance, well-bred and well-suited for the rigors of world travel. However, nothing in his background had prepared him for braving the frontier, and he found the unbroken West quite distasteful.

As a reward for contending with the hardships he had endured, Harrington chose to spend two glorious days of civilized living in Winnipeg to recharge his spirit before touring the immigrant homesteads in southeastern Manitoba. He was surprised and delighted with the sophisticated culture available in the provincial capital and had enjoyed two matinee touring plays from New York, as well as a concert by some excellent local musicians.

Winnipeg had an energetic and youthful flair and appeared to be a fine and stylish place to make a home. There also seemed to be a good deal of money about. In all, the city was positively vibrant compared to Ottawa. He was hopeful he would have a chance to enjoy more of Winnipeg's charms and perhaps see another play or concert when he returned from Dominion City.

The thought sustained him as he set his jaw and entered the dingy wooden building that served as the city's CPR train station. Almost immediately he found himself caught in a heavy crowd of travelers. Rolling his eyes, he brought his handkerchief to his nose. The station was positively teeming with the bedraggled masses disembarking from the one o'clock train. It had gathered its passengers from Quebec City, Montreal and Toronto. One colony car after another disgorged its human cargo. Harvest time was getting underway, so in addition to the immigrants, hundreds of working men from the East were arriving, expecting to make a year's wages in the coming weeks.

Harrington grimaced against the noise and the crowd and searched the departure signs to locate his platform. A cacophony of voices went up around him in a variety of languages as the passengers found their way to employment agents, family, or connecting trains. Most appeared worn from months of travel. Having arrived on steamships, the majority of the immigrants had boarded the train in Halifax or Quebec City for the final leg of their journey.

Harrington felt badly for them, but sorrier for himself, and he longed for his comfortable office on Parliament Hill. These people were peasants, accustomed to privations and discomfort. He, on the other hand, was a city man with fine tastes and sensibilities. Gathering his resolve, he steeled himself and plunged into the sea of bodies, desperately hoping to avoid soiling his coat. Holding his breath, he squeezed through the pack out onto the platform, just in time to hear the first call for his train.

"All aboard for Dominion City! All aboard!" Harrington stepped up his pace.

He ascended the steps of the car thinking how underpaid he was for his duties. He quickly found his seat and sat back, pressing his handkerchief against his perspiring brow. To quiet his anxiety, he set about making sure he had everything he needed. He checked that his ticket said Dominion City and slipped it into the pocket of his trousers. He placed his new hat in the overhead rack and then took his time inspecting and smoothing his jacket before folding it and placing it next to the bowler.

Just as he took his seat again, a bustling assemblage of peasants entered the car and headed down the aisle. The men wore thick moustaches and carried bundled sheepskin coats. The women covered their heads with flowered or black scarves and wore skirts of a coarse material. All were laden with baskets and bundles. The children were scrawny urchins, many of them blonde and sandy-haired moppets; all had dirt under their nails and dirty black rings around the collars of their white shirts. They, too, carried bundles. He recognized their costumes as typical of the Ukrainian-speaking immigrants from Galicia and he winced at their smell, a sharp mix of garlic and body odor.

Fearing for the safety of his expensive jacket, and needing air, he leaped to his feet and struggled to lower the window. Just then, the conductor rushed in, shouting.

"Hey, there, mister," he called to the tall man at the end of the line of peasants. "You are on the wrong car. This is the first class car. You must come with me. Tell them to turn around and come with me." The conductor motioned to the peasants in the aisle and then saw the look of dismay on the man's face. Clearly they didn't understand a word of English.

The conductor shouted louder. "Come with me! Turn around! I will take you to the correct car. This is not your car! Wrong seats!" The shouting was accompanied by wild gestures.

Turning to the others, the weary peasant led them out of the car with nothing more than a few quiet comments.

Harrington was weak with relief. He would have plenty of time to acquaint himself with the trials of the Manitoba immigrants but was delighted that acquaintance wasn't to start this very minute. He intended to enjoy the ride.

He pulled out his valise to check again that everything was properly organized. In it was a thick pile of notes from the immigration office in Winnipeg; from the files he learned that he would be visiting Manitoba's first group of Ukrainian-speaking settlers. The Stuartburn Colony had been established the previous summer, in August of 1896. Though the pioneers spoke Ukrainian, there was no country called Ukraine. These immigrants were more commonly called Galicians and Bukovinians, for they came from the Austrian provinces of Galicia and Bukovina. They had farmed for generations and, according to Mr. Sifton, were considered excellent immigrants for Canada's Western prairies.

Harrington read in his notes that the lead party of twenty-seven families had arrived at Quebec City just a year ago, on July 22, 1896, having sailed on the SS *Sicilia* from Hamburg by way of Antwerp. After a few days in the immigration sheds in Winnipeg, six men in their group went to Stuartburn, about seventy miles southeast of the city, to approve the location and the colony was established. Each family then chose their homestead from a map shown to them by government officials. It was also noted in the file that, as it was so late in the summer by the time they got to Stuartburn, there had been no time to plant a crop. Another ten Ukrainian families from Galicia had joined the group a few weeks later.

The government was hoping that tens of thousands more farmers from Galicia and Bukovina and other nearby provinces would be attracted to the Prairie Provinces in the coming years. Officials were counting on the new immigrants sending letters home telling of their great success in Canada.

Harrington returned the notes to the file and sorted through the other materials in his leather case.

He had pens and two bottles of ink and plenty of stationery, as well as a portable folding desk. There was also a letter from the immigration agent in Winnipeg confirming that one of the leaders of this group, a man by the name of Cyril Genyk, would meet him in Dominion City to act as his guide and interpreter. The agent had spoken highly of Genyk, who was a member of the Stuartburn colony. Harrington only hoped that Genyk also understood the value of bathing regularly.

Harrington also had in his possession several official documents related to the rules of the homestead program. Every homesteading family was given one hundred sixty acres of free land for a registration fee of just ten dollars. Within three years they would have to build homes and barns and to have cleared enough land to be growing crops. There was a great emphasis on their need to be self-sufficient.

Harrington removed his spectacles and polished them as he thought about the newcomers and the requirements of the government program. He pledged to himself that he would see that every rule was followed to the letter. He wouldn't hesitate to tell the homesteaders they might lose their land if they didn't work hard to see those crops established. This was no country for layabouts. Indeed, Roger Harrington wanted nothing but a stellar career in government and he would do everything possible to urge the success of the immigrant program.

He looked into his neatly organized case and hesitated just a moment before reaching for his little stack of calling cards. He allowed himself a moment to enjoy the pride he felt in handling them and anticipated how he would feel giving them to the settlers, seeing the look of respect in their eyes for the man from Ottawa. Surely these people were different from the ranchers near Calgary.

The urgency of Mr. Sifton's new immigration scheme came in answer to the astonishing fact that a million former Canadians had drifted south to the United States to find their fortunes. With a current population of only five million in the Dominion, this was a devastating loss. There was active discussion that the Americans were scheming to annex the whole of Western Canada. The Dominion was bleeding to death and Sifton was determined to stop it. His answer was to simplify the homesteading program and to advertise heavily to attract the right kind of immigrants from Europe and the United States. His aim was "to place a large producing population upon the Western prairies."

It was clear that the mass migration was underway. There were reports that people were on the move out of Europe by the tens of thousands, destined for the United States, Canada and South America. Sifton's immigration campaign was poised for overwhelming success.

"Dominion City!" The conductor called as he moved through the car. "Next stop, Dominion City!" Harrington woke with a start and saw that his papers had slid off of his lap and onto the floor when he dozed off. He rushed to scoop them up before they were trampled and was dismayed at the resulting disorder in his valise.

"Mr. Harrington! Is Mr. Harrington here?" A tall man with broad shoulders was calling into the rail car in a heavy Ukrainian accent.

"Yes, I am here," Harrington called back while donning his bowler and struggling into his jacket.

"I am Genyk." The friendly man gripped Harrington's hand and pumped it with enthusiasm.

Within moments the men were off the train and standing beside two saddled horses. The whining pitch of sawflies rose around them, competing with the rhythmic blasts of the steam engine as the train pulled away down the track. The sun blazed down and Harrington felt the searing heat on the back of his neck. He slipped out of his coat as Genyk lashed his new leather valise to a saddlebag.

"You want coat in bag on horse?" Genyk asked.

"You mean to say we will ride, then?" Harrington looked about to see what other options they might have and saw two Red River ox carts as well as a horse and wagon nearby.

"Sure, we ride. Is better than to walk. Too far."

"I see. I rather thought there might be a buggy, or a buckboard," answered Harrington. Seeing the questioning look on Genyk's face, he raised his voice. "Perhaps there is a wagon we can hire." He mimed holding reins when driving a carriage and bounced up and down a bit as he motioned to the nearby horse and wagon. Genyk turned to take a look but said nothing. He knew what was coming and enjoyed it. He started to whistle.

Believing that Genyk did not understand him, Harrington did the only thing he could think to do. He tried to shout his way through the language barrier.

"If it is money, Mr. Genyk, please, I have money to hire a wagon!"

Genyk turned and laughed, not with malice, but because these English people always did the same thing and he simply could not stop himself from laughing.

"Mr. Harrington, I am not deaf," he thumped his heavy hand on Harrington's shoulder a couple of times. "Shouting is no help. Also wagon is no help."

Harrington could only sputter, "I see. I mean, I don't see. Why can we not hire a wagon?"

"No road between farms. No bridge to cross river. Horses better."

"Oh. I see."

The two had plenty of time to become acquainted before finding the homesteaders' farms. The first part of the journey was relatively easy. There was a road, of sorts, full of gooey mud in the low parts and spotted with stones in other areas. The trail ran the eighteen miles from Dominion City to Stuartburn, and Genyk proved to be a most amiable companion and a fountain of knowledge. He told the story of the first group of families leaving their homes in Galicia for Canada the previous summer, of people saying good-bye to parents and other family members they knew they would never see again.

Harrington listened. At first he listened because he was tired and it was easy to let the words just slide off of his weary body, but soon he listened because the story was compelling and it shamed him. He realized that it was he who had resisted understanding the enormity of what the immigrants had been through and how much more difficulty lay ahead of them. He was wrong in the way he had been so quick to judge the people in Calgary. Most impressive was Genyk's passion for Canada and his great desire to see his fellow settlers make a success of their new homeland. He was a natural leader and a major ally for the government.

After many hours, they arrived at the Roseau River and saw a solid frame house and barn. The farm looked well-established and prosperous with thirty or more cows grazing in a large fenced pasture beyond the barn. Harrington looked at the tidy enterprise with admiration, and Genyk quickly explained that this farm was not one that belonged to a Ukrainian homesteader.

"This is cattle ranch of Mr. Ramsay. He built good farm over many years. Here is also post office in house. Mr. Ramsey is postmaster."

There was also a store nearby. Genyk told him they had arrived at Stuartburn, which the Ukrainians pronounced "Shtombur". Harrington slid off his horse, certain that he would never again be able to walk in a normal fashion. He was tired, he was dirty, and he felt badly that his new valise had taken a beating while strapped to the saddlebag. Goodness knows what his jacket would look like.

"From here we go toward Vita," said Genyk, pointing past the farm and speaking as though he had just had a good night's sleep. He turned to Harrington, who was white with exhaustion. "But first we rest. Yes?" He laughed and gave his government man a shove. "We stay tonight here."

The two spent the evening in the company of Mr. Ramsay and his family. Potatoes, green beans, and pork chops were served. It was plain and plentiful, and Mr. Harrington felt he had never had a more delicious meal.

They rose early the next day and set out on their way. Despite his sore muscles, Harrington found the early part of the ride enormously pleasant. He breathed in the delicate, moist fragrance of the trees and underbrush and delighted in the way the poplar leaves danced in the morning light. But as the sun warmed the trail and brought the biting horseflies to life, his pleasure in communing with nature was quickly extinguished.

Together Harrington and Genyk fought their way through the bush and mud and the ever-present mosquitoes from one farm to the next. As hard as he tried to spot the hatchet marks that had been notched on trees to mark the trail, he couldn't see them unless they were first pointed out by Genyk. He realized that were he to travel on his own in this country he would be hopelessly lost in minutes. He had assumed there would be roads. How do you bring people out to bush country and expect them to build farms without even a road to bring in lumber or farm animals?

The two traveled through acre after acre of bush where poplar, oak, and ash trees grew in thick abundance. They came upon a black bear and her cub, which was more startling to Harrington than to the bears, who looked on with curiosity before shuffling away.

The bush opened onto fields dotted with rocks. This poor land was in sharp contrast to the expansive open fields that had been settled by the Mennonites closer to Winnipeg, where rich meadows stretched for mile after mile ready to accept the plough.

They stopped to talk to farmers in the midst of their backbreaking clearing of the land and watched small children working alongside their parents, laboriously hauling one stone after another out of the dirt. He heard the settlers singing. Some of the songs were fast-paced and cheerful; others were plaintive, mournful tunes. One was about war and men leaving to become soldiers, Genyk explained, never again to see their lovers who waited for them or their mothers who stitched them a special scarf called a *rushnichok* to carry for remembrance.

Harrington marveled at the lonely little houses, each a two-hour walk or more from the nearest neighbor. He had never seen anything like it. The pioneers had carved their homes out of the ground, raising small cottages with thatched roofs that were plastered with prairie gumbo that they had somehow painted white. Each family had helped the next to be sure they would all be ready for winter. Little gardens, neat and productive, were set out next to the houses. The settlers had built clay ovens in the yards near the houses. Genyk said this type of oven was called a *pich,* which sounded like "peach" to Harrington's ear, and that they were built in addition to the ones in the houses used for heat and cooking in the winter. In summer, with the temperature often climbing well into the nineties, it was too hot to cook indoors.

Most of the Ukrainians had come to Canada with little or no money. This created additional hardship as it meant there was no money to buy farm animals, tools or basic necessities like flour unless the men found work that would pay wages. For this reason, most of the men had to leave their families in winter to find work. Some found jobs in nearby towns, or were hired to cut cordwood for fuel. Harrington heard stories about the trials of the women, who were alone with their children through the winter months while their men were away.

By evening, they had arrived at the farm of Peter Strumbicky. A large smudge had been lit near the house to provide relief from the mosquitoes. Peter, at sixty, was among the oldest of the immigrants at Stuartburn. His wife, Irena Goyman, was forty-two. They introduced their five children ranging from their oldest son, Nikola who was twenty-one, to little Rose, who had just turned two. The travelers were warmly welcomed and sat down with the family to a meal of beet soup that Irena called *borscht*. She served it with bread. There was no butter, they were told, because as yet, there was no cow.

"What do you do for milk for the children?" he asked. There was an exchange in Ukrainian between Genyk and their hosts. Mrs. Strumbicky shrugged at the question.

"No milk. Sometime, not often, she go to neighbor, Mr. Pidhirny, to bring pail of milk for children," Genyk interpreted.

"Does she take the children with her?" Harrington asked, looking at the smiling clean faces nearby. There was another exchange in Ukrainian. He watched Irena shake her head and pat the table as she spoke.

Genyk turned to him with the translation.

"She say if men are away working, and she is alone, she tie small children, Rose and Mattay, to table legs in house if she need to go to neighbor."

"Ties them up?" Harrington said in disbelief.

"To keep children safe. No go outside to get lost," Genyk smiled at the little ones.

"Why don't the older children look after the small ones?"

"Children working in fields. Four-years-old can carry rocks with older children."

Harrington felt a knot in his throat as he looked at the toddler who smiled and turned away shyly to her mother. Peter interrupted and said something to Mr. Genyk, then motioned he should tell the government man.

"Next month, they will have a cow. Next winter will be easier for the Missus. Also they will have big celebration. Nikola will be married to Aksana Shmigelsky who is coming with her family from the old country."

"Then they already know each other?" asked Mr. Harrington.

"*Tak*. Yes," said Genyk. "The Strumbicky family from Zalischyky in Galicia and just a few miles from them is Blischanka, where is coming the Shmigelsky family. They are friends for many years. Generations they are knowing each other."

When he asked how it was they had decided to come to Canada, Irena was given to tears. The story took the better part of an hour to tell and was punctuated by the hair-raising cries of coyotes howling in the night.

In the end, Harrington was transformed into a sympathetic champion of the new Canadians. What he learned was that their motivations for leaving their homeland were rooted in their history of serfdom over hundreds of years. Reforms had finally released them from obligations to noblemen but had left them with only small plots of land on which to survive. It became the custom in the old country that when a son was old enough to marry, his father would section off a piece of the little land he had to give to the son to start his new life. Through the subsequent generations, the area the Ukrainian peasants came from became seriously overpopulated, with too few resources left to support extended families. There also a severe shortage of trees for fuel and for construction.

Genyk explained that with the news of free land in Canada, coupled with their terrible hardship in the old country, the Strumbicky family, like others, believed their only hope was to leave. They prayed to God for their safety and sold everything they owned to come. As for the hard land they took up as their homesteads, to the Ukrainians, the abundance of trees in the area was itself a source of riches, providing wood for fuel, and rabbits and partridges to trap for food.

"To have this one hundred sixty acres, where before in old country they had one, maybe two?" Genyk raised two fingers in the air, then sighed, held is hands wide, and shook his head. "It is everything to own this land. With land you don't starve."

Irena was rocking Rose and quietly started singing a song. Genyk whispered to Harrington she was singing about a *bandura*, a Ukrainian stringed instrument. It had a lilting, haunting melody. The others joined in and soon they were all laughing and talking about the upcoming wedding celebration of Nikola and Aksana and speaking of the little baby Canadians that would be born into their family.

Harrington was deeply moved by their pride and determination to tame this unbroken wilderness and establish their families here. *Korinchikeh*, Peter called it. "Little roots," Genyk interpreted, "for the generations that will come after us."

Over the next long day, farmer after farmer spoke with Harrington. He learned that each faced the same struggles with the same resolve to succeed, and he came to understand the vast and overwhelming task before them.

Remarkably, in just one year, each family now had some kind of dwelling and each had put in a vegetable garden. Some had dug wells. The land was being cleared, one stone at a time, one tree at a time.

Winter had been especially hard for the settlers. At times the temperature dipped to thirty-five or forty degrees below zero, adding to the isolation of the homesteaders and the fear of dying from exposure.

What he had learned over the last few days weighed heavily on Roger Harrington's conscience as he made his way to the train platform in Dominion City.

"*Chikai, chikai!* Wait, Mr. Harrington! *Chikai!* I have something for to give to you, Mr. Government Man." Cyril Genyk, shouted in a mix of Ukrainian and English against the noisy arrival of the train as he strode toward him on the platform.

"Please to take it. It is special bread from Mrs. Strumbicky." He thrust a small parcel forward.

"How very kind." Harrington was quite taken aback. A family with barely enough to feed their children was giving him bread.

"It is paska, special for you from Ukrainian tradition," Genyk explained. "Usually it is just for Easter but she say to tell you she make it special to send prayers and good luck for you for journey to Ottawa."

"*Dock-yoo*, Mr. Genyk," Harrington tried his best to say thank you in Ukrainian. "Please say *doo-zha-dock-yoo*, thank you very much, to Mrs. Strumbicky and her husband for me." He stumbled through the unusual words and felt embarrassment rising under his shirt collar. He vowed to himself that by his next visit to the Ukrainian colony at Stuartburn, he would be able to express his gratitude correctly.

"*Dyacayu*, Mr. Harrington. Until next time. I am glad you come. Safe traveling for you, Mr. Harrington." Genyk shook the visitor's hand. As he turned to leave, Harrington stopped him.

"Wait!" he called. "Mr. Genyk, I also have a present." He unfolded his carefully protected coat that had cost him one month's salary.

"This jacket, could you please give it to Nikola Strumbicky so he will have it for his wedding to Aksana?" Genyk nodded and gently accepted the gift. He smiled and waved as Harrington boarded the train.

Evening was approaching and Harrington had about a two-hour ride to Winnipeg. He ached with fatigue and let out a long sigh. It would be late when he got to his hotel and he had much to prepare to be ready for his meetings in Winnipeg. He pulled out his notes. First to catch his attention was the list he made of the villages the Ukrainian settlers had left behind in the old country, Melnytsia, Zviniacha, Synkiv, Bereziv and many other names. All were new to him; all unpronounceable.

He shook his head. One hundred twenty people had set out for the golden new country a year ago and now all were fighting to take root in an inhospitable land with an impossible climate. Was this to be the foundation of the Canadian grain industry? These hardworking determined souls, picking rocks and boulders out of the soil, day in and day out, in the hope that one day a crop would be harvested. It seemed utterly impracticable.

Harrington could only shake his head. This is what Canada was advertising in Europe as the breadbasket of North America.

It seemed Ottawa knew nothing about what they were dealing with here.

11
Arriving in Winnipeg
July 29, 1897

The smell of the orchard, with its blossoming fruit trees, filled Hannah with delight. It would be a good harvest. It was always good when the stork made her nest on the roof of the barn. The old ones were right. It is a sign for good luck, the stork in her nest. Cherries, apples and plums danced from the trees and flew into the house, piling so high they dropped off the table. Clack, clack, clack. Hannah ran after the apples and plums but could not catch the flying fruit. Clack, clack, clack.

"Vinnipago, Vinnipago!" Someone shouted, startling Hannah and waking her. The acrid stench from travel-weary immigrants burned away the sweet fragrance of her dream orchard. Her neck hurt. Her back ached. But suddenly her aches and pains seemed utterly unimportant. They were just ten miles out of Winnipeg according to the marker that had been spotted next to the track. Soon she would be reunited with her husband; nothing else in the world mattered.

Eight days had already passed on the uncomfortable colonist car carrying them west from the port of Quebec City to Winnipeg. She found it was very warm in July on the prairies, much warmer than it would be at home. Hannah's matted hair and crusted clothing stuck to her skin. She longed for a proper bath. She tried to think when it was that she last felt clean or even the shame of not being clean. She shifted sleeping Mendel who was draped over her lap. How was it possible that a baby could weigh so much when he slept? She smiled wearily at her mother-in-law. Despite the travel, Bayla appeared bright-eyed, and youthful, belying her fifty-three years.

Across from Hannah, the three older children slept on. She settled back and looked out at the endless miles of prairie. It seemed a very long time since the family had said their goodbyes in Zalischyky and climbed aboard the cart with their bundles of belongings.

For more than two months they had journeyed. Hannah fixed on the memory of the hoof beats and the creaking wagon that had carried them along the familiar paths, past the cherry tree orchard and finally onto the big road to the train station in Chortkiv. From there, they had embarked for Hamburg. Bayla had been frightened of the train at first, Hannah recalled. The huffing and puffing of the great steam engine was more than she could have imagined.

Hamburg was a bustling center filled with noise, hucksters, and confusion. At the dock, Hannah watched in horror as people who said they were agents made their way through the crowd and sorted who would board and who would not. She saw Jewish neighbors turned away in favor of Ukrainian peasants. She counted herself fortunate to have received clear instructions from her husband. She knew how to process the documents and purchase the passports. She also knew how the bribes worked and how to avoid the confidence men.

Zev's most important advice, it turned out, was to dress the family as Ukrainian peasants and to speak only in Ukrainian on the dock. Zev had learned that the agents were paid a fee for every immigrant they placed on the ships and that a premium fee was paid for the farmers. He told her that she was to say that she was taking her family to Manitoba to join her husband on the farm at *Shtombur*.

Both Hannah and Bayla found the medical exam distressing, but soon their papers were stamped. They gathered up the children, and together they were shoved along through the crowd and onto the steamship.

The children were thrilled with the ship. They could not wait to clamber aboard to make new friends among the other children. At the dock, there were many people who spoke Yiddish and Ukrainian. Others spoke languages they did not recognize. Some wore clothes that were different and had light blonde hair and blue eyes. It was a startling sight for Hannah and Bayla who had never seen skin that light with bright eyes and hair to match.

The only thing all the passengers had in common was that they were immigrants, saying good-bye forever to the only life they had ever known, and leaving people they would touch and hug for the last time. Their heartache was the same no matter what language they spoke.

In the weeks before the trip, Hannah had successfully overcome her fear of the passage by focusing on the tremendous amount of work that needed to be done to prepare for the voyage. She was confident that the family was as ready as it would ever be, with food and clothing and the few treasures brought from home. As they all made their way down the stairs to the steerage deck, she thought only of Zev and how their long separation would come to an end.

She was fine until she saw the sleeping accommodations. There were no separate rooms, but one large space filled with cots placed side-by-side and stacked three high. Each cot was only two-and-a-half feet wide and six feet long, and connected to the next with sturdy metal bars. This formed the berth for each passenger.

Hannah and Bayle had huddled down in their assigned births with the children in the middle tier. For privacy, they placed sheets between themselves and the strangers, but so tightly packed were they that all through the night the jostling passengers bumped together. Bayla, ever practical and optimistic, praised the tight arrangement for it helped them stay warm and kept them from being pitched onto the floor by the movement of the ship.

Hannah was so unnerved she didn't sleep at all for the first two nights and Bayla had stern words for her, telling her that she must get some rest for the sake of the children. Think of the baby, Bayla scolded her, for her milk would stop and he would go hungry if she didn't eat and drink enough. Hannah did as she was told.

She was thankful for the fresh air on the deck. In the first few days, there was singing and dancing on deck, for there was great excitement about going to the golden land. A young man had a fiddle and another a *balalaika* and a third a *symbalis*. The familiar songs were full of hope and happiness.

112

All of that changed when the storm came up on their eighth day at sea. Hannah shivered with the memory. The ship had pitched and lurched through the rise and fall of the waves in the North Atlantic. Water splashed down on the deck, driving everyone inside for cover. In a short time, the already putrid air of the steerage deck became laden with sharp, bilious smells from vomiting passengers. There was no place to get away. She hunkered down in the berths with the children and together with Bayla, comforted them as best she could through the ordeal. Hannah was astounded at Bayla's resolute bearing through the height of the violent storm and ashamed at her own feelings of terror.

Hour after hour, the ship climbed the crests and crashed down between the swells. People who were not squashed into the bunks or clinging tightly were thrown about like rag dolls. Gripped with fear, Hannah could hardly breathe. With every groaning sway, she believed the ship would split apart and scatter them over the water like so much refuse.

She prayed that if this would be her time and that if the ship were to sink, that death would come swiftly to spare suffering. She imagined floating in the ocean and considered what it would be like to drown in that cold black water, helpless to protect her children. Her body went rigid with fear as the passengers around her moaned and cried out with each violent shudder of the ship.

At the worst of it, Hannah had become so ill that she bordered on being delirious. Her fear of dying changed into an oddly appealing resignation; perhaps her misery was near an end. Had it not been for the children, she might truly have welcomed drowning. When the storm finally ended, Hannah had firmly resolved that never again would she set foot on a ship: not even a boat if she could avoid it. Remarkably, the children and Bayla came through the frightful night seemingly unaffected, their spirits apparently completely restored by the brilliant dawn of a new day that brought calm seas and a bright blue sky, as if the storm had never happened at all.

Sitting on the train and remembering the horrible experience, Hannah shivered. By comparison, the discomfort of the train was little more than an inconvenience. Now, it was almost over.

Bayla smiled to herself and turned to the window to quiet the waves of feeling rising in her chest as she thought of Baruch. What sacrifices he had made. It had been so many years, almost fourteen, since she had seen her husband. Would he still love her? Would he still think her pretty? Would they have enough time and enough health to enjoy their lives in this new country, in this Canada that had no czar?

She reached out her hand and gripped Hannah's arm as happiness rose within her, her eyes lighting up in a way Hannah could not remember seeing before.

"After all these years, Hannah." The two women hugged each other. Nothing more needed to be said.

The passengers were starting to move about and gather their bundles. Expressions of joy and prayers of thanks in a dozen or more languages bubbled into the thick air of the railcar. A Christian woman struggled to her feet and started to sing in Ukrainian. Very soon others joined in. They sang in a solemn way, but the song was one of hope, called *Mnohaya Lita*, which translated into "Many Happy Years". It was a very old song that Hannah had heard sung many times at celebrations in Zalischyky. The tears ran down their faces and their voices were choked with emotion.

Winnipeg was finally coming into view. Little Mendel stirred and started to fuss in Hannah's arms. Heaped together, the other three children seemed more like a bundle of rags than future citizens of the new country. Now the exhausted travelers were rearranging their aching bones on the hard wooden seats and coming to life with excitement and anticipation. To start anew, to reunite with family, to see what life would bring as the future spilled out before them like the endless grass of the prairie. Would they finally have peace? Was it possible the violence would now truly be part of the past? Would they be left alone to live their lives as a family? Would there be no more fear? No czar telling them where to live and how to die?

Hannah felt her heart quicken. Sixteen months had passed since she had seen Zev. Would he be waiting there in Winnipeg? How would she know where to find him? So many people lived here in this modern city. Would anyone know where to look for him? Would anyone speak Yiddish? Of course, there would be many people speaking Yiddish. Zev had said so. Now she was worrying just to be worrying. But what if he is not there? Where should she go? Oh, yes, Patrick Street. Ask for Patrick Street. They might even be at the train station in this minute! Tears welled in Hannah's eyes. Eagerness filled her and numbed the aching weariness.

"Isaac, Ziporah," she called gently, so as not to startle them. "We are here. Wake up, Aaron. It is time to get our things together."

So, this is the new land. Would she ever see her home in Russia again? Or her sister and her family?

Hannah accepted that blessings and burdens were her life, her torment at times. To be so thoroughly happy and miserable all at the same time and for so much of the time, you needed to be a Jew, she thought. Only the Jewish heart can ache in this way at the same time it is bursting with love for the thought of seeing her family again together.

What if he is not there? What if he is sick or hurt? It had been four months since the tickets had arrived.

The clacking of the train on the track was slower now. The tall grass gave way to little wooden shacks. Finally, they crossed a big river that curved just like the Dniestr in Zalishchiky. The travelers craned to see out the windows and catch their first glimpse of the city. They marveled at the neat little wooden houses, packed tightly together. They twittered with wonder at the flowing robes and bare feet of the Indians leading heavily laden horses.

Finally, slowly, the train chugged to stop. The gasping steam engine and the shriek of steel on steel made it seem as if the train was a great beast that had expired with the weight of the past sufferings of every passenger on board. It was a fitting announcement to mark both the end of the voyage and the start of a new life.

Baruch drew the cart up to the corner and stopped.

"This is good enough," he said to Zev. "I don't want the horse should get too nervous with so much excitement with the people. I will wait with her."

"But Mama will want to see you, Papa," Zev said gently, seeing how anxious his father was. "You should come inside the station."

"Ach, maybe again we are waiting and they are not coming on the train," he answered. The two had met every train that had come into Winnipeg in the last four days. "Look, the train is stopping. Go now." Baruch nudged his son. "Is better for the horse for me to stay. You go on, Zev." Baruch jumped down from the wagon and brought a feedbag with a handful of oats to the mare.

Zev saw his father's tumbling emotions. After a lifetime of hardship and disappointment, these last few days of anticipating the arrival of his wife had been almost more than he could bear. Baruch had not spoken his feelings aloud, yet Zev knew that his father was worried that having been away from his wife so many years would leave little left of his marriage. It is a lot to ask of a woman to wait so long, and Zev knew no matter what he told his father, only seeing his mother would erase the fears in his heart.

Baruch stretched his hand up to rub the mare's muzzle and turned and smiled at his son. "Maybe this is the right train, Zev. Go find our family."

Zev smiled back. Though his father was barely over five feet tall, Zev saw him as a quiet giant of a man. No one in the family had suffered more than Baruch Zigman. He turned to elbow his way through the crowd. Everything would be different now that the family was again together. Surely they would arrive on this train. But what if they were not? Had they been delayed at the medical inspection in Quebec City? Maybe they were all in quarantine.

He worried about Hannah and the trials she had undergone. How many months had his wife carried the full weight of providing for the family? How would she look? How would they all look? How tall must his children be! And what of little Mendel? Who knew that God would bless him with the new son when he left for the New World? Poor Hannah, so hard she worked. One day his Hannah would live like a lady. Now, at least, she would be here so that he could take care of her and the children. His heart filled with pride and excitement as he searched the crowd.

"Children, don't be going far. You stay close to me. Ziporah, you hold on to Aaron!" Hannah shouted orders over the noise and confusion of people disembarking. She felt the ground sway beneath her and realized it was that every ounce of her flesh and bone had been imbued with the movement of the train. She steadied herself under the weight of Mendel. "Where are our bundles? Isaac? Do you have the small trunk?" There were so many people, so much shouting and confusion.

"Rooms for rent! Lady, come with me this way, I will take you to the fine home you need here in Winnipeg. A bargain for you and your children," a man called out to Hannah in Yiddish. A second appeared at her elbow.

"You need food? Come eat at my place. Just here across the street by the station. Good food. Food from the old country, and then we find you a room for your family, no?" This one spoke fast, switching from Ukrainian to Yiddish and even English, as one traveler after another shook him off. Hannah had come to learn a couple of words in English on the ship. She also knew enough to talk to no one, that there would be scoundrels and conmen waiting for the immigrant train.

"No, no, thank you. My husband is here. Do you know him? Zev Zigman. Do you know Zev Zigman?"

Isaac was the first to spot him.

"Mama, Mama! Look, it's Papa! Isaac pushed hard through the crowd to reach him, and Hannah waved wildly to catch his attention. Zev's face broke into a grin as he shoved along through the horde to reach them. Finally, as Isaac leapt out of the crowd, Zev swept him off his feet. Then he stepped back to proudly appraise his height and strength. In the next instant, the family fell into one great embrace, the children jumping with excitement. Hannah drank in the vision of her husband's face, so close to hers at last. She was so thankful to see him and to feel the strength of his arms around her. Tears overcame her as she realized that they had made it. All of them were alive and in the same place at last.

"Is it really true? Am I not dreaming, Zev?" Hannah laughed and cried and held out shy little Mendel to meet his father. For several minutes they were caught in the rush of happiness that came with the simple fact of finally being together once again. In a flurry of emotion, everyone was talking at once.

"And where is Baruch?" Bayla asked quietly, unable to hold back her tears. Zev grabbed his mother into an embrace.

"He is here, Mama, and he is well. He is nearby with a surprise," he said, kissing her wet cheeks, delighting in seeing her and holding her close.

"A surprise?" Bayla was annoyed and relieved all at once. "And me at the station, he doesn't come to see!" Zev laughed and hugged her again and she smiled back.

"You will see him, Mama. In just a few moments, you will see him." With this, Zev moved his family through the throng and out to the street in front.

The train station's doors fronted onto Fonseca Street, which was bathed in sunshine and gaily dressed with flags. The air was sweet and the breeze warm and light.

The children quickly forgot their tiredness as they gawked at the buildings and the people. Hannah was overwhelmed with the enormity of the moment as she listened to her children all talking over each other, so delighted to see their father at last. The questions splashed down on Zev like a welcome summer rain. Hannah watched and was replenished by the easy patter back and forth. The time apart was maybe not so long after all.

And now, what life would their children make for themselves in the new country? What life would there be for all of them here?

They had come to a building where a long line of travelers stood. "Zev, what is this place?" Hannah asked. "Do we have to go through yet another line to talk to officials?" She was horrified at the thought.

"This is the immigration shed. No, you finished your papers

when you arrived in Quebec City. These people are registering to get their farms."

"Why is there a tent there?" asked Ziporah.

"There is not enough space for all of the people who are coming to stay in the immigration sheds," Zev answered. "They need to sleep somewhere until they can find their parcels of land and start building. It is already August next week. There is no time to put in a crop. They will be lucky to have time to build shelter to protect them through the winter. The government will allow them to stay here for two or three weeks but most will be on their way as soon as they can."

"And who will help them?" Ziporah was pained to think that their fellow immigrants would have to now regain their strength in a few days in a shed or a tent, only then to go out to build a house somewhere out in the country while she was going to a house and a meal that had been prepared for them.

"It is as always," Papa said. "They will help each other, like we help each other."

"Hello there! Do you not have a kind word for an old man?" A small man with a long beard and familiar droop in his shoulders called out in Yiddish to the family. He stood next to a peddler's cart with an impatient young horse, stamping against the noise of the crowd.

"Who is that, Papa?" asked Ziporah.

"That is your Zaida!" Baba shouted and then burst into tears. Picking up her skirts, she ran for all she was worth. The others stood and watched the old man sweep his wife into his arms and hold her as if he was hanging on to life itself. He kissed her and held her out to look again at her as if he held a miracle in his arms. Then Baruch laughed out loud in a way that shed the many long years of loneliness. Holding each other tight, the couple turned to the children.

"And who are these handsome young people?" Baruch teased, embarrassed at his tears.

Zev introduced each of them, from oldest to youngest and expressed his delight in his strong, wonderful family.

Baruch looked carefully into each of the faces of the grandchildren he was finally meeting, and God smiled back at him through their eyes. The old man shook his head. He cleared his throat.

"That's enough now. Now we go home." His heart was bursting with happiness at the thought that he would have his dear, beautiful Bayla by his side for the rest of his life. That he was also blessed to hear the name *Zaida*, from these fine children, *his grandchildren*, was almost too much.

Zev and the children made quick work of stowing the little bundles and the wooden trunk in the wagon. Baruch turned and started to whistle an old tune as he helped Bayla take her seat next to him.

"Zaida! Zaida!" Isaac cried. "What is the name of the horse?"

"She has a good Canadian name," answered Baruch. "Queenie."

Baby Mendel was the only one who held back. Still warily sizing up his father, he was even more hesitant with his grandfather.

"Come, now, Mendel," Hannah laughed as she tickled the chubby baby. "You will soon get used to the voices of men. Your grandfather has waited too many years to meet his grandchildren."

"Come along," said Zaida. "We go now to our new home on Patrick Street. I will show you the synagogue on the way. It is very close to here." The little cart, now heavily laden with the family, rode along Fonseca and turned right onto a very wide and dusty street.

"Papa, I've never seen a street so big across. It would be hard to throw a rock from one side all the way to the other side," said Isaac.

"It is true. This is Main Street and it is the mud that makes it so wide," Zev told him.

"The mud? That sounds silly, Papa!"

"It's a BOOBY MEISTER!" shouted Aaron. Zaida, who had been quietly enjoying the conversation, suddenly burst out laughing. He laughed so hard and so long that soon everyone was laughing.

"You mean a little nonsense story, Aaron?" Baba said to her

red-faced grandson who quickly nodded. "The way to say it is *bubbe meiser*, but I think I like your way better."

"Well is it a funny story, Papa?" Aaron wanted to know.

"It's a true story," Papa answered enthusiastically. "I don't know how funny it is, but it will answer the riddle of why the streets are so wide. Do you see down there is a cart with very large wheels pulled by oxen? It is called a Red River ox cart. There are many still here. They are very good way to move slowly but steadily to where you need to go, especially if it is wet and muddy, because even if you have to go slowly, you will never get stuck with those big wheels and big, patient animals. The mud here in Winnipeg is the worst I have ever seen. The name "Winnipeg" even comes from the name the Indians use for mud. In the springtime especially, it is easy to get stuck. The English call it prairie gumbo. I won't tell you the word that it is called by just about everyone who gets stuck in it. It's not nice for children to say. In the summer the mud turns to dust. Today is not so bad, but soon you will see that when even a tiny bit of wind is in the air, the dust is so thick behind the cart that the people behind choke into their sleeves. So, now who can guess how the mud makes the road wide?" he asked.

Ziporah strained to see up Main Street one way, and then the other. She saw lots of carts riding side by side.

"If the carts are next to each other, then no one chokes from the dust!" she shouted and Isaac laughed.

"Whoever heard such a stupid thing?" he teased his sister.

Baruch laughed and smiled at his grandson. This one had a thing or two to learn, but he seemed to be a good boy.

"Your sister is right," said Zev. "The roads are wide here because people ride beside each other to avoid the dust. You will see that Portage Avenue, which we will see in the coming days, is even wider. You can put sixteen carts beside each other. And I'm told that in the old days you would see the carts moving that way through Winnipeg on their way west. It's been that way for over thirty years, when there were just a couple of hundred fur traders living here. Now all we have left of the old times is the souvenir of the wide roads and Red River ox carts, like those you see.

"I think this is a very interesting place to live, Papa," said

Isaac, as they turned left onto Henry Street.

"It is that. Now here coming up is King Street and we have a fine synagogue, already six years on this corner. This is the Shaarey Zedek, where Zaida is spending time teaching and learning," Zev said with obvious pride. "You, too, will come to study soon, yes?"

This led to many more questions, one on top of another. Baruch was overcome with joy. "Children, have patience. We cannot tell every story all at once," he laughed. "In time you will know all of the answers, and all of the stories. I want you should know what we have done in keeping our ways, yes? But, today is for settling in your new home, no?"

A few minutes later, the wagon stopped in front of a tiny wooden house, one in a row of other little houses that appeared to have popped out of the bald prairie along with the dandelions. Hannah's mouth dropped open. There were hollyhocks growing in the small patch of a front yard. And while there were no trees, there was a neat and orderly vegetable garden on the side of the house.

"It looks like a "just new" house," she said at last. "This is beautiful," she smiled at Zev.

The family crowded into the house filled with excitement and appraised the clean little rooms.

To Baruch, the many years of sacrifice were suddenly worth everything. The crowded little house was spilling over with the joy of having his wife and this large excited family before him. To have this reunion and to have succeeded at long last in his quest to bring his family out of Russia were deeply humbling. His life had taken an excruciatingly difficult path, filled with losses, loneliness, deprivation and much cruelty. Now he stood before God with his heart brimming with gratitude absorbing the holiness of this moment. He held his hands up to quiet them.

"First, please come and we will sing the *Shehecheyanu* to give thanks for our miracle, yes?"

They joined together and in one voice sang the ancient Hebrew blessing.

Baruch atah adonai eloheinu melech ha'olam

Shehecheyanu v'kiy'manu v'higyanu lasman hazeh. Amen.

Bayla looked into her husband's eyes and reflected on the words as she sang them. "Blessed are You, Adonai our God, Ruler of the Universe who has given us life, sustained us, and allowed us to reach this moment in time."

She believed with all her heart that God had indeed sustained them and brought them together in Winnipeg to reach this moment in time.

Then the exploration of the tiny home began in earnest. The rented house had four rooms, two small bedrooms for the two couples, a front room, and a kitchen. A small wood-burning stove sat between the two front windows. The children staked out their sleeping places. The boys would have the front room, which Hannah laughingly insisted on calling the parlor, and Ziporah would make her bed near the kitchen stove.

The kitchen was in the back of the house. Against the outside wall there was an iron cook stove. A wood box and small table were next it and on the adjacent wall, a cupboard and work stand. Near the door, a tidy washstand held a metal bowl with a pitcher. Two towels hung neatly on the rack attached to it. Zev showed them that the kitchen door leading outside actually opened into a well-organized porch-like extension on the house. Firewood was stacked along the wall, and Zev explained that in the winter only this entrance would be used so that the cold air would not rush into the house. He showed them all the trap door, with its big iron ring, in the kitchen. Taking hold of the ring, he pulled the door up to reveal stacks of potatoes, turnips, and carrots in the dugout under the kitchen. Baba nodded her head with approval, and Hannah was filled with happiness. She said she couldn't wait to fill the storage space with jars of fruits and pickles she and Baba would can for the winter. After the many weeks of travel, the family was delighted with their new surroundings.

They turned their attention to the backyard where there was a small shed and six chickens scavenging about in a pen. On one side of the shed was a stable for Queenie. And in back of it was a small workroom with Papa's carpentry tools.

Next to the stable was a chicken coop with a sharply angled

roof and two rows of nests. "We will never go hungry with the number of eggs we have coming from those chickens," said Papa. He was quickly overwhelmed with volunteers to collect them.

Along the back lane was a narrow structure with a slanted roof similar to the chicken coop. "Is that the outhouse?" Aaron wanted to know.

"It is, though here the English call it a 'box closet'. You see how crowded the street is. Each yard is only twenty-five feet or so across and perhaps forty feet deep. In the old country we used to dig a deep hole, and every few years when the hole was filled, we dug a new hole and moved the little outhouse over top," Zev explained. "Here, the houses are too crowded to do that. So the English who run the city came up with the plan to put a box in there that has be the emptied by the city workers. It is emptied not so often as you will think is good, Hannah, I tell you that now. So this is how they call it a box closet. In the fancy houses they have a room in the house with a bathtub, a sink, and a porcelain toilet with water for flushing. This they call a water closet because the waste is flushed with the water from the house to the sewer. You understand?"

"I understand that one day I would very much like a water closet," observed Hannah, nodding as she considered the backyard. "Where is the well?"

"This, too, is different. All of these homes on this street and the two near us, which are called Lizzie and Laura, share the water from a well that is two blocks from here. I bring the water in a barrel."

Hannah took her time as she surveyed her surroundings and saw in every detail how hard her husband and his father had worked to make this home for her and the family.

"Zev, this will be a wonderful house for us," she said, encircling her husband with her arms. "We will be very happy here. Now show me the garden."

12
The Immigrant Problem
August 6, 1897

Roger Harrington's week of meetings in Winnipeg had yet to pay off, and he hoped that his session with Rupert Willows would be the turning point. He checked his pocket watch and rushed out of the Manitoba Hotel, happy to see a string of cabs waiting. There was too much at stake to risk being late for his appointment.

"Do you know Ravenscraig Hall?" he asked the driver as he climbed into the carriage. "It's on Assiniboine Avenue in Armstrong's Point."

"Yes, of course, sir," answered the Irish cabbie as he took up the reins. "That would be the home of Alderman Willows."

"That's right. How long to get there, do you think?"

"Oh, I'd say about no more than twenty minutes, sir," the driver responded cheerfully as he eyed the fine clothes of his customer. "Would you care for a wee bit of a tour of downtown, sir? No extra charge. There's great things goin' on with all of the building and all," he enthused, his gold tooth glinting in the morning sun. "Yes, indeed, Winnipeg is going to be the Chicago of the North, without doubt."

"No, thank you. Not this time," Harrington smiled patronizingly at the chatty driver. Everyone had a hand out for a tip in this town. "Just the direct route would be fine, thank you." Harrington was already on edge and had no interest in hearing yet one more person infected with Winnipeg boosterism talk his ear off. He needed time to think through his presentation. So, he pulled out a newspaper, polished his reading glasses and settled back into his seat, pretending to read. His most important work had yet to be completed, and he was afraid his career might be in peril upon his return to Ottawa.

As an emissary for the federal immigration minister in Ottawa, Harrington's primary responsibility was to help ensure the success of the government's ambitious immigration program. The goal was to get great numbers of immigrants to settle the prairies and create productive farms. In this round of meetings in Winnipeg, his chief task was to inspire support for the onslaught of foreigners who would soon be arriving.

It was a confounding situation. Newspapers, politicians and cabbies alike were consistently boastful and positive about how quickly the Western cities of Winnipeg, Calgary, and Edmonton were growing. Everything seemed perfect on the surface, but inevitably in his discussions he would hear complaints about the foreign-born immigrants. The problem was enormous. It had become obvious that it would be immigrants from East Europe who would be the backbone of the farming industry in Western Canada, yet these were the people least likely to find open arms to greet them.

Here in the Keystone Province, as Manitoba was known, Harrington needed commitments from civic leaders, local businesses, and community do-gooders to assist in the transition of the immigrants and to help them get settled in the new country. So far, his discussions in Winnipeg were going poorly.

Aside from the odd charitable organization, the local people were quite vocal about their preference for English-speaking people from Ontario, Great Britain, and the United States take up the plow in the West. The resistance against the Slavic newcomers, in particular, was already firmly established. Greenhorns, they were called. Most were very poor, more than half were illiterate, and almost none spoke any English. Prejudice had quickly hardened against them, prompted by the simple fact that their customs were considered backwards at best, and at worst, boisterously inappropriate.

Religion, too, was often an issue for the many cultures migrating out of east and central Europe. Harrington was repeatedly asked, who were these people and what customs did they have? He had come to learn that one dared not be the first to say the word "Jew" out loud, for fear of starting an argument.

There were other complications associated with the ambitious plan to populate the countryside. To get enough capable farmers, Canada was going to have to cope with its cities being choked with immigrants who could not, or would not, farm. In addition, there was a disproportionate flood of men entering the country. Many of the immigrants were married and expected to send for their families as soon as they were settled. There were also large numbers of single men looking for opportunity in the New World.

This lack of women and children in the West had given rise to the seamier side of the economy, involving booze halls and brothels. The social reformers and temperance movement leaders were becoming particularly concerned about the number of saloons and houses of ill-fame that were popping up like weeds in communities all along the rail line.

Almost every politician and business leader Harrington had spoken to seemed to be too busy with his own worries to think about new settlers. Their message was clear: the foreign born were reluctantly welcome. Getting them settled would be the federal government's problem.

It was going to be extremely challenging for all concerned.

The driver turned the carriage into the large gates of Armstrong's Point and the gelding clipped smartly along beneath the young elms and willows of the stately neighborhood. Harrington was impressed. He pulled out his pocket watch and saw that he was going to be about a quarter of an hour early for his appointment with Mr. Willows. He hoped it would go well.

They turned through a second gate and Harrington choked when he saw the mammoth dark house appear before them. Oh, dear God. Was this Ravenscraig?

Harrington regarded the ornate patterns in the silver tray before him. He took his time in carefully placing his calling card in it.

"Mr. Willows is on the telephone," the butler informed him, and then motioned to a large, well-upholstered chair, indicating that Harrington should sit. Harrington looked at the chair and then turned to ask a question, but found himself alone. It was as though the butler had vanished.

Harrington shook himself back to his task at hand. He consulted his notes and went through his prepared talk in his mind one more time. He imagined Mr. Willows leaning forward to hear more. He would tell them about the earnest hard work to clear the land at Stuartburn and of the fine quality of the immigrants settling the land. He was determined to win over the alderman.

Twenty-five minutes later, well prepared and anxious to get his meeting underway, Harrington set his papers back into his case and turned his attention to the details of the stylish front hall of the Willows home. He was particularly impressed with the circular stairway and the rich choice of furnishings and artwork. He quite liked the chandelier and the way the light from the windows above the front door danced on the crystal. He checked his watch again. Another ten minutes had passed. He took a deep breath and stood to stretch his legs. He moved toward a massive portrait of Rupert Willows staring down at him. He recognized the alderman from a photograph he had seen in the morning newspaper. In the painting, Willows was portrayed in full riding costume, a scarlet jacket handsomely cut to accent his broad shoulders and athleticism. With the hounds to the side, he posed with perfect posture next to a black thoroughbred.

There was something strikingly familiar about the portrait. Could it be by the famous British artist, Heywood Hardy? It certainly looked like it might be, but something wasn't right. Harrington stepped closer and strained to see the subtle signs of Hardy's style. He couldn't find them. Nor could he find a signature. It seemed to be a fine copy that would pass with the less educated; and as he studied the painting, he grew increasingly certain that Rupert's smiling face had been expertly set upon the body of a youthful rider.

"Well, the cheeky devil," Harrington muttered to himself, staring at the painting.

"Excuse me, sir. Mr. Willows will see you now, Mr. Harrington." Chadwick had entered the room so quietly Harrington jumped at the sound of his voice. How long had he been standing there?

"Yes, thank you." He turned to pick up his briefcase. "Excuse me, Mr. Chadwick. Might I ask you a question? Do you happen to know anything about this painting?"

"I can tell you only that Mr. Willows considers it his favorite likeness of himself, sir. It was painted last year." Mr. Chadwick spoke in the sincere and hushed tones one might expect from an undertaker.

"It looks rather like a Heywood Hardy."

"Yes. It does, rather," answered the butler with an educated air.

Aha. Harrington smiled as he picked up his case. Why would the man have created a fake Heywood Hardy?

"Please do come this way, Mr. Harrington." Chadwick glided into a turn and they proceeded down the corridor to a large, ornate wooden door. Chadwick knocked and entered first, then nodded and held the door for the guest. Harrington was amused by the utter pretentiousness of it all.

"Well, hello, Mr. Harrington." Rupert extended his hand and forced a jovial greeting. He was annoyed that his telephone conversation had been a short one. Rupert felt he looked more important to certain of his callers if he kept them waiting; he had chosen to treat Harrington in this way. He had even gone as far as killing time with a game of solitaire, so as not to appear too eager to see the government man. Cards that didn't involve betting were his least favorite games.

The men exchanged customary flattery and small talk before easing into their meeting. It began well enough. Listening to Willows list his many accomplishments, Harrington recognized an opportunity and made great show of offering greetings from the minister, adding that Ottawa considered men like Rupert to be among the "New Breed" of politicians that were so needed to build the country. Emboldened with the praise, Rupert saw it was time to educate the man from Ottawa on the nation's immigration policies, and demonstrate that he would not be manipulated into becoming a puppet for Mr. Sifton. The mood of the room quickly bristled into confrontation.

"I tell you, Harrington, this immigration policy is all wrong. There are no measures to keep these heathens from taking over." Rupert paced about his library in anger, jabbing the air and glaring at the bureaucrat seated before him. "I can't possibly support this notion of the Dominion just throwing its doors open to bring in all manner of suffering and pestilence. It will be the ruin of our city and the ruin of the nation, I say."

Harrington patiently presented the opposite view, attempting to explain that the plan would result in the creation of a vibrant, prosperous nation, a true leader among the Dominions of the British Empire.

"I rather thought that you were a fan of Clifford Sifton, Mr. Willows. Everyone in Ottawa is raving about his capabilities as a champion for the growth of Western Canada."

"Manitoba politics are different from federal politics, Harrington. I will grant you that Sifton was very skilled in his handling of his duties as attorney general of our Manitoba legislature, particularly in the way that he put a stop to that French language nonsense in the schools. And indeed he had a firm hand in outlawing French in the whole province, for which I do say I am very thankful. How absurd was it that the province was made to accept that the use of French was as important as English? I never did understand the Catholics on that one. My God, man! Here we are subjects of the British Crown, for heaven's sake. So, yes, Sifton was very good in setting that right, and I'm very happy about his putting the French in their proper place. However, his take on immigration is all wrong."

Harrington could only nod quietly during what he saw as a highly offensive over-simplification of the clash between the French and English in Manitoba. He chose to move on rather than respond and coughed lightly.

"Perhaps I haven't been clear in my explanation," he said with deference. "Mr. Sifton is deeply concerned about the future of the West, and particularly that our great expanse of open prairie is now of prime interest to our southern neighbors."

"That nonsense with the Americans wanting to annex Western Canada, you mean?" Rupert huffed. "Do you really believe that, Harrington? It sounds preposterous. Who would want all that empty space?" He flipped the air with a manicured hand and reached for his cigar.

"There have been discussions, Mr. Willows. This is a very real threat. I can assure you that the minister believes that by putting enough people on the land as British subjects, the Dominion will protect the West from takeover by the United States and he means to do it. The advertising campaign in Europe shows signs of great success and the settlers are starting to come. Thousands will be here before the end of this shipping season."

"And from what I read in the papers, I take it most of them are not coming from jolly old England."

"Well, as you also probably know, we are advertising heavily in the British Isles, but we do not seem to be getting the numbers of experienced farmers that are needed."

"Naturally that means the government will hold its nose and go after the great unwashed in the sewers of East Europe to populate the West. Is that it, then?" Rupert puffed a smoke ring.

Harrington felt his patience wearing down. "Begging your pardon, sir, but, do you not see that as just a bit uncharitable? There are great troubles in East Europe with the political situation with the Russian czar and the poverty and of course the violence against, uh, certain groups, I should say."

"You mean the Jews?" asked Rupert.

"Well, yes, but that is quite aside from the issue. The point I am trying to make is that the misfortunes of the common man in those countries become the opportunity for the Dominion of Canada to grow and prosper. These are people who are desperate to find a home and to make a living. They know how to farm and we need farmers."

"The Jews don't farm. Why should we pay for the Jew to come here and become a burden?"

Harrington, now deeply offended at the callous and racist pronouncements from his host, was in danger of losing control and fought to mask his increasing discomfort in the face of Rupert's bigotry and blatant ignorance. Steeling himself, he rose with new determination to turn him into an ally.

"Perhaps you don't know about the special arrangements for the Jews. There is a movement through a Jewish philanthropist named Baron de Hirsch who is helping to pay the way for the Jews to move to Canada and other countries, so there really is no cost in having them settle here. There is only the promise of valuable new citizens."

"Well, isn't that just fine for you to say, as you are ready to board the train tomorrow morning and head back east leaving us to cope with the burden of these East European newcomers. How many will go to Ottawa? A fraction of what will be coming west, I dare say."

"Sir, I well understand your concerns, but let's move to the advantages that exist directly for you in this, shall we? There is another part of this that you might find of interest," Harrington said, ignoring Rupert's question. He barreled on with enthusiasm. "You see the federal government is intent on building a tremendous grain industry on all of that open land you speak of. Now, if a person of your means were to make a small investment in the grain business at this time, you may be very well rewarded, I should think."

"Now it's my money you want as well?" Rupert threw his head back and laughed.

"You would have an opportunity to get in at the beginning, just as you did in the land boom here, Mr. Willows. There are great demands for the limited amount of grain grown in the West. The quality is good and the future is strong."

Rupert leaned forward and looked at his guest with new interest. He had heard discussion about plans to create a major grain industry recently at the Manitoba Club.

"What do you know about it?"

"Growing grain will be the foundation of Manitoba's economy. The expectation is to build an industry that will not only feed the nation but will be a lucrative export. There is big money to be made."

"Well, perhaps, I might look into it." Rupert stroked his chin as he savored his cigar. "But you digress. You have a problem. You need me to help you sell this immigration policy the way Sifton sold you. 'Yes, Mr. Sifton. You are so right, Mr. Sifton,'" Rupert mocked.

He glanced at Harrington and saw him grimace. "So! My good man, please excuse my bad behavior, Harrington. It has been rather frustrating to be so far away from the powers that make these decisions in Ottawa on our behalf, and I'm afraid I must admit it raises the bile. So tell me again, where is it that this latest bunch is coming from? Galoshes or something?"

"Galicia, and also Bukovina. Provinces in Austria."

"And do any of them learn to speak and write English over there?"

"Well, I must tell you honestly, the answer is not likely. They speak Ukrainian, although you will generally hear them referred to as Galicians, Bukovinians, and Ruthenians. There have been many border changes in recent times. But, I can tell you they are hard-working, honest people. I've seen it for myself." Watching Rupert's expression he hastened to add, "and they are Christians, this group. The founders of the first colony are managing quite well at Stuartburn."

"How many of them are there?"

"In the two parties that arrived last year, there were about one hundred twenty people. This year and every year forward will have a much greater number of immigrants. Tens of thousands in future years, we believe."

"And they don't speak our language? That's preposterous, don't you think?" Rupert was now enjoying Harrington's discomfort.

"As I understand it, the depth of their poverty precludes education. The majority, as I mentioned, would be unable to read or write even in their own language, but of course there are some exceptions." Harrington paused for a second and, understanding the value of a full disclosure quietly added, "Oh, and there will also be a handful of Jews arriving in Winnipeg this summer. More of the Jews are literate, though not in English."

"Wonderful!" Rupert clapped his hands and laughed out loud. "Just fantastic! And while we are at it, let's not stop with those who grunt their way through life in Ukrainian and whatever other languages come out of the Slavic countries of Europe. Let's just throw away the future of the entire Dominion and hand the whole bloody thing over to the Jews!" Rupert was shouting now.

Obviously, winning over Rupert Willows was more of a difficulty than Harrington had anticipated. Yet there was so much at stake, both in Harrington's job and in the desperate needs of the immigrants. As ugly as the prospect was, he had to fashion some way of enticing Willows into coming on side. Harrington took a deep breath, then swallowed hard against the vile words he knew would bring Rupert around.

"It's not as if they will be setting up their little sod huts and rag picking businesses right here in your garden at Ravenscraig Hall," Harrington sniggered. "I'm sure you will never see a trace of them anywhere near your home." He inwardly cringed at his own words. The things one had to do when one's bread was buttered with a political knife.

A slight smile played at Rupert's lips. The officious Ottawa bureaucrat was starting to see his point. "And what is there to prevent it?" He arched an eyebrow as he challenged his guest.

"Well, the gates on your neighborhood entrance for one thing." Harrington risked a wisecrack and felt his heart flutter. Silence, but for the clock ticking.

Then suddenly, Rupert threw his hand to his knee and laughed out loud.

Harrington joined his laughter, with what he hoped would be heard as genuine amusement. "Come on now, Alderman, you know more about this immigration policy than most of the citizens of Winnipeg. Where do you see that there is anything but good to come from getting people into this province? So they are poor and they don't speak English. What of it? Most of them are going to be out on the land anyway. We have one hell of a future in the grain industry here, and we just cannot grow wheat without farmers."

"Yes, yes, Harrington, I will concede that it is a way of the future, and I agree we need to populate the area. But is there any reason why we cannot attract better immigrants? Must we be stuck with the dregs of Europe, and Eastern Europe at that? I know it is a pipe dream to think that we would have droves of capable farmers coming to us from England and Scotland and Ireland and other parts of the British Empire. Lord knows we already spend a fortune on advertising to them, but would that not be the ideal? They speak our language. They share our dreams. They live under the British flag. And if there aren't enough of them, well, then what about the Germans? The

Mennonites do very well here, as you know. They make wonderful farmers. They are clean, good, solid Christian citizens, who seem very well-suited for the purpose of farming. Do you understand? You have to see the problems we have here in the West. Yes, we need people to farm the land, grow the wheat and buy the goods, I grant you that, but you see my point as well, Roger, don't you?"

Harrington's eyebrows went up. He had been called by his first name for the first time in the entire discussion. He was making progress. "Believe me, if we could find them, we would," he quickly agreed. "But there is a limit on how much time we have to get that land settled before the Americans just annex the Canadian West. At some point, we won't be able to stop them."

"I see what you are saying, but I don't like it." Rupert was on his feet pacing again. "You know what will happen, don't you? You will have one shipload after another of Eastern Europeans landing in Canada, and all of these lost souls will wind up cramming our cities with their filth and poverty. Mark my words. They will not be on the land. They will be in the cities and in the way. Winnipeg will go from being the bull's-eye of the Dominion to the black eye of the nation."

Rupert tugged at his sleeves before discreetly stopping at the corner of his desk to hit a button. But he no longer wanted to get rid of Harrington as quickly as he had when his visitor had first arrived. The thought of making a fortune in the new grain industry was starting to take some of the edge off of his prejudice against foreigners, and he wanted to learn more about it. "I'll tell you what. Stay for dinner, will you? We can continue this discussion and you can meet my wife. Beth would love to hear all your news about the fashionable class in Ottawa."

"Oh, thank you so much, but I would never think of putting you out this way." Harrington was delighted with the invitation but did not want to appear to be overly eager.

"Nonsense. There is no point in us having anything but a civilized discussion, of course, and I mean to see to it that you hear me out on these immigration problems before you return to Parliament Hill. I have plenty to tell you about the head tax on the Chinaman."

At this moment, as if produced by an illusionist, Mr. Chadwick materialized in the room.

"Do please tell Mrs. Butterfield that we will have another guest for dinner this evening, Chadwick. Mr. Harrington will be joining us as well."

"Very good, sir," said Chadwick, bowing and disappearing.

"Well, if you insist, Mr. Willows," Harrington said.

"I do indeed. Please call me Rupert. And to help you enjoy the evening, I can tell you that we will also be hosting Mayor McCreary and James Ashdown. Both have solid ideas about the development of the city, and I'm sure they will be very interested in your news from Minister Sifton."

Harrington was suddenly aware he had struck a home run and smiled broadly. "You are very kind. Please forgive me, but who is Mr. Ashdown?"

"Who is Ashdown? For heaven's sake, man! You really must start paying more attention to the Winnipeg papers. James Ashdown is synonymous with Winnipeg itself. He's been here for a couple of decades and owns the hugely successful Ashdown store on Main Street. Ashdown will be mayor one day, you'll see. Practically everything that comes through Winnipeg comes through that store. If anyone should have a keen eye on what opportunities there are to make a dollar on this immigration scheme we seem to be stuck with, then I say that Ashdown is the one to be heard."

"Well, then, I must say I am very pleased to join you, and I thank you for this opportunity, Rupert."

Harrington smiled to himself. He would have a good report to take back to Minister Sifton, after all.

13
Ragpicker

November 14, 1898

It was only the middle of November, but already winter had taken hold of Winnipeg and pummeled the city with enough snow that ruts had formed in the streets and slick ice patches had formed on the wooden sidewalks. Queenie picked her way over the uneven road and plodded steadily along with the pans rattling musically in the cart. Zev Zigman whistled a happy tune to keep time with the mare's steps. It had been a good day for sales, and he was heartened by the extra coins in his pocket.

Zev had easily adapted to the cold in Winnipeg and had learned to enjoy the brilliant blue skies of the prairies and the sparkling ice crystals reflecting in the snow. He decided he would make just one more stop for the mail and head home early.

Zev's enterprise had been a great help to the family. Money was slower in coming than he would have liked, but they weren't starving. He made enough to pay the rent, and much of the rest of what the family needed came from bartering. Potatoes, onions, cabbage, and garlic were staples of their diet along with the eggs and chickens from their yard. Once in a while he would trade something he had on the wagon for herring scraped from the bottom of the barrel at Weidman's Grocery to take home as a treat for his family.

Overall, the Zigman family was making progress. In addition to the peddler's cart, they had taken in boarders. It was crowded, but they were sustained by their dreams. The debt Zev had incurred to pay for his family's tickets to come to Canada was slowly being paid down, and Zev had started a special savings jar to send for his brother Leib's family in England.

Six days a week, Zev traveled with Queenie and his loaded wagon through the neighborhood streets, selling his goods and collecting castoffs. Pots and pans, old clothing, blankets, buttons, and even jars of pickles found their way onto his cart. He took anything he thought he could sell for a profit. His customers called him a rag picker. Zev hated the term. He called himself a peddler, or a traveling salesman. Though he thought it pretentious to admit it, Zev especially liked the term used by his French-speaking customers. They called him a *colporteur*.

There was just one letter waiting when he stopped to pick up the mail and it was gaily decorated with British stamps. He scooped it up and waved to the postmaster as he climbed back up into the wagon to open it, anxious for the news from his brother. But the letter was not from Esther and Leib. It was from his brother's neighbor in London, Mrs. Zlotinsky, and it was filled with heartache.

Zev felt his chest tighten as he folded the letter and put it in his pocket. He dropped his head into his hands and worked to stop the stinging in his eyes. Finally he nudged Queenie into motion for the ride home.

As he pulled into the Patrick Street yard and began to settle the horse, Ziporah bounded out of the house to greet him. He pushed the letter farther into his pocket, out of sight. He knew what she was going to ask.

"Papa, did you go to the post office? Mama is worried; it has been too long since she had a letter from Aunt Esther. There should have been a reply by now."

Deep worry lines etched his face. "Hmmm. Your mother seems to always be one step ahead in these things. I have with me a letter."

Watching him, Ziporah's beaming face wilted. "Is my cousin Malka all right? Is she well?"

Through the family letters back and forth to England, Ziporah had come to know and love her cousin like a sister she had never met.

"Ziporah, we must talk in private with your mother and grandparents before the house is filled with the boarders."

She could see by her father's expression that he would say nothing more until they were in the house. Bad news was not so unusual in their lives, but she wished it was not bad today. It would be too much for her mother.

While her father took care of Queenie, Ziporah filled a basket with the vegetables. Nothing was ever left to freeze and go to waste.

Ziporah marveled at how her father remained strong, no matter what went on around him. Papa was steady and patient, and seemed less affected by the trials of their life than her mother. Nor was he quick to share his emotions.

Zev sat down with Hannah and his parents while Ziporah silently finished making supper. The news was very hard. He told it plainly, and held his wife tightly as grief overcame her. Ziporah fetched the tea and a cool towel for Mama's head. Then Mama read the letter for herself, in the faint hope that it was different from what Zev had told them. It was not.

Dear Mr. and Mrs. Zigman,

It pains me to have to write this very sad news to you, but I made a promise to your brother, Leib, when he became sick that I would. I am so very sorry to tell you that the typhoid fever in Whitechapel has been very hard and that your brother and his dear wife have died. They died within two days of each other. First your brother on September 2 and then Esther on September 4. The child, Malka, who had taken it upon herself to care for her parents, has survived and is well, and this good news is a miracle, as she, too, was stricken with typhus. Leib and Esther have had a proper Jewish burial, you will be comforted to know.

Malka was nursed back to health in the hospital, thanks to the help provided by the synagogue. From the hospital she has come to stay with me, but with no room and no money to keep her, I have been able to make arrangements for her to go to the home of Dr. Babcock and his wife. You are not to worry that she is on the streets with the beggars and street orphans of London. Malka has shown early talents with a thread and needle and is helpful in the kitchen.

Dr. Babcock has taken the girl in as a maid. She is learning to be a laundress. She has enough food to eat and a safe place to sleep. Malka will get only a small wage, but she will be all right until arrangements can be made for her to join you in Canada.

My deepest sympathies to you and your family in this difficult time. My address and Malka's address are on the back of this letter. I will keep an eye on the child to be sure she is fine until you can send for her. God willing, it will be soon.

Sincerely,

Mrs. S. Zlotinsky

"The world is a hard place," said Hannah and blew her nose loudly. "Esther and Leib both gone. I so wanted them to meet our children. It was always my wish that my sister and I would sit together under a tree and tell each other secrets just one more time." She wept and hugged Ziporah. "Who knew I would never set my eyes on her again?"

There was little time for grieving as the boys rushed in from school and the boarders began to arrive.

The younger boys did their best to be respectful during the supper conversation, but had little attachment to these relatives they knew only from letters. Isaac, though, was deeply moved by the thought of his orphaned cousin.

"Malka can have my place to sleep, Mama," he insisted. "I can sleep on the chairs in the kitchen."

Mama said she was blessed with good children. She cried again.

14
Hard Times on Patrick Street
January 17, 1899

annah stood in the back yard in the dying light of the January afternoon and swore at her laundry as the north wind cut through her heavy shawl. She swore in Yiddish, but it wasn't enough, so she added a couple of epithets in Ukrainian. One frozen shirt after another taunted her as they flapped like loose shingles on a barn, stinging her fingers with bitter cold. The clothes were neatly pegged on the frayed string that ran from the house to the metal hook on the stable. She stamped her feet and then blew into her hands to revive her stiff, aching fingers. Her hands moved steadily over the line, snatching the pegs from the shirts and towels and flinging them into a wooden pail. As she worked, she felt her dark mood closing in on her. She stepped cautiously around the tally of woes that ran freely though her thoughts, fighting for something positive to think about. Plick, plick, plick. The pins dropped into the pail.

Nothing.

Think again.

Plick, plick, plick.

Then, finally, a wisp of an image slipped through the emptiness. It wasn't much, but it was a start. Collecting the clean laundry was much easier than hanging the wet clothes when the temperature dipped to forty below zero. Hannah reserved special words for that job.

It was her second winter in Canada and she hated it. Nothing she had ever experienced in the old country had prepared her for the severity of the climate in Winnipeg. With tears from the wind blurring her vision and her feet pained by the cold, she made fast work of stacking the pieces into her basket.

"Oy," she said to the clothes pegs. "Hard winter. Hard work." When the last piece of clothing was placed on the basket,

Hannah hurried into the stable to feed the chickens. The hens squawked and fluttered as she tossed grain into the little pen of their winter confinement. It's a good life to be a chicken, she thought. Eat and lay eggs. Day in and day out. Eat and lay eggs.

"Who would have ever thought that Hannah Zigman would envy the life of a chicken?" she muttered to the hens as they competed for the scattered food. She put her hand on the door and brought her head to rest on the rough wood. The darkness moved through her and Hannah could sense the familiar seduction of defeat dancing at the edge of her consciousness. With defeat, she would be able to stop fighting. She would be numb and float through life without caring. Delicious, sweet, inviting defeat.

She sighed. Who had time to be depressed? Too many others would suffer if she couldn't keep up her workload.

Irksome thoughts stabbed at her and brought her back to the work before her. Was it a mistake to have come here? She thought about Mrs. White on Ellen Street. She gave up on Canada and went back. From England you could go back. From Russia, you learned to live in whatever country you landed; thankful to get out from under the czar. To freeze to death in Canada would be better than to go back to Russia.

No, there would be no going back for the Zigmans.

But to stand outside with laundry that froze before it could dry, this she still hated. And to run through the cold to use the outhouse in the winter, that she hated with special feeling.

She sighed heavily as tears welled in her eyes. It's not so good to complain. What's the use? Of course she had many blessings, and it would be a sin to forget them. She thanked God for the safety and health of her family. But, this weather? It's so necessary to have a wind so cruel? For what?

The careful efforts she had made to line her worn shoes with newspaper now seemed a stupid waste of time. She swore again. Above the hole in her shoe, wet newspaper sat under the ball of her foot. She swung the laundry basket onto her left hip and stomped up the icy path and the two wooden steps to the back porch.

One day, she would maybe have a nice thick wool coat and

a big fur hat. She would have fine boots with sheepskin inside to protect her from the cold. She relished the dream. Maybe she could trade a feather quilt for such a pair of boots. One day. After the children had proper boots.

Maybe.

Or maybe this was it.

Maybe this was the best she would ever have out of life.

A fragrant cloud of warm vapor met Hannah as she pulled the kitchen door open. Ziporah was tending to a large pot of soup on the small cast iron stove, pushing it aside to gain access to the heavy iron lid of the firebox. The frosty piece of wood crackled and popped, sending out a hiss of steam as she dropped it into the flames. Though still shy of her twelfth birthday, Ziporah was well beyond her years in her capabilities in the house. One day, when they had more money, there would be time for her to go to school like her brothers. For now there was only work. Like so many other girls her age, she was needed at home. Another sadness for Hannah to add to her list. A child without a childhood.

"Ach, Ziporah. I can't take it." Hannah pulled off her shawl and scarf and hung them slowly on the first peg in the row next to the door. Gaunt and hollow-eyed, she rubbed her dry red hands together briskly. Ziporah looked up from stirring the soup to see the familiar strain on her mother's face and recognized she was building into one of her spells. Pain and despair weighed down the four short steps Hannah took to cross the kitchen. She sat down in the wooden chair against the wall and stared at her feet.

"Will you taste it, Mama?" Ziporah asked gently and held out a spoon.

"In a bit," she sighed and forced a smile. She pulled a large white handkerchief out from behind the top flap of her apron and blew her nose loudly. Then she balled up the hankie and stuffed it back under her apron. She exhaled deeply. It was greater than a sigh and just short of a groan. Ziporah was worried. The last time Mama had one of her spells it went on for a long time. She seemed to be sad all of the time, and it made Papa sick with grief.

Hannah regarded the newspaper poking out of the side of her shoe. Like her shoes, she too, was worn to the breaking point. All the sacrifice and hard work for so many years had led them where? To be overrun with boarders. To have no privacy. To have no rest from the endless work. As her feet and hands warmed, Hannah gave way. She felt herself being swallowed by defeat and had no strength to stop it. She was no match for this relentless foe beating down on her. She longed to drown in the darkness and block out the reality of her life as she stared blankly out of the kitchen window.

Twelve people lived in the house the Zigmans rented on Patrick Street, eight family members and four lodgers. Hannah had put her foot down in insisting that there would never be more than four boarders at one time, as twelve people were as many as she thought humane to pack into the tiny house. With the exception of the time they took in a Jewish family of six who were on their way to farm in Saskatchewan, the Zigmans never did have more than four strangers sleeping on the narrow cots in the front room.

The house with just four rooms was a hastily constructed, one-story wooden building, twenty feet wide by twenty-nine deep. It was typical of hundreds of homes in the area. Hannah sometimes felt guilty about her distress with being crowded. So many people were worse off. In truth, by the standards of the neighborhood their living conditions were not considered severe. Two doors down, a house just double the size of the Zigman home sheltered twenty-eight people. Mrs. Bricknell, the owner, was quick to brag about how much money she was making every time she saw Hannah. "Good for you," Hannah thought. "You are a stronger woman than me." Hannah could only think about how Mrs. Bricknell's outhouse was overused and overflowing into the back lane all summer. She didn't even want to think about what it must be like to be inside that house.

There were many such houses in Winnipeg, and more were being built all the time. There were hundreds, maybe even thousands of people boarding on streets like Patrick, Laura, Ellen, and dozens of others that were all within a short walk of the Canadian Pacific Railway station. She knew because her son,

Isaac, had told the family he often read stories in the newspaper of overcrowding. He read of dirty little houses with ceilings so low you couldn't stand up and jammed so tight with people there was no air to breathe. Landlords were brought to court, but that didn't seem to change anything. What could they do? Push them out into the cold to freeze to death? Most of the boarders were men in their twenties or thirties who had recently arrived in Winnipeg. Most were single, but many were married men, working to bring their families, like her husband Zev had done. Where else would the greenhorns go if it weren't for the boarding houses? Welcome to Canada, the land with streets of gold. Ha! Some joke.

Hannah rubbed her aching feet and felt the numbness of freezing slowly give way to the prickling pain of thawing. She sighed. The family and then the boarders would be coming home soon. No, Hannah was no Mrs. Bricknell, counting her riches with that smug smile on her English face. After a year of running a boarding house for ten cents a place by the night, or two-and-a-half dollars a month, Hannah was well past irritable. She cried often and easily.

Who was she fooling? This wasn't a house. This was a hovel. A glorified tool shed packed to the walls with everyone stepping on each other, smelling each other's sweat and living in each other's noise. The house was as clean and tidy as she could manage, but it always reeked of the stench of unwashed working men. The little stand with the basin in the kitchen was no match against the grime caked on the boarders arriving dirty and exhausted from their daily labor.

Hannah kept careful records. In the time since they had started taking in boarders, the Zigman family had seen 162 different people taking their places in the lodgers' beds. She was very strict and wouldn't tolerate drunks or any fighting, so more than a few had been sent packing and Hannah kept a list of them, too.

She thanked God for the relief that came in the few quiet hours in the daytime when the house was not so crowded. The boarders were working or looking for jobs and most of her family was away at work or school. Though she was on her feet working the entire day, cooking and doing laundry, at least she had room to move. In the evenings, the only privacy they had for even a confidential conversation came in whispered tones and the limited refuge offered by speaking in Yiddish or Ukrainian, in the hopes their boarders would not understand. Usually this was the case. In this neighborhood more than twenty languages were spoken, but English was the predominant among their boarders, which the Zigman children seemed to be soaking up like sponges. Isaac was the most fluent and often acted as the official translator for the family.

She was proud of her children, but on a day like this when she felt particularly low, Hannah saw their success as small consolation for a weary woman pining for privacy. She was desperate for quiet, desperate for a moment to sit without work in her hands, desperate to smell the blossoms on a cherry tree.

She was tired, she ached, and she was sad. Hannah sat back on the chair and motioned to Ziporah for the spoon. She tasted the soup and nodded her approval.

"The soup is good. Very good. You are like your Baba. A much better cook than I am. You have a gift," she said softly.

"Thank you, Mama. Why don't you rest a bit before everyone comes in?"

The tender words from her loving child tore open the floodgates. Hannah started to cry. At first it was in a silent stifled crumple, her shoulders heaving with emotion. She squeezed her eyes tightly against the ache in her soul. She badly wanted to be strong in her daughter's presence but was powerless to stop the rush of tears. She inhaled deeply and held her breath. She looked at Ziporah. What would become of her *tchotchkeleh*? It was all work, work, and more work for all of them. What had become of them? What had happened to her family? How long could they go on without rest?

"Rest. Ach. The only rest this old woman will get is when she is dead," she said before she realized she had spoken her thoughts out loud.

"Mama! Thirty-one is not old, and you are a long way from saying goodbye to life."

"Life," she scoffed. "And what kind of life is this? There is

146

not room to turn around in this stinking shack with all of us here. It's not so bad in summer when the lodgers stay in the loft in the stable, but this is too much. Washing, cooking, cleaning. And then scrubbing this hateful wooden floor. Look now at your hands, Ziporah. Chapped and bleeding with the cold and swollen from the splinters." Hannah's voice rose in anger and gave way to deep wracking sobs. "Is this a life for my daughter who is now working herself to a thin bone? For my fine sons? My husband who is gone from morning to night? This is a life? So cold that the frost piles in the corners inside the house. Where have we landed? In Siberia?" Her crying triggered a hoarse and phlegmy coughing fit.

Ziporah's eyes went wide with fright. Hannah fought for her breath and gradually regained control. She gripped her apron and pressed it hard into her face. Ziporah drew a chair near her mother's and extended her thin arms. Hannah rocked in her daughter's embrace and cried until she was spent.

"I'm sorry to be so weak Ziporah." She drew back and sniffed, pulling out the handkerchief. "I feel like this cold is going to finish me."

"Mama. You are still not well from the flu. You go lie down. I will finish with the laundry when it thaws and hang it here near the stove. Let me look after you."

Hannah sighed heavily. "All right. I will rest a bit. You are a good girl, Ziporah. You should not have a life so hard."

"Mama. It will be better soon. In summer it is always better."

"Ha! Summer in Winnipeg. Then the air will be thick with mosquitoes and we'll have mud up to our noses and people all around us will be dropping dead from typhoid, scarlet fever, consumption, and who knows what else. I can't wait," Mama snorted. Her hand flew out to swipe at her disgust.

Ziporah heard the door close, then the groan of the cot, and sighed with relief. A few minutes off of her feet would help Mama to rebound. It almost always did. She worried a lot about her mother. There was too much on her shoulders, it was plain to see. Ever since the news from London of the deaths of Aunt Esther and Uncle Leib, Mama seemed different. Something seemed to have broken in her. Ziporah longed for the mother she had when they were still in the old country, when Ziporah was a little girl. She was different then. She was strong and determined then. She had hope.

Ziporah sat down to think. What could she do? She was almost twelve. She would soon be a woman by Jewish law, Zaida had said. Slowly it came to her that her talks with her grandfather were more than nice stories about the responsibilities of Jewish men and Jewish women. She thought of Malka in England, just a year older than she was and working as a grown woman works. Ziporah knew she was ready, also, to have more responsibility in the family.

She glanced about the kitchen looking hard to find what her mother would instantly see to do. She straightened up a towel and gave the floor a quick sweep. As she lit the lamp on the table, an idea began to take shape in her mind. It came simply and unexpectedly like an answer to a prayer. It was the seed of a monumental plan, the kind of idea that Papa would think of. She became so excited thinking about it that she laughed with happiness and hopped up and down. She would have to speak to her father about it first.

Moving efficiently about, she set the table for the family. She sliced the bread and was careful to count that there were just enough slices, with thicker pieces for Papa and Zaida. Her mind was on fire with her plan. Finally she heard the familiar clank of the door latch on the stable and looked out to see Papa was unhitching Queenie. She wrapped herself in Mama's heavy shawl and ran out to have a private word with him.

"We finished a little bit early today. It is easier to come when there is still light," he said smiling in reaction to her obvious delight in seeing him. "How is Mama feeling today? Is she better with the coughing?"

"The coughing is a little better, Papa," she answered. "I made the special tea with the Seneca root, and she thinks it helped her. She is lying down for a few minutes."

Zev turned to Ziporah with worry in his eyes. "Lying down? Is she all right?"

Ziporah hesitated. "I think so. She is sad, but I think she'll feel better with a little rest."

He rubbed down the mare and worked silently in his thoughts while Ziporah scrambled into the wagon to find out what treasures her father had brought home from his peddling rounds.

"Papa, before we go in, there is something I would like to talk with you about."

"*Nu?* So, then tell me." He saw the determination in her face and tried to guess if what he was going to hear was going to be good or bad. One could never tell with this child.

"You see, Papa, I worry that there is too much for Mama to cope with."

Zev listened carefully to Ziporah, who lit up with an animated rush of words as she summarized her plan articulately and with maturity well beyond her years. He thought about how quickly his children were growing up and shook his head. By the time she finally got to the end of telling the details, her arms were flailing with the kind of exuberance that can only come from one too young to have ever faced failure. Zev nodded and smiled and reached over to rub her head with pride and affection. Wasn't it yesterday that she held his hands and took her first steps?

"Not only a beauty, but a head for business, my daughter has." He reached his strong arms around her and hugged her hard. "I like your thinking, Ziporah. We'll discuss it at the table." he said as they closed the stable.

Ziporah raced up the path to greet her grandparents, and together they all went into the house.

They said their prayers and Mama ladled supper into their bowls at the crowded family table. With the few minutes of privacy before the arrival of the boarders, the family discussed their business of the day. Zaida had a new student coming to study with him at the synagogue. Baba said she might be getting an increase in wages at the sewing factory. And Mama worried about her orphaned niece, toiling away, 'doing God knows what', on the other side of the ocean. The jar of coins to pay for her voyage to Canada was still pitifully short of what was needed. At the rate they were able to save it would be at least two years before they would have the money for Malka's voyage.

At this, Zev nodded to Ziporah. "Perhaps there is a better way to save the money more quickly. Ziporah has an idea."

"We can open a restaurant!" she squealed.

"Oy!" came in unison from Baba and Mama.

Ziporah carefully explained that the burden of the boarders was obviously too much and that they could make just as much or even more by running a café in the house.

"I could do the cooking, Mama. You know I can do it. You said yourself that I can cook well," Ziporah said proudly. Mama sat quietly and considered how this would work and what impact it might have on the family. She saw nothing but problems.

"First, you are a child," she said. "This is too much work for a child, even with me working along with you. Then we must look at this house. Where would they sit? On the floor?"

Mama was very practical and would have to know all of the logistics before she would be able to give her approval. Zev had already been thinking about this and offered a solution that involved two long benches that he could make. The table would be fashioned from a pair of boards that could be arranged over the storage barrels. He swiftly calculated that they would be able to sit ten people at a time at this makeshift table. At the end of the evening they would take the table apart and take the benches outside. This way the front room would be available for Isaac, Aaron and Mendel to sleep in as they had before the family had started taking in boarders. Ziporah would have a cot in the kitchen.

"It will be so cozy and warm for me by the stove, Mama!" she pleaded. Zev and Hannah would finally reclaim their bedroom, which had been given over to storage as well as two bunk beds for all four children since they opened the boarding house. Everyone looked at Hannah and waited. They watched while she took a deep breath, and then finally spoke.

"Maybe," she shrugged. "We would need a new stove."

Zev stroked his wife's arm and looked into her eyes.

"I want my house back." She reached for his hand. "I want a life with my family back. Maybe we should think about this, Zev. Maybe while we are young enough and strong enough, we

150

can do this. Maybe. But we would need a bigger stove."

Zev looked as Ziporah and winked.

Baba's eyes were twinkling with anticipation. If things went well with the restaurant she would be able to leave her job in the coat factory to come and help. The constant crowding and living with strangers had been extremely difficult for all of them. The very thought, to have the little house back just for the family – it would be a joy of joys.

Ziporah let out a cry for happiness. "So we are going to open our restaurant?"

"We will see, Ziporah," Zev said, stroking his beard. "You must have patience. A decision like this takes lots of thinking and planning. Tomorrow, I will go to see Hiram and Mordecai Weidman. If we open a restaurant, they would be our supplier for the food we would need to buy. No one knows more about the wholesale grocery business in Winnipeg than the Weidman brothers. They would have some good advice, and they will allow us to buy on credit. We don't have the money to just go into business like this."

At this, there was the sound of heavy steps and men's voices at the kitchen door. Mama quickly shooed her family off the little kitchen table so she could feed the lodgers.

In the coming days, the idea quickly grew into determination to open the Zigman Café in the Patrick Street home. Mr. Lee, who owned the Chinese Laundry on the corner, was the first to suggest he would put up a sign in his shop, if Hannah would be so kind as to advertise his business in her restaurant. The planning dominated all of the family conversations, and there was much excitement as they worked out every little detail.

Free of the obligation to boarders, the family would finally be able to reclaim a proper celebration of Shabbat. The Sabbath was extremely important to Zaida Baruch, and the family heartily agreed anything to do with the café business would come after their obligations to God.

As she planned menus and worked out costs, Hannah gradually became consumed by the new project, and her mood started to brighten with the possibilities that would be presented.

She would get her privacy back. She would have a chance to be happy again. And her poor orphaned niece would soon have a loving family in Winnipeg to come home to earlier than scheduled.

The stumbling block was the stove. It was just too small to handle the large cooking pots that would be needed. Mama fretted. Papa brought out the jar with the emergency savings. They talked. They pulled out sheets of paper with columns of numbers on them. They talked louder. The jar went back. The café dream almost came to an end. Isaac was the one to find the creative solution. It would not be convenient, but they could arrange to use the stove at the Levine home next door. He had asked Mrs. Levine and she had told him, that if she could share a little in the food from the café she wouldn't mind sharing her stove.

With vigor and determination the family formed a united front to face the many obstacles that lay ahead.

And then, out of the blue, came the potential for a fantastic windfall. Zev found it at the *shvitz*.

15
The Shvitz
April 27, 1899

I t was almost May, but the evening air still snapped with the bite of winter. Zev drew his shoulders up to brace against a sharp north wind and stepped smartly along in anticipation of the pleasures ahead. He allowed himself only one luxury, and it was never questioned or disapproved of by his wife. Once a week he would wrap a towel around a small jar of herring and a large loaf of bread and make the twenty-minute walk from his house on Patrick Street north across the tracks to King and Dufferin.

At the edge of the farmers' market stood an odd-shaped brick building with a big sign in English proclaiming it to be Solly Silverstein's Bath House. No one who went there called it that. They called it the shvitz. Mondays and Wednesdays were for ladies only. The rest of the time it was clearly a men's club, a social center for the immigrant community that populated the densely crowded slums of Winnipeg's foreign quarter.

With no indoor plumbing and little more than a washstand in most of the homes in the area, public bathing houses were generally good businesses and the best of them was Solly's. Fashioned in the traditional banya style of Russia, Solly's Shvitz was a familiar and much loved piece of the old life.

On entering Solly's, visitors were immersed in thick, humid air, out of which bubbled a rich blend of languages—Ukrainian, Russian, and Polish among them—with Yiddish emerging loudest of all to dominate the shouting of greetings and telling of jokes.

Zev's recent visits to the shvitz had taken on a new enjoyment with his increasing status as a businessman. Word had quickly spread about the new Zigman Café and Zev took pride in the recognition of his family's success. In truth, the money earned was not a lot better than what they had made from the boarding house business, but they were learning quickly, and the future looked promising. Zev continued his peddling business and had calculated that in four more months he would have enough money saved to buy the new cook stove Hannah had picked out. She already had the delivery date circled on the calendar.

Even with his growing reputation, Zev was a long way from being seen as one of Solly's star customers. In fact, with his shy nature and small, wiry frame, he remained largely invisible against the boisterous personalities that set the tone at the shvitz. He much admired the confidence and witty lines of the master storytellers: men like Max "Scrap Iron" Spiegelman and Mike "Bunzy" Benzelock, who competed to be the center of attention and provided spirited entertainment for the willing audience. Zev, with his reserved nature, wasn't the kind of man who would be given a clever nickname. His gift was for numbers and computations, not for entertaining. He secretly wished that he could have just a little of that charm that seemed to come so easily to some. His own clever retorts to the banter and chiding remained unspoken, coming to mind only on his walk home as he recalled the teasing one-liners of the evening. He wondered what it felt like to be that popular. Take Solly, for example. He had to do nothing more than say hello to bring a smile and a feeling of special importance to everyone around him. Now that was true power.

The shvitz was not a place to rush. Often a visit to Solly's would last several hours, depending on whether it involved a poker game. Typically, the patrons would alternate between the steam room and the side room. The side room was equipped with tables and chairs where the men, draped in towels, would take a break and talk and eat or smoke and play cards before returning to the steam for their second and sometimes third sweats. It was here in the smoky card room that they shared stories and news about the community.

It was understood that in the steam, talking was kept at a minimum so people could hear themselves think. Here, the bathers would savor the sensation of the vapor billowing off hot rocks, purging their bodies of pent up poisons and tensions as

154

they sweated in temperatures that climbed near one hundred and ten degrees.

Solly's place had class and low prices. The class came from the presence of a *parchik*. He was a big Russian named Grigori, a burly giant of a man whose job was to soap down the patrons with a leafy broom.

Zev filled a bucket with cold water and carried it up to the upper bench, the clouds hissing around him as he sat in his favorite spot in the corner.

"You want *playtza*?" The parchik held up a fresh oak leaf broom and motioned to Zev.

"Not today, thanks, Grigori," said Zev, mindful of every extra expense.

"I'll take his turn." A heavy man unfamiliar to Zev waved his hand from the lower bench. He groaned his way into a standing position and then carefully settled onto Grigori's wooden massage table as a walrus might take comfort on a warm rock. The parchik raised the bundle of soapy wet leaves and spun the wide short broom against the man's back. He then began rhythmically slapping it down on his naked hide, flinging the soap as he worked. Solly's recent hiring of Grigori had been met with great approval from his wealthier clients who could afford the special service of the professional rubdown. To the others, the fresh smell of the oak leaves, shipped in all the way from Chicago, was alone, an unpaid extra benefit.

The shvitz renewed them, cleansed them and gave them strength to cope with their daily struggles. Among the Jews, the word *mechiah* was often used to describe the pleasure of the experience. No English word could come close to that description. That sense, that wonderful sensation of ultimate comfort, hummed through the place and gave them all the belief that, one way or another, they would make it in the new world. There were no limits on what they could accomplish here. In Winnipeg, Solly's Shvitz was to the Jews what the Manitoba Club was to the wealthy English. It was a home away from home, a place to trade stories with friends, to laugh in the unguarded company of men and to make the odd deal.

Such was the case for Zev on that fateful evening in April,

1899. Lightheaded and in need of relief from the steam, he double wrapped his towel around his skinny body and emerged in the card room. Solly was just back from a visit to New York and was in fine form as he delivered the punch line of a story to a group of regulars lounging between sweats. As the laughter reached its peak, Solly spotted Zev and turned to say hello.

"Hey, Zev!" His voice boomed out over the crowd. "You couldn't arrange for the warm weather a little earlier for me to enjoy on my return to Winnipeg? Irving, get my friend Zev a shot of the special vodka, will you?" Solly called out to the man behind the counter, who was dispensing sandwiches.

"Good to see you back, Solly." Zev shook his hand, swelling with pleasure to be singled out so publicly. "The shvitz is not the same without you. What's new in New York?"

Solly glanced over his shoulder and lowered his voice. "You won't believe my luck. My brother, Max, has found for me a pot of gold."

"Gold?"

"Zev. Not gold. But good as gold. He found for me a syndicate. A syndicate making big money in the stock market. And you know what? It makes for the investor ten percent a week. I put all the interest back in and can you imagine what is happening? In the three weeks, me, I made almost thirty dollars on my investment."

"Thirty dollars? A fortune!" That was as much as Zev used to make in an entire year in the old country. Zev locked onto the numbers and instantly realized Solly would have had to have invested the fantastic amount of almost one hundred dollars to make that kind of interest. It was an astounding story. "Good for you to be so lucky. Must be a big risk to make that kind of money."

Solly stopped for a moment as though hoping to learn something from Zev and then angled closer to draw him into his secret. Max was right. Hard working, struggling immigrants like Zev would sell the investment scheme for him if he played it right.

"Zev. You are smart with money. You could be rich on this."

"What are you saying? Rich?" Zev laughed. "Solly, a man like me has only the money he can earn with his own hands. I don't have that kind of luck that is given special to people like you."

"Zev, this is not luck. This is good business. It is called the Franklin Syndicate. It is advertised in the newspapers. My brother found the place and he looked into it. He's careful, my brother. Very good in business. So, Max learns this very smart young man named Miller runs it. Max invested, he made good money and he says it is legitimate. He told me and now I am telling you. You should try. I only tell you because I know you have plans to move to your own house and to bring your niece to Canada. Zev. Think about this. You could be owning your own house, completely paid, in no time. And now, you know what Max tells me? People are making so much money in New York they are selling their businesses and retiring. Imagine that!"

Solly turned his attention to his drink to let Zev absorb the dream. Then he raised his eyes and looked into Zev's flushed face. "Zev. Here's what I am going to do for you. I will connect you with the syndicate as a special favor, only to accept just a small fee for my service for this. What do you say?"

Zev laughed.

Solly held his hands wide and appeared insulted. "You laugh? You pass on ten percent?"

"Ten percent a week?" Zev shook his head. "Who pays ten percent a week?"

"Yes. I know it sounds like crazy talk. But I have the money to prove it is true. Minimum investment is ten dollars."

"That is a lot of money for me to invest, Solly." Zev hunched his bony shoulders into his neck and looked about to see who might be listening.

Solly breathed deeply and spread his arms wide on the table. "Why should it be only the big shots in New York like that Carnegie and J.P. Morgan and Rockefeller that make the money? Why not the boys in Winnipeg, too, Zev? You think about it. I only mention this to you because I like you. You are a good peddler and always fair with me. I appreciate it when you find me deals when I need something. This time, I can find for you a deal. But, I understand. Maybe your missus is not so happy to have money invested. Still, you think about it. I am wiring again my money to New York next week. You let me know." Solly's large hand patted Zev's knobby shoulder as he left the table.

The bait found its mark. Excitement built in Zev as he ate his herring and toyed with the idea. By the time he returned to the steam for his second sweat, his mind was swirling with the thought of the money he could make. Numbers ran in his head as he calculated what ten percent a week would make for him over just a few weeks. He picked up the pail of cold water and dumped it on his head. It could be a small investment. Then again, a bigger amount would perhaps make a year's wages in just a few months. But, there was risk. All investment had risk. Hannah would never approve. It was ridiculous to even think about it, and he shoved it from his mind.

Zev wasn't the only one who had been taken into a whispered conversation with Solly. Very soon, people at the steam bath started bragging about overnight riches they had made through Solly's connections in New York. This was the golden land they had been promised and gold was landing on people all around Zev. He was tormented every time he thought about it. But it was only when that *zhlub* Zonigbaum boasted that he had made seventy dollars that Zev made up his mind to get into the game.

What was there to lose? Should Zev Zigman be the only one not to benefit from the riches that came without work?

He worried about what Hannah would think and was immediately reminded of Solly's biting comment. Could he not make a decision without his wife's involvement? His mind was made up.

Five weeks later, with a newly delivered wad of cash in his pocket, he went to the Busy Bee dry goods store on Main Street. When Hannah saw her husband and sons unloading her new cook stove, months earlier than the date she had circled on her calendar, she cried for joy and showered Zev with kisses.

He almost told her about the syndicate, but decided the time wasn't right. At the rate he was investing, by the end of the year, he would have enough to pay for Malka's ticket to Winnipeg,

158

and he could soon start thinking of building a house on Selkirk Avenue.

The Zigmans were on the path to a wealthy future.

16
The Invitation

November 9, 1899

Beth was deep in concentration, scrutinizing a list of names as she wandered into the front hall and came upon Mr. Chadwick.

"Mr. Chadwick, has Mr. Willows returned from his appointment?"

"Yes, madam. He is in the library. I believe he is engaged on the telephone," answered the butler.

"Oh, dear. That dratted invention is going to ruin our lives. Well, please do tell him I need a few minutes of his time in the drawing room when he has finished his conversation. I must make arrangements for our upcoming dinner party, and I cannot do a single thing until he confirms the guest list."

"Of course, madam."

"Oh, and would you please tell Mrs. Butterfield to send in my tea. No crumpets, today, thank you."

"Right away, Mrs. Willows."

Beth shook her head in dismay. She could hardly keep up with her obligations, with her husband's demanding social calendar. One dinner party after another seemed to be on their schedule. And what benefit had they reaped for all their trouble? Had the favors been returned? Had Mrs. Willows ever been invited to the Lieutenant Governor's home to drink tea with the society divas? On how many guest lists did the name Willows appear? Did Lady Ashbury even know her name, let alone consider adding it to her social registry?

Lady Ashbury was the most influential of the society women in Winnipeg. Her Blue List, as it was called, was the only one that mattered. To be named to the list was seen as the golden key to all the society functions in Winnipeg. For Beth, however, the celebrated doyenne was impossible. She had turned down three invitations from the Willows in the past eighteen months and Beth knew there was no point in punishing herself further. The name Ashbury was off the list at the Willows home.

It didn't matter what Rupert said about it. Two years of building up their social circle one invitation at a time and they had yet to break through to the Ashbury blue list. You would think that their efforts would have at least yielded the coveted invitation to join the Board of Trade that Rupert was so determined to have. What on earth were they doing wrong?

"Mrs. Willows, will you care for anything other than the tea?" Mrs. Butterfield carefully placed the tray with the pot of tea and china cup and saucer on the table near the window as Beth looked up from her embroidery.

"Oh, no, thank you, Mrs. Butterfield. I am afraid I won't be able to get into my ball gowns when we sail to London. I do so enjoy your pastries. Too much, I am afraid." As she was about to turn back to her lists, a thought suddenly occurred to Beth. "Mrs. Butterfield, may I have a moment of your time?"

"Certainly, ma'am." Mrs. Butterfield felt her cheeks flushing. What fresh trouble could this be?

"With all the entertaining Mr. Willows intends to do in the New Year—the new century, as he keeps reminding me—I think we may find ourselves inadequately prepared for larger parties, and I am wondering if you think there might be a maid or two that we should add to our staff. Only the best qualified, you understand. They must have had excellent training, preferably in London, of course. I've heard that our neighbor, Mrs. MacDonald, is moving back to Toronto. Do you think any of her girls are worth bringing here?"

"Of course." Mrs. Butterfield answered more quickly than necessary, still shamed that she had lied about her own credentials. "Yes, ma'am. There are two girls who come to mind. Shall I arrange to have them come by?"

"Yes. But please do be exceedingly discreet. I would like Mr. Chadwick to speak with them on your recommendation to be sure they would be a proper fit in our house, of course."

"Yes, ma'am."

"That will be all."

There was a light knocking, and Mr. Chadwick arrived

carrying his silver tray.

"Excuse me, Mrs. Willows," he spoke softly. "A letter has arrived from Redwood House to your attention."

Beth picked up the envelope and smiled.

"Thank you, Mr. Chadwick." She looked at the clock again. "Please, do go find out when my husband expects to be able to see me."

Alone, she turned the letter over and saw the elegant seal. It was larger than a thank you note, so could it be an invitation? She reached for her letter opener and gently broke through the red wax. Her eyes opened wide and she raised a dainty hand to her mouth, suddenly filled with delight. She started to giggle.

She heard Rupert before she saw him. Bellowing his way through the door, he strode impatiently toward her.

"Beth, I don't know why you think every matter regarding every party has to be approved by me. I have a business to run, you are aware."

She jumped out of her chair and threw her arms around him. "Oh, Rupert, I'm so sorry to be such a bother."

Puzzled at her gleeful welcome, he reigned in his temper. Feeling a wee bit churlish for having been so quick to shout at her, he responded, "Do pardon my rudeness, darling. Now, what it is it?"

"Care for tea?" Her eyes twinkled with happiness.

"Brandy."

"I'll ring."

"No, Beth, let me do it."

"Oh, please let me ring for him. It's my turn." Beth enjoyed the secret game Rupert had created. To amuse himself and his guests, Rupert had worked out a code in ringing for Chadwick so that the butler would know what beverage to bring and how many to serve. The buttons were hidden in strategic locations throughout the house and the bells rang below stairs, never to be heard by the guests. It became utterly complicated when Mr. Chadwick was not within hearing range of the bells, for it set off an awkward chain of communication. Rupert had been known to laugh uproariously at the sight of a kitchen maid dashing through the main corridor in search of the butler.

Chadwick detested the ringing game. Aside from the inconvenience, he thought the little pretense so boorishly American he could hardly bear it. But, if that's what his master wanted, that is what he would have, though it made the butler cringe at being treated like an organ grinder's monkey every time he heard the bells ring out their cheery little tunes.

Comfortably seated with his brandy, Rupert gave his full attention to his wife. "Now what could possibly so brighten your mood on a gloomy, icy November day?"

"A party. A party to celebrate the ringing in of the New Year. You will never guess who is hosting it."

"The Ashburys?"

"Don't be silly. They'll be in New York. Guess again."

"The Queen of England?"

"Oh, Rupert, don't be ridiculous. The invitation is from Redwood House! Can you imagine? We've finally been invited to be guests of the Drewrys."

Rupert was enormously pleased. "Well, how positively splendid. That will be quite an event, I can assure you. I've heard stories at the club about his wonderful parties and stunning guest list."

"It's very unusual, Rupert. Not only have we been invited, but the invitation has been extended to our children! Have you ever heard of such a thing?"

"Edward Drewry is a very unusual man, and an excellent member of City Council. He could care less about doing what everyone else does. He makes his own social rules and from what I hear, his entertainments and celebrations are second to none. Why, the debutante balls he has hosted have been noted as being the most lively and extravagant events in town."

Beth laughed. "Oh, Rupert, do you still read those society columns?"

"Well, certainly I do, my sweet lady. As to why our children have been invited, just consider this for a moment. We have very attractive children," he said, thinking of his own good looks. "I think Drewry and his wife believe there is great worth in bringing the young people together to meet each other at such a celebratory social occasion. To do this when the parents are about gives everyone an opportunity to see what matches might be made in the future. You see? Our sons will no doubt add to the atmosphere of the party. Alfred and James are soon going to be of marriageable age. Alfred is doing well in the business, and James will be a doctor in some years. Elliot is clearly the best looking of the three, though still a bit young for the matrons to take seriously for their marriageable daughters. I daresay it is likely because of our sons that we have been invited at all, don't you see?"

"Hmm. I see what you mean. They've even made special mention of Emma. Don't you find that odd?"

"Why should I? Just look to her classmates at Havergal. There are benefits in having her enrolled in an exclusive school and this is one of them. It is certain that many of the school families will be invited as well. I think it's going to be a very important evening."

Beth smiled. "I have just the right dress to wear!" Beth smiled.

"Perhaps." Rupert held his hand up to slow her pace. "I want a full inventory of every last stitch of clothing that you propose will be on each member of this family. Can you do that by next week?"

Beth twirled with excitement and threw her arms open. "Oh, Rupert, I do think we have finally arrived!"

17
The Franklin Syndicate

November 16, 1899

The hot summer had run too quickly into fall and the short weeks of autumn had disappeared; suddenly it was mid-November. An overnight snowfall announced that winter had arrived and intended to stay. The city was transformed into an expanse of white, with grey wooden houses in neat rows. Spindly dark trees, denuded of their summer splendor, poked out along the roadway.

Zev breathed in deeply, comforted by the quiet. He relished the still blue dawn as he loaded his wagon. This was honest work and he took solace in the fact he still had a taste for it. He was heading out to Gimli, a fishing village fifty miles north on Lake Winnipeg. He looked forward to the long ride ahead, badly needing some time alone to wrestle with his conscience.

In Gimli, he would meet Mr. Gislason, who would buy all of the household goods loaded on Zev's wagon and in return would sell him a shipment of whitefish and pickerel, packed in ice, for Zev to bring back to the city. Throughout the winter, he had a standing appointment with the fisherman; he knew that if he was late, the fish would be sold to someone else.

He thought of Hannah and the restaurant. She would hardly miss him with all her work. In fact, she was probably happy he'd be out of the house for a few days, with the way things were at home.

Hannah was very pleased with her new stove and the ease it brought in cooking large quantities of food. Over the summer months, word had gone around about the tasty meals served by the lively Mrs. Zigman, and the café had a growing number of regular visitors. To Zev, the venture's immediate value was the change it brought in his wife. Her dark spells had been pushed aside by her new enterprise. She bustled through her long workday, bossing around both her children and her customers, seemingly energized by the praise for her hearty meals.

Her optimism was infectious. It had brightened the spirits of the entire family. When Mama was in a good mood, everyone was in a good mood. Hannah was already working on new ways to expand her business. Pestered with requests, she was now planning to make soups and bread for take-away customers who would bring their empty jars to the kitchen door for her to fill them.

They were a long way from being rich, but they were no longer as dirt poor as they had been in their early years.

Every week throughout the summer, Hannah made great ceremony of presenting her profits to Zev, stacking the neat piles of coins in front of her at their tiny kitchen table.

"I cook, you count the money!" she joked as she pushed the coins across to him, listening with pride to his reports of how much money they had put away. Then suddenly, the ritual stopped. Zev made excuses about time, but there was so much more to it. He had created a terrible problem and it was ruining him. Now, he was the one who carried the dark mood as 1899 was drawing to a close.

For the first time in all of his years with Hannah, he had allowed an odious secret to be wedged into their marriage. He had started lying to Hannah in the spring, about two weeks after Solly Silverstein had first told him of the Franklin Syndicate. He remembered the look in her eyes. There was a small question in her glance, but nothing more. With money hidden deep in his pocket, he told her he was going to the fishmonger. In fact, he was on his way to see Solly. His reason for lying was not complicated. He knew she wouldn't like the idea of investing in Wall Street and he didn't want to have to defend his decision. He wanted to make money, like everyone else was doing. According to Solly, immigrants all over North America were making money on the investment plan. As for his keeping it from Hannah, Zev rationalized that it wasn't entirely a lie, just a deception. But he knew what she would say and how strongly she would object to it. This is what was eating at him. She would consider it gambling, plain and simple. Money came only from the hard work that passed through their hands, she would say. She didn't trust banks, and she certainly was not going to have any confidence in the stock market.

The big lie he told the family was that he had bought Hannah's new cook stove with their savings. Baruch was genuinely surprised by the announcement, but Zev shrugged off his father's skeptical look, knowing the old man would never question him about his personal finances. He had never intended for the secret to grow so big. It just got away from him somehow.

Zev had planned to tell Hannah about the Franklin Syndicate on the day he brought her the stove, but in all of the excitement, he couldn't seem to find the right moment. Even late that night, in the quiet of their bed, he couldn't bring himself to tell her. She was so elated with the surprise. He convinced himself it would be best not to say anything rather than to chance spoiling her mood. After all she'd been through, Hannah was suddenly blossoming; a sunflower pushing upward to follow her dreams. She was once again the Hannah she'd been in their early years together. Who was he to stomp on her happiness?

So, he kept silent and on Solly's advice, re-invested the money. He couldn't lose. He had proof. The interest was paid, just as Solly said it would be. It had taken almost no time to have the money to buy the stove. Cash. Paid in full. Powerful words, feeding an even more powerful greed. To his utter surprise, after a while, it had become easier to keep his secret. His mind turned to new bothersome thoughts. How much was he losing by not increasing his investment?

Driving the peddling cart everyday, Zev had lots of time to ponder his problems and to rationalize his motives. It wasn't greed after all, it was good business. The family needed the money. He worried about his young niece, Malka, and was anxious to bring her to Canada. Because of the syndicate, he would soon have enough to pay for her steamship ticket. Then he would save to make a deposit on a new home for his family. He would have money to send his boys to university when they were old enough. God willing they should earn the marks to be accepted. He could help his parents ease their burden, maybe even stop working entirely. The image of his mother bending over her sewing machine in the coat factory played in his thoughts. So, in mid-summer of 1899, Zev made a decision. He resolved to stay in the syndicate just until the end of the year. He would start the new century with a load of money to pave the way for their future. And by December he figured he would come up with a way to tell the family what he had done. It was an exciting plan that made solid sense.

Every week, he secretly slipped money out of the savings jar to give to Solly to invest. Every week the investment money grew, his records matching Solly's accounting to the penny. It was astronomical. The money was all he thought about.

But as time passed, his joy in secretly building his financial security began to erode into fear that he might lose it. Alone with his thoughts on the cart, Zev's misgivings began to grow as he puzzled over the Franklin Syndicate. As proof of the program's legitimacy, Solly had showed him a poster for the syndicate boldly proclaiming profits of "520 percent per year" and articles in *The New York Times* that talked of people lining up in the street to bring their investments to its founder, William Miller. A "blizzard" of ten dollar bills had landed on the syndicate, the newspaper stated. Laughing loudly, Solly had pointed to a quote indicating that the stoop of the syndicate office had collapsed under the weight of the investors lining up to get their money into Miller's hands.

Instead of bringing comfort, however, Solly's words only escalated Zev's apprehensions. It made no sense that a syndicate could pay ten percent a week. The truth of it bore down on Zev and ultimately made him feel sick. It truly was gambling. He could see it now. It had to be. He felt the sin tightening around his throat. The only way it could work was if early investors were being paid their interest with money from later investors as new people came into the scheme. No other explanation made any sense.

Hannah watched Zev's mood slip into constant ill humor. She worried about his weight loss and his sleeplessness. He became critical and sharp-tongued with the children. Yet he assured her nothing was wrong. She pushed food at him. He pushed back, demanding to be left alone.

168

Angry and upset, she threw her energy into developing new dishes for the restaurant. Family meals became quiet as the children warily eyed their father, fearing an outburst, and Bayla sat with raised eyebrows and tight lips. Her unspoken criticisms were saved to discuss privately with Baruch.

Zev's nightmares began about the time the leaves started to change color. He realized his nerves couldn't take it anymore; the secret investment was ruining his life and hurting his family. At the end of October, he went to Solly to tell him he was quitting the syndicate. Solly said he was terribly disappointed, but he did as Zev asked and the following week he handed Zev his windfall. Every penny of it. He counted out the money behind the closed door in his office at the steam bath. Five hundred three dollars and twelve cents. Solly also emphasized that Zev had already lost the additional fifty dollars that would have come from another week of interest. He told Zev he was making a big mistake getting out so early, but that any time he wanted to get back into the syndicate, Solly would be there for him.

To his horror, Zev found no relief in pulling his money out, for his thoughts turned to calculations of the interest he was losing every day. He had taken the money home, wrapped it in a leather pouch and hidden it away. He stewed, he worried and he began to feel a persistent pain in his stomach.

He was frozen in despair. He could neither tell Hannah of his dilemma, nor could he take the money back to Solly to put back into the market. He felt foolish and he felt dirty. He had stashed the leather pouch deep in a corner of the cellar, behind the pickle barrels, exactly where Hannah had happened across a garter snake two summers before. She had run shrieking from the house and had refused to enter the root cellar since, sending the children to fetch the vegetables when needed. No, she wouldn't be likely to discover his secret.

Fortunately, he had to make the trip to Gimli. If the weather held, it would take him between four and six days. The time alone would do him a world of good. One way or another, he would work out a way to tell Hannah about his secret. Then he would be done with the syndicate and its frightful power over his life. And he had the five hundred dollars to make the guilt go away.

As he was climbing up to the driver's seat, he caught sight of Solly Silverstein, wrestling his bulk out of a cab and waving a paper high over his head.

"Zev! Where are you going, so early? I have to show you something!" Solly was weighed down more than usual. Wearing a new silver fox coat, he closely resembled a shambling bear. He huffed along in his rolling gait as fast his short legs could carry him.

"Not today, Solly, I am already late to get on my way. I'm going up to the lake and should have left an hour ago."

"You work too hard, my friend. Here this is the answer to your dreams. I am holding your future in my hands."

"What is it?"

"Look for yourself. A gold mine." Solly handed him a telegram.

IMPORTANT. WE HAVE INSIDE INFORMATION OF A BIG TRANSACTION TO BEGIN SATURDAY OR MONDAY MORNING. BIG PROFITS. REMIT AT ONCE, SO AS TO SECURE THE PROFITS.
WILLIAM F. MILLER, FRANKLIN SYNDICATE.

Zev felt his muscles tighten and his heart quicken. His resolve weakened under Solly's enthusiastic bragging about how much money he had made, along with his news that he was rich enough that he might sell the shvitz and retire to California. Zev was stunned. Solly was ready with all the answers. The Vanderbilts and Astors didn't feel guilty about being rich, and they shouldn't either, Solly told him. But Zev wasn't like Solly.

"Solly, I don't know. I have go to Gimli."

"Zev, did you not already collect a bundle with your investment?"

"You know exactly how much, Solly. As you know that my money earned for your pocket as well."

"So why stop now? A little for me, a lot more for you."

"I don't know, Solly. I really am happy with the money I have."

"Zev, for you I am going to give special rate. Yes? I will charge you only half of my regular fee. Instead of one dollar for every ten you earn, I will charge you only fifty cents. You give me the money, just the five hundred dollars, and we leave it for just four weeks, and at the end of that I will come back with a profit of ..." Solly poked a finger in the air and mouthed his calculations.

"About two hundred and thirty dollars before I pay you your fees," Zev supplied the number as if as if it was written on a paper before him.

Solly whistled. "No one can do sums faster than you, Zev. Such a talent." His gold tooth glinted in the sun. "So? A quick two hundred and thirty, minus a few bucks for your buddy Solly. How much you gonna make on poor Queenie dragging this cart to Gimli and back? Fifteen dollars? Maybe twenty?"

Zev was too honest to hide his grimace. "Maybe. If the fish is top quality."

Solly lowered his voice and came in so close that Zev could feel the moist heat of his breath before he could smell the garlic.

"You've seen for yourself how good this works. It's money to reach out and just take. No work."

Zev's mind filled with numbers as he felt himself drawn into analyzing the risk. Solly had attached his silver thread and was spinning his web.

"This is guaranteed?" Zev asked.

"Sure it's guaranteed. Why not? You know you can trust me. But just don't tell nobody, because I don't want to be causing trouble for those who will ask me how it is you get such special rate, no?"

Solly read the consternation on Zev's face and chuckled. "Look. You go take care of your business, Zev. You did all right with the money you already made. You're right." He waved at the waiting cab driver and slapped Zev on the shoulder. "Have a good ride up to Gimli. If you change your mind, have somebody get your money to my place before four o'clock today. I am wiring the new investments to New York before the close of business." His diamond ring caught the sun as he turned to wave good-bye.

Damn it to hell. Zev watched the cab jiggling under the weight of the shvitzing Solly, overly warmed by his expensive fur coat. He stood next to his cart listening to the sparrows singing his shame. "Cheap, cheap cheap," is how Zev heard them, and felt a vein popping up on his forehead. It was a lot of money to make in a short period of time. Was he pushing his luck? But, he didn't have to do it Solly's way. He wouldn't have to stay in the full four weeks. Just a single week would bring in more than double what he was going to make on the trip to Gimli. He yanked his pocket watch out and glanced at the light in the kitchen window. He could catch Isaac before he left for school.

The time away had worked wonders for Zev, and he was in a good mood as he made his way back into Winnipeg. With many solitary hours of tortured thinking behind him, and the comfort of having a full load of good quality fish to deliver, Zev had worked his mind around to the conclusion that his decision had been in the best interest of the family and that it would all work out. In another few days he would have all of his money back, along with the new profit. He would waste no time in going directly to buy the ticket to bring Malka to Canada—a year ahead of schedule. It was the greatest justification he had for risking all of their savings. Hannah would understand. He would persuade her with the solid reasoning he had rehearsed, over and over, in his long discussions with Queenie.

He winced in shame at the memory of lying to his son. He had handed Isaac the leather bound parcel of money and instructed him to take the package straight to Solly Silverstein. He told Isaac it was a book, a gift that Solly wanted to send to his mother in New York. Isaac, unfledged and innocent, had tucked the package into his coat and gathered up his schoolbooks. He had wished his papa a safe journey and waved as he ran off to do his errand.

Now, as he pulled into the market in Winnipeg's North End to unload the fish Zev was both exhausted and greatly relieved by his decision. He would go to Solly's right after he had emptied his cart and tell him he was pulling his money out. In just a few days he would have his profit and he would leave his troubles behind. It didn't matter what Solly had to say. Zev was done with the syndicate.

He pulled up to the rear of the Winnipeg Fish Market and Feivel the fishmonger leaped from the doorway to help him unload.

"So Zev, what do you think of what happened to Solly Silverstein? Do you think he'll serve time?"

"What? Serve time?" The words made no sense to Zev.

"You know, all that money he ran off with," Feivel said, as he pried open a crate and shoved the ice aside. "Nice looking pickerel, Zev."

Zev couldn't speak. He looked anxiously at Feivel and felt dread pouring through his body.

"I forgot. Of course, you've been traveling, Zev, so you probably don't even know. It's all over the papers. Solly got involved in some investment scheme and the story is that he had a dozen or so folks in Winnipeg hooked into believing they were going to be rich. They just threw their money at Solly. Thousands of dollars they gave him for something called the Franklin Syndicate. Now the syndicate has been closed down. The guy running it, Miller, his name is, has disappeared to Montreal, they say, and is being hunted by the police. Millions of dollars are involved with something like forty thousand investors from all over the United States and Canada. No one has seen Solly in three days. They want to arrest him, Zev. A lot people around here want to hang him. Suckers. Imagine if you'd put money into that."

"Imagine." Zev whispered.

The few blocks left to ride home seemed an eternity as Zev reeled under the blow, his knees weak with knowing he had had lost a fortune. There wasn't ten dollars left in the savings jar.

As he rounded the corner to Main Street he happened across Isaac, running towards home with his empty newspaper bag. He called out and the boy turned and saw him and waved. Then as if stricken he suddenly dropped his head. Zev wondered if he had somehow already learned of his father's evil deed. That couldn't be possible.

Isaac climbed into the cart with barely a hello, his eyes cast downward.

"Isaac, what is it? You are as pale as a ghost. You are not well?"

"I am not sick. Your trip was good, Papa?" Zev could barely hear him.

"What is it, Isaac? Why are you acting so strangely?" Zev's mind started to race.

"I have something to tell you, Papa."

Zev turned to his son and gripped his arm. "What has happened? Is Mama sick?"

"No one is sick, Papa. Oh, please understand, Papa, I did not mean to disobey you. I just forgot!"

"Forgot what?"

"The package for Mr. Silverstein." Watching his father suck in his breath, Isaac braced himself for his anger. "Papa, I was on my way to deliver it, and then I was late for school, and I meant to go at lunch time, and then I had to run to the market for Mama, so I put it away in a special hiding place because you said it was really valuable and I should be careful, and ..."

"The leather package?" Zev shook his son.

"Yes, Papa. I am so sorry. I am so ashamed I forgot about it."

"And where is it now?"

"Inside my mattress with my stamp collection."

Zev took a moment to absorb the news, then threw his head back and laughed until he almost fell from the wagon. God had spared him and he would forever be in debt for His grace.

He would announce tonight that he would buy a steamship ticket for Malka to join them in summer. They would cut back on other expenses to advance the date.

Later that night, in the darkness of their room, Zev took Hannah's hand and lowered his eyes under the weight of his shame and his sin of deception. He told her how sorry he was and then he told her why. He told her the entire story, leaving out nothing, but adding no embellishments to gain her sympathy. Stunned, she said nothing. Finally he finished and rubbed his fingertips into his aching temples. He waited in the moonlit stillness for her to speak and heard only the ticking of the clock, as if it were counting off the seconds to an explosion.

Silence.

Ticking.

A tiny sigh in the dark.

Ticking.

Blood pounding in his ears.

Ticking.

An eternity of ticking.

Finally she turned to him. There were no words, just Hannah's gentle touch drawing him into the warmth of her embrace to release the pain and restore comfort in their union.

He wrapped his arms around his wife and wept with relief.

18

The New Century Begins

December 31, 1899

Thee sound of someone chopping wood downriver split the frozen air and summoned Emma Willows to her bedroom window. She climbed onto the window seat and rubbed her little fist in a circle in the frosty windowpane to clear a peephole. The fresh snow lit up with sparkles against the indigo sky of the late prairie afternoon. Henry was bringing the coach around to the front door, the horses stamping and snorting blasts of vapor. Emma could hardly contain herself. Though just eight-years-old, she had been given permission to accompany her parents to her first evening party. It was almost too much to bear.

A sharp rapping startled her as the door flew open and in bustled Lizzie Gallagher, the new maid.

"Good heavens, child. Are ye nae going to the dancin' party? Yer parents is puttin' on their coats and yer father is in no mood to be kept waiting, lass!" Lizzie chided her little mistress while scooping up dropped clothes and fluffing a pillow.

"I'm all ready to go, Lizzie. See?" Emma hopped down from the window seat and let her arms fly as she spun around to show off her new dress.

"Well, now, my goodness, Miss Emma, how fetching! Here, let me tie that bow properly in the back. I daresay that you'll be makin' a smashin' impression in this lovely frock. You mind the boys now. They'll be runnin' after you to pinch yer cheeks, or steal a kiss, I'll bet."

"Lizzie!" Emma shrieked and slapped a hand against her mouth. "Father will have kittens!"

"Kittens? Oh, I think not. He'll have a cow or maybe a dragon. Aye, he'll have a dragon if he sees boys chasin' after you!"

"A fire breathing dragon!" Emma shouted in delight.

"Aye, little missy, so no flirtin' with silly rascals," Lizzie teased with a twinkle in her eyes.

Emma adored Lizzie and was thrilled that the spirited Irish girl had come to Ravenscraig. Young and pretty with bright red hair and deep green eyes, she was nothing like the older, more serious members of the housekeeping staff. She was the only one who didn't treat her as though she were too young for everything.

Father's voice carried to the top of the stairs as he barked orders at Mrs. Butterfield and Mr. Chadwick. A grand dinner party was to be held at Ravenscraig in honor of the new mayor in just three days and there was apparently much to yell about this early on.

"Oh, don't even give him a second thought," Emma patted Lizzie's arm, as though she was very grown up. "Father is always yelling. He doesn't really mean anything by it."

"Well, that's fine, but we don't want any unneeded delays addin' to his concerns," Lizzie urged her along. "Here's yer coat, Miss Emma."

Rupert Willows loved control almost as much as he adored being the center of attention. Hence, the order was given to the stable that he would drive the sleigh himself this evening. He was intent on setting the gossips atwitter upon his entrance at the Drewry party and arriving in the driver's seat would accomplish this most directly.

The entire party would know in short order that he had acquired a new, fantastically expensive coach, and most important, that he had the dash to take the place of his driver. He had instructed his eldest sons, Alfred and James, to go on ahead to the party in a hired sleigh. In this way his own rig would not be overloaded and his sons would be on hand to gauge the reaction to his arrival.

While Rupert reprimanded the household staff, Henry readied the coach, absent-mindedly muttering and whistling as he settled the horses into position. The excitement, or perhaps it was better described as tension, was felt equally by the family upstairs and by the servants below stairs at the Willows home.

Horses were so much easier than people, Henry mulled.

One had to stay on one's toes around the likes of Rupert J. Willows, Esquire, but after six years in his employ, Henry could read the signs and catch the signals.

Tonight the Willows family would travel up to Redwood House to ring in the New Year—the new century, in fact. This was the famed home of Edward Drewry, a respected city leader and alderman as well as owner of the highly profitable Red River Brewery, risibly known as the Drewry Brewery. There was no doubt this party ranked at the top of the list of society events being held in the city on this special night.

"Not the usual class of party for His Nibs, wouldn't you say, Charlie?" Henry reflected as he affectionately rubbed the lead horse's muzzle, and puzzled over how this invitation must have come about. Willows was a tyrant dressed as a gentleman. Oh, he knew his way to a dollar all right, but God help those who stumbled into his path.

As Henry heaved the buffalo robes into the sleigh, he thought about the strange world of the wealthy in Winnipeg. There would be no fewer than eight millionaires at this party. Willows was not officially part of that elite club of successful leaders, Henry knew, but he was clearly desperate to gain his way in.

"He's a study, that one," commented Henry to the horses as he rubbed their necks and cast a practiced eye over the rig to see that everything was in perfect order. Mr. Willows had been quite sharp in delivering his instructions. Henry patted the chestnut gelding and pulled out a cloth to give the brass door handle a swift polish. He glanced at his pocket watch then moved into the expected military posture. One minute to go. Henry stood at attention, his shoulders squared, eyes forward.

As if on cue for a grand entrance, the heavy front door of the house swung open and Mr. Willows appeared with his wife at his side. He stood for just a moment, as if applause would follow, and she paused at his side, much as a well-trained poodle might wait to match the step of her master. Then with great show, he gallantly escorted her down the grand stone staircase and brought her to the carriage. She smiled and Henry tipped his hat in greeting, quite relieved that so far everything seemed to be trouble free. Just as Mrs. Willows was getting settled in her seat, the door of the house was flung wide, and fifteen-year-old Elliot bounded down the stairs and hopped up into the driver seat, grabbing at the reins.

"Move aside, Elliot, I'll be taking those reins," called his father, as he helped Beth arrange her dress in the carriage. "Now, where is Emma?"

"I'm here, Father. I'm here."

Emma clambered up through the doorway into the coach and snuggled down, the fur of her mother's new mink coat tickling her nose.

"Mummy, I could just burst, I am so happy. I will remember this evening for the rest of my life," she gushed.

Radiating beauty and fine taste, Beth knew that no one at the gala would capture her husband's attention the way she would this evening. She almost giggled as she hugged her daughter close. "I, too, expect we shall have a wonderful time. Now, Emma, I do know you will be careful to remember your manners, you know how important this party is to your father."

Redwood House was magnificent. It was very modern, one of the first in the city to have electric lights, steam heat and a telephone. The Drewry parties were known to be exceptional, and the details were often discussed in the society pages.

Father was terribly anxious that they would make a good impression. He had spared no expense in selecting the clothes they wore that night. So there they were, dressed like the Rockefellers and warned to be on their very best behavior as they made their arrival. Rupert had determined that tonight he would change the course of his future.

The footman lifted Emma from the sleigh and placed her down gently on the packed snow of the roadway. Elliot gathered her up, tossed her up onto the crook of his arm and headed smartly up the path following the others, the enticing sound of scrunching snow beneath his footsteps.

"A lady can't be getting her new button-down shoes wet on the eve of the new century," he whispered into her ear.

"Elliot, do you think I'm old enough to dance tonight? Do

you think I will be allowed? I've been practicing so much. Do you think I could?"

"Emma, dear Emma, what would be the point of wearing your pretty new shoes from Chicago if it were not for the opportunity to dance in them?" he smiled into her frowning concern. "Of course you must dance! And I would be truly honored to show our fellow guests what a fine dancer you are. Shall it be a *schottische* or the Red River Reel? Or would you fancy a jig?"

Relief and anticipation washed over Emma as she broke into a giggle. Emma "oohed" at the lights spilling out onto the snow from every room in the house. She strained to look into the drawing room, filled with finely dressed guests as the Willows family rounded the corner to the grand entrance of the home.

She saw her brother, Alfred, ahead of them, and they waved at each other. James must have already disappeared into the house. Emma knew her older brothers had more important things on their minds than to worry about their little sister tonight. This was, after all, such a delicious opportunity for wealthy young men to show off. In fact, Father would expect it.

Everyone who was important was there. Emma knew this because her father had told them so. Since Alfred was a little boy, Rupert had been in the habit of picking out highlights from the newspapers to read out loud after dinner, determined to ensure that his children would understand that their position in life was a privilege and in many ways now a birthright that needed to be protected at all costs. They needed to know with whom they could associate and with whom they could not. The daily discourse on the goings on of the upper class was considered part of their education. The Willows children all learned at a very young age that what others thought of you was more important than anything. That was the key to success according to R.J. Willows, Esquire.

Emma reminded herself not to get too carried away with having fun. Father wouldn't be pleased.

Rupert guided his wife into the drawing room and swelled at the approving and envious glances. The exquisite emerald velvet dress he had chosen for Beth had been dreadfully expensive and well over his intended budget, but was clearly worth the investment. Hand-made in Paris and trimmed in Austrian crystals, it was not only the latest European fashion, but the most splendid gown in the room. Beth, accustomed to Rupert's expectations, carried it magnificently. She beamed at her admirers as if the party was in her husband's honor. Rupert was greatly pleased and made an elegant show of placing his name on her dance card.

"There's the new mayor," Rupert whispered as he interrupted his scan of the ballroom to raise his glass in acknowledgment of the nodded greeting from Horace Wilson.

Rupert had a system. Upon arriving at a social gathering, he always took the time needed to look the room over and rank the people there in the order of their importance. He discovered, early on, that this way he would minimize the amount of time he would have to spend with people "who had nothing to offer" and maximize his opportunity to exploit the acquaintances that might advance his growing business and political ambitions. The fact that he was able to do this without being truly offensive was evidence of the degree of sophistication he had cultivated so carefully to mask his past and secure his ascent to wealth. He was shrewd, ruthless and callous, but carried it off in a way that allowed him to garner the admiration of his peers.

Rupert was a natural at creating an impression. He drew eyes as a flame draws moths. The power was in the fact that there was never the slightest hint that he did anything deliberately to gain attention. It was not an act. It was an aura.

Now, watching an intoxicating display of wealth and beauty at this glittering party, Rupert positively brimmed with his own cleverness and magnetism. Life was grand indeed. And here he was, now an alderman in one of the fastest growing cities in the Dominion and, perhaps, in all of North America. If things went as planned, not only would his position on city council give him a direct line to new business, it would also lead him to take the mayor's chair. What possibly could hold him back? Perhaps he would even be prime minister of Canada. The opportunities were limitless.

Intent on getting across the room to be seen speaking with Sir James Aikins, a leading member of Winnipeg society, Rupert gently guided his wife past polite hellos, stopping only long enough with the no-accounts not to be thought entirely rude. Beth was a well-mannered asset. While in Rupert's presence, she knew to say as little as possible and look as pretty as possible at all times.

"Good evening, Mr. Aikins. Do you remember my wife, Beth?" he asked.

"Of course, how lovely you look this evening, Mrs. Willows," replied Aikins, as he took her hand with a slight bow. With a smile and nod he turned his attention to Rupert. "I had the most interesting discussion with your son, Alfred. That young man has a real sense for business, I say."

Swiftly calculating the best opportunity to heighten his profile with this influential icon, Rupert considered how much pride to manifest and decided a humble and quiet laugh would be the perfect prelude, "Yes, indeed. Now that he has graduated from Harvard, there's no telling how quickly he'll be wanting to push me aside and take over the company." The discussion went directly to business and droned on as young Emma slipped away from her mother's skirts and headed off to find Elliot.

Her heart danced with the spectacle of it all. She tried to remember not to gawk as she worked at burning every detail of the evening into her memory. She noted the songs the orchestra played and the pungent linger of cigar smoke as she made her way past the conservatory to the entrance to the billiards room. She peeked through the doorway and saw several men in a heated discussion on the cost of labor, waving off white-gloved servants offering hors d'oeuvres.

"I hear that McEwan fellow is planning to increase wages to twelve dollars a week at his furniture factory. You know how fast word will get around. I'm expecting to lose my best foreman to him," harrumphed a stout man while chewing on his cigar.

"Good God. That's more than six hundred dollars a year!" came the boisterous response. "And McEwan"'s already got his workers leaving at four o'clock on Saturdays. They barely put in fifty hours a week."

Emma's eyes opened wide, as she eased back behind the doorway so as not to be seen. Six hundred dollars for a year's wages? She must have heard wrong. That's what she heard Father tell Mummy he had paid for her pretty green dress.

"He must be daft." A third man hawked and spit, just making the spittoon by the corner of the table. "Even five hundred dollars a year is too much. We are overflowing with people flooding into the West, wanting to make a home here and looking for work. Have you been to the railway station lately? You can't breathe for the smell of them. And the federal government is just heating up its campaign to bring in tens of thousands more. You mark my words. Nothing is ever going to stop Winnipeg's growth and that means an endless supply of workers."

Emma recognized the speaker as Archibald Montgomery. He was an alderman, and she had seen him in her home playing cards with father and some other businessmen. Mr. Montgomery's heavy face, rimmed with bushy auburn sideburns, was getting very red. She wondered if the thick vein in his neck would pop open and spurt blood all over his white shirt. Shaking with rage, and chewing hard on his tobacco, a tiny stream of spittle started to leak out of the corner of his mouth as he continued his tirade.

"They need jobs. They come from poverty. Peasants and paupers they are. Most of them don't even speak English for pity's sake. They expect a hard life here. Why would we want to spoil them? No, sir. Ten dollars a week is the top wage I would ever pay. They can take it or leave it."

"Right you are, Archibald." The man with the cigar slapped him on the shoulder in agreement. "There are plenty more immigrants who will take the work for even lower pay. To hell with the greedy bastards."

"To hell with the greedy bastards," Emma repeated softly to herself, tasting the words of angry men and wondering what a bastard was as she moved along the hallway back toward the drawing room.

Emma stood back against the mahogany wall and watched a group of women descend the grand staircase returning from the ladies' lounge. She was captivated by the sparkle of the jewelry, the swish of the bustled skirts and the expensive perfumes wafting by. The empty chatter about fashion and children from the society matrons stood in sharp contrast to the bluster and ranting from the men. Emma continued on to the drawing room and near the door she came upon her mother who was conversing gaily with a group of well-dressed women. Mummy seemed quite at home amidst all the glamour, and Emma wondered if she would ever grow up to become as much of a lady.

Beth fluttered about, dropping her flowery words about nothing into one conversation after another as one might scatter seeds for pigeons. In time she found it tiring to be so charming, and it came to her that a glass of sherry would be most enjoyable. How on earth was she to manage that among these drumbeaters for the temperance movement? She glanced about and spotted one of the younger members of the wait staff. Then, like a southern belle holding court among suitors on a cotton plantation, she flashed a smile and danced her fan coquettishly against her bosom. Oh, yes. It appeared the young man would only be too happy to accommodate Mrs. Willows.

On the other side of the grand hall, Emma soaked up details and impressions of her fellow guests. Ethel Fortune, beautiful in burgundy silk and pink cheeks, gained quite a bit of notice from the available young men. Emma rolled her eyes at the silly look on Clifford Young's face, as he stuttered his way through a besotted attempt to gain Ethel's attention. Making her way back to the drawing room, Emma wondered at what age boys lost their ability to think. Or was it a spell that pretty young debutantes had the ability to cast? She thought she must take this up with Lizzie tomorrow. Lizzie certainly knew a lot about boys.

The sound of the music in the drawing room redirected her attention. The orchestra broke from the standard fare of popular quadrilles and struck up a toe-tapping favorite she had been practicing with Elliot. It was a spirited new song called *The Maple Leaf Rag*. Unfamiliar to the audience, a few brave young dancers remained on the floor and jumped along to the rollicking music while skirts flew in a garden of colors.

"It's ragtime music!" shouted the orchestra leader. "Does anyone know how to dance the Turkey Trot?"

"It's our dance, Emma!" Elliot's strong arms encircled her and suddenly he was wheeling her about in the center of the room. Elliot had learned the new dance on a recent visit to New York, and he was so enchanted with ragtime music that he had brought home a phonograph recording to practice with Emma.

"I can't believe they are playing this!" Emma squealed.

"I asked them to play it!" he answered, and she shrieked with enjoyment at the very courage of such a thing. Emma hopped and whirled, guided by her brother's superb dance style. The others cleared the floor to admire the performance of the talented youngsters. Round and round they spun with the confidence and freedom known only to those who never give a second thought to creating the right impression. The intricate steps and perfectly timed flicking of their heels prompted hearty approval. Hoots of encouragement came from their fellow party guests entertained by the skill and grace of the elfin dancer among them. Thoroughly enjoying her vainglorious venture into the world of grownups, Emma looked across the floor to find her father.

As her eyes met his, she felt the blood drain out of her tiny body.

He stood quietly seething, glaring his disapproval in the face of the horror that she, his only daughter, would be making a spectacle of herself by crossing into the adults-only territory of the dance floor. Terror slithered into Emma's chest and tightened around her heart. She gasped sharply, preparing for the bolt of lightening that would surely explode through the chandelier and strike her dead on the spot.

"Elliot, we have to stop!" Emma insisted, digging her fingernails into Elliot's coat sleeve and feeling her stomach flip as the music segued into the Viennese Waltz.

Her savior was the most unlikely of people. As the crowd stepped back to allow the significance of his presence to be known and with the slightest tap on her brother's shoulder, Sir Rodman Roblin, premier of Manitoba, smiled down at her, offering a deep bow and asking, "May I have the pleasure of a place on your dance card Miss Willows?"

Emma snapped her gaping mouth shut. She smiled weakly in reply and forced her eyes to travel across to her father who, to her utter relief, smiled broadly.

Rupert could hardly contain himself. What a charmer that Emma was turning into. He beamed with opportunity and desperately hoped to pass it off as a look of pride in his unusually gifted daughter.

Saved from certain death, she accepted the invitation of the premier with a feminine flutter of her fan. She arched into a graceful posture as he took her spinning about the room, in a polished and awe-inspiring display of talent. Applause rose around Emma and her esteemed dance partner. Her heart pounding with happiness, she finished the waltz by dropping into an exaggerated bow, inspired by one of the ballet performances she had attended and was escorted back to her father. She did all of the things she knew mother would expect. She smiled at her father, she thanked the premier, then bobbed into a curtsey for a quick exit as her father slipped into a discussion with Sir Rodman about current building projects of Willows and Sons.

On the second floor she found a chair near the powder room and sat down to recover from the shaking in her knees. Only when her heartbeat returned to normal did she hear the voices of the women around the corner.

She recognized Mrs. Anderson's voice. She had been to tea at Ravenscraig on more than a few occasions. Mother once commented to Emma that Mrs. Anderson had more jewelry than any other woman in the city.

"Surely, what we hear is exaggerated," Mrs. Anderson said with distress in her voice. "Children are no longer dying of Red River Fever. We have improvements everywhere in the sanitation system. If there were a problem my husband would know about it."

"Mrs. Anderson, I implore you. Red River Fever is a dressed up name for typhoid," a soft and cultured voice replied. "By the spring thaw we think we are going to see a terrible number of

186

cases, yet again. If women like you and your friends were to take an interest in helping, we would save many lives."

"Dr. Yeomans, I am afraid I wouldn't know where to begin."

Dr. Yeomans? A woman is a Dr. Yeomans? Emma's eyes widened as she leaned toward the corner doorway to better hear the conversation.

"Mrs. Anderson, if you would be generous enough to host a gathering of some of the women in your circle, perhaps I could come with Dr. Crawford, Dr. Mary Crawford, and talk with them about the wretched conditions that exist just a short distance from this home."

Mary? Two women doctors? Had she heard right? Emma slid off the chair and edged her way to the doorway.

"There are houses with just three rooms where four families are crammed in tight, fighting for air," continued Dr. Yeomans. "They are desperately poor and they live in overcrowded, filthy conditions that are impossible to imagine. They are cold, they are hungry, and they won't ask for help."

"You're talking about that awful place we read about, New Jerusalem. I've heard it called in the *Winnipeg Star.*"

"New Jerusalem, the foreign ghetto or the tenement slums. It doesn't matter what it is called. These are all names for a dreadful place that you wouldn't allow livestock to live in."

"But the people who live there are the Hebrews and those Galicians. They don't even speak English," protested Mrs. Anderson, her voice taking on a whine.

"They are simply people who need help."

"Dr. Yeomans, I don't know." Emma could hear the anxiety rising in Mrs. Anderson's voice. "My husband wouldn't like it. He told me stories about drinking and disease and bad things that happen over there. Violent things. Forgive me, but *Dirty Jew* and *Bohunk* are the kinds of expressions he has used. No, I don't think he would like it," Mrs. Anderson slowly shook her head.

Dr. Yeomans pushed on. "Please, Mrs. Anderson. You have children. Please don't close your mind and your heart."

With warmth and dignity and an understanding that came from many, many conversations just like this one, the doctor eased into her closing.

"Thank you for being so gracious as to listen to me. I'm sorry I took so much of your time."

Emma peeked around the doorway and glanced up at the red face of Mrs. Anderson. She watched as the regal woman bowed her head and closed her eyes very tightly. Then she did the most amazing thing Emma could have imagined. Mrs. Anderson slipped her diamond bracelet off her wrist and pressed it into the hand of Dr. Yeomans.

19
To Be a Jew
April 25, 1900

Every day before school and most days after school, Isaac hawked newspapers for the *Winnipeg Star*. He had been selling papers for almost three years now, ever since his family's arrival in Winnipeg. The morning edition was the big money maker, and if Isaac got up early enough, he had no trouble securing a prime street corner, such as Main and Bannatyne in front of Ashdown's Hardware Store. A great many office workers, tradesmen, candy makers, and garment workers passed by Ashdown's on their way to their Exchange District jobs and there was considerable competition among the newsboys for this particular corner.

Suddenly a new attraction caught the attention of all the boys. Mr. Ashdown had placed a brand new bicycle in his shop window and Isaac, at fourteen, was instantly burning with desire to own it.

When he went into the store to get a good look at it, Mr. Ashdown happily pulled it out of the window and explained all of the bike's features. Manufactured by the Canada Cycle and Motor Company, the CCM two-wheeler was the epitome of modernity. He encouraged Isaac to touch it, to sit on it, to examine the fine bicycle chain and the leather seat, and to admire the updated design of the diamond shaped frame carrying two wheels of identical size. So much safer, he explained, than high-wheeled bicycles and much more comfortable than the teeth-rattling vehicles, known as "boneshakers", that had started the craze for bicycles.

Isaac was so enthralled he couldn't speak. He ran his hand over the frame and imagined riding it. Mr. Ashdown pointed out the convenience of the large basket on the front and an endless list of other impressive details. With all of that, it was the smell of the tires that proved of greatest appeal to Isaac. Mr. Ashdown was amused and shook his head as he watched the intense young man close his eyes and touch his nose to the pneumatic tire, breathing in the smell of the new rubber as if he were drawing in the scent of freshly baked cookies. The storekeeper promised him a special price of fifty dollars, and Isaac's heart sank. He might as well have said five hundred; it was so far beyond a newsboy's reach.

Mr. Ashdown seemed undaunted, however, and spoke as though he fully expected Isaac to be back to buy the bike.

"Isaac, as plain as I can see the nose on your face, I can see that you are worried about how you ever might pay for the bicycle."

Flushed with embarrassment, Isaac dropped his eyes.

"I've known you, for at least three years, Isaac, standing out front, selling your newspapers, and what I see is a hard working young man, determined to make something of himself. That's all you really need in life, son. You'll find a way to earn your way to acquiring the bicycle. I'm certain of it."

Isaac met the gaze of the dapper storekeeper and found his voice.

"Thank you, Mr. Ashdown, but with respect, sir, I don't think you know what it is like to be, well, I mean ..." Isaac's words caught in his shame.

"Poor?" the storeowner asked gently.

"Yes, poor. I have to walk everywhere I go and, well, I can't imagine with all of your success that you have to walk anywhere you don't want."

James Ashdown clapped his hands together and laughed until tears came to his eyes, leaving Isaac to twist his cap in his sweaty hands, mortified and perplexed.

"Isaac, please understand that I am not making fun of you. I need to tell you something, son. When I first got to Winnipeg there were just a hundred people or so living here. That was more than thirty years ago, before Manitoba was a province and when Winnipeg was a tiny settlement called Fort Garry. Imagine it. No railroad, no roads. How do you think I got here?"

"Riverboat?" Isaac offered.

"No, sir. I walked. I walked for nineteen days next to a

string of Red River ox carts all the way from St. Cloud, Minnesota. Grasshoppers were so thick in the air that summer that we were almost breathing them in. And I can tell you that I sincerely doubt that ever in your lifetime will you have to walk that far to get somewhere you wish to go."

"I'm sorry, if I was rude, Mr. Ashdown."

Isaac considered telling him about the walk out of Russia, but thought better of the idea. He had learned it was best to not discuss his background with people who weren't from the old country.

"Nothing rude about it. We are all quick to make assumptions based on what we see. You'll go far in life, Isaac, if you learn to look past a first impression. I can tell you most people don't, and they miss opportunities because of it. Do you understand?"

"Yes, sir."

Isaac watched as Ashdown lifted the bike and placed it carefully back into the window.

"And from my own experience, I can tell you that if a man wants something badly enough, he'll find a way to get it." He smiled and shook the boy's hand. "You're a smart lad, Isaac. You just need a little gumption, I'd say."

Isaac spent hours thinking about what Mr. Ashdown had said to him. He thought of his father's and grandfather's gumption in leading them out of Russia. Every morning, he stared at the bike through the window between selling papers. He admired every spoke and bolt on the shiny black machine and ached with envy at the very sight of it. It suddenly seemed that bicycles were everywhere in Winnipeg. Every time he turned his head he would see another jaunty cyclist speeding expertly down the street atop the two-wheeled wonder. In his mind's eye, he saw himself flying down the roadway with the wind in his face enjoying the magic of traveling so quickly. And he couldn't help but also think of his admiring friends and how it would raise his stock with girls he never dared approach, girls like Bessie Greenberg who were too beautiful to notice boys like Isaac Zigman. It was overpowering. To own such a vehicle would completely change his life. He would be free to travel anywhere he wished, anytime at all. But the hard truth remained. The cost was so great it would take him months, even years, to save the money. He was already putting aside money for university and just could not see finding the additional time to earn what was needed for this extravagance.

He awoke thinking of the bicycle and fell asleep dreaming about it. Three days after first seeing it, Isaac was completely preoccupied with the matter during his long walk home from school. He was obsessed with figuring out how to earn the needed money. He could do his homework faster and sleep less. Maybe he could work as a hot-walker at the racetrack. Then, imagining what it would be like to control a lathered horse fighting to regain its breath after a race, he dismissed the idea. Besides, a lot of the races were on Saturday, and his father would never permit it. Maybe the newspaper needed extra people to clean the office after hours, or Mr. Gunn might need help in the bakery. So deep was his concentration on his problem that he didn't notice the boys behind him. He heard the voices before he understood the words.

"Hey, Jew boy. Hey, Kike, I'm talking to you."

Ace Patterson, tall and gangly with pimply cheeks and sunken, red-rimmed eyes was yelling at him. Isaac stepped back; he could see what was coming. He knew all about Ace, a local tough guy who was known to be lucky at cards and skilled at shooting pool. His father owned one of the lower class saloons on Main Street, a joint called Hangman's Bar. The story was that his old man first taught Ace to shoot craps when he was just six. Isaac also recognized Ace's sidekick, Vic Stanky, another troublemaker who had dropped out of school the year before. But the third boy, short and dirty with thick green snot clotted in his nostrils, was new to him.

"Hey, leave me alone, eh?" Isaac shrank into his coat and moved along a little faster.

"Leave you alone? Why, Jew boy?" Stanky thrust his jaw out. "You goin' home to count your money?"

The boys looped behind and surrounded Isaac as Ace dived for Isaac's books and yanked them out of his grasp.

"Dirty Jew. I see that long line of folks goin' into your

family's restaurant everyday. You must be loaded with money by now. Rich dirty Jews. I guess that makes you filthy rich, right?" Ace found his witticism hilarious and started to snort at his own humor.

The new kid slipped in and kicked the books to the side before Isaac could grab for the strap that held them together.

Stanky came up into Isaac's face and sneered at him while working a large wad of chewing tobacco in his cheek.

"You folks *Jewing* them customers of yours out of their hard earned money?"

Isaac's muscles tightened as he circled with the boys, looking for an opening so he could break through and run away.

"I don't know what you are talking about. It's a restaurant. People pay for meals," he said evenly, not wanting to further agitate his aggressors.

Ace moved in close and cracked his knuckles.

"Jews are all cheats," he said calmly. "I'll bet y'are cheatin' your customers. I'll just bet y'are, just like Solly Silverstein stole money from my old man, Jew boy. My pop lost everything we had. He was so mad he bust up the house and my ma took off and ain't come back yet. Ya think that's fair? Eh? Ya think that's fair?"

Ace was screaming now. Isaac said nothing, but his heart pounded and he began to pant as the boys worked him back into a corner between a garage wall and a woodpile.

"Somebody's gotta pay for that, and it may as well be you, Kike," Stanky spat out the words as he pushed his face into Isaac's, the black tobacco juice running like blood from the corners of his mouth.

The first punch landed solidly on Isaac's rib cage under his left arm and forced him off balance. Three or four hard blows left him staggering; he swung wildly to defend himself. The boys moved in, jeering and laughing. Tightening his small frame, Isaac ducked one punch and took a second on his shoulder. Then a third hit him squarely on the nose and blood gushed from his face.

Stanky laughed, pointing. "If I hit you, do you not bleed, Shylock?" he taunted.

Anger rose in Isaac as never before and unleashed a power he didn't know he had. He sprang like a wounded tiger, kicking fiercely at the hands scrambling to get a grip on him. His legs were knocked from under him and he went down on his back. As he fell, his boot clipped the side of Ace's head, knocking him into the garage wall.

"My teeth! Son of a bitch! He broke my tooth!" Ace was spitting blood.

Stanky reached into his boot. The glint of steel caught Isaac's eye and he scrambled to his feet. He sidestepped the thrust of the blade and smashed a swinging blow into Stanky's jaw, knocking him off his feet. The snot-nosed kid saw the knife and stepped back out of the way. Isaac bent to grab his books but before he reached them, Stanky lunged at him with the knife raised to strike. Isaac grabbed his attacker's arm with both hands and fought to keep the blade from his face. Locking his grip on Stanky's elbow, he twisted his arm back with all his force, and slammed his knee up into the kid's crotch. A piercing shriek filled the alley and the knife flew from Stanky's hand as he doubled over. Gulping for air, he fell, writhing in the dirt like a snake with a severed head. With the others momentarily glued to the horror before them, Isaac shot through the opening. Snatching his book strap in full flight, he cleared a fence and tore for home.

The family supper at the Zigman home was electric with tension. Everyone was silent in the aftermath of Isaac's terrible story. Each had much to say, but they were all quiet for fear of setting off Mama. The dinner table was not the place for the Zigman men to sort out the many complexities of such an attack. Thoughts of revenge raged beneath the surface, but were kept in check by Hannah's vehement opposition to acts of retaliation. She had been close to hysterics the last time Isaac had suffered a schoolyard beating.

Unexpectedly, it was little Mendel who broke the tension and bridged the emotions around the supper table.

"I want to talk. I have something to say!" Mendel

announced loudly.

Zev motioned to his youngest child to go ahead.

"Teacher says we should all be Christians and we would have no more problems!" Mendel, attended the neighborhood kindergarten. He hopped up and down with his good news. "She was talking about Jews today. She says we should come to church, then we can get free food and all kinds of stuff. Even clothes! Wouldn't that be swell? She says that in Canada we are all supposed to be Christians now."

"What?" cried Mama. "Why would she say such a thing?"

"Because they want to get rid of the Jews." Zaida Baruch measured his words. "The same thing could happen here as happened in the old country."

"Papa, it would never happen," Zev spoke quietly, with respect for his father. "Here, it is different. Too many people suffered terribly in the old country. Those attitudes will never grow here. Not in the same way. This is a new world. The government would not allow Jews to be pushed away from Judaism."

"Oh, yes they would," Aaron said. "I've heard the same speech from my teacher. She says we all need to be "God fearing Christians" and then we'll be good citizens and make a great success of our growing country. She says there is no room for us to hold on to our old ways."

"This is what they are teaching you in school?" Zev stared at his younger sons.

"Yup," answered Mendel. "We even learn songs and sometimes we march. I like when we sing *Onward Christian Soldiers.*" At this Mendel jumped up and started singing and marching in place. A dark curtain seemed to fall over Zaida Baruch's face. Baba shook her head and brought her napkin to her lips as Mama put a hand on Mendel's shoulder to quiet him. Zev spoke first.

"Mendel, it is good that the Christian children should have their songs and their religion, but it is also important that you and other Jewish children will have a school where you can learn to be proud to be Jew. We will one day have such a school in Winnipeg."

Shifting in his seat, Aaron looked at Isaac's bruised, swollen face and then at his father.

"You have something you would like to say, Aaron?" Zev nodded to his son.

"Yes, Papa. How come we can't be Jews at home and more like everyone else when we are at school? It's hard to be a Jew when so many people think it's bad. Look what happened to Isaac. You know my friend, Petie? See, he's a Christian but he likes me and I like him. His pop saw me playing tippy sticks with Petie and all of a sudden it's like I was caught stealin' or something. Petie's father started hollerin' and chased me away. Oh, was he yelling! You know what he said?" Aaron caught his mother's stern look out of the corner of his eye and his voice trailed off as he wound up his story. "He was yelling words I can't say at the table."

"This happens. It is complicated." Zev answered quietly.

"Papa, we're just a couple of kids playing a game," Aaron continued. "We don't care that we don't say the same prayers or celebrate the same holidays. We never talk about it. Why is it wrong for us to be friends?"

Zev rubbed his brow and took his time before responding. "Aaron, there is nothing wrong with you being friends with Petie. It is very sad that you have these problems that come from adults who only know hatred toward anyone who is different. Your zaida is right. There are people who hate Jews. Some live only to see Judaism destroyed. You need to know these stories, this history. The truth is you haven't been properly educated. It is my fault."

Zev caught himself as he saw the pain on his father's face.

"My dear family, this is not the time to discuss this," Zev said.

"No, Zev, you are right to talk to the children about these things." Baruch told him. "Without knowledge, we cannot know what to believe. Already you see how it starts, hmm? These little invitations to stand and march and sing a pretty song. Then in two or three generations, who will count himself as a Jew? Will you? Will your grandchildren be raised to know and love Torah?"

196

The weight of his words had quieted the clatter of cutlery. When he continued, it was in Yiddish so the language could flow easily in the telling of a difficult part of his history.

"Aaron, and Mendel, I am going to tell you a story so you should understand that it is not so easy to just throw away what it means to be a Jew. This story is not like the ones you know from the Torah. This story is from Russia."

The family sat quietly as Baruch calmly told the story of the czar's army of boys, the *cantonists* as they were known, in Russia. It had started under Tsar Nicholas. In 1827 he had issued a decree requiring the conscription of Jewish boys between the ages of twelve and twenty-five. Younger boys, often as young as eight or nine, were also taken into the czar's army.

His goal was to strip the Jewish boys of their religious and national identity. In this way, the government created divisions in the Jewish communities, setting quotas for new inductees and demanding that selecting the boys be the job of the Jewish leaders in the villages. It was a dreadful time in Russia for the Jews. Parents hid their children with relatives. Some resorted to cutting off the index fingers of their sons, so that they would be unable to shoot a rifle, and therefore be unsuitable to be a soldier.

Once inducted into the army, most of the boys never returned home. Their mandatory service of twenty-five years officially started only after they turned eighteen. Not only were they denied kosher food and the opportunity to pray, they were also beaten and tortured to accept baptism to the Orthodox Church. Only when Czar Nicholas died in 1855 did the kidnapping of Jewish children for the army come to an end.

Baruch closed his hands in front of his plate and said nothing more. Isaac, familiar with the story, answered the question he knew was on Aaron's mind.

"Zaida served in the Russian army for ten years. He was kidnapped and forced to be a soldier at age nine. The same age as you are now, Aaron."

Nine-years-old, and taken from his family. Aaron couldn't imagine how he would survive such a terrible thing. "How did you get out of the army, Zaida?" he asked.

His grandfather hesitated and seemed suddenly very tired.

Isaac picked up the story. "It's only because of the change in the law that Zaida was able to leave the army in 1859, when he was nineteen. All the *cantonists* under twenty were released. Zaida went home and very soon after, he married Baba. He remained a Jew, despite all of the suffering. It is a miracle that we are here, because it is a miracle he survived."

"You know your history very well, Isaac," Zev said approvingly. "Even the dates."

Isaac shrugged. "I think that if we have to memorize all of this business about the Magna Carta at school, I should at least remember my own history."

The story hit Aaron like a thunderbolt. He searched his grandfather's face for validation. "This is true, Zaida?"

Baruch nodded and spoke softly. "Yes. That is all correct. Isaac you are a good boy to want to know and to remember these things. You make your zaida proud. It is only if we know and we tell the stories that we will remember and we will have a way to be sure it does not happen again."

Aaron was dumbfounded. Many of the kids from school went to the Greek Orthodox Church on Stella Avenue. "You think some of these *goyim* who beat us up might have had grandfathers who were Jews who were forced to convert?" His mind filled with thoughts of every boy that had ever swung a fist at him.

Baruch considered before answering. "This, I do not know. What I do know is that many thousands of men and boys were forced to convert. A few later went back to their families. Others never found them again. And here we are, so many years later in a new country with no thought about that suffering. Old country, old stories. New country, new opportunities. But never forget what came before. If you do, the suffering was paid for nothing. It is not so easy to be a Jew. This is true. It has always been true. It is what we are, and what we always will be." He shook his head. "That's enough now."

Aaron and Mendel turned to whisper to each other. "I can't wait to ask Petie if he thinks his family might be Jewish instead of Ukrainian!" Aaron's words were loud enough that the entire table heard him.

Isaac backhanded him across the shoulder and before he had a chance to return the strike he felt the familiar thump of his mother's hand on the back of his head. "Stop that!" She glared at them.

"Well, I'm just sayin' that a lot of *goyim* like Petie's father, who hate Jews, might be Jews themselves," Aaron defended himself.

"Ignorance and bigotry are hard to remedy. There will always be difficult people touching your life," Zev said. "Don't make them more important than necessary. You miss the interesting people when you worry too much about the ones who make you angry. Enjoy your friend Petie. Stay out of trouble with his father."

The next day Isaac went to see Mr. Gunn at his bakery and got lucky. One of his employees had just quit to take a higher paying job in Rat Portage and Mr. Gunn needed help right away. Isaac was hired to help stoke the fires for the baking ovens and to get things ready to start the bread rising.

In no time, Mr. Gunn was so pleased with Isaac's work that he had Isaac working as many hours as the boy could manage. He got up at two o'clock and worked at the bakery for three hours in the early morning before running to sell his papers. He worked another three or four hours after school. On Sundays he got up early and went from one door to the next looking for all the extra work he could find. He dug a garden for Mrs. Fuga, cleaned out a shed for Mrs. Bachynsky, and helped deliver grocery orders for Mr. Matas, who had a meat shop over in Point Douglas. Mr. Ripstein sent him to his mother's house to help with her spring cleaning. The dimes, nickels and occasional dollars started to add up.

Every day, Isaac admired the new bicycles Mr. Ashdown brought into his store. They were selling like hotcakes, he said. But he told Isaac that he had put the special black bike in storage for him, for when he was ready.

His sleep suffered, but he tossed off Mama's worried looks. He caught a few hours here and there and somehow managed to keep up with his schoolwork and his chores around the house.

One night in mid-June, Zev came in from a late meeting at the synagogue and found Isaac asleep on top of his books at the tiny table in the front room that he used for studying. The oil lamp had burned low and his brothers were sound asleep in their makeshift beds in the room. Zev watched Isaac for a time and considered how fortunate he was to have dreams of success burning so brightly in his sons. This was what he had fought for in their desperate flight from Russia.

Isaac stirred and slipped from the table, jarring himself awake.

"Papa! What time is it?"

"It's after eleven. You should get to bed."

"I'm fine Papa. I have to study for a test in history for tomorrow."

"How are you doing with your savings for the bicycle?"

Isaac grinned widely. "Three more weeks, Papa. I just need eight more dollars."

Zev looked at his determined son, and the words he wanted to say got stuck in his throat. He rubbed Isaac on the head as he left the room to go to his own bed.

An hour later, Isaac jolted awake again. He looked at the clock and saw it was close to midnight. His picked up his books and underneath them was startled to see a fresh, crisp five-dollar bill. A short note in his father's neat writing was under the bill.

"Isaac, you make me proud to be your papa."

20
Blackmail
April 26, 1900

The letters of congratulation and the invitations for social engagements came in almost faster than Beth Willows could keep up with them.

The national magazine, *The Dominion Coast to Coast,* had published a very flattering story about Rupert's success as a politician and his great influence as a new member of the Winnipeg Board of Trade. The writer had identified him as a fine example of "the new breed of man" that was shaking things up in Manitoba.

Beth was overjoyed at the instant fame that the article brought and was only too happy to respond to the letters on his behalf. To facilitate the task, Rupert had installed a temporary desk for Beth in his library at Ravenscraig.

"Rupert, dear, take a look at this one," she called to him from across the room. "It's in some foreign language. I can't make out a single word. They've got your name right, though."

"Is it local?"

"No. The postmark is from Toronto. Quite a lengthy letter, though," she said as she peered at the writing.

"Beth, darling, I'm terribly busy. You can't bother me for each of the letters. If you don't know who it is, put it aside. Or throw it out. I needn't respond to every immigrant who aspires to find his fortune in Canada. I'm sure the bloke is looking for free advice. Imagine not even taking the time to write in English. Give it the toss, will you?"

Beth scrutinized the envelope and touched it to her nose.

"Smells like cheap cigars. No wonder. Let's see, the return address is to a Mr. I. Volinsky. The handwriting on the envelope is not very neat but it is legible. Yes, that's it. V-O-L-I-N-S-K-Y. Let's see if I can't pitch it into the fire from here."

The hair had come up on the back of Rupert's neck and his

heart was hammering.

"No, Beth!" he shouted as leapt for the letter. "You don't want to be scattering ashes all over my lovely carpet now do you?"

"Oh, Rupert, you never let me have any fun!"

"Beth, dear, you have been at this all afternoon. That is quite enough for one day. Off you go, I have a couple of telephone calls to make and I will see you for cocktails in about forty-five minutes. How would that suit you?"

"Splendidly. I'll go up and change for dinner, darling. You do know me so well."

She reached her arms out to him and he obliged with an affectionate embrace and kissed her on the cheek as she swished her way to the door and winked back over her shoulder.

"Don't work too hard, my love," she cooed.

"I'll be right along. The faster I get through my work, the sooner I'll be able to listen to all your news over drinks."

As the door closed, he sat down with the letter. It was in Russian. Rupert looked at the familiar handwriting and felt his skin prickle. This was the last thing he ever expected to have to contend with. The poison of the message was the same as that which flowed in the blood of the writer.

Hello Rupert,

How surprised you must be to be to reading this letter. I am writing in Russian because there is an obvious advantage to keeping this little secret for the time being. I can imagine how happy you are that all of those years ago I forced you to learn to read and write in the language of the old country. You must also be happy I chose Russian and not Yiddish for this correspondence.

Such plans I had for us in those years. I believed we would leave our stupid little farm and go to New York. I believed we would be in the diamond business with my uncle and that by now I would be rich and sitting in a beautiful home, working only if and when I pleased.

Your mother, that whore, ruined everything for me. Every dream, every plan, every opportunity. Here I sit in Toronto, working on Bloor Street. A captain of industry? No. Just a regular slob with a magazine stand in the financial district. But I see that there is hope. There is a wonderful opportunity that came to me in one of those magazines. Imagine that. I believe it was my destiny.

You see, all of the years I searched to find that woman who bore you came to nothing.

Don't misunderstand. I did not want her back. I wanted to not be working so hard and I had reason to believe her family had money. That turned out to not be true. But, now it seems that I was looking for the wrong family member.

Last Monday started as every day. I was selling the papers and calling out to my regular customers. What should happen, but one comes running back to the newsstand, shouting and laughing. What is it? I asked of him. Look, he told me. Here you are in the magazine, the spitting image of you, with a fancy costume. This Rupert Willows in Winnipeg looks so much like you.

I looked at the magazine and I saw it for myself. It was a big enough photo that I could bring a spyglass to it and I saw the scar on your neck. Why did you not hide it? It must be you wanted me to find you. Is that right, Reuben?

So now, it seems the great Rupert Willows has lots of money of his own. And now, with your slut of a mother dead and buried, here is my chance, a second chance to find my way to an easier life. I understand it must be very important for you to have a quiet and respectable life. I don't wish to disrupt this. Naturally, if I did, there would be no hope for my plan.

My idea is simply this. With all your money, there must be enough there to afford a little help for your father who with his seed gave life to you.

I want money, "Rupert". Not enough that will break you because it is my idea to live with comfort for many years, and I am not stupid. So this is what you will do, my long lost son. You will send to me, to the post office address in the bottom of this letter, the amount of sixty dollars a month. Not a great amount you will see. Just maybe three times what I am making at the newspaper stand. If you decide not to go along with the plan, I have the copies of all of the documents that attest to the birth and name change of Reuben Volinsky to Rupert Willows. I found everything I needed and have it in a safe place. I also have my own documents that will prove that I am your father.

How proud are you that the blood of a Jew flows in your veins, Rupert?

Yours truly,

I. Volinsky

Rupert folded the letter and placed it in his desk. He opened his liquor cabinet and poured a stiff drink. Then, he picked up the phone and called his lawyer. Grenville Doddsworth had proven his worth as a most trusted professional and he was the only one who could help him.

"Doddsworth. I expect to see you here in twenty minutes. No. I will tell you when you get here. No, not thirty. Twenty."

Rupert went to his safe and pulled out a stack of bills and divided them into two piles. He then put two envelopes on his desk. On one he wrote "Doddsworth". On the other, he wrote "from R.J.W.". By the time Doddsworth arrived, Rupert had every aspect of the plan in place.

It would be Doddsworth's responsibility to handle the payment and all future correspondence from Mr. Volinsky. This turned out to be a most appropriate solution that was to work very well for a good many years.

It was only when Mr. Volinsky became too greedy that matters changed.

21
Alrightniks and Dreamers
July 15, 1900

Malka waited, but no one came. It was only a hope. But hope was what she had lived on for most of her life. She watched as the Winnipeg train station went from being jammed to the walls with passengers and the families meeting them until almost empty. The train had pulled out of the station and no one had come for her. Well, on with it then. Maybe the letter she wrote about the change in her schedule never got to them.

The immigration line was like all of the others she had experienced along her journey, and the young teenager knew exactly what was expected of her. First she tidied her hair and smoothed her clothing as best as she was able. She checked her reflection in a window and pinched her cheeks to bring a healthier hue to her sallow complexion. She took time to adjust her hat on her black thick hair. She loved the hat. It was a gift from Mrs. Babcock, her employer in London. The hat made her feel grown up and gave the impression that she looked like a somebody instead of a greenhorn. She stood up straight and determined she would walk as the English walked. They moved with a purpose and a style that said they were people who mattered. She picked up her carpetbag and with her head held high, strode forward into the line before the immigration agent. She, too, would be a somebody. Now was as good a time as any to step into her new identity. The agent was all business and it was clear he had no enthusiasm for his job.

"Name?"

"Maisie Rosedale."

"Country?"

"England."

"What city?"

"London."

"Religion?"

She hesitated.

"Religion?" He repeated and looked up at her.

"Anglican," she answered clearly.

"Where are you going?"

"I'm stopping here at Winnipeg."

"Any family with you?"

"No."

"Family here?"

"Well, um. I'm afraid not."

"You have work?"

"Yes. I will be working as a maid."

"Where will you stay?"

"I have lodging on Patrick Street."

"A young girl like you? You're going to a boarding house?" He shook his head. "Make sure a good woman is running it." With that he stamped her papers and yelled, "Next!"

Maisie Rosedale was off to find her future in Canada. She clutched her bag to her chest to defend it against pickpockets and felt her heart flutter as she pushed her way through the hawkers and confidence men who worked the sidewalk near the train station. She found her way along to Main Street and walked quickly past the saloons and rough looking hotels, turning onto Henry Avenue. When she passed the Shaarey Zedek Synagogue at King Street, she knew she was very close and quickened her pace. The directions and map from her uncle were exactly right. She went past the Chinese laundry on Patrick Street and found the house with the hollyhocks, just as he said she would. Excitement rose within her as she climbed the three little steps to knock on the front door. It opened and standing before her was a young woman who looked strikingly like herself.

"Hello?" said the efficient girl in the apron. "I'm sorry we don't serve supper until five o'clock, miss."

Malka stared back and was speechless.

"Could you come back ..." Ziporah's hand flew to her cheek. "Malka?" The two girls froze and stared at each other.

Malka's head bobbed up and down and the teenagers hugged each other, shrieking with joy.

"We thought your train was coming next week! We would have been there to greet you. Oh, please come in and sit down. I'm so happy. Mama, come quick. It's Malka!"

"Dear child!" Hannah came running and stopped in her tracks on seeing her niece for the first time, then grabbed her up in an embrace. Her eyes brimmed with tears as she swayed gently with the girl wrapped warmly in her arms.

"Malka, darling little Malka, how long I have waited to see you." She pulled away and held her out at arms length to get a good at the young girl. "Look how beautiful you are. Just like your sweet mother was. Come, child, let me hold you some more."

Hannah sobbed with joy and a surprised Malka was left reeling with the happy realization she was an orphan no longer. She had family who accepted and wanted her. With her aunt holding her and stroking her like a long lost kitten, suddenly all of the strength went out of the weary traveler, and she gave way to the tears she had fought to keep from falling for so many years.

Malka's arrival turned the house upside down as one by one the family members came home and flew into the happy welcome of the long-awaited cousin from London. Baruch was astonished at how similar in appearance his teenage granddaughters were.

"Well, of course," said Baba. "Two beauties, just like their grandmother!"

Everyone laughed and the Zigman home took on a special holiday feeling despite the clamor of business as the evening customers filed in for dinner. Hannah and Ziporah whirled about the kitchen, bringing large bowls of food onto the long table that ran the length of the small front room as the parade of evening clientele came and went.

Energized by the warmth of family surrounding her, Malka insisted on helping with the meal. Hannah and Bayla were thoroughly impressed with how much she knew and how well she worked, not once complaining of being tired from her long journey. With all forty-three of the evening café customers fed through five different sittings, the family finally gathered at their own supper table to learn about their enchanting niece with the English accent.

Zaida Baruch shook his head with amazement. He led the prayers of thanks and Hannah quickly ladled soup into bowls.

"It really is a special blessing that our mothers were sisters, and our fathers were brothers," said Malka. "I heard that dozens of times from my parents, but now I really understand it. It makes me feel like a sister, not a cousin. Thank you for bringing me here to be with you, Uncle Zev. The people I worked for were very nice, but it has been a long time since I felt I had a family."

"So this way we can make fun of you like a sister?" asked Isaac.

Ziporah gave him a playful shove. "At least give her some time to recover from her train ride, not to mention that voyage on the steamship!"

As the bread was passed and the soup bowls refilled, lively conversations flowed over the table in English and Yiddish punctuated by much teasing and laughter, as was the custom of the Zigman family. Everyone was talking at once, and Malka found the noise and confusion and warmth utterly wonderful.

Little Mendel, quiet and pale, couldn't stop staring at her sitting next to him. Shyly, he slipped his hand into hers and she smiled into his eyes.

"Can I ask you a question, cousin Malka?"

"Yes, of course, Mendel."

"Malka, when you talk in Yiddish you sound like us. When you speak in English you sound like the fancy people. You don't sound like you are like us at all. You don't sound Jewish. How come?"

In an instant, all eyes were on Malka and the table went silent.

"I've never known anything else," she blushed. "I was born in Spitalfields, which is a very Jewish area of London. Most everyone there speaks Yiddish, as did my parents, of course. Later, when my parents died, I was working for Dr. Babcock, and no one in that house spoke Yiddish. I learned to speak English from them. I learned a lot from the housekeeper and from the children as well. They shared their books with me and taught me to read in English," she said softly. Her eyes dropped to her hands in her lap.

"They were good to you, these people?" Hannah could plainly see that she was missing her adopted London family.

"Very good. I was more fortunate than most. Is it terrible that I sound English when I speak?" Malka searched for assurance in their faces.

"Not at all. In a city like Winnipeg, you will learn quickly that you have been blessed with a gift," said Zev.

"What do you mean?"

Isaac jumped in. "There are two kinds of people here, the English and everyone else. If you are English you get a good job. If you're not, life is not so easy."

"And what is wrong with being Isaac Zigman?" asked his grandfather sternly.

"Isaac Zigman would like to be a lawyer and for that you need to go to university," he answered respectfully. "According to my friends, Zaida, if you have a Jewish name you are not on the top of the list to be accepted."

"Nonsense."

"Isaac, don't borrow trouble from tomorrow. You don't know yet that you will have a problem with being accepted at university," Mama said.

"And you will give up your dream so quickly?" asked Zev. "Because it is hard, you won't try? That doesn't sound like the boy who almost killed himself just to own a bicycle."

"Papa, all I'm saying is that when the time comes that I finish high school and go to university, no one is going to be quick to welcome a Jew if they have English students to choose instead. It's the way it is. I'm just being realistic."

Zev shook his head at the realization of how far ahead they were by the simple fact they were no longer under the rule of Russia. "Isaac. It seems to me you are perhaps one of the smartest boys in your high school. You are just fourteen."

"So is Malka," interrupted Ziporah.

Zev nodded at his niece. "Yes, Malka, too, is fourteen already. So grown up for one so young. What I was going to say is many things can happen in a few short years, Isaac. I would be proud to have my sons all go to university. I will work and save. You will work and study. Maybe even to be a lawyer, hmm?" Zev couldn't hide his pride in his children and their ever-improving status.

"And what about your daughter? Will she go to university, too?" Ziporah knew her father's hopes for her, too.

"Perhaps, if it is what you must do," Papa smiled. "And Malka, too. You are the fifth child in our family now."

He put a sugar cube between his teeth and raised his glass of tea. Hannah could see that Zev was unusually happy and that it was more than Malka's arrival that was in his thoughts. It was as if he had something to say but was waiting. She reached over and affectionately patted her husband's hand. He smiled back and winked at her. Yes, he had something to say.

Aaron had been listening to all of this talk of hopes and dreams with great interest. He, too, hoped to go on to university and was starting to understand that without all of the sacrifices made by his parents and grandparents he would still be in Russia and there would be no discussions about education at all.

"Thank you, Zaida," he said quietly to his grandfather.

"For what?" Baruch asked, surprised.

"For bringing us to Canada," said Aaron. The old man nodded and squeezed his grandson's hand.

"Hear, hear!" said Isaac and raised his glass of tea and they all joined in with their good wishes for Zaida, that he should live for a hundred and twenty years.

"Zaida, do you have a dream?" Aaron asked.

Baruch's wrinkled face split into a smile. "Yes. A new dream I have. But first you must know how much happiness it brings to me to see Malka here with us. I am overjoyed, and it is for me a dream come true to see her smiling, loving face." He patted Malka's hair and again her eyes welled with tears.

Baruch turned to Bayla and took her hand. Bringing it to his face he kissed it and locked his eyes onto hers, as a young man on bended knee might look at the most beautiful woman he had ever known.

"Yes, a new dream, I have. I would like to make *aliyah* with my wife. I would like to move across the ocean to the Promised Land, and to be living in *Yerushalayim*, Jerusalem, with your Baba."

No one spoke. Jerusalem! The weight of the love and the strength of the moment unified them and confirmed their success in the new world. They had made it.

For a time, Baruch and Bayla talked of their plans and the many conversations Baruch had had with other Winnipeg Zionists who had relatives now living in *Eretz Yisrael*, the Land of Israel. He told how plans were already being made for two prominent citizens, Dov Beryl and Rachel Weidman, to make the great move after almost twenty years in Canada. Their family was now firmly established in Winnipeg with their sons, Mordecai and Hiram Leib, operating a successful grocery wholesale business and very ably looking after their growing families. The older couple would finish the journey they began in Bialystock with one more move to the land of their ancestors. It was an inspiration to the entire community, Zaida explained.

Malka was utterly floored by the idea that these families, who had worked so hard to leave Russia and put down roots in Canada, would want to again uproot their lives and travel thousands of miles.

Her uncle stepped in to explain.

"You are following what is going on with Theodor Hertzl?"

"I know who he is, of course, and that he is working very hard for the Jewish people, but I am afraid I don't know very much about him," she responded.

"Malka, there is much talk in Canada of the work of Dr. Hertzl, who is leading the Zionist movement to encourage Jews to claim their homeland," Zev explained. "There is growing support for the Jewish colonies in Palestine. Your zaida has been very active with the men here in Winnipeg who are involved in the Zionist cause."

"All the way from Canada, people are working for this dream of a Jewish homeland?" Malka was surprised.

"Oh, yes," Zaida answered. "It is very important to Jewry in Canada that this should happen. A strong organization was started in Montreal by a great rabbi named Clarence de Sola," he said, passion rising in his voice as he spoke. "You see, in Canada the Jewish community connects very well from one city to the next, despite the thousands of miles across the Dominion. Here in Winnipeg we have many leaders, like Mr. Ripstein, Mr. Finkelstein and Mr. Weidman, who are working hard for this Zionist cause. They travel to these meetings in Montreal and in Europe, and in this way they are helping Winnipeg Jews participate in the world congress to establish this homeland. In time, many Jews will move to Palestine. You will see."

"I wish you good luck with your dream, Zaida," said Malka.

By this time little Mendel, Baba's special little boy, had climbed into her lap with worry on his face.

"You would leave us, Baba and Zaida?" he asked.

"I will go where God leads me and with his blessing, so too, will go my beautiful wife, but it is not in a big rush that we are going, Mendel." Baruch patted his grandson on the head.

"What is your dream, Malka?" Isaac asked.

"Oh, my. I think I am living my dream, to have so much family around. It is hard to tell you how this feels to me to have a place in a family, to live in Canada where you can have a life, maybe one day even a romance and a husband." She looked down, suddenly feeling embarrassed at having spoken out about such personal desires.

"Of course you will have a romance and a husband!" announced Hannah and everyone laughed. "Such a pretty girl, just like my Ziporah. You both will have many suitors, I am sure."

"Malka, I can only wish you good luck in making your life in Canada," Zev said. "You, too, should have an education if that is what you wish."

"You are too generous, Uncle Zev. In the meantime, I will find work," said Malka with certainty.

"Well, we saw for ourselves tonight that you have many skills," said Hannah.

"Isaac is right," Ziporah jumped in. "You can work anywhere. You pass as English," she said with admiration.

"I was thinking of getting a job in a big house with lots of servants to work in housekeeping or cooking," Malka said. "I

212

would look to have my lodging there also, to not be a burden to you here."

"Excuse me, cousin," said Isaac. "I mean no disrespect to you, but do you think they would hire a girl named Malka Zigman to work in one of those fancy houses?"

"Well, no, I don't think so," she admitted and was immediately embarrassed. So direct was this family in what they had to say! English people would never sit down to a family conversation like this. She rushed on and just blurted out her plan.

"I have made up a new name, just for the purpose of having a job. I hope you all understand."

"What name did you choose?" Ziporah thought this wonderfully intriguing.

"Maisie Rosedale," said Malka.

"Oy," said Hannah. "What is that name?"

"Well, Maisie was the name of the housekeeper in Dr. Babcock's home. She was of great help to me, and I feel comfortable borrowing her name."

"What about Rosedale?" asked Isaac.

"I heard it on the train. Apparently it is a very nice neighborhood in Toronto."

"Maisie Rosedale," Ziporah said. "It sounds like an important name. Could we call you Maisie, too?"

"I would like that. Yes, if you would like." She glimpsed Aunt Hannah's frown and brightly added, "Of course, I don't mind being called Malka as well."

Her Uncle Zev interrupted and reached for Malka's hand.

"What a blessing to have you here with us. Whether you call yourself Malka or Maisie or Millicent is of no matter. We will call you family. Even if you work outside, I must have you know that there is always room in our house for you. I promised this to my brother, may he rest in peace. You are to me, as one of our children. It will be that way all of my life."

"There is plenty of room in the kitchen next to the stove, where I make my bed," said Ziporah. "There is enough space for you to sleep there, too."

Quite overwhelmed by all the kindnesses she'd been shown,

Malka was again close to tears. "You are all very nice to want to help me, but I must do my share to look after myself. Do you think it would be hard to find such a job?"

"I think you will be in great demand. Many homes are looking for this kind of worker. But it is a different world out there," said Hannah.

Malka could plainly see that her grandfather was troubled. Despite her young age, she had become something of an expert at reading trouble. "Is it bad, to have this plan, Zaida? To lie this way? To have even another name to go with the lie?"

He stroked his beard and thought for a time before he spoke. "Dear child. In life we make decisions that sometimes make us appear on the outside to be something we are not. This is not always bad. This is sometimes survival, yes?" He waited and she nodded and wiped the tears from her eyes. "I see in the way you say your prayers you have a sense of what it means to be a Jewish woman. I would only say to you that if you go into the world as English, just be careful to not lose what you are hiding on the inside."

Hannah nudged Ziporah and while Baruch and Zev helped Malka make her plans to look for a job, she and her daughter brought a fresh pot of tea and an apple *kugel*, still warm from the oven, to celebrate Malka's arrival.

Through all of this talk, Zev had been itching to break his big news. Only today had all of the arrangements come together. He clapped his hands and rubbed them with enthusiasm as the mouth-watering smell of the *kugel* prompted happy murmurings at the table.

"A special treat for a special celebration," he announced. "This is a day for big news. I, too, have something to tell. Malka, your arrival has brought us great luck. I wish to tell you that even if you live during the week in the house where you go to find work, you are, of course, going to be coming to us on your day off. I think it only right that you and Ziporah should have your own room, a proper room for sleeping, with two beds and a desk for study. Just as my sons should also have bedrooms with real beds instead of having every night to make up a place to sleep."

"Zev!" Hannah snorted. "What nonsense are you talking

about?"

"No," he held up his hand to silence her. "I was going to wait to tell all of you the news, but with so much talk of dreaming and planning and such joy to have Malka here with us, I cannot wait to tell you." He put his hands down on the table and looked into their expectant faces. This set off a boisterous chorus. Zev stood up to address them, holding his thumbs high in his suspenders as he had seen important men do when making speeches.

"Dear family, in a few months, we are going to move to a new house on Selkirk Avenue."

A cheer went up. Then everyone talked at once demanding details.

"Did someone give to you a sack of gold for your handsome smile today?" Hannah flipped her hands to dismiss his comments, certain he was playing a game with them.

"It is no joke. Our little restaurant has done very well. And my business with the cart has also been good, very good, in the last two years and a few other things have been lucky for us as well," he shrugged thinking of his windfall from the Franklin Syndicate investment. "Today, I had a talk with a contractor and gave a down payment for building our new house, a big house with lots of rooms for all of us."

The questions flew at Zev, everyone laughing and talking over one another. He held out his hands to shush them and continued. "The house will be on Selkirk Avenue just near King Street. Construction will begin next month. Before winter comes we should be able to move over there.

"Where is Selkirk Avenue?" asked Malka.

"On the other side of the tracks, just a few blocks north of here," answered Isaac.

"Who will come north across the tracks to have a meal? There are just farms up there." Hannah was skeptical.

"There are more houses on Selkirk than you think. On Pritchard, too, even on Manitoba Avenue, there are some." Zev's hands flew with excitement as he spoke. "I have been watching. All along Main Street from Sutherland up past Selkirk Avenue will be many businesses. It will feel like a real *shtetl*, you will see. It will be full of houses and full of businesses in the years ahead. It is all the talk at the synagogue that the whole community is moving north of the tracks," answered Zev. "It's going to be a very important neighborhood. Everything will be new. You'll see how quickly our friends will be coming north. And don't forget all of the people still to come from the old country. We will have a very good business there."

Hannah could see that her husband had been planning this for a long time and that his information was, as always, to be trusted. Zev never spoke before he knew what he was talking about.

"Oh, my, Zev. A new house?" She took his hand.

"It's true. A big two-storey house, we will have, with a restaurant and a little grocery store together, facing out to Selkirk and lots of space upstairs for all of the bedrooms we need. Behind the store and the restaurant will be the kitchen and we will have also a real dining room, just for our family and even with a special cupboard I will build just for the dishes for Passover, Hannah."

Everyone was laughing and shouting about the news. They had made it. They truly were *alrightniks* in the new country.

"You see," said Zev, "It is not just for us that we will have our home and business." He smiled at his family. "We have all of these fine young people coming up. All of you, one day, God willing, will be married. Like Malka says, you will find romance in the new country."

She covered her face with her hands and everyone laughed. Zev enjoyed the moment, then broke in to finish his thought. "We will have a big table with lots of room for the little ones in the next generation that we will one day celebrate Shabbat and all of the other holidays with us. What do you say about that?"

Hannah was beside herself with happiness.

"Zev, don't be thinking I am spoiled being in the new country, but might I ask one question?"

He nodded and stroked her cheek. "Ask many. It is your house you are moving to, my dear one. We will ourselves be the owners of this house. No more renting."

She played with her fingers and asked shyly, "Do you think

in all of those rooms we might somewhere have a water closet?"

"Yes. A water closet you will have."

"With flushing?"

"Yes, with flushing," Zev announced loudly, to much approval. "It might take some time for the city to connect it to the water supply, but I guarantee you, that we'll be ready for the modern world!"

22
The New Maid
July 22, 1900

Malka was almost walking on air as she followed the energetic Mrs. Butterfield. She had just been accepted as the new maid at Ravenscraig Hall. Now all she had to do was remember to answer to the name Maisie and everything would be fine. She hadn't counted on such difficulty in assuming her new identity.

By the time they were on the second floor and halfway through the tour of the mansion, she knew she was going to adore working with the no-nonsense housekeeper. Mrs. Butterfield was kind, accommodating and very thorough in her comments and instructions.

"Miss Emma's room is at the end of the hall on the left. Her parents' rooms are opposite hers. I'm sure you will find her an agreeable child, but you must be careful not to spoil her." Mrs. Butterfield turned and peered over her spectacles. "She will test you, I can assure you, Maisie."

"She seems very bright, Mrs. Butterfield."

"Oh, indeed, that she is. The term strong willed comes to mind as well. But, she truly is a fine little girl, and I think the two of you will get on very well." She bustled down the hallway, stopping to inspect an ornate side table to be sure that the housemaids had done a proper job in dusting it. Satisfied, she pulled out a key and worked the lock on door. It opened into a brightly decorated room with a beautiful view of the river. "The guestrooms are all on the second floor," Mrs. Butterfield explained. "Mrs. Willows thought it too much to have her company climb any higher."

Maisie fought to avoid gawking at the rooms as she followed Mrs. Butterfield. Surely, Kensington Palace in London could not be finer than Ravenscraig Hall's lush interior. She would have quite a story to tell her family. Imagine! She had a job! The interview with Mr. Chadwick had been quite unnerving at the outset, for his manner was so formal, but she quickly realized what he wanted to hear. Everything she had learned during her time with the Babcocks would help her at Ravenscraig. At the end of the interview, he had offered warm words of encouragement and told her that he was very comfortable recommending that she be hired. She almost hopped with joy.

"Only two rooms on the third floor are in regular use," the housekeeper said, eyeing the stairs and lifting her skirts to make the climb. "Mr. Elliot and Mr. James both have their suites up here. Very nice accommodations they are, with full water closets in each. There are also some storage rooms for linens and household supplies, and a few rooms that are locked and never in use on the north side of the third floor. Too many bloody rooms," she whispered. "Not worth heating in the winter."

Mrs. Butterfield stopped for a moment to catch her breath at the top of the stairs. "Mr. James attends the University of Manitoba and it is his father's desire that he have as few distractions as possible so that he is able to study."

Mrs. Butterfield turned, frowning, to face Malka. "Maisie, tell me again, how old are you?"

"Seventeen, mum," she answered with more haste than she intended.

"I see."

Maisie flushed under the searching gaze. Had she stretched her story beyond believability by adding three years to her age?

She had. Mrs. Butterfield saw a girl not a day over fifteen, a lass who might even be as young as thirteen. The child was well-trained though, knowledgeable and most important, respectful. The housekeeper found herself immediately liking the capable girl with the intelligent look in her eyes. If she had been lucky enough to have a daughter herself, she would have been proud to have one like this Maisie girl. She was not one of those know-it-all missies, who bounce their empty heads up and down like little birds but can't accomplish the simplest task without supervision. Maisie seemed most anxious to have the job and to prove that she would do well at it. It was also apparent from her tardy response to her name that Maisie was something she had made up. No matter. A chosen name for a new beginning. Well, she'd done it herself, hadn't she? Rescued from a Chicago brothel by Mr. Butterfield, she was. He had put her on the train for Winnipeg himself with a purse filled with enough money to give her a new start. No one had to know she really wasn't his widow and that he was in good health with the real Mrs. Butterfield at home. All these years later, she missed him, still.

"Do you have any questions, Maisie?" Mrs. Butterfield brought her hands together in front of her apron and smiled.

Malka had many, but didn't want to ask any for fear of jeopardizing her new job. She would stick with the essentials.

"Just one, Mrs. Butterfield. The uniform is very fine and I do believe it will take me some time to have enough money to pay for one. Do you think I might borrow a uniform in the meantime?"

Mrs. Butterfield was taken aback. "Dear girl. You are not to concern yourself with that. Mr. Willows is very particular about appearances, as you will learn. Your uniforms will be provided to you at no cost. You will need both housekeeping and parlor uniforms, as Mr. Chadwick wishes to train you for dining room service. Now, listen to me, Maisie. It is of the utmost importance that you take scrupulously good care of your uniforms and never allow yourself to appear improperly groomed or dressed. Mr. Willows is exceptionally sensitive about these things. Any offence in this area, I can tell you, will get you sacked on the spot."

Mrs. Butterfield peeked over Maisie to be sure they were alone in the hallway. Raising her hand to keep Maisie quiet, she spoke barely above a whisper. "I can also tell you that you will hear and see a good deal at Ravenscraig that you might find offensive or even shocking. Mr. Willows has a temper. You are to pay no mind to his eruptions. If he should set off in your presence, just do your duties and slip away as quickly as possible. There is a clear divide between upstairs and downstairs in Ravenscraig and as long as you keep that in mind you will be fine. If you have any questions, you come directly to me. And never discuss what you might have overheard from the family with the other servants."

She stopped and listened intently for a moment, then cupped her hands around her mouth as she mouthed the words, "Especially not with Mr. Chadwick!"

"Yes, mum." Maisie drew back and felt her skin prickle.

Mrs. Butterfield smiled slowly as she patted the girl on the shoulder.

"Come along then," she said, loudly enough to be heard if Mr. Chadwick was in earshot, as she suspected. "At the south end of the hall is the service stairway, which goes directly from the attic down to the kitchen. In the attic there is storage space and additional quarters for some of the household staff. It's a bit of a climb, but you'll get used to it. You're taking Lizzie's place up there and she will be moving downstairs next to the kitchen. I'll show you where the cleaning supply cupboard is on this floor and then we'll go up to see your room."

Mrs. Butterfield swung the door open and Maisie caught her breath. It was a narrow room with a round window at the end. A little cot with a pretty green coverlet and large feather pillow sat on one side of the window. On the opposite wall were a small writing table, a lamp and chair. A trunk sat at the foot of the bed and a row of neatly arranged clothing hooks adorned the wall adjacent to the door. A thickly woven wool rug was centered in the tiny room. Maisie could hardly believe her luck. Having slept on chairs in the kitchen with the Babcock family, she had dared to hope for a bed here at Ravenscraig, but it never occurred to her that she might be given her own room!

"It's a bit cold in here in winter, I must tell you," Mrs. Butterfield told her. "But I have some big quilts to keep you from freezing to death. Summer afternoons can be quite hot up in this attic, but the window does open and you will find you get a nice breeze off the river. That's about all that I can think of to tell you. I trust you will find the bed comfortable enough."

As Maisie's gaze traveled the room in obvious appreciation, Mrs. Butterfield knew this was the right girl for Ravenscraig.

"Do you have any questions, Maisie?"

"No. Thank you, Mrs. Butterfield. It's absolutely splendid and I shall be very comfortable here, I am sure."

"Well, then. I just have one question for you." The housekeeper brought her hands together and looked straight into Maisie's eyes. "Are you a church-going girl?"

Maisie was struck with terror; certain Mrs. Butterfield had caught her in her lie.

"I, well, I … yes, that is … I used to be, that is when I was in England," she stammered, "and I, well, I haven't as yet, joined or found a church here, not the right church that is, so, no I suppose I am not, at this particular moment, a church-going girl." She snapped her mouth shut to prevent further damage, suddenly aware that she must sound like a complete idiot.

"Good!" said Mrs. Butterfield. Seeing the look on Maisie's face she hastened to add, "Oh dear, I didn't mean to upset you. It matters not at all whether you attend church. No one in this house will judge you on that. My question is entirely of a practical nature as, you see, there is the matter of scheduling your day off. I, myself, go to church only once in a while, but I like my Sundays off. Most of the others do as well, and that sometimes leaves us a problem with who will work on Sundays."

"Oh, my goodness, Mrs. Butterfield. I am so very happy to have this job. I would be pleased to work Sundays. All Sundays, if you wish."

"Well, that's very good of you. It would make things easier. Very well then, you will be off on Friday evenings and if you choose to leave the house, you will have to be back on Saturday night."

"Thank you, Mrs. Butterfield." Maisie couldn't believe her good fortune. It was as if God had taken her by the hand and led her to Ravenscraig. That she would have this job and also time off that would allow her to join her family on the Sabbath was a spectacular gift.

Maisie's first few weeks at Ravenscraig Hall flew by as she worked to learn everything she could about the proper care and smooth management of the house. True to her word, Mrs. Butterfield had taken care to school her in every aspect of the household work that she needed to learn. This guidance helped to make a seamless transition for Maisie with the Willows family and she quickly learned their habits and how to best serve their needs. She found the family to be a little pretentious, as the English often were, but it was not anything she was unaccustomed to seeing.

She was ever alert for signs that her secret might be exposed, but not once had anyone hinted that she was anything but a proper English girl. Her cousins had been so right about the benefit of her accent. She talked to Lizzie about London and the Babcocks but said not a word about the Zigmans of Patrick Street. No one seemed interested in learning more. She assumed they were busy with their own lives and protecting their own secrets. Lizzie was an expert. She simply refused to talk of her past. Maisie learned from her example and adopted the same behavior. They all lived a lie, in one way or another. It was the only way any of them would get ahead.

She was a little wary of Mr. Chadwick, who clearly ran the house, but found Mrs. Butterfield easy to accommodate. Things went smoothly as long as everything was done precisely her way.

Just when Maisie had found a comfortable rhythm, Mrs. Willows threw the house into complete chaos with the packing for the Grand Tour. Lizzie bore the brunt of the work, as well as Mrs. Willows' frequent fits of frustration, so Maisie was left to take on Lizzie's usual housework. Maisie was greatly impressed by Lizzie, who had a knack for calming the mistress's nerves. She was also a helpful friend and ally and Maisie was saddened when she winked and cheerily waved good-bye as they embarked on their journey. They would be gone for ten to twelve weeks, and Maisie wondered if she would die of boredom in the house.

Then came the day when the books rained down on her head. It was a particularly quiet day and Maisie was in the kitchen scraping carrots, when providence came calling.

"Do you know anything of gardening, Maisie?" Mrs. Butterfield stood on her toes and peeked out the kitchen window. The groundskeepers were almost finished with tidying the perennial gardens for winter and would soon be heading to her kitchen garden.

"I know a little," answered Maisie.

"Well, dear girl, we are about to lose the last of the treasures in our little herb garden. Would you mind going about with a basket to see what you might find to save before those men get in there and destroy what's left?"

Happily working among the plants, Maisie watched the river lazily moving beyond the garden. It was a perfect fall afternoon, and she was glad to be outside. The poplars and willows along the riverbanks were turning yellow but the air felt light and deliciously warm for September. She checked the bushes near the house and saw that the rosehips were not quite ready to be gathered. She would have to remind the gardeners to delay pruning until the bright red berries had been picked.

Suddenly, she was startled by the sound of shouting. She turned to see that it was coming from the third floor, where Mr. James was flinging a book from his window. It was followed by another and another and several more after that. All the while, he was yelling something about his miserable schooling. Maisie heard the window slam shut as she ducked for cover. Slowly, she stood and stared horror-struck at the scattered books, their pages lying crumpled against the freshly tilled flowerbeds. Heavy, expensive textbooks, they were. She picked her way over and found that they were books on anatomy, biology and common diseases. Gently gathering them up, she dusted the dirt from one, surveyed the cracked spine on another and discovered wet pages on a third. She was aghast. Why would anyone do such a terrible thing? She carried the heavy stack into the kitchen and excitedly explained what happened to Mrs. Butterfield.

"Did they land on you? Are you hurt?" The housekeeper demanded.

"Oh, no, I'm fine, Mrs. Butterfield, but I'm afraid some of Mr. James' books are damaged rather badly. I'll clean them as best I can and take them back up to him."

"No, you will not, Miss Maisie! You will march them straight out to the trash bin."

"The trash? Mrs. Butterfield! I can't put books in the garbage."

"Yes, you can, and you must. Let me explain what is going to happen here, if you don't do as I suggest. If you clean the books and take them to Mr. James, he will yell at you. He will demand that you remove the books from his sight, and threaten to set fire to them before he tosses them out of the window again." She lowered her voice at Maisie's shocked expression. "You see, he is quite spoiled. It's best not to upset him further."

"Oh, my," said Maisie. "What if he calms down and then wants them back?"

"Well, I can only tell you what happened last time. A few months before you came, young Mr. James was taking a run at law school, you see. Whilst Mr. Willows was working in the library, Mr. James had become frustrated and tossed his books, one by one, out of his bedroom window up there, exactly as he did today. Well, don't you know that they flew down right in front of the library window, where Mr. Willows was sitting? Mr. Willows became very angry, indeed. He summoned Mr. James and there was a good deal of shouting. Mr. Willows told his son he was behaving in a boorish and ridiculous fashion. This time, Mr. Willows is abroad, and we will miss out on the entertainment. Mr. James must sort this out on his own. He has an allowance to buy new books, so don't you worry about it."

"But they are books! I must take them and ask him if he wants them back. Maybe he is less angry now."

Seeing Maisie's determination, the housekeeper threw her hands up. "Well, you suit yourself, but be ready to move quickly in case he throws something at you."

Twenty minutes later, Maisie was back in the kitchen with the books.

"Oh, Mrs. Butterfield!" she spluttered. "He is terribly rude and most frightening."

"Well, I told you so." She planted her knuckles on her round hips. "Now, off you go. I told you he doesn't want them back. Hurry along now and get rid of them. It's time to start mixing up the bread dough."

"Mrs. Butterfield," Maisie looked down at the books and felt her heart pounding.

"What is it? We don't have all day, child." She dropped the big flour sack onto the table and sent a cloud of white up around them both.

"Do you think I might put them away in my room? I think it is a sin to throw out books."

"Suit yourself. I don't see any harm in it. Just don't let him catch you with them, as you will learn, when Mr. James pitches a tantrum there is generally another one coming behind it. He has all of the bad temper of his father and none of the charm. Horrible little snot." She looked at the clock near the stove and reached for the flour. "Now come along, Maisie. Let's set the bread dough to rising."

Maisie was thrilled. Books! Books she could keep. She would have real medical texts to read at night. Her life was filled with good fortune.

23
A Spring Ride
April 16, 1902

Maisie poured steaming coffee into the silver pot she'd so carefully polished, and smoothly set it into position next to the warm scones. She took a brief moment to admire the tray, which she believed was the picture of sophistication with lace edged linens setting off the delicate Limoges china and the jams arranged precisely the way she had been taught. With Mrs. Butterfield quarantined in her room with illness, and Lizzie away with Mrs. Willows, today was the day Maisie would move up in rank to parlor maid. Even if it was a temporary assignment, she felt almost giddy with accomplishment.

It had been almost two years since she had come to Ravenscraig and she'd learned a good deal about the lowly jobs in the kitchen and in housekeeping. Parlor duties were a significant step up and she was determined to show Mr. Chadwick that she was ready for promotion. All was in perfect readiness, as she looked up into the approving face of the butler.

"Now, remember, Mr. James does not care to be involved in conversation, especially when he is studying. It is unlikely that he will speak to you at all. When you go up, be sure to put the tray down on the hall table next to the newspaper and not on top of it. Do not take in the newspaper unless he requests it. You will rap twice on the door, gently, so as not to disturb him more than necessary. Do not enter until he has beckoned. If he does not answer, knock again, but do remember to apologize for interrupting his work. Place the tray on the table to the right of his desk, and ask him if he wishes to have the curtains opened. On occasion, the morning light disturbs him. Do not pour the coffee. He prefers to do it himself. Ask if there is anything else he might desire. He may ask for the newspaper. You will then curtsy and remove yourself, closing the door with as little noise as is humanly possible. He is not likely to look up from his work. Do you understand?"

"Yes, Mr. Chadwick," Maisie nodded and carried the silver tray up to the third floor.

James exhaled deeply as he reached for the book on infectious diseases. He refilled his inkwell and carefully inspected the pen nib for damage. Satisfied, he turned his attention to the paper. He counted out the sheets, as was his habit, and carefully restacked them. He was ready. He sighed. Now he'd have to actually get to the assignment. How he wished the work came more readily to him; the pressure of medical school was starting to wear at him. It was one thing to have so easily gained entrance to the Manitoba Medical College. The right family name opens doors faster than academic ability, he had learned, grimacing as he thought about it. The painful truth was that it was quite another thing to earn the title of doctor. But earn it, he would. With new resolve, he picked up his book and dove into the text.

Resolve or not, the light rapping at the door a few minutes later was more relief than bother, as it gave him a new excuse to escape from his work. Mrs. Butterfield was always punctual with his morning coffee.

"Good morning, sir, may I draw the coffee for you? Shall I pour the curtains?" To her utter horror, Maisie's tongue had flown a good ten feet free of her brain.

"The curtains are open, and thank you, I shall be fine to pour my own coffee." A smile formed at the corner of James' mouth. He was surprised how pleased he was at the unexpected sight of Maisie, as he could not remember seeing her in parlor duties in the morning. And here she was, a lovely fluttering bird, discombobulated and fretting over her new tasks.

"What's this now, Maisie? Where is Mrs. Butterfield?" he asked politely.

"She is confined to her room with the bronchitis, Mr. Willows." Maisie's eyes were on the lace on the tray.

"Ah, an infectious disease of the thoracic cavity, within our midst." James poked his pen into the air for emphasis and glanced at Maisie, hoping to see that he had impressed her.

Her blank stare was a crushing blow. James was instantly appalled with what he saw as confirmation that he had just made a complete ass of himself. He felt heat rise under his collar as he thought of how pompous and stupid his remark must have sounded to her. Maisie, however, still unsteady from her blundered entry, remained unaware of any embarrassment in the room but her own. She wrestled her wits together and forced on.

"Well, it isn't contagious any more, thankfully," she said. "Mrs. Butterfield reports that she is feeling a good deal better and expects to be fully recovered in a day or two."

"That is certainly good news."

"Will there be anything else, sir?"

His pulse having returned to a normal rate, James unexpectedly found himself looking to delay her departure. Casting about for something sane to say, he glanced into his textbook and smiled back at Maisie.

"Not unless you can tell me what the tuberculosis authority, uh, yes, Dr. Sigard Adolphus Knopf has to say about dietary requirements for consumptive patients."

"Oh, yes, of course." Maisie was instantly back on her home turf and responded automatically, as a well-prepared student to a professor. "He recommends that broth or soups should be taken at the principal meal, which he believes should be between noon and two, but a full four hours after breakfast. If the patient has a fever, he says it is best to wait for the fever to reach a low point before food is given and only to give the most easily digested foods. He says the consumptive must be encouraged to chew his food well."

James was flabbergasted. "Anything else?"

Entirely engrossed in her passion for her studies, Maisie continued on. "Yes. Dr. Knopf thinks highly of feeding raw meat, particularly beef, to tuberculosis patients, very finely chopped or scraped and then mixed with a raw egg yolk."

She tapped her finger on her chin as she took a moment to think, keeping her head down and her gaze fixed on her fingers playing with the edge of her apron. "If I may say so, I strongly disagree with this, as I believe raw food may cause additional problems. It would seem odd that Dr. Knopf would include that recommendation when the vast majority of patients suffering tuberculosis are from the poorer classes who may not have proper ice boxes or the money to spend on high quality fresh meat."

Satisfied with the thoroughness of her explanation, Maisie pulled her mind from her medical thoughts and turned to face the young Mr. Willows. She was suddenly consumed with the notion that she must have sounded cheeky in adding her criticism of the great Dr. Knopf and instantly felt shame heating her face. She looked first into the bright blue eyes of the young man and then her brain shifted to register his slack-jawed stare back at her. The shock of realization pierced her, as a bubble pops when stabbed with a knife. What a stupid mistake to reveal her secret studies! How on earth had she let it happen?

Maisie's hands flew to her face, as she felt her whole life disintegrating before her.

"If there is nothing further, sir, good day!" She abruptly excused herself and bolted for the door.

"Here now, just one moment." James could not believe what he was hearing. "How is it you have so much knowledge? Is this Florence Nightingale in our midst?" Maisie felt her chest constrict and cursed her unchecked conceit. How could she have behaved in such a manner?

"Well, I ... well, I learned ..." Maisie's heart pounded as she braced herself to be fired on the spot. "Oh, my, I am so sorry to have disturbed you, Mr. Willows, please, do forgive my dreadful behavior."

Dropping into a hasty curtsy she wheeled to face the door and only then realized that her foot had become tangled in her skirt. She was sent soaring headlong into the doorway. As fate would have it, she hit the opening at the exact same moment as James's father was entering the room. Completely unprepared for the blow, Rupert went down as if tackled in a rugby match with Maisie coming to rest flat on top of him. Maisie shrieked, Rupert gasped, and James let out a laugh, loud enough to be heard throughout the house.

Chadwick, who had been concealed in the next doorway so

that he could spy on the apprentice parlor maid, exploded onto the scene, tossing Maisie onto her feet and assisting Mr. Willows all in one movement. Everyone spoke apologies at once, and again James laughed heartily.

"I assure you it was I who caused the accident," explained James as he reached to calm his flustered father. "It was entirely my fault, and I should be severely reprimanded for tormenting such a hard working member of our household staff."

"James, what on earth is going on here?" demanded Rupert.

"Well, you see, I embarrassed poor Maisie through my teasing, and she was only trying to extricate herself as quickly as possible, and wouldn't it be my luck that you, Father, would be entering the room at the same moment that Maisie was beating a hasty retreat, so you see this is truly all my fault."

James' explanation burbled forth with such youthful enthusiasm that Rupert's anger immediately subsided and he was prompted to inject his own humor into the fray.

"I rather thought that we were going to learn something exciting about Maisie's past. Have you ever worked with cattle, Maisie? Or, perhaps wrestled alligators?"

"Father, please, I do think poor Maisie has suffered enough this morning," James insisted.

Maisie's eyes locked onto the younger Mr. Willows with a gratitude that warmed him like the heat of the summer sun.

"I am ever so sorry! Please, do excuse me," she stammered and barely remembered a curtsy before dashing from the room.

Any sign that there had been a mishap was by now erased from Rupert's bearing. He turned to his manservant.

"I'm just fine, Chadwick. Accidents do happen, after all, and it would appear there has been no harm done."

"Again, my apologies for being so wicked to Maisie," James added. She is very conscientious in her duties and it was most unfair of me. Mr. Chadwick, please be sure to tell her."

"Certainly, sir. Will there be anything else, sir?" Chadwick held his head high and spoke as if nothing untoward had occurred.

"No, thank you. The time is wasting and we are off to enjoy a morning ride," Rupert answered on behalf of his son.

"Very good, sir."

Chadwick bowed and with heightened dignity aimed at dulling the fresh memory of the disruptive scene, made his way elegantly on to his next duty. He would most certainly be having a chat with young Maisie! The thing of it was she had presented such a dilemma. He would first have to decide whether the exchange he had overheard about the medical issue was appalling or to be admired. What else was going on in this house that he did not know about?

"Well, now." Rupert was all business. "You promised me you would leave that infernal studying and join me for a ride this morning. Let's have a bit of fun, shall we? The weather could not be better, old chap, and our horses are certainly not going to be getting ready for the hunting season on their own."

James was now completely thrown off his studies, not just by the eventful morning but even more so by the staggering display of knowledge from the housemaid. He groaned as he looked at the homework that beckoned and then toward the puckish smile on his father's face.

"Father, it would give me great pleasure to accompany you on a ride this glorious April morning," he enthused.

It was, indeed, a spectacular morning. The two rode out of Armstrong's Point and made their way over the Assiniboine River by way of the Osborne Bridge.

"Everywhere you turn there is new construction in the city," Rupert said as he admired the new mansions that were going up on Roslyn Road. "Just look at this colossal home, will you? Gus Nanton is building it and it's to be called Kilmorie, if you hadn't heard the news. He told me it would be the finest home on Roslyn, and I daresay the old boy has done it. It's very exclusive with the five acres of land he has set it on. Oh, it does remind me of England. Why, the stables are the finest money can build and the gatehouse itself is larger than many of the homes along Broadway. Winnipeg is the place to be, James. We did well making our move here when you and your brothers were young lads."

"Well, it certainly is the place to be if you have money," responded James.

"And you do, so what of it?"

"What of it? Father, I cannot believe you just said that."

"Well, perhaps not as much as Nanton, but ..."

"I don't care about the money. Don't you understand?" James rolled his eyes.

"Oh, yes, here we are again. You, who had the good fortune to have been born into a family that enjoys the comforts of wealth and power. You, my socially conscious son, are going to start ranting about the foreigners in our midst, "the strangers within our gates" as the Bible thumpers like to call them. I swear that you and Alfred must be in a conspiracy to see your father to an early grave with all this concern to be looking after the under classes. It confounds me, James," Rupert shook his fist. "I tell you, this attitude of yours is a great disappointment to me."

"Father, please. Alfred and I do see things a little differently than you do, of course, but there are very good reasons to look at these problems."

"You are about to tell me, yet again, about the poverty and the muddy streets and the dirty little hovels that breed disease. Must you be such a, well, such a social reformer, James? It's so tiresome. I can hardly believe you and Alfred are my sons. How is it possible you don't see the many benefits of capitalism as I do? I find it astonishing that I have had so little influence on your thinking."

Setting aside the stinging comment about his comforts, James was determined to make his point. "Father, just hear what I have to say. These are problems that affect the whole city. Winnipeg has a very serious health problem because of the lack of a proper supply of good water."

"Ah! A variation on the theme. Today it is the water supply. Well, James, allow me to enlighten you. That is a very old problem and it is now solved. You really need to update your knowledge."

"Solved? How is it solved if there is not an adequate supply of water to go to all homes in the city?"

"It is solved, my dear son, because the city has a new artesian well in operation which is feeding top quality water into the water mains, and as we are discussing this, new water mains are being dug as fast as we can put them in. In time, we will have all the water we need. I am quite surprised you don't know this. Do you not read the newspapers anymore?"

"I was going to ask you the same question, Father. Water is going only to the better neighborhoods. What about north of the tracks? I read that not one of those water mains is scheduled to connect to homes in the foreign quarter."

"Patience! In time, the North End will have water and sewers, too. Council is talking about it, but there just is not enough money in the budget to serve every need all at once. There are priorities and money is limited."

"People are dying in astounding numbers, Father. Tuberculosis, scarlet fever, diphtheria, and not to mention typhoid rates in this city are astronomical. How is it not a priority of council to address this problem?"

"Understand, James, that every growing city has this problem, and the thing of it is that Winnipeg is growing the fastest, which is bloody fantastic, don't you agree? So, of course we have a problem. It is because of progress and these are just ordinary growing pains, I'd say. It will all come out right in the end. You just wait and see. Let's end this discussion, shall we? Now, come on then, a little canter will brighten your mood."

"Father, please do listen. I really do not wish to be disrespectful, but I do feel very strongly about this, and you are, after all, an alderman. You can make a difference with your leadership on this issue."

Rupert pulled his horse to a halt and James, who took this as a sign he was getting through, looked expectantly into his father's face.

Rupert laughed. "Really, James, I don't know what has happened to you since you got into this dreary pursuit of becoming a doctor. You'll never make any decent money at it, you know. I do wish you would just chuck the whole thing and come to work with me. The company is called Willows and Sons, you remember, and only Alfred is working with the firm. Elliot is still years off."

"Thank you, no, Father. I really don't believe I have the instinct for it."

The two rode on in silence for a time, Rupert frustrated that his morning was being spoiled by this unpleasant confrontation, and James seething at his father's adamant refusal to see the seriousness of the city's health problems.

"Father, this is a crisis and I cannot understand how city council can turn its back on thousands of people this way."

"Because, my son, this is not a crisis!" Rupert had now lost his patience and was shouting. "This is a way of life for them. Don't you see? They are immigrants! They are accustomed to living in filth, like swine. They are accustomed to starving in their old country. These people are Hebrews, and Slavs from Russia and Poland and Galicia and Hungary and so many other unpronounceable countries where the life they left was worse. They did not have to come here. They chose to come. Don't you see how much better life is for them being here instead of having their skulls crushed and their women raped in Eastern Europe? Their conditions here are not perfect, I grant you, but they are fine for the time being."

"Rampant disease and babies dying? No water or sewage connections to the majority of their homes? That is fine to a city alderman?"

"James, you are missing the larger picture. Why are you so resistant to understanding that for them, the privilege of living in this city is a gift?"

"Father, but you've been on city council for a number of years, and now that you are also on the Board of Trade, you have the power to change the way things are done."

"Change? And what would you have me change? Has it not occurred to you that if we give the lower classes too much comfort that they will stop working and just expect to be looked after? Think about it. Your beloved foreigners aren't used to the finer things in life, so why should we spoil them? They are here to work. There are plenty of jobs for them digging sewers, building roads, working in manufacturing, farming. Why, even the foreign women are finding that work for them is highly available. They are in the sewing factories and even working as servants in those homes where the employers don't mind the Slav or Hebrew. God help them.

"Now if there is a crisis at all concerned with the water supply, you will find it in the area of fire insurance. That is a crisis."

"Fire insurance? I'm not following," James said.

"Winnipeg does not have enough fire hydrants, and perhaps not even the volume of water needed to feed the hydrants that do exist in the case of a major fire. Thus, the insurance companies charge exorbitant prices, and this is a tremendous hardship to the business community."

"How is it possible that the fastest growing city in the country did not plan to have enough fire hydrants? It is not as if Winnipeg suddenly started growing. This has been a boomtown for years. Everyone knows that, why didn't the city look after the hydrants years ago?"

"Because more than twenty years ago, Winnipeg City Council signed an idiotic agreement with the hopeless Winnipeg Water Works Company, and we had our hands tied right up until that agreement finally expired a couple of years ago. The company was supposed to build a certain number of water mains, provide a certain volume of water – all from the Assiniboine River, mind you, and provide hydrants. They fell terribly short on their commitment and therefore the hydrants, even today, are almost non-existent."

"Why didn't the city buy out the contract?"

"It was a question of price. The Water Works Company wanted a king's ransom. Council refused to pay it. Council then decided to wait it out and then, of course as the end of the contract was approaching, the Water Works people wised up to the fact their holdings would be worthless. They finally sold the mains and the equipment to the city for a reasonable price. Now that the city is in control of the water resources, we can move ahead, but as we have been discussing, it will take time. So, the insurance industry has us over a barrel and we have no choice but to watch them continue to charge higher and higher premiums. Now, *that* is a very serious problem. It hurts business, and it could hurt the continued growth of the city. And the truth is that until we are sure there is water for fire control in the business district and, of course, to protect the homes of the

236

better citizens, then there really is no point in taking the limited resources we have and putting money into the foreign quarter."

"Father, it is shameful and despicable that a city would not provide basic services for all of its citizens."

"Despicable? Have you not heard a word that I've said? That is about as thorough an explanation as I can give you, and quite frankly, the whole issue bores me to tears. Why are you worrying so about immigrants? They are foreigners. They don't speak English. These impoverished city dwellers you care so much about are a tremendous blight on Winnipeg and other cities, and we never should have allowed them in. They belong out on the land as farmers, not sucking up sympathy in the city. This miserable lot is only here because of the good graces of the Dominion government and their value to our country is yet to be determined!"

James raised his hand to calm his father, but as he opened his mouth to make a follow up point, Rupert cut him off.

"James, could we please leave this subject? I've really had quite enough of it, and it is ruining my day. Let's move on, shall we? We are to have drinks with Robert Fortune at the club later. He and some other chaps including Roderick Ballantyne want to get a proper country club established and we are among the few who have been invited to lead the development of this venture. It is to be called the St. Charles Country Club. Rather exciting, isn't it? The early talk is to have a polo field, a hunt club complete with facilities for the hounds and a full-time hounds master, and, of course, there would be a top man brought in to design the golf course.

"I'm not sure you are aware that Fortune truly has a passion for golf. His whole family plays. Even his young sister Alice is catching the attention of the professionals, and she is not yet sixteen years of age. She will be playing at Pinehurst in North Carolina this summer. Now, mark my words, that young lady would be quite a trophy, herself, one day for a man of your background. I say, now, there's a peach of a girl."

With that, Rupert cantered off, signaling an official end to the conversation. James needed some time alone and held his horse back. He returned to his own thoughts, not the least of which was the question of where and how Maisie had come by her medical knowledge.

24
Strangers Within Our Gates
April 18, 1902

Ziporah stood with a potato and a knife in her hands and appeared momentarily paralyzed as she listened in wide-eyed wonder to the story Maisie had to tell.

"You didn't!"

"I most certainly did," answered Maisie. "There I was, flat on top of Mr. Willows, both of us writhing in the throes of imminent death and suddenly, as if God's hand had come from above to my rescue, Mr. Chadwick, who is quite strong, had me and Mr. Willows, on our feet in just one second."

"And you still have your job!"

"I do! Oh, Ziporah, I really did think I was going to die. Right there on the spot! I thought my heart would explode and it would be the end of me; that it would 'finish me up', as Mrs. Bachynsky says."

Both girls howled with laughter. Ziporah took a quick look at the clock and gasped.

"Mama will be here any minute. We have to get these potatoes cooking or we will both be "finished up". But, truly, Maisie, how do you expect to explain how you know so much about treating illnesses? Are you going to tell them the truth?"

"Oh, goodness, no! The truth would never do."

Ziporah viewed her cousin as a hero. In another time she would have been the leader of a revolution or saved an entire village from a pogrom. She was the embodiment of greatness. "Well, what are you going to tell them?"

"Why should I tell them anything?" came the quick response.

"Have you lost your mind, Maisie? Do you think you can just recite medical information that the family's student doctor doesn't even know and expect to not be questioned?"

Ziporah's practicality always got to Maisie. There was no

point in pretending she could just ignore the problem.

"All right. It will have to be something that at least has some link to the truth or I will foul it up entirely."

Maisie dropped the remaining potatoes into the water and slid the heavy pot to the front of the cast iron stove while she contemplated her dilemma.

"So?" Ziporah couldn't hide her impatience as she shook out the tablecloth and smoothed it onto the table.

"Well, this is only if I have to say something, you understand," Maisie answered slowly. "Then I think I should tell them that I am the daughter of a physician and that he died in some terrible way, perhaps from an accident, leaving me to fend for myself in coming to Canada. What do you think?"

"Oy. What do they know now?"

"What did I tell them? Only that I grew up in England and that family circumstances required me to work, and that I was an eager learner and had some experience in the kitchen."

"So they really know nothing of your life?"

"Ziporah, that is the truth. Well, mostly. Besides, this summer I will have been there for two full years. No one in the Willows family has the time or the interest to worry so much about what happens in the lives of the servants. They just truly don't care. So I don't see how this will ever be a problem."

"What about the other servants? Don't they wonder where you go on weekends?"

"Not really. Everyone goes somewhere. I told them I have an elderly Aunt Rose I see on weekends and no one cares to know more."

"But what if they press for more? The Willows family might be more curious now that you have revealed your interest in medicine."

"Well, then I'll tell them this yarn about being the daughter of a doctor. It's not all that far-fetched. Dr. Babcock was so much nicer to me than an employer would be expected to be. He was a wonderful doctor, and no doubt his passion for medicine sparked something in me. Don't worry, Ziporah. I'm a very believable liar. Trust me."

The Zigman table was filled with large bowls of simple

foods. The rich beet soup called *borscht*, boiled potatoes, a buckwheat dish called *kasha varnischke,* and freshly baked bread were mainstays at their supper table. Tonight there was also a platter of roasted chicken to round out the menu.

Maisie breathed in deeply, filling herself with the comfort of family and traditions. Hannah took great pride in her big new house on Selkirk Avenue and the table was always beautifully set for the Friday night welcoming of Shabbat. The candles were lit, the prayers and blessings were sung, and the *challah* was passed around with a deep and loving sense of home. The family conversation rose through the house as bowls were passed and news shared.

It was here that Maisie was most troubled by the reality of her double life. Ziporah's questions had gotten to her. Her deep affection for the traditions of Judaism and the warmth of family both nourished and pained her as she confronted the lies she had spun to make a life for herself in Canada.

Baruch had been watching his granddaughter and saw that she was unusually uncomfortable this evening.

"You have something to say, Malka. Don't be shy. If we don't talk, we don't learn."

"It's a little complicated. Oh dear, I don't want to sound like I am complaining, Zaida. I am just so grateful to have found my way to you, to have a future here. I suppose my trouble is that because I live one way during the week and another when I am here in your house, I don't really know who I truly am. I know you always talk about how our family's history in Russia is the foundation on which we are shaping our future, but what shape must that be now that we are in a new country?"

Baruch sipped his tea and considered the delicate question before he answered.

"We have new responsibilities both to our heritage as Jews, and to our survival," he said at last. "Each of us must find our own path. I cannot tell you how you must live your life. You are young, and there are many years ahead for you and no doubt many choices as well. All of us at this table must choose, as I have, where you wish to be. To decide is a gift, and to make a decision comes also with obligation. For me, it is easy to find guidance. I look first to God and my duty as a Jew."

There was a long pause. Hannah looked at her brood with a worried face, but caught a subtle sign to wait from her mother-in-law, Bayla.

Maisie was the first to speak. "Zaida, I think that is both helpful and true. I think my struggle is with how to be what I am meant to be. Perhaps there is value in being a Canadian first. I don't mean to not be a Jew, but to be assimilated." She chose her words carefully, not wanting to upset her grandfather. "Zaida, to be a Canadian first and then everything else—Jewish, Ukrainian, Polish, or Mennonite—would that be so terrible?"

Baruch considered these questions, then nodded to Isaac, who was burning to speak.

"The people from England, Scotland, the United States, Ontario, and anyplace where English is their language do better than everyone else," Isaac said. "No one but a Jew will hire a Jew first if there are other people to hire. All of the leftovers get the worst jobs. Look at us here in the North End. Look at the ditch diggers, the railroad workers and even more, the sewing factories. Jews and Ukrainians are working those machines all day long. What great benefit is there in fighting to maintain an old country identity that so many people hate? Isn't it better to create a new direction? To be Canadian, like our cousin says?"

Listening carefully to the words of his eldest grandchildren, Baruch reluctantly acknowledged that his world was changing. "And what would you have us do, Malka?"

"Well, for me, I want to be Canadian."

"You do, hmm?" Baruch peered from under hooded brows. "And what might that be? What is it to you to be Canadian?"

"I want to be seen for the person I am, not that which I represent. I want to go to school. I want to be a doctor."

"A doctor? Whoa!" shouted Aaron. "Women can't be doctors. They can be nurses and teachers. They can make clothes and cook, but they can't be doctors!"

"Shut up, Aaron. You don't know anything." Ziporah smacked her little brother.

"Stop it! Both of you!" Hannah scolded. "This is no way to behave at the table. Aaron, you must never underestimate what a woman can do. I am surprised at you."

"Sorry, Cousin Malka," he said sheepishly.

Maisie returned to Ravenscraig the following evening and slipped in through the kitchen door, as was her habit on Saturdays. She was happy to see that the only note that had been left to her attention was that Mr. and Mrs. Willows were out for the evening and that Miss Emma was in the care of her governess at a music concert but would require hot milk and cookies upon her return. Mr. Chadwick was the wild card. Although he was not required to work on Saturday nights, he frequently stayed in and could be found snooping about the hallways searching for the tidbits of information that made him seem all-knowing. The man needed a new hobby, was Maisie's thought. In any case she got on well with the butler despite her wariness of his probing personality.

Maisie looked forward to an evening ahead with light demands on her time. Lovely. She would have at least an hour to study, maybe longer. In the time that had passed since she rescued the medical texts that young Mr. Willows had tossed from his window, she had made her way through them twice and was ready to start a review of the most interesting chapters.

As she came up the last few stairs to the attic, she saw there was a book sitting in front of her door. She knelt down to pick it up, and her heart almost leapt from her bosom when she saw that it was a textbook on the spread of infectious diseases in urban centers. There was a note sticking out from it with her name formally and neatly written on it. Looking about to be sure no one was watching, she slipped into her room and locked the door before carefully breaking the wax seal on the letter.

April 19, 1902

Dear Miss Rosedale,

Please excuse my bold and inappropriate behavior in seeking to ask a special kindness from you. It is with the greatest respect for your position that I chance offending you with my request, and I do hope you don't think poorly of me as a result.

It would please me greatly if you would accept this book as payment in advance for assisting me with my studies. I would be ever so grateful if you would consider reading chapter three and giving me your thoughts on the four assignment questions you will find at the end of the chapter.

I feel this material is hopelessly beyond my understanding, and I was greatly impressed by the knowledge you displayed in my presence the other day.

If you would consider it, it is my hope that we shall be able to enter into an arrangement to study together under the cloak of secrecy, of course, so as to protect us both.

With my sincere gratitude and my promise to uphold discretion of the highest order, I beg to remain,

Your fellow student,

James Willows

James had left his door ajar to enable him to hear Maisie's return. His room on the third floor was near the end of the hall and he would easily be able to hear her on the stairs. With the other staff members away on Saturday evenings, James knew there was little chance that the surprise he had left for Maisie would be found by anyone but her. She was always prompt in her return. He was utterly consumed with delight in anticipating her reaction.

Finally his patience was rewarded with the sound of her footsteps on the stairs, marching energetically, as she hummed a tune. He waited. It couldn't take but a minute before she would be back down the stairs. The minute passed, and several more after that. Had she missed it? How would that be possible? James paced about impatiently in his room before heading for the door to the service stairway. As he reached it, it flew open and hit him soundly on the head, sending him reeling backward and bringing stars to his eyes as he hit the wall and slumped to the floor. He looked up into the starry darkness and saw an angel, fluttering about in a terrible state of angst.

"Dear me, Mr. James! Please let me help you!" Maisie was horrified at the accident she caused. The second in less than a week! The book flew from her hands as she reached to help young Mr. Willows. "I'm so dreadfully sorry! Are you all right?" She helped him struggle to his feet.

"I'm fine, really I am. Just bad timing is all." James rubbed the rising knot on his forehead, desperately trying to hide his embarrassment.

"I must be the clumsiest person on earth!" Maisie exclaimed. "Oh, I am so terribly sorry." Her face had turned crimson and he quickly forgot his embarrassment in his desire to ease her concerns.

"Please, Maisie, it was an accident. Calm yourself. No harm was done. There now," he said as he straightened his tie and smoothed his jacket. "See, everything is fine."

"Thank you, Mr. James," she said in full voice, certain they were not alone. "It seems this book was misplaced. I found it and believe it belongs in your collection." The words streamed rapidly out of her mouth as she thrust the book forward.

Unable to mask his disappointment, he took the book from her hands. He opened the cover to see if she had retrieved his note, and was immediately heartened to see she had replaced his note with her own.

She smiled and immediately dropped her gaze onto the floor as she curtsied. "I do believe Mr. Chadwick is likely to have returned and may well have need for my assistance. Is there anything I might do for you Mr. James?"

"No, that will be all. Thank you, Maisie. I shall retire to my studies."

"Goodnight, Mr. James."

She hummed as she turned and disappeared in search of the elusive, ever present Mr. Chadwick, whom she suspected was lurking nearby, as James turned back to his room and closed the door. He held the note and felt his heart beating in his chest. He took his time getting settled at his desk before he opened it and discovered it held an astonishing surprise.

Dear Mr. Willows,

Thank you for the gift, but I already have this textbook. It fell into my hands shortly after I arrived at Ravenscraig, as luck would have it.

I completed all of the exercises in this book some months ago, and have written extensive notes. Here are the answers I wrote for chapter three.

With great appreciation, I most humbly accept your offer to study together, in secret, of course. I await your further instructions.

Sincerely,

Maisie Rosedale

25
A Letter from Elliot
January 18, 1903

While James was studying medicine in Manitoba, his younger brother, Elliot, was in Paris, studying architecture at the *Ecole des Beaux Arts*. At least Rupert believed he was.

Only Emma knew the truth, and it was enough to consume the child with both excitement and worry. Elliot had sent her a letter with his news, and she had been carrying it with her for ten days, not having told a soul about it. Their father was going to be most upset when he learned what Elliot had done. But Emma could only admire her brother for following his dreams.

Today, at last, she would be able to unburden her secret on her dearest friend. Mary Doogie was in her grade six class at Havergal School. She was finally home from her Christmas vacation travels with her parents and her arrival for a visit at Ravenscraig was a cause for great celebration between the two.

"Mary, I have missed you so!" Emma threw her arms around Mary, and the two hugged and laughed, as they spilled compliments over one another while desperate to hear all of the news each had to share.

"I have a secret!" Emma whispered when they were settled in the parlor. She checked over her shoulder to be sure none of the servants was about.

"Well, out with it then! Don't keep me in suspense," insisted Mary.

"You have to promise not to tell anyone. My brother's very future depends on it!"

"Alfred is getting married?"

"No. This is not about Alfred."

"James?"

"No, no, this is about Elliot!"

"Elliot! How is he enjoying Paris? Is it fantastic?"

Emma glanced around. "Yes," she said, louder than necessary, suspecting they were not alone. "Elliot is loving Paris. Imagine studying architecture at the Beaux Arts!"

Mary stifled a giggle. "Are you sure it is safe to talk here?"

Mary put her finger to her lips. "Shh. This is extremely important to him and you are the only person on earth that I can tell. He gave me permission."

"My goodness, Emma, whatever is it?"

"Shh! First you have to pinky swear that you won't tell a soul!"

The girls linked fingers and swished their locked hands in the oath to secrecy.

Mary drew in very close as Emma cupped her hands and whispered in her ear.

"What?!" Mary clapped her hand over her mouth and squealed. "Your father is going to have a canary!"

"Well, that canary won't be appearing anytime soon, because no one is going to tell him," Emma whispered. "Mr. Chadwick might be nearby. Be careful what you say out loud." She reached into her dress pocket and brought out an envelope. "Elliot sent me the most exquisite dancing slippers and tucked inside the package was this letter. You read it for yourself."

Mary handled the letter as if it were a great and fragile treasure. She hesitated, then gently pulled the letter from the envelope.

December 5, 1902

Ma chère petite sœur,

Paris is absolutely wonderful! I feel so alive and happy in this city with its charming cafés, vibrant art displays and endless museums. I see you reading this and shaking your head, wondering what has happened to change the dark and gloomy circumstances I wrote about in my last letter. I'm so sorry to have worried you with all of my troubles, Emma. Those days are gone. Now I feel as if I have absolutely become another person!

Dear Emma, please know that what I am about to tell you must be kept the strictest secret. My entire life will be turned upside down if our parents should learn my plans. Do you swear to keep my secret? I know you do. You are the only person at home that I am sharing this with. Now, because I trust you, I will say that if you absolutely must tell Mary, that is fine, as I know how close she is to you and I know she is of good character. However, if either of you betray me, you should have no doubt that it will be the last that I will ever speak to you. I am quite serious. I would never, ever forgive you.

My secret is that I am no longer attending the *Ecole des Beaux Arts*. As you know, I positively loathed it for every day of the sixteen months that I was there. Architecture is just not for me. I am still in school, though, but this is a different school, a dream school. Here is how it came about.

There is a café near my apartment that has the most scrumptious delicacies in the entire world. I take most of my meals there. The pastry is beyond imagination in both the beauty of presentation and superb taste. I am in seventh heaven the moment I step through the door and breathe in the fantastic aromas emanating from the kitchen. I very quickly became friends with the owners who are also the cooks. They are Henri and Solange Bouvier, and you could not find a more creative and talented duo.

So, here is what happened. One day, while dining, I suggested a technique to Henri to enhance the flavor of the Crème Caramel. He looked at me with surprise and asked how I would know the method I was describing to him, and I admitted my fondness for culinary pursuits and told him of my experimentations below stairs at Ravenscraig. He immediately invited me into the kitchen and since then I have practically become a fixture there, regularly experimenting with creating new dishes. Henri was so delighted with what he calls my "innate talent" that he offered to introduce me to one of the directors of the school where he studied. Emma, this school I speak of is the famous Cordon Bleu! I am floating above the ground in telling you that I have been accepted as a student. Your brother Elliot is going to be a chef!

Now, of course, I have no desire to cut short the life of our father, so you must allow me to tell him this news myself, at the time when I determine would be appropriate. I am so thrilled to tell you about this wonderful development. I absolutely had to share my news with you.

I do hope all is well with you and your studies. I know the winter is dreadfully long in Winnipeg and hope you have been cheered by my little present of the dancing slippers. I saw them in a shop on the Champs Élysées and could not resist buying them for you.

Affectionately yours,

Elliot

"Oh, Emma!" exclaimed Mary. "How utterly brave he is!"

"He certainly is. He won't let anything stop him!"

"What did he mean about his experimentations below stairs at Ravenscraig?"

"He used to have trouble sleeping sometimes and he would go downstairs and bake. Can you imagine? Scones and cakes and things."

"Surely he couldn't keep that a secret!" Mary exclaimed.

"Well, no. He did get caught, but only by Mrs. Butterfield who came down early one morning. But he told me he traded his scones recipe for her silence."

"You're joking," said Mary

"No. But she would never tell. You can trust Mrs. B."

"Are you going to tell her?"

"About Elliot's decision? Of course not. You are the only person who knows except for me. Oh, Mary, I do feel so much better now that I have confided in you. It is such a weight to carry a secret all by myself."

The girls went on to chat about their schoolmates and Mr. Chadwick grew frustrated. He had arrived in his eavesdropping spot too late to learn much about anything. All he knew was that Mr. Elliot was up to something and that somehow Mrs. Butterfield had information that he did not.

26
Aaron's Essay
April 12, 1903

The noon bell rang out through the school and Miss Mitchell touched her handkerchief delicately to her nose. The limited lunch offerings the children brought out of the tin pails they carried to school included garlic and goose fat sandwiches, bread and butter, and rarely, a chunk of cheese. She smiled sympathetically at those who were too poor to have been provided a lunch from home, and excused them to play out of doors.

Miss Edith Mitchell had devoted her life to her students and her devotion was being tested. She strained under her ambitions and unmet goals, as she considered the collection of unwashed children crammed into her classroom.

Her class currently included forty-two children from ages ten to sixteen in three different grades: four, five and six. Grades were assigned according to ability, not age. Hence, among her grade four students there were some boys taller than she was herself. Language was always the greatest challenge as most of the children struggled to learn enough English to understand their lessons. Of her class, only seven spoke English as a first language. Eighteen other languages were represented in the homes of the immigrant children. In the mix, the Jews were greatest in number, but close behind them were the Germans, then the Ukrainians and other Slavs. None of them rich, many of them undernourished, some of them bright stars in the midst of the most difficult circumstances. It broke her heart.

Miss Mitchell had found her purpose in life in her dedication to help these children raise themselves out of poverty. With her guidance, she believed that they would, one day, leave behind the grime, the lice, and the strings of garlic suspended around their necks, and assimilate to become productive contributors to the British Empire. She was very disappointed that eight students had already left the class during the school year. In almost all cases, the impetus for departure was a family's desperate need of wage earners, thus dashing any hopes for further education for the child. It was particularly disheartening when she lost the children who were naturally good students. She took every loss as a sign of personal failure. With each child who dropped out, one more little foreigner was missing the opportunity to be transformed, under her tutelage, into a proper Canadian citizen.

Miss Mitchell took great satisfaction in the accomplishments of her pupils; chief among them was how capable they had become in English over the year. Her class was well ahead of the others at Selkirk Avenue School. She had pushed them hard and the proof of her method was in their conversations in the schoolyard. English conversations. She had done it. She was proud of them, and even more so, she was proud of herself. A spinster of twenty-nine, she had vigorously committed her life to excellence in education.

Her reward came in unusual payment. She saw it in the admiring eyes of the pale-faced girls who worked to imitate her British accent and in the teenage boys who removed their caps and said "Good morning, Teacher," when she happened across them in the market. Most significant, and a fact she kept to herself, was that she saw her influence in their growing shame for their origins; the shame they felt for their illiterate parents. The evidence of this embarrassment was in the increasing number of report cards that got "lost" on the way back to school for lack of a parent's ability to read and sign the documents.

She allowed her students their dignity and accepted their explanations. Secretly, she counted their unreturned report cards as a sign of validation for her techniques.

From shame came ambition. In Miss Mitchell's view this was the golden ticket to becoming Canadian. Shame allowed the children to distance themselves from their backward ways and embrace the culture and work ethic of the Anglo Saxon founders of the country. Some of the children were even considering changing their names to anglicize them. Yes, years from now, many of these young people would undoubtedly remember her for having had a profound impact on their lives.

When the children returned to their seats after recess, Miss Mitchell's special guest was waiting for them. Mr. Sisler, the principal, had been invited to hear the results of the school essay contest.

The essay was part of a national competition, whereupon the best essay from each school would be sent to King Edward VII. Affection for the monarchy was deeply rooted in the Dominion, and held great appeal for the immigrants. Miss Mitchell had taken charge of the contest thinking it an ideal opportunity to show Mr. Sisler how valuable she was as a teacher. Sadly, it had not worked out as she had planned.

She was hoping Aaron Zigman would be the one to represent the school, as he was far and away the best writer. But what he had turned in for the essay assignment was shockingly disappointing, and defiantly off topic, in her view. This afternoon, she would have to make an example of him, to help him get back on track. She had no choice. The essay assignment was neatly written on the large black chalkboard behind her desk.

Selkirk Avenue Public School
Writing Assignment: Canadian Heroes

The Dominion of Canada is a shining jewel in the British Empire with a strong future. Among the loyal subjects who dwell here, there are many heroes. Choose a hero in Canada and explain how he is important to the future of the Dominion. This person can be someone you have read about in the newspaper, a historical figure or someone in the community whom you believe to be a hero. Be sure to include many details about your hero's life.

"Class, I have graded all the essays for the national contest," Miss Mitchell called out as the students settled. "As promised, the one with the highest mark will be sent to England with the best essays from schools across the country for King Edward to read. Aaron, would you please read the assignment out loud."

Aaron stood and read, fluently and easily in a strong voice.

He knew immediately that he had aced the assignment. When he finished, Miss Mitchell started handing out the marked essays and excited chatter rose among the students. She shook her head slightly as she dropped his essay on his desk. He was stunned to see he had received a C.

Miss Mitchell had not intended to speak to Aaron, but could not stop herself as she was sure no one but him would hear her. "Aaron," she said in a very quiet voice. "The man you wrote about is not a hero. A hero is someone everyone knows. Your writing is excellent and deserves an A, but this is not what you were asked to write. You will be more careful next time, I'm sure."

Jake Grady kicked Aaron's chair and snickered as Miss Mitchell made her way to the front of the class. Aaron hunched down over his desk and held his temper.

"Class, I am pleased to announce that the winning essay from our school is about our first prime minister, Sir John A. Macdonald, written by Janey Shroeder," Miss Mitchell announced in her clear voice. "Congratulations, Janey. Please come up to the front and read your essay to the class."

As the youngest child in the Zigman family, and one who easily found himself at the receiving end of his mother's anger, Mendel enjoyed the rare opportunities when he could watch one of his older brothers "get it" from Mama. Such an occasion presented itself after school that afternoon. Hannah was working behind the counter in the little store they had set up in the corner of the Zigman Café. Mendel was on hand to see Aaron slip into the kitchen door with a bloody nose. It wasn't that his brother needed his mother immediately, but Mendel just couldn't resist the sweet taste of schadenfreude that came with volunteering to be the one to bring the news to her.

"He what? He's fighting again!" Mama was instantly in full fury as she slammed the cash register closed and shouted to Baba Bayla to take over the counter.

"It's all right, Mama. Ziporah's cleaning him up. He ain't hurt too bad this time," Mendel said, a little too sweetly.

Meanwhile, in the kitchen, Ziporah had reached for a clean towel and, with a furrowed brow had started to work on Aaron's bloodied and swollen face.

"Aw, come on, I don't even have any loose teeth. I'm all right," Aaron fought his sister's hold. "You should see Jake Grady. Boy, I'll tell you, he'll never come after me again."

Hannah swooped into the kitchen, eyes blazing and apron flying. Steady in her flight, she folded around Aaron to scrutinize his injuries.

"You breathing? If not, I'm going to kill you."

"I'm breathing, I'm breathing!" Aaron shrank from his mother's powerful grip, bracing himself for her quick temper. "I'm fine. This time I really got him. There isn't much chance I have to go back to that stupid school. I can work in the store like a man. Maybe earn a man's wages, Ma."

"Aaron," Mama pleaded, choosing her English words carefully. "My dahlink little cabbage head. You are a boy. You are twelve-years-old only, and somehow you have to stay alive to go to school until you have that paper, that what do you call it? That graduating paper. You go to school, we will look after the work. Now tell me how it is you should come home with blood when I forbid you to fight and when your father tells you not to be so stupid to get involved with those bad boys."

"It was the essay. It's a long story, but she asked me to read it out loud to everyone."

"So, Mazel Tov on the good work!" Her rage instantly dissipated. "Oy, to be thinking his royaltyness the King of England himself would read the work of Aaron Zigman, my son!"

"Mama, stop. Let me explain."

But Hannah was too excited to stop. "You brought home for your mama an egg?"

"Do you mean an A, Mama?"

She swatted the back of his head. "You know what I mean, you smarty pants! Yes! An A you brought for me, yes?" Mama dragged out the A sound to make her point and Aaron put his hands up in anticipation of the next blow.

"No, Mama, I brought home a C, but she said the writing

was good enough, it should have been an A, and that's why she made me read it out loud after the winning essay was read. She did it to embarrass me, Ma. She said she wanted to teach the class how important it was to pay attention to the assignment. But, I did pay attention and I did it right. Then Mr. Sisler got involved and had something to say. It was a real mess."

"The principal! And then a black eye on top of everything!"

"I didn't start the fight, Mama. As soon as school let out, Jake Grady and his pals came after me. I'm sick of getting beat up, so I put my fists up the way Isaac showed me."

"Aaron!" Mama was shocked.

"Sorry, Ma, I had to!" Aaron dropped his head and Mama looked at the clock.

"There is no time for this now and this is too much for a tired woman. Save it for supper time and we will see what the family has to say. Where is that essay?"

"I have it with my books," Aaron said.

"Good. Bring it to the table. Now, go wash your hands. Where is that Isaac?"

"He told me the newspaper needed him in the composing room today after school," Ziporah said.

"That newspaper is swallowing him up." Mama shook her head. "Ziporah, go tell Zaida and Baba supper is ready. We will start without the big shot newspaperman. If he can't show up for supper, maybe he can eat a newspaper." Mama's words trailed off into a mix of worry and annoyance about Aaron's schooling while Ziporah hurried off to find her grandparents.

By the time the family had come to the table, Aaron's left eye had swollen shut. He sat tall and shrugged off Baba's sympathetic mutterings. The truth was he felt like a man for the first time in his life.

The family ate and talked about the day's activities. Finally, at the end of the meal it was time for Aaron's story. The sound of boots stomping at the kitchen door brought a smile to Aaron's face. Isaac was not going to miss his moment. Usually Aaron felt his stories were never important enough to take the attention from his older brother's re-telling of the exciting events at the newspaper. Since he had started training at the *Winnipeg*

Star's Linotype machine, he suddenly seemed older, someone to be more respected. Aaron was ashamed of the envy he felt as Papa and Zaida hung on Isaac's every word. Today would be different! Let him top this one.

Isaac settled at the table with a large bowl of soup and a plate of bread before him, and Zev nodded at Aaron. The family quieted as he quickly went through the facts of the assignment. The class had been talking about how the Dominion of Canada had come to be created with the passing of the British North America Act in 1867. Miss Mitchell reviewed a number of significant events that had happened since Confederation and had introduced the contest. Then Zev asked him to read his essay to the family. "Baruch Zigman, a Hero in Canada, by Aaron Zigman," he read, and Baba smiled. Aaron continued reading:

Baruch Zigman is a hero, a leader and a great citizen for Canada and the United Kingdom. Without him and his sacrifice to face hardships to come here to this country, my family would yet be starving in Russia. I would not have the chance to be sitting and writing in English about our heroes. I would not have a life to be growing up to make of myself a somebody in a free country where you can own a house, learn many things, and raise yourself up to be a success.

If my family would still be now in Russia, we would live in fear of violence and we would have little chance to make enough money to live. In the new country you can be safe behind your door. Baruch Zigman believes even a Jew can have a good life and a job and money and family together in Canada and can be free from trouble, even at school or outside where we play sports as long as we mind our own business. He was the person in our family who decided we would come to make a new life here and for this reason he is a hero. There are other reasons, too. I will explain them.

Canada is growing with many people from many places. It is because of the difference in what all of these greenhorns bring to Canada with what God has put into their talents and their thinking that Canada will grow to be a strong and important country. Here people can be free from starving and from governments that do not believe in freedom and opportunity for ordinary people. Here people are free to work at what they choose and free to help each other without the government or the police looking to bring you pain and punishment, and even death.

Let me tell you about Baruch Zigman. He is the father of my father. He left Russia to come to Winnipeg in 1883 when the Czar Alexander III, on whose name we spit, made it very bad for Jews to live in Russia. In case you do not study what is history in the old country, I will tell you what happened. The czar known as Alexander II was killed by a bomb. There came lots of anger and beatings and killings in our village and in many villages. It was not a Jew who brought death to the czar, but it does not matter because it is only the Jews that were blamed. I was not yet born, but Baruch Zigman says it is very important to know the story and to tell the story, and for this reason I am telling you about it in this essay.

My grandfather worked for many years by himself and then with my father, before it was possible to buy the tickets for my grandmother, my mother, my brothers and sister, and me to come to Canada.

My grandfather is also a hero because he helps people who need help. He gives them money. He gives them food. He teaches his grandchildren to respect everybody and to be good citizens and to make our place and earn our living in the new country.

I am very proud to be a grandson of Baruch Zigman. He is my hero. One day I wish to be a good man like him to help make a good future for my family and my country, Canada.

Aaron folded the paper and placed it on the table. The family sat quietly as Mama raised her apron to wipe a tear. Baruch said nothing. With his eyes cast down, he silently nodded his appreciation and cleared his throat.

Zev spoke first. "And what is the reason Miss Mitchell gave you the lower grade for this essay?"

"Miss Mitchell says a grandfather is not important enough to be a hero. She says I did not understand the assignment."

"How did you get into a fight?" Zev asked.

Aaron clenched his jaw as he recalled the horrible afternoon. "Mr. Sisler came back at the end of the afternoon when class was dismissed. He asked me to stay and wait in the hall. Then he closed the door and had a talk with Miss Mitchell. A few minutes later they called me in. Miss Mitchell said she was ashamed, and she was practically crying. She said she made a mistake and my essay should have been chosen. But, she had announced Janey as the winner and she said hers would be the one to represent the school. She said Mr. Sisler had recommended she change my grade to an A but that that was her decision, and she said she would think about it."

"And how did you end up in a fight?"

"Jake and his friends were waiting for me in the schoolyard. Jake said I was never going to amount to much as a Canadian because Canada needs people who want to be like the British and they don't need Jews. I started walking away, Ma, I really did. Then he started in on Zaida and said ... " Aaron dropped his eyes. "He said something very insulting and I hit him."

"Well, then," Zev paused then considered the matter while he drank his tea. The family waited in silence. "First you must know I am very proud of you, Aaron," Zev said quietly.

"It is a wonderful essay, Aaron," Ziporah beamed and got up to hug him.

"And the fighting?" Hannah asked loudly, with her eyebrows up.

"The fighting is a man's business, Hannah," Zev answered. "We will not speak any further about it."

"Papa. I really don't want to go back to school. I really hate it. Even if Mr. Sisler makes Miss Mitchell give me an A, it really doesn't mean a lot to me."

"If Mr. Sisler thinks you should have the A, then you should have it. To be given proper credit for correctly doing the assignment is very important," Zev answered. "To graduate from high school is even more important. Unfortunately, it is not a question of what is fair, but what is necessary."

"I hate that school." Aaron looked at his father. "I only like my friends. Papa, would it be so terrible for me to work in the store? I could study on my own."

Zev shook his head. "Aaron, we are still working at the synagogue toward having a school for the Jewish community, but it will be some years before we have it. For now, we must accept what we have. You must be educated."

Isaac gave his brother a weak punch in the shoulder and forced enthusiasm into his voice.

"Your essay is very good, Aaron. You need a little help with getting the Yiddish rhythms out of your English, but you are quite a good writer."

"Well, don't be so overjoyed, Mr. Newspaper-Know-It-All," Ziporah chided.

"I'm sorry, I guess I'm distracted. It is just that it is very sad that much of the trouble you write about, Aaron, is not any different now than it was twenty years ago when Zaida first left."

"What is it, Isaac? Do you have news from the old country?" Zev asked.

"It is terrible news. There are more pogroms. This time in Kishinev."

"Oh, dear God. No!" Hannah shouted.

"It happened last week. It's very bad. A massacre. We printed an article from *The New York Times* about it today. I brought it home."

At his father's urging, Isaac read the article out loud.

"The anti-Jewish riots in Kishinev are worse than the censor will permit to be publish. There was a well-laid out plan for the general massacre of Jews on the day following the Orthodox Easter. The mob was led by priests and the general cry, 'Kill the Jews,' was taken up all over the city. The Jews were taken wholly unaware and were slaughtered like sheep. The dead number 120 and the injured about 500. The scenes of horror attending this massacre are beyond description. Babies were literally torn to pieces by the frenzied and bloodthirsty mob. The local police made no attempt to check the reign of terror. At sunset the streets were piled with corpses and wounded. Those who could make their escape fled in terror and the city is now practically deserted of Jews."

Zev and Baruch talked quietly with Isaac as the table was cleared and Mendel and Aaron went off to do their homework. Soon there was a knock at the door. The men were wanted for a meeting at the synagogue to discuss raising money for those in need in the old country.

27
The Scarlet Sin

November 16, 1903

The Linotype machine clattered away as Isaac tapped the keys. He watched with contentment as the brass matrices, each with a different letter, slid through the channels and clinked into place to form precise lines of words. In his capable hands, the machine's astonishing arrangement of ingenious elevators and tiny conveyor belts transformed the words of copy on the scrap of paper before him into the lines of metal type, called slugs, that would be inked to become the printed words of the newspaper. To Isaac, this seven-foot behemoth, part typing apparatus and part metal foundry, was the most amazing machine ever invented; a monument to human creativity. Arms flew, wheels turned, and the smell of molten lead wafted up around him as the hulking machine swallowed the brass lines of letters and smoothly spit them out as words. One hot metal piece after another was neatly stacked and made ready to go to print.

Isaac thought himself extremely fortunate to have been promoted from selling newspapers to working in the composing room at The *Winnipeg Star*. His job promotion had come out of the blue. One of the Linotype operators had suddenly left to go to The *Manitoba Free Press*, leaving a vacancy that needed to be filled immediately. The *Star's* manager had asked Isaac to show them what he could do. He took to the work like a duck to water. An added benefit was the increase in pay that allowed him to start putting more money aside to go to university. The only downside was that with high school, homework, and the newspaper job, there wasn't much time left for anything else. He considered it a minor inconvenience.

What Isaac liked best, however, was the opportunity to get to know the reporters and editors. As a newsboy selling the papers on the street, he almost never entered the *Star* building.

Now that he was a composer, he couldn't soak up the atmosphere fast enough. Isaac thought it an utterly fascinating place, filled with wildly interesting characters who talked about everything imaginable. There were no taboo subjects here. Especially intriguing in recent days was the civic election campaign, which clashed with the crusade of the social reformers and temperance leaders whose aim was to clean up Winnipeg's immorality. With the election less than a month away, these were hot times in the big city.

"Hey, kid!" Jim McGraw, his hat pushed back on his head, shouted over the din of the machines. "Hey Ziggy! You gonna work all night?"

McGraw was a brash young reporter with a quick mind and a faster mouth. With an easy laugh and an enviable swagger, he seemed to liven up the whole newsroom the second he walked through the door. He had a boisterous, affable way about him and always greeted people loudly, seeming to be truly happy to see them. His height and build seemed average, until he put his fists up. Though just a few years older than Isaac, it was clear that Jim McGraw was a seasoned man of the world. Isaac immediately liked him and the two had quickly become friends.

"Hey there, Jim!" Isaac yelled over the noise. "Hold your horses." Isaac's hands flew over the machine and the mechanical arms whizzed overhead as the letters found their way home. The machine clanked to a halt.

"Listen, Ziggy, I'm going out to cover a story," said McGraw. "Wanna come along?"

"When?"

"Tonight."

"Sure, I'm almost done." Isaac's fatigue was instantly gone. "What's the story?"

"Reverend Du Val and his Social Reformers are holding a rally at the Winnipeg Theater. It's gonna be huge. They've booked Westminster Church for the overflow and looks like they'll fill that, too. Word is that the holy-rollers are whippin' this election campaign into a frenzy and Mayor Arbuthnot is on his way out after all these years."

"You think so? He's been elected three times already. I

thought he was very well liked."

"He is liked, if you don't take into account this moral crusade," said McGraw. "The word on the street is that Reverend Du Val has all the support he needs to push city council to shut down the bawdy houses. The reformers are looking to blame Arbuthnot for letting the problem go so long and they've built up a lot of steam. The way I see it, the flesh pots are going to bring this mayor down."

"I thought the morality problem was about drinking and the number of saloons around, not, well, not those women." Isaac's cheeks went bright red.

"Whores!" McGraw said loudly, pronouncing it HOO-ers, the way it was commonly said in Winnipeg. "Whores, they are, lad." He laughed out loud. "Well, yes, right you are my friend, the hard drinking in this town is a much bigger problem, but the way Du Val and his followers have it, the brothels are a major part of that booze trade, so they figure on getting rid of the Thomas Street bawdy houses and the inmates therein, and in so doing, they are counting on cutting down on the boozing."

"What do you, figure, Jim?"

"I figure it's going to make for an interesting shouting match at the rally tonight. Those ladies have been conducting business out on that road for more than twenty years and they aren't going to take this lying down, if you pardon the pun." McGraw snorted at his own humor. "When are you gonna be outta here?"

"Just wrapping up the last page now. Give me ten minutes," answered Isaac, grinning broadly.

"Make it five. I'll meet you out front."

Isaac scrambled into his coat and tugged his hat onto his head as he flew from the building to find McGraw chewing on a cigar and chatting with a beat cop outside the *Star's* front door.

"Hey, Ziggy. Meet my buddy, Officer McLanahan," McGraw greeted his friend. "This is Isaac Zigman."

"Glad to know you." The cop towered over them, resembling a bear in his heavy buffalo coat and fur hat.

264

"I was just telling the officer here that with your sense of a good story, I'm betting you'll end up writing for this rag one day," said McGraw.

"Oh, I don't think so," answered Isaac, surprised and pleased at the compliment. "I think I might be a lawyer and that you'll be writing about me one day, McGraw."

The men all had a laugh and McLanahan raised his hand in a wave as he continued on his patrol.

"Here's the dope," McGraw told Isaac, as the two started their walk to the theater. "McLanahan says extra forces have been called in tonight to keep the rally from getting out of hand. This Du Val is a real hellfire and brimstone kind of preacher. He's got a way with words, he does."

"I don't understand." Isaac jammed his hands into his pockets and hurried along to match the pace of the reporter. "I thought that the brothels had been left alone because they are out on the edge of town and segregated from the rest of the population. What's all the fuss?"

Jim turned and looked at Isaac. "Well, whadda ya know, the lad has a feel for the predicament of the ladies of the scarlet sin. Yes. The good and solid leaders of the fine City of Winnipeg have indeed turned a blind eye to the goings-on over on Thomas Street."

"What do you mean a blind eye? Aren't prostitutes legal if they stay out there in the brothel district?"

"Well now, that takes us right to the heart of the matter," answered McGraw. "Segregate the prostitutes and there's no problem. Out of sight, out of mind." He waved his hands as though pretending to be addressing a crowd and then turned to look Isaac in the eye. "Yes, that's most definitely the policy the city fathers adopted. But no, it ain't legal. It's against the criminal code for gawd's sake!"

"So if it is not legal, why don't they just enforce the law?" Isaac was confused.

"Isaac." McGraw stopped and put his hand on the boy's shoulder. "I gotta tell you that you are just dumber than shit." McGraw shook his head and started to hoot with laughter.

Deeply embarrassed, Isaac shrugged him off and sharpened

his tone. "Well, if I'm so stupid, why are you taking me along?"

"Aw, c'mon. I'm just bustin' your chops." McGraw slapped playfully at his friend's cap. "Look, here's how it is. I'll explain it slowly so you can understand."

Isaac snapped. With a yell, he tucked his head down and charged full force into McGraw, slamming him into a snow bank.

"Hey! What the hell are you doing?" McGraw rolled and twisted around to grab Isaac's fists.

"Don't you make fun of me!" Isaac was faster, and slipping through his grasp, pinned his opponent face down in the snow. With his knee planted between McGraw's shoulder blades he grabbed his right arm and wrenched it as hard as he could.

"YOWCH! All right, all right! Lemme loose!"

"Stop insulting me! I'm not a kid." Isaac gave McGraw one more shove and stood up.

"You're an asshole! Look at, me! I'm all covered in snow!"

Isaac raised his fists. "Say you're sorry!" he shouted, weaving and bobbing, ready with his next punch.

"Oh, for gawd's sake." McGraw plopped back down onto the snow. "Stop it, Isaac."

"Say you're sorry!"

"All right! I'll say it," McGraw held his hand up and Isaac helped him to his feet. "I'm sorry you're an asshole."

Isaac rushed him again, but this time McGraw was ready. Dodging out of the way, he stuck his foot out and sent Isaac flying.

Now, both covered in snow like two small boys, they started to laugh.

"Jumpin' Jehosaphat, Isaac! Where'd you learn to fight like that?"

"I had lots of practice in the schoolyard."

"All right. I give up. You hear? So, let's be friends and be on the same side, eh?" McGraw held his hands up to signal a truce. "Turn around and I'll brush the snow off your coat. We gotta move along here. I'll explain the whole story."

They quickened their pace to the theater while Jim, with a new respect for Isaac, outlined the history of the brothel problem.

"You see, this town is pretty much the 'Wild West' that easterners read about in their dime novels. You don't have to look hard to see how men outnumber women by a substantial margin."

Isaac nodded his head. Even in school, there were very few girls in Isaac's grade twelve class.

"All those fellas comin' west for jobs just ain't gonna find an abundance of decent and eligible women around to marry. So, this gives rise, you should pardon the expression, to a rather lucrative industry for the sportin' women who are more than willing to offer up paid entertainment to an endless supply of strong healthy men who want to blow off a little steam. Now, from the city's point of view, you have to know, this also brings in a lot of money. Think about it! If our good city fathers ever are successful in shuttin' them bawdy houses down, how much money is gonna be chopped right out of the Winnipeg economy? Those whores like to spend a dollar. Believe me, some of our department stores just about throw out a red carpet to greet 'em."

"But how can the city just decide to not enforce the law?" Isaac couldn't make sense of it. "How do you turn away from the Criminal Code of Canada?"

"You already lawyerin' up with those books, Ziggy?" McGraw shook his head. "Man, oh, man, do you ever need to have a little fun. Holy cow, you're wasting your youth with all that hard work."

Isaac turned red, and McGraw gave him a shove and laughed. "Here's how it came to be. Bear with me here, Ziggy, I figure this stuff isn't in those law books you read in your spare time. In 1870, there was no Winnipeg. There was a little fur trading settlement here at the forks of the Red and Assiniboine Rivers that was called Fort Garry. It was home to about two hundred people, fur traders and Indians mostly.

"Three years later, the population had exploded to almost two thousand people and Winnipeg was incorporated as a city. Think about it. That's only thirty years ago. Well, way back when Winnipeg was startin' to attract all this population, a group of enterprising women set up a nice little string of whore houses on Colony Street near Portage Avenue. A bunch of 'em had come up from South Dakota, from a place called Deadwood Gulch—famous for its gamblers and gunslingers.

"Anyhow, Winnipeg continues to grow like crazy, real estate prices go through the roof, and suddenly there's a need to build Manitoba College. Where'd they decide to put it? Right next to those little houses on Colony Creek. No one said much at first, but soon enough it came out that the students were getting a little distracted and there was a big ol' fuss about the fallen women fallin' all over the fine young men of the moneyed class. It hit the newspapers, and suddenly everyone in town knew there were prostitutes among us. Good God, Almighty! The citizenry was all just shocked right down to their toenails to learn of it!" McGraw threw up his hands to emphasize his point.

"So what happened?"

"So, they sent in the police chief to push them whores out of there. He was a new man, by the name of John Ingram. And you know what happened?" McGraw started to snicker like a schoolboy.

"They fought him off?" guessed Isaac.

"No, sir, they set him up! The doxies made him real welcome. So, good old John thought he'd sample some of the delectable pleasantries offered, and there he was, caught with his pants down, and I mean it in the most direct way possible."

McGraw laughed and slapped Isaac on the shoulder. "The mayor and council ran his sorry ass right out of town."

"Then what happened? Did they close down the brothels?"

"Well, we finally got some order restored when City Council decided the thing to do was just push the problem out of sight. So they segregated the women in a brothel district out on Thomas Street. It's a full two miles west of downtown, and at the time, it was out on the bald-ass prairie. Not a bad location, especially because the streetcar service ran all the way down Portage to their establishments. Everything was just tickety-boo for more than twenty years. The cops kept an eye on the prairie nymphs and made sure they kept to themselves. Women who drifted into downtown were quickly treated to a clear explanation of the rules and sent in the right direction and somehow everything remained in balance."

"So, why did it change?" Isaac asked.

"Where've you been for the last few years, Ziggy? Hiding under a rock? When did you come to Winnipeg?"

"1897."

"And what do you suppose the population was six years ago when you jumped off that train with your eyes all wide and innocent?"

"Somewhere around thirty-five thousand." Isaac set his jaw and tried to ignore the insult.

"Very good. I oughta know that if anyone would keep track of shit like that, it would be a bookworm like you. Anyhow, yes, that's right, thirty-five thousand. And now going into 1904, we stand at something more than sixty-five thousand.

"Now you tell me, when we add thirty thousand people in just six years, where're we gonna put 'em all? I'll tell you where. One street after another has been built heading west out there toward Thomas Street until the city grew right up to the front doors of those whorehouses. Thomas Street ain't out on the prairie any more.

"That's the whole problem, you see. All those decent church-going women living out that way are madder than hell because their little kiddies are playing in yards just a stone's throw away from cowboys haulin' up their drawers and snappin' their suspenders after a bit of frolic with the floozies."

Isaac was hanging on every word as they hustled through the fresh snow, his head swimming with images he'd never entertained before.

"You with me so far, Ziggy?"

"Oh, yes." Isaac's head bobbed up and down.

"So, enter one little fireball of a preacher with rather fine chin whiskers by the name of Reverend Frederic Du Val.

"Now, Ziggy, when you see him, you're going to think this man is just not big enough to cause any trouble at all. But, don't be lettin' his small stature cloud your judgment. This man stands tall among the righteous. Educated at Princeton, winner of all kinds of oratorical contests, he is not a narrator to ignore. Yes, sir, you are in for one fine speech tonight. He has those temperance women fainting in the aisles the second he opens his mouth."

"He's the one I've been reading about as leading all the city pastors in the moral reform movement."

"Yes! He is the very one. And he's well cut out for the job. The man could run for mayor and beat out all the competition. Do you know that yesterday alone he got more than eight hundred men to stick around after church services for his blistering speech on what they're now all callin' the Scarlet Sin? He got that audience so wound up that they decided to have this big rally at the Winnipeg Theater tonight. So, now the good preacher has got himself a regular army of do-gooders bangin' the drum for this crusade of his. And they can all hold an audience, I tell ya. These are great speakers, these preachers. Men like Reverend Charles Gordon and J.B. Silcox. They're all pounding the same message. It's expected to be standing room only, tonight, and the place holds over fourteen hundred people. How do you like them apples?"

"Do you think Mayor Arbuthnot is going to be re-elected?"

"Not a chance," answered McGraw. "This Du Val has a lot of influence right now and he's favoring Alderman Thomas Sharpe because he promised to actually close out the Thomas Street houses."

"Well, maybe that would be good for Winnipeg, to move the prostitutes out of town."

"I don't know if Sharpe has the guts to do it. Besides, according to the cops, it's only going to cause even more problems if all these social reformers get their way."

"How so?" asked Isaac.

"The cops I talk to say the women are just not gonna leave town like Du Val is insisting. You know what'll happen, Ziggy? The whores are going to quietly move into the heart of the city and carry on business in decent neighborhoods everywhere. They'll be scattered all over tarnation and believe you me, all manner of complaints are going to come up about the whores sullying the fine image of Winnipeg by being on every street corner through town.

"You wait and see. This is just a real bad idea, and it looks like there is no way to stop it. It won't be any time at all before we get farmhands comin' into town, and gettin' good and liquored up, then looking for a little bump and grind. You wait for the fireworks then. You're gonna see all manner of decent women being mistaken for sporting gals. It's going to be hellfire and damnation of a whole new kind." McGraw rubbed his hands with glee. "I can't wait!"

They rounded the corner and came upon a mob of people pushing to get through the doors of the Winnipeg Theater.

"Wow," said Isaac. "You sure are right about the crowd."

"Yeehaw! Hold onto your hat, Ziggy. History will be written tonight."

28
Rupert's Secret Investment
December 9, 1903

Rupert rose early the morning after the election. He sat alone at the table in the breakfast room, poring over a stack of newspapers neatly piled next to his coffee. The good news was that he had held on to his seat as alderman, though it was the narrowest victory in the entire slate of winning candidates. The hard news was that his friend and colleague, John Arbuthnot, was no longer mayor. In fact, Arbuthnot had been forced by fire-breathing moral crusaders to withdraw from the race altogether.

It was a mess. Reverend Dr. Du Val, that power hungry little zealot, had practically carried Mayor-elect Thomas Sharpe into office on his own shoulders. Not that Sharpe was a bad sort, but this moral crusade of his had grown completely out of control. Good God! Du Val had no idea what a hornet's nest he was stirring up.

Now council would have to go through the ugly business of shutting down the Thomas Street resorts. What did the reformers know of the workings of the brothel trade? If the population was so frenzied to get rid of the girls, why had the turnout at the polls been so pitifully low? The entire vice issue had been blown right out of proportion. That's why.

All this malarkey that the bawdyhouse inmates would be driven from town by the simple act of shutting down the Thomas resorts was so much naïve nonsense.

The worst of it was that all this scrutiny had brought Rupert to the very precipice of a political scandal that could ruin him. As the owner of five of the houses rented out to the madams on Thomas Street, Rupert lived in fear of being discovered. This was so much worse than the quiet matter of sending blackmail money to his wretched father. For more than three years, the checks to Ira Volinsky had been cashed every month with not a word, or a hint of trouble, since the arrangement began.

The problem of potential political ruin, however, was monumental by comparison. To hide the truth, Rupert had been forced to appear to be in support of the ridiculous moral crusade.

Then there was the matter of having to use his own son to distance himself from the segregated colony. Though Alfred didn't know it, Rupert had transferred all five of his whorehouses into his son's name. It was sound advice from his old real estate friend, Percival Wright, who had helped him in his purchase of Ravenscraig Hall so many years before. He had hated to do it, particularly since he had no intention of telling Alfred, but if a problem erupted, Alfred would have to take the fall. It was simply the only solution. It wouldn't be so bad. He was a good lad with a lot of ability. He could start again down east. He had much less to lose, after all, than Rupert did. No, starting over would not be difficult for him, if it ever came to that, and Toronto would suit him well.

The thoughts and the justifications flew through Rupert's head. But surely it would never come to that. Wright had assured him that it was only precautionary. It was unlikely that the newspapers would pay any attention to such things.

Next on Rupert's agenda would be to persuade the new mayor to give him a seat on the police commission. Then, he could be seen to be visibly campaigning against the social evil. It was an ideal solution. This way, Rupert would rise above the whispered rumors of his connection to vice in the city and at the same time have access to city hall's most confidential information. Minnie Woods and her sisters in the brothel business deserved to at least know when the raids were coming.

Rupert removed his spectacles and rubbed the ache in his eyes. It was all so dreary to keep it all going.

"Good morning, darling," Beth sang out as she poked her head into the room. "May I join you for breakfast, Mr. Alderman?"

"Of course, my dear." Rupert stood to help her take her seat. "Don't you look as fresh as a daisy on this cold December morning?"

"Well, thank you," she said, tucking her chin down and fluttering her eyelashes.

"Ah, I see you have something to tell me, Beth." Rupert couldn't help but smile at his wife's transparency.

"Well, if you insist." She reached into the pocket of her dressing gown. "I have a present for you, Rupert. Close your eyes."

"Oh, come now, Beth."

"Oh, please, do play along, or it will spoil my fun," she pouted. He closed his eyes as Beth placed two tickets on the table. They were theatre tickets for *Babes in Toyland* at New York's Majestic Theatre. They were front row center, for January 7, 1904, at eight o'clock. "I so wanted to get tickets for the *Wonderful Wizard of Oz*," Beth gushed, "but it will be touring. I hear that *Babes in Toyland* is equally delightful. Are you pleased, darling?"

"Beth! My goodness, what joke is this? We can't be in New York on such short notice."

"Oh, yes we can." She placed two train tickets in front of him.

"We leave on December twenty-sixth?" He stared at her as he calculated what appointments he would have to reschedule.

"Rupert, dear, I have it all worked out," she tapped the table. "City Council will be in recess for the Christmas holiday of course. We will have a few days to allow my favorite alderman to relax and enjoy a little time with his wife. Won't that be grand? I've made arrangements for us to stay at the Waldorf Astoria. Henry Flagler and his wife will be available to dine with us on January fifth just before they leave for Palm Beach, and we are all set to leave New York on the ninth for our return to Winnipeg. You see how considerate I was in making the arrangements? What could be better than allowing me to take charge of your social engagements, my darling?" She took his hand.

Rupert looked at the tickets, then raised his eyes to Beth's fresh, open smile. Honest and true to the end, she was. He knew that she truly did love him, whether he deserved it or not. He was genuinely pleased at such an unexpected gift and made an instant decision to risk the time away.

"Oh, Beth, I am lucky to have you in my life. You have such a wonderful way of pulling me away from the tedious workings of business and politics. I shall be ever so glad to have you whisk me away on holiday."

29
Raid on the Resorts of Thomas Street
January 9, 1904

Ziporah pounded up the stairs to knock on the door of her brothers' bedroom. "Isaac! Come quick! You have a visitor waiting for you. His name's Jim McGraw and he says it's important."

"What's Jim doing here? And on a Saturday night?" Isaac threw his books aside and reached for his boots.

"He didn't say. He just asked for you. And he was very polite to Mama. He said the chicken soup smelled delicious and I'm sure she's loading his bowl with matzah balls this very minute. He's your friend from the paper, isn't he?"

"The one and only Jim McGraw." Isaac dashed past his sister and flew down the stairs to the restaurant.

"Hey, Ziggy," Jim greeted his friend. "Your ma is taking awful good care of me, here. This is one fine place to grab a good meal."

"Isaac's friends are welcome anytime." Mama was blushing at the compliment.

"Just look at all the people in here," Jim nodded toward the tables that were rapidly filling up.

"We open the restaurant on Saturday night after sundown so the people can come in for a little *nosh* after the end of the Sabbath, you see," said Hannah proudly. "We are now calling our restaurant a *delicatessen*."

"Well, thank you, ma'am, for the nosh soup. It's delicious." Jim stood and tipped his hat as Mama giggled into her hands.

"Did I say it wrong?"

"Close enough," Isaac told him with a laugh. "What brings you to Selkirk Avenue?"

"I came for you!" Jim announced, his eyes dancing with excitement. "The story of the year is about to break, and I thought you'd want to come and see it for yourself. I'll tell you about it on the way. Wanna come?"

Isaacs heart leaped. "You bet I do!"

"We have to hurry. Thanks again, Mrs. Zigman." Jim eased out past the customers who were crowding at the door waiting for a seat.

"Don't wait up for me, Ma!" Isaac shouted back over his shoulder.

"We have to take the streetcar," Jim explained as they made their way to Main Street to wait for the southbound car. "Every hack in town is tied up this evening."

"Where are we going?"

"Thomas Street."

"What?" Isaac's eyes flew open. "Oh, you mean, well, I uh … gosh."

Jim laughed out loud. "No, it's not anything like you're thinking, Ziggy. This is an actual news story." He looked around to be sure that no one was listening. "There is going to be a raid on the brothels tonight. The cops are gonna close 'em down and bring all those women in for a special court session tonight."

"What?" Isaac could feel his ears turning red.

"It's going to happen about seven when the night shift coppers come in. Every man on the force will be involved. Nobody knows anythin' about it."

"How do you know, then?"

"I can't tell you who told me. I gave my word. But it's true, all right. Here's the deal. The police commission had a special meeting this afternoon, and there was quite a bit of shouting going on. In the end, the order came down to Police Chief John McRae to shut the brothels down and to do it tonight. They've got every cab in town on standby to bring in the ladies of the trade. The days of Winnipeg's segregated red light district are coming to a close tonight, my friend. It's over."

"Why'd they pick a weekend night? Are they going to bring in the customers as well?"

"Hell, no!" Jim's head swiveled at the question. "Can you imagine the ruckus if they ever did that? How many families and businesses would be ruined? No, they would never even fine the customers, let alone arrest them. I'm not saying I agree with it, but the way our city fathers see it, this is one-sided sinning and it's only the whores that gotta pay up."

"It doesn't seem fair."

"Isaac," Jim looked at his young friend. "Now I ask you, just what can you show me that's fair in life? Fair has nothin' to do with it."

"So, why did they pick tonight?"

"Because Alderman Willows is out of town. Fact is, despite his going on about the need to clean up the vice in Winnipeg, it's an open secret that he has a lot of friends on Thomas Street. There's good reason to believe he'd tip off Minnie Woods and the other keepers and spoil the raid."

"You mean he's a customer?"

"I never heard that. I've got a list of regular customers with some pretty big names on it, but I've never seen him on it. Willows plays cards down there, but I don't know if he dabbles in the delights, if you catch my meaning. In any case, he does have some connection to the madams. Maybe he owns houses there. Whatever it is, the members of the police commission don't trust him to keep his mouth shut. It's just more likely that this raid will go smoothly without him around."

Isaac was puzzled. Why hadn't he heard any of this from his cousin, Maisie, who worked for the alderman? "So, are they going to put all the women in jail?"

"Nope," said McGraw. "Even if they wanted to, where would they put them? In with men?" He snorted at the thought. "They'll come before Magistrate Daly tonight. He's on the police commission, too. He'll hold a special session at the courthouse once they've rounded 'em all up. They'll all plead guilty and pay some fines and then they'll be encouraged to leave town."

"Do you think they will?" Isaac was picturing a line of prostitutes at the train station.

"Naw. I wouldn't count on seeing them rushin' to get out of town. One or two might, but the others are just gonna disappear into houses all over the city and start up again. They make a good pile of money in this town. They'll be harder to get rid of than ants."

"There's the streetcar," said Isaac. "I'm glad you thought to ask me along, Jim. Why did you?"

"You're smart and you got a nose for news, Ziggy. You might see something that will help me out, so keep your eyes and ears open. A lot is going to happen pretty fast. Now, don't talk about it anymore 'cause we can't risk bein' overheard."

"Boy, this will be some story for you to write." The thought of a front seat on history, especially history with such juicy appeal, thrilled seventeen-year-old Isaac to the core.

"Damn straight, Ziggy. And tomorrow being Sunday, with no paper being published, it'll give me time to write a real humdinger of a tale. I tell ya, Ziggy, we'll be talking about what we see tonight for the rest of our lives."

The next night, Isaac volunteered to switch shifts with the compositor so he could personally see to Jim's story being set properly in the *Star*.

HARLOTS HEAVED FROM HOUSES
OF ILL-FAME
Thomas Street Brothels Closed after Twenty-Two Years of Protected Existence
Eighty-four Arrested in Raid
Criminal Code to be Strictly Enforced
Painted Women Weep Woefully in Court

Winnipeg, January 11, 1904—As the sun went down on the prairie on Saturday afternoon, so too came the end of peace in the valley for keepers and inmates of the houses of ill-fame situated in the brothel colony on Thomas Street.

Lights flickered behind red curtains as brightly dressed women painted their faces for customers that they were never to see again in those houses. A well-planned secret raid by the constabulary of Winnipeg brought the swift and shocking end to a twenty-two year history of harlotry on Thomas Street, effectively snuffing out the red light district like a blazing bonfire being extinguished in a drenching downpour.

According to the new police commission, hereafter, the law relating to disorderly houses will be rigidly and entirely enforced. This was decided and unanimously agreed upon Saturday afternoon at a special meeting of the police commission. Immediately afterwards, at five-thirty o'clock, with the echoes of the shouting commissioners still lingering in the air, orders were handed to the Chief of Police to close out the social evil. His instructions were to enforce the law as it is written!

SURPRISE RAID

While the fate of the Luscious Lulus was being decided upon during the heated session of the police commission, on Thomas Street it seemed to be a Saturday afternoon like any other.

The music and loud voices had yet to take over the stillness of the street, as the sleepy inmates of the brothels roused from their slumber. As is their habit on any given day, their late hours preclude any wakeful enjoyment of the early morning light, or even the early afternoon light. On this Saturday, their Chinese houseboys had gone about their normal business, fixing meals and mending costumes.

By the time the ladies were adorned in their finery and ready for their evening visitors, by which is meant, their clientele, there had been not one sign of any unusual activity. A few early gay blades had already made their way to the seat of social evil ahead of the usual Saturday crowd and were chatting and visiting with the prairie nymphs.

Someone sat down at a piano to play a spirited tune as the evening party was warming up. One of the soiled doves stood outside refreshing herself in the brisk evening air. As she looked out across the prairie, a mournful whistle of a passing train sent a chill through her as it signaled a death knell on Thomas Street.

It was the sleigh bells she heard next and indeed there was not just one, but a string of sleighs making its way in a steady advance toward the bawdy houses.

"What's this?" said the dove as she threw her hand to forehead. "Can this be the end?"

RAIDERS NOT TOLD DESTINATION

The raiders themselves had been kept in strict secret, not being told their destination for fear that the keepers and inmates of the Thomas resorts would be warned and would spirit themselves away under the cover of darkness. One or two officers were seen shaking their heads, saying they were in disagreement with the plan to bust up the brothel district.

"It ain't fair to suddenly be changing the rules on the dolls, in this way," one policeman was heard to say. "We just can't be looking out for all of them if they up and move into town to all kinds of different streets. It ain't right at all to be doing this with no warning at all."

Meanwhile, officers had also been posted in livery stables, warned to be ready to stop carriages from leaving, should there be telephone calls for transportation to come fetch the harlots.

Upon arrival, Police Chief John McRae posted guards on the back lane to keep a watchful eye for anyone who might try to leave by the back doors. Then at each house, an officer entered from the front door and shouted out the announcement that "all within, except the customers, are now under arrest!"

It was then that the sporting women shrank back in their colorful evening dresses, shrieking in disbelief as they were gripped by the realization that the iron hand of the law had formed a fist that was about to smash down hard on the Scarlet Sin in Winnipeg!

SPECIAL COURT SESSION SATURDAY NIGHT

In all, eighty women and four men were arrested. The men were all let go. As the police sorted out the criminals and escorted them into the taxis to be transported to the courthouse, there was soon among them a large gathering of onlookers and unsatisfied customers watching the uproar on Thomas Street. With truth, it can be said that a goodly number of them joined in the rumpus with jeering and shouting. It can also be said that there were equal numbers of people yelling in defense of the ladies.

As there were many more arrested ladies to bring into town than there were cabs available, several trips had to be made to transport all of the madams and their girls. Down at the courthouse, it wasn't long before the onlookers formed a sort of parade, picking up more folks as they went along until the crowd at the court was three and four deep, maybe numbering up to five hundred of these sightseers lining up to get a good look at the fallen women. And look they did, upon the jewelry and fine furs and great hats with jewels and feathers atop golden tresses. With rouged cheeks and bright red lips, the ladies of the evening marched past the gaping onlookers and filed into night court to appear before Magistrate Thomas Daly.

All of the women pleaded guilty except one, a little old gray-haired lady who said her name was Mary Johnson. She cried out loud and was in just a plain awful state. Mrs. Johnson told the court she had been employed as a seamstress and that she had been out there "just to do sewing work for a couple of weeks because she needed the money real bad". She was presently allowed to leave after the girls vouched for her story.

FORTY DOLLAR FINES FOR FLOOZIES

Having sorted out the affairs of Mrs. Johnson, Magistrate Daly then had to work some to get the crowded courtroom quieted down so he could conduct the business for which they had been assembled.

"Am I to understand now that you all plead guilty?" Magistrate Daly bawled from the bench, having had all the arrested stand at once and answer to their charges as one.

The answer came in a chorus of affirmation, whereat the Magistrate meted out fines of $40 plus costs to the keepers of the houses, of which there were twelve. Each of the inmates was fined $20 and costs. All were given a stern warning that should they come back to his court the fines would be much worse and that there would be no mercy against the promoters of the scarlet sin. He urged them to get out of town.

CUSTOMERS FIND CLOSED DOORS

Later on Saturday night, Thomas Street was crowded with men who had come by the brothels knowing nothing of the closing. Also in attendance were many other folks who came to watch the hapless would-be patrons as they rang doorbells and knocked on doors and shouted aloud in the street, only to be turned away from the houses where the lights were turned low and the fortunes had turned dark.

As the social evil on Thomas Street has fallen to the law of the land, so too has silence fallen on the thunderous denunciations from the pulpits of Winnipeg against the lack of political will to enforce the Criminal Code of Canada. Sunday morning sermons following the raid brought words of praise for the police action of Saturday night.

ACTION FOLLOWS PLEAS FROM THE PULPITS

The raid on the Thomas Street brothels follows months of impassioned sermons from the group of clergy banded together to crusade for moral reform under the organization known as the Ministerial Association. Their scathing denunciation of the police commission for allowing the evil to continue unimpeded in the face of the law was of great concern in the campaigns leading up to civic elections last month that brought in the new city council.

Among the most eloquent of those Sunday sermons was a roaring oration delivered by the Rev. J.B. Silcox on November 15, 1903, of which the following is quoted directly from the sermon, for the benefit of readers who do not go to church: "On the western suburbs of our fair city, defiant of the nation's laws against their existence, there stands in unblushing impudence the house of her whose steps take hold on hell. The city has allowed that monstrous iniquity to exist and thrive year after year. Into their swinish precincts the youth of the city are lured to debauchery and death. The malaria of that foul and festering mass of moral rottenness spreads its blight over every hearth and home.

"We quarantine the house where scarlet fever rages, why not the house where the scarlet sin is rampant? For three years the Ministerial Association has been trying in quiet ways to enforce the law of the land against this plague spot of iniquity, this hell-hole of licentiousness, this cesspool of damnable corruption, that with cancerous persistency had festered itself as an institution on our fair young city. We have not asked for new laws, simply for the impartial enforcement of laws already enacted.

"The blame and the shame must be fastened on the men

who are responsible for it—the police commissioners."

NEW ERA AHEAD

The Ministerial Association believes the decisive action in closing down Thomas Street leaves no doubt that a new era of superior morality has begun in the great City of Winnipeg.

As for the painted ladies, it appears that they may still be quietly living among the good folks of Winnipeg, as following the raid, newspaper men waiting about the train station have seen no evidence of a flock of soiled doves taking flight to leave these here parts by train or any other form of transportation. There was a report of just one woman, an American sporting lady, who was seen at the train station on Sunday, quitting Winnipeg to head for Deadwood Gulch, South Dakota, from whence she came.

30
Grand Opening
July 20, 1904

Ater a full year of construction, the new office building of Willows and Sons was ready to be officially opened. That the weather had cooperated with a stunningly beautiful day, bathed in sunshine, was taken as a sign of good luck by Rupert, who was almost giddy with excitement.

"Alfred! Please, do hurry. We are going to be late for our own celebration!" Rupert shouted up to the second floor while pacing the entrance hall at Ravenscraig.

"I'm right here, Father." Alfred emerged not from upstairs, but from the library. "I was just on the telephone with the mayor's office. He has had a change in schedule and can join us for the ribbon cutting but will have to leave before the reception with the newspapermen. However, Mayor Sharpe promises he will not miss the opportunity to congratulate you tonight at the celebration dinner at the Manitoba Club."

"Fine, fine, Alfred. I see no disadvantage to that. The newspapers will have me to quote for their stories for the morning editions, and not the mayor. Not a bad outcome for us, old chap!"

The timing of the opening was critical and Rupert had removed every barrier in order to not delay the launch. The Eaton's company was set to have its groundbreaking ceremony for its grand new department store on Portage Avenue the following week. By having the Grand Opening of the Willows building today, Rupert would have the chance to focus attention on his part in the construction of the mammoth store.

Why on earth John Craig Eaton decided to build on Portage Avenue, so far from the commercial centre on Main, Rupert could not imagine. However, while Eaton might have made a mistake, as long as his money was good, who cared where he built his store?

Rupert was in exceptionally good humor. He joked and sang all the way to the office, and Alfred slowly felt the tension of the last few months start to ease. He took a deep breath and smiled as they bumped along Main Street in his father's new vehicle, the only Packard in Winnipeg.

"I see you are much better acquainted with the workings of the motorcar, Father," Alfred said. "But given the number of times it stalls, would it not be faster to have had Henry drive us in the carriage?"

"Of course it would have been faster," Rupert laughed. "But that's hardly the point, dear lad. Just look at all of these people staring at us. There is no equaling the feeling of being conspicuously successful! Don't you agree?"

Alfred felt his jaw tighten. Father did know how to boast.

The Willows Building was an impressive addition to the heart of the commercial district. Sitting in grand prominence on Main Street next to Ashdown's Store, it was positioned to catch the attention of all the Main Street traffic heading to City Hall or into the wholesale district. Rupert had taken particular care to be sure the Willows name would also be grandly displayed, making the bronze sign large enough to be clearly seen, yet small enough to not be accused of looking overly showy. He wanted to be recognized, not criticized, and deciding this seemingly small detail took days of agony. He was extremely pleased with the result, judging the sign to look perfectly elegant, as it stood bracketed by marble pillars and enhanced by the intricate ironwork over the main entrance.

Willows and Sons occupied the top two floors, while offices on the lower two were leased to other businesses. Rupert had spared no expense in the design and furnishings and already the building had been declared by the *Winnipeg Star* to be the most impressive new office address in Winnipeg.

Everything was going wonderfully. After months of worry, Rupert was allowing himself to believe he had escaped the long reach of scandal from the brothel raids as ably as he had the blackmail matter. The payments to Ira Volinsky continued and he had heard nothing more from the man. He rarely thought of either issue any more. Not one word had been published regarding the ownership of the former bordellos on Thomas Street. The only mention of Thomas Street at all concerned the street's name change to Minto, to honor Lord Minto, Canada's retiring governor general.

It was Rupert's idea to commemorate Lord Minto's visit to Winnipeg with the street naming, and City Council quickly agreed. The memory of that happy afternoon, filled as it was with pomp and circumstance, brought a smile to Rupert's lips. Lord Minto appeared deeply touched by the recognition bestowed upon him and he had spoken very warmly about the large and enthusiastic crowds that came out to see him in Winnipeg. It was the perfect solution to bury the insalubrious past of the street, and of course Lord Minto would never be told a thing about the former brothels.

Indeed, Rupert felt he had acted too hastily in transferring the property titles to Alfred and was now sorry that he had done it. It was not that he was concerned about enriching his son's holdings at the expense of his own. That was of no issue at all. His only concern was that he was unable to tell Alfred about the transfer for fear of doing serious damage to their relationship. Alfred was blessed with a keen intellect and a sharp mind. He would see immediately that Rupert had set him up to take the fall should there have been a scandal. Rupert would have to find a clever way to either transfer the houses back to himself or to tell Alfred about his new holdings without upsetting his son. In any case, that would be a problem for another day. Today was for celebration.

He pulled the car up in front of the office and shooed his son inside to ensure that all was in readiness. A doorman rushed out to place stands with ropes at both the front and the rear of the Packard to be sure no drayman would attempt to bring a wagon too close to the car.

"Good afternoon, Rodney," Rupert addressed the uniformed man. "Please be sure to extend your barriers to allow space for the carriages to drop their passengers directly in front of my car. Mrs. Willows and the rest of my family will be along shortly, and the dignitaries will be arriving at any time. And do give a quick sweep to this unsightly dust on the boardwalk. Oh, and you'll find cleaning cloths and the like in the boot of the car. Be sure to attend immediately to any splashes. Don't let any of those street urchins get near my automobile!"

Rupert reached into the rear seat and pulled out a package. "Here." He thrust the parcel into the doorman's hands. "I brought a sack of candy to help you persuade those young hoodlums to keep their bloody hands off my car."

Before entering the building, Rupert walked across Main Street to see for himself how impressive the new building looked with the Packard sitting in front like an expensive piece of art. The sidewalk was crowded with shoppers streaming into the Ashdown Store. He watched as people slowed to point at the car and he imagined their conversations. In his mind all of their talk was about how Rupert Willows was making a grand contribution to Winnipeg's growing commercial sector. He was almost bursting with pride.

As Rupert luxuriated in his moment, Alfred took charge inside. He surveyed the lobby with a well-informed eye and immediately set to work to adjust the setting to meet his father's expectations. The flowers were in the wrong place. There was no riser behind the podium to bring Rupert to the height he would insist was correct. And worst of all, there were too many chairs. Rupert had been quite adamant that there be "standing room only" for the newspapermen to write about. That would have to be engineered. Alfred snapped his fingers and half the chairs were removed. As the employees bustled about under his direction, Alfred took heart in the fact that in just ninety minutes all the tension would be behind them, the ribbon will have been cut and the newsmen would be running along to their next stories.

The stress of getting the Willows Building finished and properly launched was wearing on the whole family, not to mention the employees of the building company. Moving the executive offices from the construction yard to Main Street was as important to Alfred as it was to his father, but for different reasons, though he had been careful not to reveal them. At long last, he could emerge from his father's shadow and define his own role as the company's operations manager. He relished the thought of his father spending less time meddling in his work and more in the boardrooms of Winnipeg and Toronto. Rupert could make the deals, leaving Alfred to run the projects. He was going to prove his worth; perhaps even his father would recognize it one day.

"Alfred!" Rupert smiled widely as he entered the building. "Wonderful job. Everything looks just right. Is my speech at the podium?"

"It is, and the water glass is filled and ready for you as well. I must say, Father, the building does look very fine and makes an impressive addition to the streetscape."

"Ah ha! And tell me again about your concerns regarding location," Rupert teased.

"Must I?" Alfred turned away from his father for a moment so that he would not be seen rolling his eyes. The man was always so greatly in need of compliments. "I do admit I am sorry that I fought so hard against your choice of address," Alfred nodded to his father. "Yes, there is enormous value in being next to Ashdown's and so close to City Hall. It was only the high price of the land that caused me concern, you understand.

"I wish you many happy and prosperous years in your new office, Father."

"Thank you, son." Rupert was genuinely touched. "I very much appreciate your talent and your wise counsel in these matters. It might not always seem that way to you, but I mean it. You are a strong asset to the company."

The thought of a giving his son a gift of appreciation suddenly came to mind and Rupert's eyes brightened with inspiration. What a perfect idea! He could drop his Thomas Street problem by creating papers with today's date instead of the true date of the property transfer. If the transfer was framed as a gift, it would result in a brilliant solution to his sticky problem.

Alfred couldn't help but notice the change in his father's demeanor.

"What is it? Do we need to change something in the room, Father? I can see you thinking."

"No, no, Alfred, everything is perfect. In fact, I have a

surprise for you, but I will save telling it to you until this evening. Alfred, the minute you see Percival Wright, tell him I need to seem him after the ceremony, will you?"

"Of course. Is there something I should know about? Are you buying more real estate?"

"All will be told in good time, son. Now, I see the newspapermen are starting to arrive and I need a little time to gather my thoughts. I'll be in my office."

Wright would certainly be able to work up the new real estate papers, and Alfred would never be the wiser. It was a perfect solution. Rupert chuckled to himself. He would tell his son the good news before the dinner reception this evening.

Rupert took a moment alone to admire his office and its rich furnishings. It almost took his breath away, it had come out so well. He loved the way the room was almost entirely covered in mirrors, ornately trimmed in heavy gold frames. It was his recent trip to Paris with Beth that led to the design decision. His son, Elliot had insisted on taking them to visit the Palace of Versailles. So impressed was Rupert with the exquisite Hall of Mirrors, that he immediately determined that his office would carry a similar rich theme. He was tremendously pleased with the look of his surroundings and couldn't wait to conduct business here.

Life was very good, indeed, this bright summer day. Oh, how wonderful to be admired for success! No one had to know how he had depleted his bank account to shore up his image. He had several projects on the go and a few irons in the fire. Rupert was a gambler who believed there was always more money to be made. All he needed was to stick to what he knew best: charming people into investing in his schemes. As long as there was enough money coming in to pay his obligations on his debts, no one would be any the wiser regarding his tight finances. He would make it work. After all, success was mostly about what people thought of you. Rupert could almost taste the money.

There was a knock at his door. "We're ready for you, Father," Alfred called. "Everyone is here."

"Excellent. Let's have a bit of fun, shall we?"

"Mr. Willows! A word with you, please, Alderman Willows!"

The newspapermen shouted out at him as he stepped off the elevator and made his way to the podium. He felt like a god. He had finally reached the goal that he'd pursued for so many years. He was a powerbroker and an admired business leader. People wanted his opinion. Rupert was beside himself with happiness.

The program went precisely as planned. The planted questions and compliments from his staff members were shouted from the floor, and Rupert made a great show of expressing his pride in Winnipeg and the future of the commercial sector. Flashbulbs popped, cigars were handed about, and the president of Willows & Sons was roundly congratulated on his speech and his wonderful new building. The afternoon newspapers were effusive in their positive comments about the grand opening and praised the new office building for its magnificence and innovation.

What Rupert didn't know was that this joyous time was to be short-lived. In just three months, his world would crumble into what he would later call the dark times. But not today. Today, it was summer in Winnipeg and Rupert Willows was the talk of the town. There were parties and dinners and important men seeking his opinion. And everywhere he turned it seemed there were beautiful women fluttering about, desirous of his attention. He had truly arrived.

31
Million Dollar Fire
Oct. 11, 1904

Ziporah's heart was pounding as she shook her snoring brother. "Isaac! Wake up. There's a fire!" She whispered loudly enough to reach through his deep sleep, but not so loud as to wake Aaron and Mendel nearby.

"What? Here?" Isaac sat bolt upright.

"No, shh. Let the boys sleep. Downtown. It's a big one. We can see it from our back lane. It might be City Hall. You better hurry. The paper will be looking for you."

Ziporah pushed her new woolen scarf at him as he flew out of the door. "Take your bicycle!"

"No, there'll be a crowd and it might get stolen," he called back.

"Be careful!"

Isaac ran along King Street, astonished by the eerie look of the golden skyline. A strong southeast wind drove the smoke straight at him as raced downtown. Cutting onto Main Street, he could see that fire was south of City Hall. Fear clutched him. Not Ashdown's! He drew the scarf over his face against the choking smoke and pounded on. The sight of the monstrous blaze stopped him in his tracks as he rounded the corner. Droves of people shouted and pushed to get a better look at the spectacle. The brand new Bulman Block, the city's most modern print shop, had turned into a roaring inferno. It was on Bannatyne, across from the Ashdown's store. Whipped hard by the wind, the flames were licking the adjacent buildings that fronted onto Main. Hundreds of people were in the street and on the rooftops working a frenzied bucket brigade to splash water on threatened buildings. Firemen shouted their frustrations as they directed weak streams of water into the blaze from fire hoses splayed in the streets. It was clear the fire was going to destroy the building, for not a drop of water reached past the second floor.

Isaac was a half-block away when the explosion happened. Windows burst, sending balls of flame into the night sky, and shooting shards of glass down into the screaming crowd that had gathered to gawk at the spectacle.

"The fire has spread to the Woodbine Hotel!" someone shouted.

"And the Duffin Block!"

"The whole street is going to go!"

Isaac counted six fire brigade rigs, their horses frothing in terror. Looking up, he watched desperate residents toss furniture and other goods from the top floors in a bid to save their possessions. He was stunned at how quickly hooligans rushed in to trample the property and carry pieces off. The hysteria of looting quickly spread through the throng.

"Look!" someone shouted. "The fire has jumped across Main to the Ashdown Store!"

Isaac was horrified. As he watched, a strong gust of wind came up and the fire instantly claimed the roof of the store. The scorching heat pushed the crowd back.

"Clear out of the way! Fire brigade coming through!" The fire captain shouted to create an opening.

Isaac jumped aside as four more rigs, hauled by wild-eyed horses, churned up Main Street with bells clanging. He turned away and began to push his way along, hoping to circle the fire to the newspaper office on McDermot, a block away.

"Ziggy! Hey Ziggy!"

It took a moment to realize it was Jim McGraw.

"Where are you going, kid?"

"The paper. They'll need help with the extra edition, Jim. I've got to get over there."

"They'll be needing help writing the story so they have something to print!" McGraw yelled over the roar. "There are bucket brigades on the rooftops all the way to McDermot, including some on the *Star* building and the fire station back there in Market Square. But there are only two other reporters here, Ziggy, and this hardware store is gonna blow! Ashdown's is loaded with paint and turpentine and all kinds of shit. And it's hunting season, so who knows how many boxes of ammunition and gunpowder he's got loaded in there."

He pulled a notebook out of his pocket and shoved it at Isaac's chest.

"Ziggy, I need your help. You know what I'm looking for, and you can find it as fast as I can. Head around back to Albert Street. That's where the big crews are right now. I'm told there's a family of Italians living in a shack back there, but don't waste too much time on them unless someone's been killed. Follow the action. Once the Bulman Block comes down, get back up front here on Main. I'm going to find James Ashdown. If you see Rupert Willows, latch on to him. His new building will go next. It's right there, next door to Ashdown's, and by the look of things, it won't be more than ten minutes before it goes up."

Isaac stood, gripped with fear. Jim grabbed his shoulder and gave him a rough shake.

"Isaac! Wake up! You ain't a kid anymore! With this wind, this fire might go all the way to Union Bank Tower and City Hall. And if that happens, God help us, we may lose the entire downtown, and maybe even everything north of here. Now go!"

Isaac ran. Gripping his notepad, he ran past the flames and across the line that separated his youth from his manhood. The smoke choked him, and his eyes were burning by the time he got to the back of Ashdown's store. There, the Italian family members were clutching one another, their store ablaze. Behind him, he heard glass breaking. Looters threw bricks through storefront windows, fighting each other for position. Scrambling over the broken glass, they grabbed at crates of fruits and vegetables, then ran wildly down the street so as not to be caught stealing what surely was going to burn. A starving family would eat apples tonight.

The chaotic scene numbed Isaac's senses. It seemed the whole world had gone mad as the wind sent sparks showering down on the crowd. Suddenly, the fire chief was there, yelling and waving furiously in the direction of the Bulman Block.

"Get the hell out of the there! Move! Move now! That building is coming down!"

Firemen scattered, dragging hoses and shouting. "Get back!

Get out of the way! Make room!" The shouting was drowned out by the deafening crash as the building thundered into the street in an avalanche of bricks and splintered timber. Screaming and crying pierced the din for a moment, as if the monstrous fire had taken a giant breath. Then the explosions began as the blaze ignited the ammunition at the front of the Ashdown store.

The crowd came alive with panic. People ran for their lives, women screaming, children crying, men cursing. Isaac sprinted from under the falling cinders and then whirled to watch the inferno, panting with fear, overcome with the certainty that he was not cut out to be a newspaperman.

He willed his nerves to settle. Jim was counting on him. Get the story. Do the job. He made his way over the fallen bricks and smoking debris on Main Street to the north side of Ashdown's where the Willows Block was now in flames.

He spotted Mayor Sharpe, who was climbing from a carriage, helped by Alderman Willows.

"Dear God in heaven, Rupert!" shouted the mayor. "Those hoses have no pressure!"

"We need more water in the mains! The pressure keeps dropping," Willows yelled back over the noise as Isaac moved closer.

"That's all the pressure we've got. There's not enough water!"

"We can get more," shouted Willows. "We can pump in river water through the old pumping station on the Assiniboine."

Mayor Sharpe shook his head.

"The one up by your house? We can't do that. The water is dirty from sewage, and that pumping station hasn't been used for years. It might not work anymore."

Willows threw up his hands and as if on cue, the flames roared through the roof of his building.

"It's all we've got, Your Worship! This could be as bad as the Chicago fire if we don't get more water. Bulman's, Ashdown's, and my building are already lost. With this wind we'll lose everything including City Hall."

Mayor Sharpe looked stricken. He nodded. "Where is the fire chief?"

Seeing his opportunity, Isaac shouted over the din.

"I know where he is! I just saw him."

Within seconds, he was off in a dead run, dispatched by the mayor to deliver the order to open the Assiniboine River pumping station to save the city.

A short time later, a cheer rang out from the crowd as the force of the streams visibly grew. And as if in answer to a prayer, the wind abated. With renewed energy the firefighters set to their task and gained control of the spreading flames. Slowly, the fire weakened, then finally submitted; the smoking, soggy ruins hissing into the darkness.

Through the night at the *Winnipeg Star*, the story took shape. With the electricity out in the building, the reporters pulled oil lamps from a closet to provide enough light to work. Isaac pounded away at his typewriter and then, as the deadline loomed, he dashed to the Linotype machine to help ready the pages for printing.

In just hours, the heart of Winnipeg's business district had been decimated by a million dollar fire. The newspapers all gave high praise to the men who fought the fire and prevented it from spreading beyond downtown. Amazingly, not one person died. The most serious injury was suffered by a fireman who lost a finger. It was pinched off in an accident with the pumping equipment.

McGraw hustled into the composing room as Isaac was getting ready to leave for home an hour before sunup.

"Hey, Ziggy! Come on! We're all going to the Marriagi Hotel. Frank, the owner, is putting up sandwiches and coffee for all the firemen and the newspaper guys. You gotta come along. You're a newspaper man, Isaac Zigman!"

Isaac smiled through his exhaustion. This is what it felt like to be intensely alive.

Two miles away in Armstrong's Point, the clock struck seven in the morning, and Rupert considered whether he wanted another brandy or a cup of coffee. He, too, had been up the whole night. His beautiful new building had been destroyed. Everything was gone. The lovely mirrored walls in his office, the paintings from Europe, the hand-crafted leather chairs, the Persian rug from Sotheby's. All gone. It would be months before he would have an office again. What was to become of his business? His only hope was his insurance, and that was a long shot. He didn't even have his policy to review, for it, too, had been claimed by the fire. Perhaps even his beloved Ravenscraig would have to be sold. He was lost in despair. With his bank account depleted in the construction of the new office building, there was little left to hold things together until he could rebuild. If he could rebuild.

He sighed deeply, vaguely aware that the telephone was ringing. Then Chadwick was looming over him. What was he saying?

"Mr. Willows, It's a call from New York," Chadwick repeated, his tone softened with sympathy. "Mr. Henry Flagler of the Standard Oil Company. Will you take it or would you prefer that I take a message?"

Rupert motioned that he would take the call. He hadn't spoken with Flagler for some time. His American friend had been busy with developing hotel properties and a railroad in Florida.

"Hello, Henry?"

"Willows, are you all right, old chap?"

"Henry. Henry, well, how very good to hear from you," Rupert fought to focus.

"You sound terrible, Rupert. Were you hurt in the fire?" Flagler's voice rose over the crackling on the telephone line.

"No, no, thank you for your concern. None of us was hurt, Henry. How do you know about the fire?"

"It's all over the front page of the *New York Times* that the whole of central Winnipeg was on fire, and I wanted to be sure that you were all right," Flagler's voice came through more strongly. "Can you hear, me?"

"Yes, I can and yes, it was a terrible disaster. Several office buildings burned to the ground. It was a great loss. It is quite amazing that no one was killed. It flared up again at half past three this morning but it's all under control now."

"And your business? Were you spared?"

"We lost our new office building, Henry. We were wiped out."

"I'm wiring some money to you to tide you over, Rupert."

Rupert was deeply moved as hope rose out of the darkness. "Oh, dear. I don't know what to say. That's very generous, Henry. I really can't accept, but how very kind of you to be thinking of us." But Henry Flagler would consider no protest from Rupert.

Listening from around the corner, Chadwick noted his employer's strengthening tone as he went on to explain the details of the tragedy, and how fortunate it was that injuries were minimal.

"Well, yes," he heard Rupert finally say into the telephone, "if you really do insist, I would be very grateful for the loan. You are a very good friend, indeed, Henry."

Chadwick could hardly contain himself. Mr. Henry Flagler! One of the richest men in America is calling to offer his assistance. Perhaps things were not so dire, after all. Chadwick was much relieved; he would have some good news to report below stairs to the worried household staff. Every one of them was wondering how long it would be before jobs were cut in the wake of the disaster.

32
Something in the Water
October 14, 1904

The fire was the largest ever seen in the Manitoba capital, and for several days it seemed the only topic of discussion among the citizenry as they came to the shocking realization that Winnipeg had come to the very brink of destruction. While there was no loss of life reported, there were many stories of financial devastation among businesses and homeowners that had little or no insurance.

The ghastly sight of the blackened ruins and heaps of debris quickly became a prime local attraction, complete with enterprising pushcart vendors loaded with fresh sandwiches and pastries to sell to the throngs of gawkers and treasure seekers who pawed through the rubble.

There was much public praise for both the brave work of the volunteer fire fighters and the quick thinking of Mayor Sharpe in ordering the use of the Assiniboine River water to increase the water pressure needed to get control of the fire. Rupert was initially miffed that his influence in convincing the mayor to take this action went unreported, but the truth was he had many more serious problems that demanded his attention.

Ravenscraig had fallen under a gloom of uncertainty that matched the somber October sky. With the terrible financial loss suffered by Willows & Sons, there was a great deal of insecurity about the future, and the household staff members did their best to move calmly through their duties despite the palpable tension.

Maisie fought to hold onto her belief that in time everything would return to normal. She opened the kitchen tap and started to fill the crystal water jug. "Mrs. Butterfield, does this water look all right to you? It seems a little off. Perhaps we ought not to be using it."

"We're in a hurry, Maisie. Madame is waiting," Mrs. Butterfield snapped as she waddled to the sink and nudged

Maisie over.

"Lets have a look. Hmm. Seems all right to me. Just a bit of a summer smell to it. Odd this time of year. Run it through a cheese cloth, and it will be fine. Mrs. Willows will be in a frightful mood if the water jug is not on her table in five minutes. When you're done, just set in on that tray and I'll take it up. And don't forget to chip the ice to put into it."

Maisie followed her orders uneasily. She closed her eyes and smelled the freshly filled water pitcher. Nothing seemed amiss. But how unusual to have poor quality water this late in October when it was too cold for algae to grow. And how would algae get into artesian wells? As soon as Mrs. Butterfield left the kitchen with the tray for Mrs. Willows, Maisie filled a large kettle and several pots with water and set them to boil. It was easy enough to bring the water up to top quality, she thought. Everyone knew that boiled water was safe from contamination. Well, everyone with a medical text tucked under a bed. It was always better to be safe than sorry.

Mrs. Willows had been particularly anxious this week; she was hoping to hear good news from her husband regarding the fire insurance. Despite the bits of positive news that had filtered in from Chadwick, the servants were also a bit on edge. Maisie twitched at the thought of the conversation she'd had with Henry, the chauffeur, about it. She had been suggesting to Henry that anyone with the low moral character of their employer deserved to suffer hard times once in a while. She added that she wouldn't mind one bit if he had to give up his fine cigars and his lavish parties to impress his friends.

Henry took no time to set her straight. "Are ya daft, lass? How long do you think you would keep yer job if His Nibs loses all that money? Time to open yer eyes and see what's goin' on around here."

Well, at least things seemed to be going well with the construction of the big Eaton's store. Thank goodness Mr. Willows had his share of that building project. The new department store was taking up almost all his time and seemed to be bringing in enough money to maintain the home in the usual manner.

In the meantime, she had her studies. And she had a study partner. Mr. Willows would likely need to be hospitalized if he knew that his son was studying with the parlor maid, but Mr. James seemed to think that with their strict rules of secrecy, that they were in no danger of being discovered. She was glad it had worked out as well as it did.

They were good study partners. Mr. James supplied the books and the assignments, and she stayed awake late into the night poring over the materials. They arranged secret meetings to discuss assignments and James always complimented her on her thoroughness. She was beginning to feel that she might really have her chance in life. She felt so fortunate. Could it be that she would truly be a doctor one day?

Mr. James was actually very smart, she had learned, but impatient about getting through the material. He was very much a gentleman and treated her respectfully. He clearly was not interested in romance, at least, not with her. But would he find it so impossible to throw her an appreciative glance once in a while? She hardly looked like a cow. Or did she? Was she plain? Unappealing, perhaps? Stop it! It was nonsense to think that a man of his standing would have anything to do with a maid. Ha! And a Jewish maid at that. There's an explosive bit of history to toss into the mix. No, he would have his fine life with one of those sappy, childish women who traveled in his circle and Maisie would achieve her dream to be a doctor. Nothing else mattered if she had that.

Now all she needed to do was figure out how to be accepted into medical school and how to pay for her education. The textbook work was one thing but without a university education and a degree in medicine she would be nowhere.

The whistling of the kettle punctured her daydreams, and she set to work providing a proper supply of safe drinking water for the Willows household. She would take things one step at a time.

Just a week later, relief came to the household. Rupert could hardly wait for the telephone connection to be made before he started to shout. "Hello, hello, Alfred? Can you hear me? Yes, yes. I have very good news. Please come home quickly so I don't have to share it with everyone who is joining us on this telephone line.

"Louise, I know you are listening, and I know you believe that as a telephone operator that is your job, but, please be a dear and wait for real news before you ring up everyone in town. Would you do that, darling?"

Rupert hung up the phone and launched into an impromptu jig, just as Beth was coming through the door.

"And which darling of yours might that have been on the telephone?" she asked with just a hint of jealousy in her voice.

Ignoring her tone, Rupert drew his wife into his arms, held her close and danced her into a waltz to music only he could hear. He looked deeply into her eyes, and she started to warm under the heat of his charm. He smiled and kissed her on the forehead. "There is only one sweetheart for me, my love, and that is you, my precious Beth."

She threw her head back and laughed. She knew it was a lie but she didn't care. He was hers. At this moment, he was hers.

"My goodness, aren't we in fine humor, Rupert."

Seduced by her husband's playfulness, she responded with restrained affection. He danced and hummed, snuggling her hair and kissing her ear. She relaxed to his rhythm and then, humming along with him, gradually melted, reminded of a dance like this one years ago when she first said yes to him.

"My, my, Rupert, we are in a frisky mood. There must be good news."

"There must be champagne, my dearest one."

"Champagne? My goodness, it is not yet four o'clock! It would be scandalous!"

"Then, let's be scandalous. Let's celebrate my good fortune to have taken out an insurance policy that will not only replace the lost building, but will allow us to enjoy a few of life's pleasures as well. Isn't life grand? Beth, my love, I do believe it is time we paid a visit to Henry Flagler in Palm Beach. I would like to pay back his loan to me in person. Winter is so very hard, darling, and he wants us to meet his new wife.

"Oh, please say yes. It will be such fun. It will be so lovely to sit beneath the palm trees and listen to the ocean. Just like a honeymoon. It would be a second honeymoon for us."

Beth fought to make a pout, "But it is such a long, dreary train ride to Florida."

"Oh, come now, darling," said Rupert as he whirled her into an elaborate turn. "Henry has just finished construction on his new home. He calls it Whitehall. It is a wedding gift, in fact, for Mary. Do you remember those fellows, Carrère and Hastings, who did the bank here? They are utterly famous now. They designed the New York Public Library. Can you believe that Flagler contracted them to build his home in Florida? It has more than fifty rooms and a ballroom for three hundred and fifty guests. He insists we must stay. He and Mary will travel there right after New Year, and so should we. Say yes, my love." He kissed her deeply.

"Yes." Feeling light as a feather, Beth gasped with happiness as she thought about the shopping she would have to do before they left for Palm Beach.

33
Epidemic
October 25, 1904

I saac hunched over his work at the Linotype machine in total concentration, his fingers flying over the keys. He needed to get home to the schoolwork that was waiting for him.

It was becoming harder to concentrate on his school assignments. He would be the first in his family to go to university, and the weight of expectations was enormous. Yet, since the fire, he could feel the newspaper taking hold of his life. A new road had opened before him. He had won praise for his writing and had been invited to apprentice as a copywriter.

Most important, since the fire he had been welcomed by the other reporters and editors to join them at their regular gatherings at the Mariaggi Hotel. All the news people met at the Mariaggi, as did the men who conducted their business in the Grain Exchange. It was the place to argue politics, current events and business trends, and Isaac Zigman had been invited to join. He could hardly believe his good fortune. Maybe they didn't know he was Jewish. Maybe they didn't care. A lot had happened in the two weeks since the fire.

Just another few minutes, and he'd be finished work. He adjusted the visor over his eyes and stretched the weariness out of his back before taking a deep breath and bending to the task of typing in the last few lines. As tired as he was, there was something about the feel of the keyboard and the rhythmic music of the Linotype machine that filled him with a sense of accomplishment. He was so caught up in his work that he jumped when Jim McGraw came up behind him and brought his fists up in a playful jab.

"Well, if it isn't our new star reporter back in the salt mines."

"Jim! I thought you were in Toronto. When did you get back?" Isaac was genuinely pleased to see his friend.

"They called me back to work on this story about the bloody typhoid. The hospital is crawling with sick folks."

"What do you mean? It's almost November. We had a bad bout of it last summer, but that's long gone."

"There ya go, thinkin' like a guy typing up stories, not reporting them, Isaac. I keep tellin' ya to open your eyes to what's goin' on around you."

Isaac smelled a trap. McGraw looked like he was gearing up for one of his practical jokes. Well, this time he wasn't going to fall for it and end up in yet another wild goose chase.

"Jim, you know I live right on Selkirk Avenue, the heart of the North End," said Isaac. "You could not ask for a more central location for typhoid in this city, and I tell you it's quiet."

"Aw, you know so much. Why don't you come with me over to the hospital and we'll see what's goin' on? I could use some extra help. I got tickets to the new vaudeville show in from New York, and Maggie is expecting me to fetch her in time for that curtain. Be a sport, will ya? Here's the thing: I'll introduce you around, you write the first draft of the story for me, see, and I'll share my fee with you. What do you say? We know you can write. Come on, I know you're itchin' to do it." He pulled a cigar from his coat pocket and slapped Isaac's shoulder in one fluid motion.

Isaac hesitated as he arranged the last few metal lines of type in the frame that would be the front page. His composing work was done, homework was waiting, and now here's McGraw with an offer too tempting to turn down.

"All right. Only, you don't think this will get me in trouble, do you?"

"Not a chance. Get that grease smudge off your face, and let's get moving. Yeehaw!"

Isaac laughed out loud at the boisterous McGraw and wondered what if felt like to take life so boldly into your hands.

The hospital was crowded with people waiting to be seen. Standing in a corner, McGraw pointed out familiar faces among the visitors in the hospital corridors, reciting who owned which business and who had come into wealth through investments in real estate.

"Look around. This ain't your ordinary epidemic. These folks have been hit hard, and I don't think we can count this as one of those plagues you studied as a kid, where God sent in locusts and floods and all that to punish people. This is going to be a big story."

"So, it's typhoid," Isaac agreed, trying hard to look grown up and sophisticated. "So what? Winnipeg gets hundreds of cases a year. Where's the story?"

"Where's the story? Are you kiddin' me? This typhoid epidemic is slamming the upper class families, you dope. Does that not strike you as a big story, lino-boy?"

Isaac flushed.

"Sure, I guess. I just never saw the paper take typhoid seriously before."

Jim pulled Isaac into a quiet corridor and put a hand on his shoulder. "I don't mean any disrespect in what I'm going to tell you, Ziggy, but, you see, no one cares about the folks in your neighborhood. Jews, Ukrainians, Poles, all those East European immigrants don't figure high on the list of attention getters for the front page. I don't say that to hurt your feelings or anything, you know."

"Oh, I understand. It's just true." Isaac dropped his eyes.

"But just wait and see what happens when word gets out these are rich families coming down with the typhoid. I tell you, folks in Winnipeg are about to have a whole different view of how serious this disease is when people with good names start droppin' dead. No offense," McGraw shrugged. "C'mon, Ziggy. I'll introduce you to some people."

The director was in a meeting and could not be disturbed, so Isaac did not have the benefit of a proper introduction. Everyone else Jim had expected to introduce him to was busy or away. Some start, thought Isaac, but Jim had full faith his friend would get the job done.

"Ziggy, you just get the details, and leave the rest to me. Now, I have to get my ass out of here, so here's what you do. Find out as much as you can about where these people live and how many in their families are sick. Get any names you can, but if they clam up don't worry. The paper won't likely let us print their names anyway because all these guys are friends with the people who own the papers and it's too embarrassing for them. Talk to the nurses. A few of 'em like to gossip." McGraw dug into his pocket and handed Isaac three neatly folded bills. His eyes flew open at the casual way Jim handled so much money.

"If they need a little extra persuasion to give you information, here's a little help." McGraw explained.

"I see." Isaac made a pretense of being calm.

"Now get in there, and get us some juice. Write what you learn, and leave it on my desk. I'll polish it up for tomorrow's morning edition and we'll be the golden boys!" McGraw raced off to get Maggie to the vaudeville show.

Isaac froze. He did not have the vaguest notion of what to do. The only thing he knew was that he was in way over his head. What was he thinking that he wanted to be a reporter? He wasn't a reporter. He was an imposter. He was a poor Jewish kid with big shot dreams of being something other than a storekeeper. He felt his cheeks go red and his stomach flip.

"Do you need something?" The voice that startled him belonged to a young woman in a starched white cap and crisp white apron. "Are you feeling faint? The admittance desk is in the waiting room. Go down the hall that way. You must have come in the wrong door."

"Um, well, thank you, but no, I'm not sick."

"Oh. Are you here to visit someone?"

"I'm a newspaperman. I'm here to write about the typhoid epidemic," he blurted.

"Oh. Well." The nurse stepped back. "Well, I can't help you. Goodnight."

"No, please, wait."

"You'll have to talk to the hospital director. Goodnight." She turned and walked briskly down the hall.

Isaac spoke to the director's secretary and made his request. Then he waited, watching the wall clock as it ticked away the minutes. He asked again. He waited again. The third time, he was told that the director had left for the day and to please try again in the morning. He went on to speak to two nurses who shook their heads and scooted away before he could show them a bribe. He talked to three neatly dressed, English-speaking visitors who said they would not talk to a newspaperman.

He knew McGraw was going to kill him. He had no facts and no story. He had nothing but fear and the realization that he was just not cut out for this kind of work. He felt a weakening in his knees and realized he needed to sit down. He made his way to the waiting room and eased down onto a bench trying to take up as little space as possible next to a portly man with a large handlebar moustache.

"I say, dear boy," the man nodded politely in Isaac's direction, "would you mind taking another seat so that my son might sit with me? He's on his way here, and I would greatly appreciate it."

They were ordinary, well-modulated words, but they stopped Isaac cold. It was the perfect English accent that did it. The words rolled forth, steeped in education and generations of wealth. Isaac could only think that this must be exactly how the King of England sounded. He'd never spoken to anyone who sounded like the king and he was immobilized as he stared blankly into the man's face. The man pushed him, repeating his request in a very loud voice.

"PLEASE MOVE. MY SON IS HERE. I WANT TO SIT WITH HIM." He ended with a gesture one might use to shoo pigeons off a park bench.

It was then that Isaac recognized the man. Mr. Barnard R. Sedgewick, one of the leading bankers in the city and a member of every important business organization as well as every social group in the city including the Granite Curling Club. He was a powerhouse both in size and by reputation.

Isaac nodded and slid down the bench. Any hope of recovering his tongue vanished; he was silenced with humiliation, consumed by dread. The blood pounded in his ears. How would he tell Jim that he couldn't do the assignment?

He gripped his aching head and swallowed the bile that was suddenly in his throat. Then, without warning, without any effort on his part, something wonderful happened. Isaac realized he had disappeared. All around him, well-dressed English people were talking freely about typhoid. Mr. Sedgewick had given him the gift of access by creating the impression he did not speak or comprehend English. Isaac didn't need to interview anyone. He would get the whole story by eavesdropping.

People came and went. Isaac moved soundlessly to different seats in the waiting room. Twice, when spoken to, he shook his head and said "No English", the same way his grandmother would. Emboldened by the reaction he received, he even added a bit of a stammer for extra effect. He made no eye-contact but stole discreet glances about the waiting room. He sat and soaked up the details for Jim McGraw.

The visitors exchanged stories, speculated about the cause of the typhoid outbreak, and gossiped about the people they knew to be ill. Isaac quietly pulled out his notebook and pencil and started making notes in Yiddish. He wrote down names and street addresses, and he learned that typhoid truly was a very serious problem in the wealthy neighborhoods of Armstrong's Point and elsewhere along the Assiniboine River where the great homes were built. He also learned it was getting worse. Many people were ill or dying. McGraw was right. Wealth and fancy homes were no protection against the horrid grip of the disease, and the people wanted answers. They were demanding to know why the city had allowed typhoid to escape from the immigrant neighborhoods.

In two hours, Isaac had all the information he needed. He slipped out of the hospital and ran back to the newspaper office to write it up for McGraw. He also had a puzzling new angle of the story to think about. How could typhoid spread so quickly through the one part of the city that had both sewer and water connections? It made no sense.

The story he left for Jim to polish stated the facts regarding the number of victims being extremely high for this time of year, and confirmed that many had died. Isaac was only too aware of the story's weaknesses. No official had been willing to say anything about what might have caused the outbreak. Neither would anyone confirm that the location of the outbreak was primarily in Armstrong's Point and the tony neighborhood on

Broadway known as the Hudson's Bay Reserve. Everything Isaac had learned was anecdotal. Just as he was finishing his draft, McGraw came bounding into the room.

"Hey lino-boy! How did the interviews go?"

"Not the way you expected. But here's what I found out," Isaac handed over his copy. McGraw eased a hip onto one corner of the desk and started reading. He let out a low whistle.

"Isaac. This is very good. This is going to be one hell of a story."

Isaac smiled and reached into his pocket.

"Thanks, Jim. Here's the money you gave me. I didn't need any of it."

"What?"

Isaac explained what had happened. McGraw slapped his hand on his knee and laughed so hard he started coughing.

"Ziggy, the invisible reporter. I tell you, we are going to be one hell of a team."

"I'd like that Jim. I think I could learn to do this."

"Learn? You'll be teaching me a trick or two. I can see that," Jim said, smiling broadly.

"I've still got homework and it's late, so I'll be seeing you. Goodnight Jim." Isaac slipped his coat on.

"Just a minute. Here's partial payment on the story." To Isaac's surprise, Jim handed him two folded two-dollar bills.

"You mean it?"

"I never joke about women or money, kid. And I won't be callin' you lino-boy anymore."

At the Zigman dinner table the next day, the entire family had plenty to say about Isaac's story and his great windfall. What made the story particularly lively was the Zigman family's analysis of the typhoid problem. No one did a better job at this sort of thing than his mother. Hannah was well known and greatly teased for her habit of hearing two words of a tale and attaching a whole new story, then passing it on. Often she would continue to add new details from her vivid imagination as new opportunities arose to tell the story. Mama should have been in the theater, Isaac mused. But, somehow her stories always got to the heart of what was going on.

"They should wash their hands, those people with so much money they can't think of what is sensible to do," she proclaimed. "They're sick because they are filthy rich. That's all there is to know. Washed hands make it hard to get sick.

Hannah muttered and sputtered while slamming her kitchen pots about in the dishpan as Isaac went to his homework. He could not get the news story off his mind. He couldn't make sense of the spread of the disease, and he worried about Maisie, knowing so many of the cases were in Armstrong's Point.

34
Darkness Descends

October 30, 1904

Emma grew restless as the weather turned colder. The thought of picking up a book or her embroidery was just too dull to consider. Too old for dolls and too young to be courted, she was longing for the day when just getting out of the house would be easier. It was not much fun being thirteen. She felt like a gosling, ugly, and awkward as she waited for her flight feathers to grow in. She hated the way everyone insisted that she be treated like a child. No, she could not go over to Mary's house without a proper invitation. No, she could not ask Henry to run her downtown for a little shopping on her own at Robinson's store. No, Mother had been having headaches this week and was not up to a game of backgammon. It was all so truly unfair to be stuck in such emptiness, she thought as she gazed out the window at the lifeless grey sky. Just when she thought she would surely die of boredom, Maisie poked her head into the room and purposefully started fluffing pillows.

"Pardon the intrusion, Miss Emma, but you appear in need of a distraction." She paused to listen for Mr. Chadwick. Satisfied he wasn't hiding nearby, Maisie nonetheless lowered her voice.

"I thought perhaps you'd like to join me in the kitchen to bake cookies."

Emma perked up immediately. The very idea was both positively risqué and enormously appealing. Dare she go below stairs with the servants?

"Oh, Maisie! What a wonderful idea!" Emma jumped from her chair, straining to keep from squealing with delight. "But Mother will be horrified. She never allows me down in the kitchen."

"Your mother has seemed a bit overwhelmed these last few days. Perhaps she won't mind you joining me if you ask her properly. Mrs. Butterfield and Lizzie are doing the marketing today so we have some time."

Emma could plainly see by the twinkle in Maisie's eye that she had already decided what would work in this matter of gaining approval from her mother. The game was familiar. It was like a riddle, and it was up to Emma to think hard to guess what would work. Maisie's clues reminded Emma of a sun shower. They would fall as though they were occasional rain droplets on a parched prairie. Never enough and never fast enough.

"It would be of great value ..." Maisie began.

Suddenly the idea burst forth in Emma's mind. "It would be of great value for me to understand how a household is run!" Emma declared with joy and saw the approval on Maisie's face. "After all, if I am to be properly prepared, in perhaps just four or five years to consider an engagement for marriage, perhaps it is best that I know what managing a home entails. Would that not require, therefore, that I spend some time below stairs to understand what is expected of properly trained servants, Maisie?"

"Dear Miss Emma, I do think you have a very good sense of your needs in household education."

Emma rushed off to find her mother in the conservatory while Maisie went on to the kitchen. Not one to waste a moment, she pulled out her textbook to continue reading as she waited for Emma. She had learned to be very efficient in order to allow time to study while she was working. She had barely put her mind into a complicated passage when the sound of Emma shouting carried down the stairwell. Maisie's textbook slammed to the floor as she flew from her chair.

"Maisie! Mr. Chadwick! Come help me!" Emma shrieked, tears streaming down her face as she tugged at her mother, who lay sprawled on the floor moaning, but not answering.

Chadwick bounded into the room a step before Maisie. "Get Master James, straightaway!"

The butler gently brought Mrs. Willows onto the settee. Heat radiated from her body.

"I'm fine, really I am, Mr. Chadwick," Beth moaned as she regained consciousness. "I was just so tired. I must be coming down with a cold."

In short order, Mrs. Willows was safely tucked into her room. The servants whispered and fretted in worried tones as Rupert met with James to decide a course of action.

Maisie was gripped with apprehension. She had known at first glance that this was not a cold. As she helped her mistress to bed she saw the rosy spots on her abdomen and knew with certainty that this was typhoid.

She instantly felt her life shifting and changing with all of the fear of an animal caught in quicksand.

James delivered the news to his father and waited for him to speak. Rupert looked grimly into the brandy swirling in his glass, his jaw pulsing rhythmically against his rising tension.

"Typhoid?" Rupert fell back into his chair, horror-stricken. His immediate thought was of his mother and the horrible days before she succumbed to the disease. No matter how he had cared for her, he had been powerless to prevent her death.

As he fought to regain his composure, beads of sweat formed on his brow. He pulled his starched and perfectly folded handkerchief from his coat pocket, opened it slowly, and carefully pressed it to his forehead, buying a moment or two to recover. Typhoid. Sweet Jesus, Mary and Joseph. Typhoid.

Unaccustomed seeing his father weakened by obvious emotion, James took a breath and placed his hand tentatively on his shoulder.

"We need to get Dr. Carruthers."

"What will he do for her?" Rupert, his pragmatism suddenly restored, looked hard at his son.

"He will likely tell us to bring her to the hospital. I think it prudent, Father."

"The hospital!" The thought of whispers in the corridors trashing his good family name sent ice running through Rupert's veins. "The hospital is a dreadful idea, James."

"Father, I understand your sensitivity to the overcrowding there because of the epidemic but, really, it's best for Mother."

"It's best? To put your mother in rooms overflowing with

disease?"

James was startled into silence.

"Will she live?" Rupert gulped hard.

"Yes. I think so," said James, fighting his own fears, and moved by his father's unconcealed concern. "Mother is strong and has been in very good health. Only about a third of typhoid patients die, and that seems to be the case whether they are treated or not."

"Then you will look after her medical needs."

James froze. The very thought of being responsible for his mother's care during a dire illness was well beyond his level of comfort.

"Father, I am not yet a doctor, and Dr. Carruthers will certainly prefer to have her in hospital."

"No!" Rupert pounded his fist on the arm of the chair. "James, we will not call Dr. Carruthers. Your mother will stay at home."

James slid into a chair, his words silenced by worry for his father's state. Rupert was almost shaking with emotion.

This is an immigrants' disease," hissed Rupert. "It would ruin me to have anyone know that this kind of filth has come into our home!"

James felt as if he had been roundly slapped. He took a moment before he spoke. "What would you have us do, Father?"

"Aside from hospitalization, what would Dr. Carruthers advise?" Rupert's tone was now all business.

"He would tell us she needs to be isolated, and he would give her a special diet and outline the needs for her care so that no one else in the house would become ill." James recited the facts coolly and waited, still reeling from the weight of his father's shocking bluntness.

"Well, then. The course is set. We will isolate her in Elliot's suite. She will need care around the clock. One of the maids will do it. You choose. Perhaps Maisie. She seems to have a good head on her shoulders and doesn't strike me as a gossip, like Lizzie. Look into those special diet needs in one of those books of yours. Hire someone else to replace the servant assigned to your mother, and find out if there is any kind of medicine she should have." Rupert rose and turned to look down at his son. "And James, this is most important. Tell no one that she is ill. We will tell her friends that she was called to Montreal and won't be back for some time."

James was looking to get a word in but Rupert would have none of it.

"That will be all, James. Tell the servants whatever you wish, but do not say typhoid. Call it pneumonia. Yes. That's it. Pneumonia."

35
Battling Typhoid
November 7, 1904

Beth's condition deteriorated rapidly. Within days, her fever rose, and she drifted in and out of consciousness. When she started to show signs of delirium, James panicked. He pleaded with his father to allow him to get her to the hospital, but Rupert angrily refused.

Maisie worked tirelessly to provide her care and comfort. Completely dedicated to her patient's recovery, she remained by her bedside around the clock, sleeping in a tiny cot just a few feet away from her. She sent notes to the kitchen for special soups to be made and gently dripped water on Beth's parched lips to keep her from dehydrating. She bathed her, combed her hair, and administered medicines. She did all her laundry to keep it apart from the household, and kept careful notes on the progression of the illness.

James was a frequent visitor to the sick room, though he prudently refrained from touching his mother, to protect against becoming infected. Having surreptitiously gained advice from Dr. Carruthers, James guided Maisie's work and marveled at her competency and courage.

As delirium took hold of his mother, James became deeply afraid that she would die. Too weak to thrash, she moaned softly, unable to communicate. In time, the moaning seemed to sap all that was left of her strength, and an eerie stillness came over her. With her eyes half closed and her chest barely rising against impending death, it seemed they would lose her. James was at a complete loss as to what to do. Paralyzed with fear, he sat with his head in his hands, prepared for the worst.

Maisie, ever practical, drew on her knowledge and created her own orders. She rang for ice and extra towels, and in a desperate move to break the fever, covered the sick woman with the cold wet cloths. All the while, she continued to talk to Beth, explaining what she was doing and why.

Maisie's determination and constant attention seemed to fuel an inner core of strength within Beth. The hours passed and gradually her breathing grew stronger. Finally, she opened her eyes and asked for water. The worst of the crisis was over, at last.

The clock in the hall chimed six, and Emma began to weep. More than two weeks had passed since her mother had taken ill and been confined behind closed doors. The chiming, which reminded her that Mother would again be missing from the dinner table, completely unnerved her. Mother always presided over the dinner table, gaily chatting and learning everyone's news, offering encouragement or empathy as required by her husband and children. They all missed her at the table, but Emma ached for her. To have her mother in the house, but quarantined, out of view, was torture. With fear suddenly rising that her mother was about to slip away into the clutches of death, a dam burst in the teenager and she sprinted up the stairs with tears streaming down her cheeks. On the second landing she came upon Mrs. Butterfield on her way down to the kitchen.

"I want to see my mother, and I want to see her now!" Emma dodged past the housekeeper.

"Now, stop! Miss Emma, please, dear girl, you must not get sick. It is not safe to see your mother right now!" Mrs. Butterfield wheeled about and gathered up her skirts. She chugged along back up the stairs to the third floor, heaving her way as fast as she could manage behind her young mistress.

"It's locked! The door is locked!" Emma knocked gently, fighting hard to restrain herself. Then, sobbing quietly, she slid to the floor. Desperation washed over her as she rested her wet cheek against the door.

"Are you there, Mother? Are you are all right? Are you alive? Oh, Mother! Please, please get well."

"Now, now, Miss Emma." Stricken by Emma's pain, Mrs. Butterfield eased her heavy frame to the floor and folded the girl into her arms. So thin, she was, like a little bird. "Now, now, hush, sweet child. Everything will be all right in time. You have to have faith. You'll see." Mrs. Butterfield held the girl tightly and swayed gently as Emma cried.

"Mrs. Butterfield, it's been so long. What if Mother is not going to get better?"

A chill ran down the housekeeper's spine. At that moment, the door opened a crack, held fast by the chain.

"Emma! Emma, don't be afraid." Maisie peeked though the opening and spoke in a whisper. "You're mother is doing all she can to get better."

"Maisie, let me come in, just for a moment. I miss her so. Oh, please let me visit Mummy, just for a minute, Maisie!"

"She must rest, Miss Emma." With the door chained, Maisie sank to the floor on the same level as Emma and the housekeeper.

"Emma, listen to me. Your mother is going to get well. She is young and strong, and you know how very determined she is."

"Well, how is it that you can be there? Are you going to get sick too, Maisie?" Emma wept through a fresh round of tears.

"Shh. No, I won't get sick. I promise. It's my job to take good care of your mother and that is just what I am doing," she answered.

"How do you know you won't get sick? Are you immune in some way?"

Mrs. Butterfield's head came up at the question and she stared at Maisie with her eyebrows glued to her hairline. The entire staff had been speculating on the matter for days. But Maisie remained cool and noncommittal.

"Perhaps I am," she said. "All I can tell you is that I am perfectly healthy, and if I were vulnerable, I believe I would be showing signs of illness by now."

The tinkling of a bell interrupted their conversation.

"Your mother is calling me. See how much stronger she is? Please excuse me, Emma and Mrs. Butterfield."

"But, when will I be able to see her?" Emma demanded.

Maisie gently pushed on the door to close it so Emma wouldn't hear her mother moaning.

"I can't tell you right now. We need to be sure she is no longer contagious. Listen, Emma, could you write a note to your mother and slip it under the door. Tell her all your news, and I'll read it to her. I'm sure it will cheer her up." The bell rang again, more insistently. "I must go. Now, please, do as Mrs. Butterfield asks."

Maisie disappeared behind the closed door, and Emma heard the lock slide home. Tears rushed anew as she allowed Mrs. Butterfield to guide her to the stairway.

The entire Willows household had been turned upside down since Beth's illness took hold. At first the house staff was kept in the dark. To throw the servants off track, Rupert set about telling stories of pneumonia, and to appease their employer, the staff outwardly talked about her illness as if it was just that. But the rumors of typhoid were too strong. One of the parlor maids and a stable hand quit without giving any notice.

Young Mr. James had taken charge immediately upon the onset of her illness. Orders came down that the house be immediately scrubbed from top to bottom. He demanded that only water that had first been boiled be used for drinking and cooking. It was a practice Maisie had started weeks before, at the first suspicion of a problem with the water, and Mrs. Butterfield thanked her lucky stars that the girl had been adamant as to its importance.

Mrs. Butterfield and the other servants were also grateful that they had no contact whatsoever with Mrs. Willows. It wasn't the same in many of the other homes, and stories circulated in the neighborhood about entire households falling ill with typhoid.

Mrs. Butterfield counted her blessings and decided it was high time that she became a regular churchgoer.

36
Censorship
December 28, 1904

Heavy snow followed by a severe cold spell wore at the patience of Winnipeg residents. Isaac could plainly see that the staff of the *Winnipeg Star* had no special immunity against the strain of a harsh winter, and he was happy his workday had come to an end. Tidying his station at the Linotype machine, he bade goodnight to the man taking his seat for the next shift and bundled warmly in his new wool coat, wrapping the scarf high on his face and over the earflaps on his hat. This was no time to take a chance on catching a cold.

These were busy times at the newspaper, and Isaac was counting on being asked to fill in as a writer for extra pay. To ensure that he would always be prepared, he had resolved to keep up with all the developing local stories. To this end, he tried to read every newspaper published in the Manitoba capital every day. He was particularly impressed with the *Manitoba Free Press* led by Editor-in-Chief, John Dafoe. It was his secret desire to work there one day.

Isaac walked down the stairs to the lobby of the *Winnipeg Star* with his newspaper open, engrossed in his reading. As he reached the bottom of the steps, Jim McGraw spotted him, and in one swift move snatched the paper out of Isaac's hand and yanked his cap down over his eyes.

"Hey, what do you think you're doing?" shouted Isaac.

"Well, look who's developing a backbone! If it isn't my polite little Jewish friend who used to be scared of his own shadow!"

"Hey, Jim. I thought you were going to be in Chicago until next week." Isaac smiled and grabbed the paper back before he shook his hand.

"Nope. The story fell apart and I got to come home. What's so intense in that paper that you gotta risk your neck to read it while you're walking downstairs?"

"Did you hear about all the fires last night? Three alarms came in from different fires, one after another. Drinkwater's Tailor shop was wiped out at Portage and Main," said Isaac.

"I just went by there," Jim responded. "Hell of a mess. The entire building is coated in icicles. They must have run pumps all night long on the sucker. Anybody killed?"

"No, thank goodness. No serious injuries. There has been one fire after another in the last two weeks. It's a record."

"No kidding. I'm sure you're gonna tell me that there are lots of problems with water pressure, too," said Jim.

"Yeah. Same problems. Jim." Isaac paused and glanced about to see who might be listening in on their conversation. "Do you have time to sit down and talk? I think I've got a lead on the typhoid epidemic story that no one is writing about."

Jim knew when to take Isaac seriously. The kid had an instinct. "Sure, let's go over to Mariaggi's and have a bite. It'll be quiet over there this time of the day. I'll buy."

Bundled and braced against the cold wind, they quickly walked down the block and into the warmth of the hotel coffee shop. Within minutes, they were settled in a back booth with sandwiches before them.

Jim leaned over the table. "Whatcha got, Ziggy?"

"A very good roast beef sandwich," Isaac said as he took a bite.

McGraw reached over the table and slapped Isaac's hat off his head.

"Hey! What did you do that for?" Isaac demanded.

"Whaddaya think, Rookie. Now tell me whatcha got."

"Oh, the story." Enjoying himself, Isaac picked up his coffee cup and sipped at it slowly.

"Isaac Zigman, you have one terrible sense of humor, and you really do know how to try a guy's patience." Jim threw his hat down in frustration.

"All right, all right!" Isaac put his hand up to shush his friend, then continued in a barely audible voice. "Here's the thing. I've been watching the typhoid story develop since you sent me in to talk to those folks at the hospital last month, and I think the whole thing started at the big Main Street fire in October."

"Not true," Jim said, shaking his head. "Look. This has been a terrible year for typhoid, the worst the city has ever seen with almost four times the cases we normally get. I got my hands on some reports from the Health Department. There were more than six hundred typhoid cases before the end of September this year. But there's a simple reason for it. Have you been following the population growth numbers?"

"Yes. It's incredible. In five years the city went from forty thousand to almost seventy thousand."

"Right you are. Seventy per cent growth," said Jim. "Think about what that means. It's only natural the typhoid numbers would reflect that growth. More immigrants, more typhoid. That's all there is to it. It's all about arithmetic." Jim bit into his sandwich. "Sorry, kid. There's no story here."

"Jim, just listen to me. Yes, it was a terrible summer. On the face of it, it seems to all be due to the exploding population. But there is a lot more to it than that. The new immigrants almost all end up in cheap housing in the North End, and that causes a bunch of problems."

"I'm waiting to hear something new here, Ziggy." Jim looked at his watch.

"Would you stop talking and let me finish?" Isaac snapped. "Yes, it's true that most newcomers end up in the North End because the housing is cheapest there. The slums grow larger, and boarding houses are bursting into the streets. With hardly any sewer connections in the North End, everywhere you look the outhouses are overflowing in the lanes." Isaac's eyes were flashing. "Last summer, the flies were thick as carpets on what amounted to open sewage and all that made for the right conditions for typhoid to spread, along with a host of other diseases. It was a terrible summer. We both know these facts. These stories have been in the papers for months."

"Okay, professor." Jim held up his hands. "I can't help it. You are killing me with details and I'm getting bored with all of this background. You got a point to make?"

"Yes. The spread of disease did not stop at the end of the

summer. I'm talking about another six hundred typhoid cases after a hard frost, which normally kills the flies and halts the spread of the disease. We've had twelve hundred typhoid cases this year, Jim. That makes Winnipeg the typhoid capital of the Western world, maybe the whole world."

Jim stopped eating, impressed with Isaac's research. "That's right." His eyebrows pulled together in concentration. "Where are you going with this?"

"That's why I think the big October fire is directly connected," Isaac spread his hands on the table and looked around again to see if anyone was listening. "The cause has got to be contaminated drinking water."

"What the hell are you talking about? What are you? A scientist now?" Jim sat back with his arms across his chest. "Are you telling me that Isaac Zigman, an eighteen-year-old kid from the North End, can figure out the source of contamination that caused hundreds of people to get sick with typhoid when the provincial health inspector missed it? Give your head a shake. I'll bet your brains have rattled loose."

"Well, now, you don't need to be so insulting before you even hear how we can prove it, Jim!" Isaac's anger flushed his cheeks as he jumped from his seat to grab his coat. "Thanks for the sandwich. I'll see you around."

"Whoa! Hey, hold on, Ziggy. I'm sorry." Jim hopped up and put his hand on Isaac's shoulder. "I'm way outta line. Maggie's mom took sick and I guess I'm a little off my game. It's got me worried for her whole family."

"Typhoid?" asked Isaac.

"Not likely from the symptoms she has, but they're all pretty worried over there. Maggie's sister is a nurse and they know how to look after each other. Gee, I'm sorry I've been so rough on you, Ziggy. Let's sit down. I want to hear what you have to say. Please, just sit."

Calmed by the apology, Isaac eased back into his seat. "All right. As you taught me, Jim, we start with what we know. We know all the sewage pipes empty into the Red and Assiniboine Rivers. No one on earth thinks it's a good idea to drink water that has sewage in it."

"For Gawd's sake, Ziggy. No one is drinking sewage-tainted water. The Winnipeg supply comes from artesian wells."

"Yes, but there is still the old pumping station in Armstrong's Point. It allows water from the Assiniboine to come into the water mains."

"It's never used. It's shut down. Has been for almost five years now."

"No. That is not true," Isaac countered, poking his index finger in the air. "I was right there the night of the fire when Mayor Sharpe gave the order to boost the water pressure by pumping in extra water from the Assiniboine. Alderman Willows was the one who thought of it and was quite insistent that it was the best solution at hand. The mayor didn't like it, but he went for it."

Jim's eyes narrowed as he thought back to the night of the fire.

"That's right," he acknowledged, thinking hard to remember the details. "I forgot about that. Well, they had no choice. They needed the water pressure to save the city from the fire. We could have lost the whole damn thing, just like Chicago when it burned down."

"Well, the price of saving the city was the typhoid epidemic," Isaac said evenly.

Jim put his sandwich down and swallowed hard against his skepticism. The kid was young, but he had good instincts and a very sharp brain. "Go on."

Isaac quickly laid out the facts he had gathered.

"It starts with the hospital story and your insistence that the number of rich folks getting typhoid was highly unusual. The hospital isn't big on giving out the numbers, but from what I've been able to get, I can tell you that there are many more typhoid cases in the better neighborhoods in the South End than there are in the foreign quarter. In fact, since October, hardly any of these cases are north of the tracks. It's never been that way in any of the outbreaks before."

"So what? We've also never had a winter outbreak of typhoid like this before. What if it just turns out the rich neighborhoods are unlucky? Maybe the typhoid is being delivered to their homes in the milk supply. There's all kinds of talk about that. All those milk wagons travel all over town. Maybe one of 'em is carrying disease around but the folks in the foreign quarter got a break, that's all."

"Jim, you are missing the point. I'd bet my last dollar that the milk wagons have nothing to do with the problem. It's the water mains that are carrying the typhoid into the wealthy neighborhoods," Isaac stated emphatically. "The foreign quarter is the land of outhouses and well water. There are very few water connections, and that's why the area is largely protected from this outbreak. That's my theory."

"Ziggy, I dunno. I think what you got here is real interesting, but, how is it possible you're the only one onto this idea? The papers are full of theories from every guy who every earned a university degree or complained about taxes, and no one's talkin' about this."

"Maybe they don't want to see it," Isaac answered. "It would be pretty embarrassing for the city. Look, it's common knowledge that typhoid is carried in many ways, so there are a dozen ways for the city to blame everything but their own actions. I say the water mains pumped disease straight into the kitchen taps of homes with running water." Isaac stopped talking.

Jim shook his head and sipped his coffee. "They tested the water. There was no problem."

"They tested the water too late. After the fire, they closed off the Assiniboine pumping station. The well water eventually flushed out the dirty water, so there was no evidence to be found by the time they did their tests." Isaac sipped his coffee.

McGraw rubbed his jaw and considered how to let his cub reporter down easily. This kid had a lot of gumption, and one day it would serve him well, no matter what job he had. "I admire your enthusiasm, Ziggy, but there's no story here. We can't prove your theory, so you got nothing."

"You go ahead and make fun of me, Jim."

"Hey, hothead, no one is makin' fun of you! I'm just tellin' ya this ain't a story."

"I am right, and the proof will come up on its own in ten

days to two weeks!" Isaac spat back. "You don't want the story, no problem, maybe I can write it myself."

"What proof?"

"Look, it's really simple," said Isaac. "There have been only two occasions that the fire department tapped into the Assiniboine River to increase water pressure for fire fighting. I went over there and talked to the fire chief, and he confirmed it. There was the big fire on October 11th, and now this one last night on Main Street. If I'm right, within the next couple of weeks, we will see another spike in the number of typhoid cases, and just like the last time, there won't be a lot of them coming out of the North End." Isaac looked at Jim.

Jim sat back and whistled through his teeth. Then he placed his hands behind his head and stretched back looking at the ceiling while he processed his young friend's hypothesis. He eased the chair away from the table, balancing on its two back legs. The creaking of the wood filled the void in their conversation. Suddenly the chair dropped with a bang and McGraw was in Isaac's face.

"Holy crap, Ziggy!" Jim saw the full potential of the story and lowered his voice. "This is some situation. Did you know the city is fixing to spend a ton of money to bring in a big name biologist from Chicago to solve this so called mystery? Professor Edwin Oakes Jordan. I had a long talk on the telephone with him last week. He confirmed he got a call from the good mayor of Winnipeg. Not only that. When I talked with him, he mentioned contaminated drinking water as one possible source of the disease that would have to be investigated. He also talked about sewers, the milk supply and sanitary conditions and a few other potential causes, but I think you are onto something, Ziggy."

Isaac felt his heart pounding with excitement. "So, we have one big story to write. We could save the city all kinds of money and stop people from getting sick by exposing the danger in the drinking water." Isaac's hands were flying as he talked.

"Now, just hold on, Ziggy. No one is gonna be writin' anything about this unless they are lookin' to get their sorry asses fired right off of the paper."

327

"What?" Isaac was astonished. "What are you talking about?"

"Think about it. If you're right and we run this story a whole bunch of folks are gonna look bad. It could get Mayor Sharpe tossed out of office. Like you said, he's the one who gave the order to use the water from the Assiniboine. Then there are all kinds of other folks who would be out for blood if this gets out. Who do you think owns this paper? Or any paper in Winnipeg for that matter. All those rich guys who run the Board of Trade and the Stock Exchange. If we go after the city fathers and their cronies, they'll run us right out of town. Not one of them good old boys wants to see Winnipeg's fine reputation harmed with headlines in newspapers saying the city deliberately poisoned folks with drinking water and caused the worst outbreak of typhoid ever seen in the Western world. You see what I mean?"

"So, we have to sit back and watch people get sick and die?" Isaac couldn't believe what he was hearing. "What about Professor Jordan? He'll find out the truth. It's just a matter of time."

"Ah! Don't count on it. You know that slogan about all the news that's fit to print? I can guarantee you that if this Dr. Jordan turns up anything really bad, the papers will just decide it is unfit to print. I've seen it lots of times. This is where you will see our dear editors at the *Star* get into a little creative writing. They aren't in business to tell the truth. They are in business to sell advertising. The news should never get in the way of a good profit, or in the way of an opportunity to promote the good name of Winnipeg. Believe me, the editors of the *Star*, and likely all of the other papers, will bury the truth in stories that are as confusing as possible so that it won't look so bad for the guilty."

"They can't do that." Isaac felt his cheeks getting hot.

"They can and they will and I tell you they do it all the time. None of these fellas that own newspapers in Winnipeg is looking to be ringing alarm bells that this is a bad place to live. Confuse the readers, and nobody will ever know who to blame. That's the way they do it. It ain't gonna change because Isaac Zigman thinks it's wrong."

"I can't believe it." Isaac shook his head. "It is wrong. It's immoral."

"It is. But it doesn't matter. They don't care," said Jim.

"So what do we do about the story?"

"We wait and see if your theory is correct and if there is a jump in the number of cases in the next couple of weeks."

"Then what?"

"Then we see if we can get an editor on side to allow the story to go forward," said Jim. "I need my job. We play this one by the rules."

Isaac sighed. "All right. I don't like it, but I understand. And hey, Jim, do me a favor and make sure you only drink boiled water. Would you do that?"

"Now, how would you have this advice, Dr. Zigman?"

"My cousin is studying to be a doctor and that's what she said," answered Isaac.

"She?" Jim was astonished.

"Oy, I meant, he." Isaac caught himself on the verge of disclosing Maisie's secret. He was carrying a letter from her in his pocket telling of the troubles at Alderman Willows' house. "Guess I'm not getting enough sleep."

"Well, you can sleep better now, my friend, knowing that I will take that advice," said Jim. "Maggie's already told me the same. 'Just in case,' is what she said. I sure hope you are wrong on this one. Hey, look at the time. I gotta get Maggie. Hey, I didn't tell you! She and I are gonna get married in April!"

"Jim! Mazel Tov! I mean congratulations. I am so very happy for you."

"I want to see you dancing at our wedding, Ziggy, so you better start working on finding a date," Jim teased as he smacked Isaac's shoulder and headed for the door.

Jim left and Isaac pulled on his coat, taking his time to arrange his scarf to protect his face for the walk home. As he walked, he prayed that his theory was wrong. How could the city pump disease-laden water into the homes of its citizens? He went over the conversation with Jim in his head, and felt dread crawl into the pit of his stomach as he thought of what Jim said about losing his job if he wrote the story.

It was only as he was rounding the corner onto Selkirk Avenue that the solution came to him, and he all but whooped for joy at the thought of it. It was so simple. None of the stories published ever carried the name of the reporter or editor who wrote it. As a compositor, he could just include the story in the paper without ever running it by an editor. No one ever looked over his shoulder to see what he was tapping into the Linotype machine. Why not just slip it in?

37
Elliot's News

December 29, 1904

Emma stood at the door of her mother's suite and listened carefully. At first there was only silence, and her breath quickened as she twisted and bruised the flower stems in her hand. When she finally heard her mother's voice, her fears lessened and she knocked quietly.

"It's all right, Miss Emma. She's awake, and she has been asking for you." Maisie smiled as she opened the door. Emma peeked into the room over her shoulder.

"Is she really all right, Maisie?" Emma asked as she retreated into the hallway, motioning to Maisie to come out so they could talk privately. Maisie closed the door behind her and the two sat together on the settee outside Beth's door. Emma played with the flowers that she had gathered into a posy for her mother. "Is she going to die?"

"No, she is getting well, Emma." Maisie was surprised at the question and gripped the child's hand. "Why ever would you ask such a thing?"

"I had a dream. A terrible nightmare, Maisie. I dreamt that I was getting ready for my debutante party and that mother was not anywhere to be found. I was so scared, Maisie." Emma's tears started to fall and she dropped her head into Maisie's lap.

"You poor thing. Please, don't be frightened." Maisie hugged her. "Now, look at me. You know what your brother James has said. She is well past the worst of the illness and is recovering very well. He is going to be a wonderful doctor, Emma, and you should be very proud. Your mother's appetite is improving, and she is getting stronger every day. Come in with me and you will see for yourself."

"It's been such a long time since I've seen her. Does she look awful?"

"She looks tired and she's thinner, but you'll see how happy she will be to see you."

A tinkling bell could be heard from within the bedroom suite.

"Come. She's ringing for me. "Maisie pushed the door open and stepped aside to let Emma lead the way.

"Emma! Oh, my dear, sweet daughter! Come here, darling," Beth called with as much strength as she could muster. She was dressed in afternoon clothes and was seated on a chaise lounge near the window.

"Mummy, I can't tell you how I've missed you," Emma cried as she rushed into her mother's arms. She held on tightly and wept as Beth stroked her hair.

"Oh, darling, you mustn't cry. I am fit as a fiddle."

Emma saw the color in her mother's cheeks and was filled with relief. "How we've all missed you, Mother."

"I'm under very good care with your brother's orders and with Maisie here," Beth nodded at the blushing maid. "I do believe I owe much to her for my recovery. Oh, I've missed you more than you will ever know, Pet. It was so annoying to be restricted to chatting with you from the other side of a door. Now, let me look at you! My, how lovely you look in your new dress. Is that the one Elliot sent to you?"

"Yes, it is. Do you like it?" Emma felt her heart soar. Mother was just as she always had been; full of joy and with her concerns about fashion rising over everything around her.

"I do like it very much, Emma." Beth admired the painstaking detail of the stitching. "I think you will be the talk of the town in this frock. Now, you must tell me that you have kept your promise to me and not told your brother of my illness," Mother said sternly.

"Yes, I have, Mother. I've not said one word about it." Emma looked down into her hands. "It was so hard for me not to write to Elliot about your trial, Mother. I was so terribly worried, and it is such a comfort to me to share my troubles with him," she said.

"Emma, dearest, I am so sorry to have put you through all of this. I really can't imagine how it was that I, of all people, was lucky enough to fall ill. But if you had told your brother, then what would have happened? He would have left his architecture studies and rushed home to my bedside for no reason. You see? Here I am, perfectly fine and almost as good as new."

Emma was thrilled to hear her mother mention Elliot's architecture school, confirming that her brother's secret remained safe.

"And I have flowers for you!" gushed Emma.

"Oh, thank you, darling." Beth smelled the flowers as if they were the most exquisite blooms she'd ever seen.

"Please, Maisie, would you mind putting these in water for me? They are so pretty." She patted Emma's hand. "You really mustn't look so worried, Emma. As a matter of fact, I have been marching about the room to get my exercise in recent days under the serious and heavy regimen that Maisie has determined to be in my best interests. I'm getting stronger all the time. Am I not, Maisie?"

"You are indeed, mum. You are an excellent patient, I must say."

"Well, I shan't be a patient for much longer. I have had quite enough of being confined to these quarters. Emma, how would you like to go shopping with me? Come to Montreal with me. We'll see what new fashions are on Sherbrooke Street and spend some time with Grandmama."

"Oh, Mother, how absolutely wonderful that would be. Are you sure you are strong enough to go?"

"I am better every day. Truly I am, Emma. And I must tell you that your father came to me with the most exquisite news. From Montreal, he and I will be traveling on to Florida for a few weeks."

Emma gasped. This was the first she had heard of the potential for a southern holiday. Her mother rushed to allay her fears.

"Now, now, Emma, I know what you are thinking. I can see it all over your face. You and I will spend every waking minute together for ten full days. You will be positively sick of me by the time you leave to return to Winnipeg."

"Florida! I thought you and Daddy were going to skip your winter holiday this year."

"Well, your father seems to think that the warm ocean breezes will hasten my full return to good health, and I must say it is too tempting to resist. Now just think, darling. Won't it be fun to travel to Montreal with me and have a bit of a holiday yourself?"

"Will I travel home alone?" Emma suddenly imagined herself as a woman of the world, boarding the train on her own, in fabulous traveling clothes, of course, for the journey.

"Certainly not! What on earth are you thinking? You're not even fourteen years old."

"I will be fourteen in just a few months, Mother."

"Alfred will be joining us in Montreal as well," her mother explained. "He will travel east a couple of days after our departure. He and your father have some business to attend to and he will escort you home on the train."

"But are you really strong enough to travel, Mother?"

"I truly am fine, and just to be sure ..." Beth stopped and looked at Maisie. "Well, I haven't asked you yet, if you would mind, Maisie, but all of this is coming along so fast. I would like you to come along with Mr. Willows and me, in the capacity of my personal maid and nurse, should the need arise, that is, just to be sure that I am well looked after under all circumstances."

Maisie's eyes flew open and her knees went weak as she fought to maintain her composure.

"Florida?"

"Yes, please do say you will come. It will make all the difference to me. I've already discussed the matter with Lizzie, so you needn't worry about her being offended. It seems she has been rather nervous about my illness and is quite happy to have you take her place to help me with my travels."

Emma was starting to feel the excitement. Mother truly was on the way to being back to her normal good humor, and getting away for the worst of the winter was probably a very good idea.

"Maisie, I think you should go. You would love St. Augustine, I'm sure."

"Oh, not St. Augustine, dear. We're going to Palm Beach."

"Palm Beach!" Maisie and Emma said in unison, and then clapped their hands over their mouths.

334

"Dear me, how funny you both are! Yes, we're traveling to Palm Beach. We are to be the guests of Mr. and Mrs. Henry Flagler at their extraordinary new mansion, which I believe is called Whitehall. It's a terribly grand residence, I'm told," Beth gushed. "Apparently there are more than fifty rooms. Imagine a private home that large! And Mr. Flagler absolutely insisted that your father bring me there so that we could relax and recover from the terrible trials of the fire. Such a dear and thoughtful man, he is. Oh, Maisie, do say you will come with us. You have taken such good care of me all these weeks. You saved my life, I do believe. I just couldn't bear the thought of traveling without having you near. You will come, won't you?"

Maisie couldn't believe her good fortune. By contrast with Winnipeg's harsh winter, the thought of warm ocean breezes was absolutely tantalizing. With shining eyes and pink cheeks she turned to her mistress and curtsied. "I would be honored to accompany you, Mrs. Willows." Wait until she told her family she was escaping a Winnipeg winter to travel to Florida!

Emma sat immobilized on the edge of the chaise lounge, her ears ringing like an alarm bell.

"Emma, child of mine," her mother reached out to comfort her daughter. "You look like you have been struck by lightning. What is it?"

"Mother, I thought you were going to St. Augustine!" said Emma as her hands flew high.

"St. Augustine?"

"Yes!" Catching herself, Emma blurted, "I thought you were intending to go to the Alcazar Hotel to enjoy the sulfur pool and the Roman baths to help you recover."

"Well, yes, that is a rather nice thought." Beth reached out to stroke Emma's hair. "Goodness, I am surprised you remember such details, darling. Sometimes I think you don't hear me at all, and look at all you remember from my prattling on. We'll see what Daddy thinks about stopping at St. Augustine on the way home.

"But really, you mustn't be concerned with any of this, Emma. You look like I've given you shocking news. Is there something I should know about?"

"Not a thing. No, not a thing, Mother."

Emma was starting to feel a little queasy. Palm Beach? She felt for the letter hidden in her dress pocket and held it, to be sure it wouldn't fall out and spill its secrets into the room. "It's just that I thought you liked St. Augustine. That's all." As she hugged her mother, she saw the clock on the mantle. "Oh, goodness. Look at the time. Mary is coming over to study with me. Please excuse me, Mother."

"Of course, darling. As a matter of fact, I am feeling so well that I will join the family in the dining room this evening. You run along. I'll rest a bit before Maisie helps me dress for dinner, and I'll see you later."

Emma embraced her mother again and left the room, the letter now squashed into a damp ball in her sweaty palm. She scooted along the hall and down the stairs to her room, locking the door behind her. Whatever should she do? How could she possibly reach Elliot to warn him?

She pulled the letter from her pocket. Like Elliot's previous letter, this one had been hidden in his gift to her. Maybe she'd only dreamed what it had said. She smoothed it out to read it again.

Paris
November 15, 1904

My dear little sister,

I have the most extraordinary and delicious news! You won't believe how fortunate I am. Of course, what I am about to tell you is to be kept secret as a matter of highest priority. You are the only person I am telling, so please understand how crucial it is that you tell absolutely no one about this. This is so top secret that you may not even tell Mary about it!

So here it is, then. By the time you are reading this I will be busy at work in a paying job! Not just any job, mind you. I have accepted employment of a temporary nature as an executive chef for a special client. I was selected through a rather large and serious competition to be the chef for "the season", as it is called, for a very important man who lives in New York but takes his winter holiday in Florida. His name is Henry Flagler. I'm sure you may know the name, as he happens to be friends with our father. I have not met him, for I was hired by one of the executives in his employ. They believe my name is Chef Louis La Chance. How do you like my new name?

Now, here is the most important part of this message. Father would be horrified to learn of my change in occupation, as he was so determined that I should become an architect. I am quite sure he would be frightfully wounded, and my relationship with him might well be irrevocably damaged were he to hear that I have chosen to cook for a living. I do plan to tell him in time, but not just yet. A great deal of finesse will be necessary. So, I am asking you, dear sister, to help me keep up my pretense that I am continuing at architecture school.

I expect that as you are reading this I will be frightfully busy running the main kitchen at Whitehall in Palm Beach, Florida. Mr. Flagler is very highly thought of in Florida and does a great deal of entertaining. I can't tell you how utterly relieved I was to receive a letter from Mother that she and Father had decided to forego a winter vacation this year due to Father's demanding schedule since the dreadful fire. Knowing that there would be no chance of my running into them made all the difference in the world. I just jumped for joy.

The season in Florida will come to an end about early March. After that I will travel to New York, and from there I plan to come to Winnipeg as a surprise for everyone. I will fill you in on the details, darling sister.

Wish me luck!

Affectionately yours,

Elliot (I mean Louis!)

Emma fell back onto her bed. Wish me luck! She thought of her brother's words. He would need more than luck. How could she keep all these secrets? First, her mother had forbidden her to tell Elliot she was ill. Then, Elliot had insisted she keep his change in professions secret to protect Father's feelings. Now all these lies had the potential to end in disaster. She thought about sending Elliot a letter from Winnipeg, but considered it far too risky. How would a Parisian chef named Louis La Chance explain a connection to Winnipeg? Talking to Mary was also out of the question. Elliot had asked her not to tell, so she could not. If she followed his instructions, she would tell no one, and he would be ambushed by his own parents! It was a huge dilemma, and there was no one she could turn to for help.

38
Travel Plans
Dec. 30, 1904

Maisie was overjoyed to finally be at the Selkirk Avenue home again, after so many weeks at Mrs. Willows' bedside. The family took time over dinner to catch up on everyone's news.

"I have something else to tell you," Maisie said, looking up from her plate with a smile. "I will be unable to see you for some weeks, again, I am afraid."

"Again? Is someone else ill?" Baba Bayla wanted to know. "It has been two months since we last saw you. The letters are nice, but it's a smiling face we like to see."

"No, no, Baba. In fact, this is a great opportunity. I will be traveling to Palm Beach, in Florida, with Mr. and Mrs. Willows." She tried not to sound like she was bragging.

"Florida!" Ziporah let out a whoop.

"Palm Beach?" Mama couldn't hide her distress. "Where is this Palm Beach, and why is it you have to be the one to go with them?"

"I'm going, Tanta Hannah, because Mrs. Willows insists that she will not travel without me to care for her, and Mr. Willows is adamant that she be given every chance to recover her full strength," Maisie explained calmly. Her cousins sat spellbound at the idea of what amounted to a holiday in warm summer weather, and by the ocean, no less.

"You don't mean you are now the official nurse in that house, do you?" Hannah waved a serving spoon in an accusing fashion.

"No, of course not." Maisie glanced at her grandparents for support.

Zaida looked amused as he exchanged knowing looks with Bayla. Maisie knew she could count on them for understanding.

"You aren't going to tell me I shouldn't go, are you, Tanta

Hannah?"

"It's the voyage I don't like." Hannah plunged the spoon firmly into the bowl of mashed potatoes in front of her and jammed her hands onto her hips. "You know how I feel about ocean travel! Your tanta will be worried for you the whole time, my darlink."

"Oh, my. If that is what you are worried about, then there is no problem. You see, we are traveling by train."

"The whole way?" Hannah was astonished. "You can go so many thousands of miles to a place where it is summer all year round and you don't have to go on the ocean? Where is this Palm Beach?"

"Mama!" shouted Mendel. "There are maps in one of Aaron's books from school. I can show you where is Palm Beach."

"And how will you get there?" Hannah asked again.

"It is quite a journey and very far south," Maisie explained. "We will travel in Mr. Willows' private rail car. He wishes to go to Montreal first and then we'll travel to New York. Mrs. Willows will do some shopping with her sister there and then we will go south to Palm Beach. Mr. Willows' friend, Mr. Flagler, built the railroad. It is quite incredible, don't you think?"

"*Oy gevalt.*" Hannah scrutinized the map Aaron showed her. "And for how long will you be there?"

"I'll be back home by the end of March. Not that long, really."

"Ach, well, you have to do what you have to do. What do you think, Zev?"

"I think Malka, excuse me, I mean Maisie, is very fortunate to travel in this way. May you go with comfort and safety, God willing," said Zev, nodding with a smile at his niece.

"Thank you, Uncle Zev."

Baruch cleared his throat and took his wife's hand. "Wonderful news. You will see something of the world and enjoy something new every step of the way. We are happy for your big opportunity." He cleared his throat again. "Well, while we are talking about far away places. Aaron, please bring to your zaida that book from school. Does it have a map also of

340

Palestine?"

"Sure, Zaida. I will find the page for you."

"Let me find it! Let me help," shouted Mendel, and together the two found the correct page.

"Well, please pass the book so everyone can see where Jerusalem is marked on the map, as I have a big announcement to make," said Baruch.

"You're going!" shouted Ziporah, clapping her hands in a rush of emotion. And suddenly everyone was talking at once.

Baruch put his hands up to silence the family.

"Yes, it is true. The time has come for your grandmother and me to leave Canada for *Eretz Yisrael*, the Land of Israel. We will go this summer. As you know, I have been writing to Dov Ber Weidman for many months now, and he assures me that he and his wife Rachael are very happy in Jerusalem. You know, it has been almost a year since they arrived there. I, too, wish to have that happiness he speaks of in his letters ... to be in Jerusalem, with my wife by my side, to be close to God in the land of our ancestors."

Bayla's eyes shone, giving her the appearance of a young woman, full of determination and passion for life.

"I was in the Weidman store yesterday, and I talked with Mordecai about his parents," Baruch continued. "We had a long conversation and he, too, assures me that both he and his brother Hiram Leib are certain their parents made the right decision to go to Palestine."

"Mazel Tov!" exclaimed Zev, who had known for some time that the announcement was coming.

"But don't you think at your age a long trip might be very hard?" Pale with fear, Hannah sat wringing her apron in her hands.

"Because we are older?" asked Baruch.

"Oh, Papa Baruch," Hannah was immediately embarrassed to be caught being so transparent in her greatest objection. "I didn't mean to be insulting in any way. It's just I worry so much."

"The Weidmans are older than we are and they made it fine. It is like the old saying: a man is not old until his regrets take the place of his dreams."

There was a great to deal to talk about and the family's conversation continued late into the night. It wasn't all planning for the future; there was also a lot of reminiscing.

When they finally said goodnight, Isaac went upstairs to his room and pulled out a brand new notebook. He opened it carefully, almost with reverence, and turned to the smooth, clean first page. As neatly as he could, in the center of the page he wrote: The Stories of the Zigman Family of Winnipeg.

Perhaps one day his own children, and even his grandchildren, would want to know how it was that the Zigmans came out of Russia. Maybe they would be excited to read how in 1905 his courageous grandparents, Baruch and Bayla would go to live in the land of Israel.

He sat for a while thinking about how happy he was for his grandparents, and how much he would miss them. What an adventure to go to Jerusalem! Gradually his thoughts turned to his own long journey to Canada and the family's arrival in Winnipeg. Then he knew where to begin his story. He dipped his pen in the inkwell and in his clear, beautiful hand, wrote the title for his first chapter: "The Day I Met My Zaida Baruch".

39
Sewer Tour
January 10, 1905

D awn broke with the promise of a brutally cold, bright January day as James sat alone in the breakfast room with his coffee and a stack of Winnipeg newspapers. He was totally engrossed in what he was reading.

"Would you care for more coffee, sir?" Chadwick appeared from nowhere, startling the young doctor.

"Good heavens, Mr. Chadwick! I almost jumped out of my skin. Must you be so silent all the time?"

The butler bowed his head in exaggerated politeness. "I'm terribly sorry, sir."

"Would you please tell my father that I'd like to see him before he leaves?"

"Certainly, sir." Chadwick bowed again as Rupert's quick footsteps could be heard coming down the stairs into the central hall.

"Good morning, Father," James called to catch him. "Do you have time to join me for a cup of coffee?"

"Good morning, James," Rupert said as he checked his pocket watch. "Yes, but just for a few minutes, I have a lot of work to get through before we leave on holiday tomorrow."

"Father, I see Alderman Willows was part of the contingent of civic officials in yesterday's sewer inspection on Assiniboine Avenue," James pointed to the newspaper before him.

Rupert was surprised and pleased. James was not usually one take an interest in his father's pronouncements to the press.

"Why, yes, I was. We went right to the heart of the district that has seen the highest number of typhoid cases in this recent outbreak, and as you no doubt have read, our party determined that the sewers are as clean as can be expected and that they have nothing to do with the epidemic. We have, therefore, come to the conclusion that the cause is contagion."

"Yes, Father. It appears that you had plenty to say about the cause of the typhoid problem."

"Oh, come now, I see you are wanting an argument. I'm really not interested in another of your rants, James. The city needs to be seen looking into the problem, and that was the reason for the tour. In truth, well, we already know the typhoid epidemic is entirely related to all those filthy immigrants and the dreadful squalor up in that foreign quarter, but of course I couldn't say that to a newspaperman. It would make me sound hard, or uncharitable at the very least. No, we talked instead about contagion as the source. It sounds better, don't you agree? I also happen to believe it is true."

"I thought the city was embarking on a true investigation," James countered after a moment of stunned silence.

"It is. The population is very worried and we, the members of City Council, need to be seen to be looking into the causes. Why can't you understand that?"

"Then perhaps you can help me understand how it is possible that the City Council would be so quick to dismiss the pollution of the drinking water supply."

"To what pollution might you be referring?" Rupert raised an eyebrow as he sipped his coffee.

"When you bring sewage into the drinking water supply, don't you think you would have a problem?"

"I'm afraid I don't follow you. What has sewage got to do with the water supply? The sewage goes into the river and the water supply comes from the artesian wells. They are not connected."

"Except when the city opens the old pumping station to bring the Assiniboine River water into the water mains. Father, have you not seen the stories about the new outbreak of typhoid in the city? Look, here it is in a story in the *Winnipeg Star*. One of their reporters seems to be quite keen on pushing the idea that water pollution is the primary cause of the fall typhoid outbreak and that it is directly linked to the more recent increase in typhoid numbers we saw this week. The writer suggests that it was caused by the necessity of opening the Assiniboine pumping station again a fortnight ago, to combat the rash of fires in the last week of December." James pushed the paper toward his father.

"Rubbish. James, that's not science. That's speculation on the part of a newspaperman."

"I've read about it several times now, and I'm just curious as to why the council would not take the charge seriously."

"James, the pumping station was only used for fire protection." Rupert's tone slid from calm to condescending. "It's rare that we need to do that. In fact, had we done it earlier on the night of the fire last October, we wouldn't have lost our office building. No, you are wrong on this one, I'm afraid. Never mind the *Star*. No one reads that scandal sheet but you, it seems. Now, let me see your copy of the *Manitoba Free Press* and I will show you."

"Ah ha. Here we are. Dr. Gordon Bell's speech to the Manitoba Medical Association last evening."

"Yes, I read that," James interrupted. "He believes the typhoid epidemic is related to air coming up from the sewers."

"That's right! Even skeptics like you, James, must admit that Dr. Bell is a credible expert. He has been chief bacteriologist in this province for the past eight years. What is more, he investigated all of these concerns that people like you have about the water. Listen to this. The paper quotes right from the report on typhoid that he gave to the provincial board of health. Bell says: "The water from the artesian well, treated as it is by milk of lime in the softening process, is remarkably germ free and there seems no possibility of it having played any part.""

Rupert smacked the paper for emphasis. "He goes on to say that the examination of the water in the taps gave no evidence of pollution. There you have it, James."

James shook his head. "That really doesn't make sense. Maybe by the time they tested the tap water, the pollution had dissipated, Father."

"Oh, please." Rupert threw up his hands.

"Father, just look at the facts. As the article in the *Star* points out, we never see problems with typhoid in January, and all of a sudden there is a huge jump in the number of cases, just as there was in late October after the downtown fire. With

Mother still recovering, and so many others in our part of the city ill, as well, the quality of the drinking water is an obvious suspect. It seems likely the reporter is right in his assertion that there must be a link to polluted drinking water."

"James, of course I understand your concern, but I must correct you there. The sewage that flows into the Red and Assiniboine is harmless."

"I beg your pardon? Harmless? How could that be, Father?"

"Ah! I'm glad you asked because I asked the same question yesterday. You see, it has to do with fresh air. There is apparently a plentiful supply of airflow in the sewers, and that is the key to making the harmful effects of the sewage disappear before the sewage enters the rivers."

Rupert could see that James was not grasping the concept, so he continued to elaborate. "You see, James, there are these bubbles floating about on top of the sewage, and we were told that when the bubbles burst the germs go away, and there is no more harm in the sewage. We had a first hand account of it when we toured the sewers."

James didn't know where to begin with this preposterous story. When he finally got his tongue untied, he stammered, "Did you go down there?"

"Oh, my dear boy! Certainly not! We walked above ground, of course, from one manhole to the next. It was frightfully cold, you know, and we just walked the one block from Smith to Garry Streets, you see, and the man inside the sewer, what was his name? Well, one of the city workers who does this sort of thing, told us all about the ghastly bubbles and we came to our own conclusions."

"Father, I mean no disrespect, but do you have any idea how ridiculous that sounds?"

"Ridiculous? There were engineers with us!" Rupert spoke as though James was a young child. "And doctors, too. It was scientific and reported in all the papers! I thought you said you read all this."

"I did. And you can't deny that it does seem there is a great interest by the esteemed leaders of the city to pretend that this problem does not exist; that somehow it might be bad for business to have the world know that Winnipeg has a typhoid epidemic that is clearly out of control!"

"Rubbish!" Rupert slammed the table with an open palm.

"How do you think Mother got sick?"

"James, please, would you mind lowering your voice? The servants will hear. Mother got sick from contagion. She had been visiting with Muriel Penneyworth. That woman is all tied up in her charity work with those dreadful, filthy children up there in Jew Town. She probably touched one of those disease-ridden little vagrants and then came to tea with your mother and there you have it."

James was stunned. "Do you really believe that?"

"Of course," answered Rupert, staring wide-eyed at his angry son. "I repeat: the health authorities believe the entire typhoid problem is based on contagion and nothing more." He picked up the stack of papers and dropped them one-by-one in front of James to emphasize his point. "Every one of these papers is filled with endless articles and letters from readers that speculate on the causes of the typhoid epidemic. Everyone who can write is being quoted, expert or not. They talk of the sewer, the milk supply, contagion, the weather, the box closets and even the phase of the moon, for goodness sake. And what does it come to in the end?"

"Oh, Father, please."

"I'll tell you what it comes to!" He bellowed into James' face. "Everyone knows that the North End is rife with typhoid because of the slovenly habits of its population!"

"Father, that's nonsense! The health authorities, as you call them, present conflicting views on what is causing the problem. There is no general agreement on this contagion idea. It's just that you, along with all of your City Council fraternity brothers, have pinned your public relations campaign to this one theory and you now send it out as fact! What I see very clearly, Father, is that the good old boys who lunch at the Manitoba Club just don't want Winnipeg to be seen as having tattered skirts and broken shoes on the world's dance floor. They don't want the truth to come out!"

Fuming, Rupert left the table and started pacing. "Oh, really,

347

James? And what might your version of that truth be?"

"The truth is that an exploding immigrant population, coupled with woefully inadequate support from the city, have created unspeakable living conditions that have led Winnipeg to become the typhoid capital of the western world. There isn't a single city in Europe or anywhere in North America that can top Winnipeg's numbers for illness and death due to typhoid. That is the truth."

"Oh, come now, James." Entirely fed up with the conversation, Rupert attempted a more convivial tone. "You are just so, well, so dreary. You're no fun at all these days."

"Father! I must tell you it is increasingly difficult to have a serious conversation with you. You can't imagine how frustrating that is. Perhaps I should seek a meeting with our mayor and leave you to your, your golf and your hunting."

"It's winter, James. No one golfs or hunts in winter. Did you mean to say curling? Our team is doing rather well at the Granite Club this year." Rupert pulled out his pocket watch, anxious to get on his way. "Please, James, you must know that I do take you seriously. And, yes, you are at least partly right."

"You will admit, then, that Winnipeg has an appalling record in typhoid management?"

Rupert so hated this kind of discussion. "Unfortunately, yes, I would agree that the numbers are high, but don't forget that we also have all of those people from the rural areas coming into Winnipeg to our hospitals and this gives Winnipeg a falsely high number. And as you so aptly pointed out, being recognized for having a typhoid epidemic is such a distasteful distinction for the city to have. We don't believe that we are hiding it, we just choose not to discuss it. Of course we are trying to put a good face on things. In the grand scheme of things, it is not that serious. It will eventually run its course and be forgotten history. It is very important that this be kept as private as possible, rather like a family matter. You really need to change your thoughts on this need for exposure of weaknesses. Some things are best kept private."

"But, Father, this is not a family matter; it's a city health matter."

"Enough! James, do you mean to tell me that every man who has a mistress should run home and tell his wife about it? Don't you think that would cause unnecessary harm? Some truths are better left untold."

"And the greatest truth, Father, is that Winnipeg is only interested in dealing with typhoid because it has become a problem in good neighborhoods and in homes like ours."

Rupert pounded on the table. A thick vein, like a small snake, appeared on his forehead as he spoke through his clenched jaw. "Stop shouting, James. You have a real talent for kicking a man when he is down. Do you think it doesn't kill me that your mother has suffered so terribly? Is that what you want me to say? That until she was over the crisis, I was frightened for her very life?"

"But you won't acknowledge that mother became ill directly because of decisions made at City Hall."

"No, I will not!" Rupert dropped his voice. "And I must say I don't like this uppity behavior you've been exhibiting since you began studying medicine. I've told you this before. It is ruining you, James. It is making you very unpleasant to be with. I'm rather glad that your mother and I are leaving for Florida tomorrow. I won't have to deal with your endless whining about how difficult life is for the poorer classes!"

James opened his mouth, but Rupert raised a hand to stop him. "Wait, James. I do appreciate your passion for the subject, but why don't you leave it to the professional investigators? I'm sure you're delighted to hear that Mayor Sharpe is insisting on paying a pretty penny to bring in that fellow, Professor Edwin Jordan, from Chicago. A waste of money, I say, in the face of the experts we have right here. But the exercise should satisfy all the malcontents and rabble-rousers like you. Now, if you will excuse me. I have had all I can take of this discussion." Rupert slapped the newspaper onto the breakfast table and stomped off.

Chadwick quickly scuttled from view and headed below stairs. He would see Mrs. Butterfield straightaway. She would just have to put up with continuing to boil the drinking water until this Dr. Jordan had completed his investigation. Worrisome times, these were. Worrisome, indeed.

40
Emma's Dilemma
January 11, 1905

Four hours out of Winnipeg, Emma's emotions finally crumbled. The train puffed along the track, through the forests of North-western Ontario. Up the hill, down the hill, round the bend, look at the lake, up the hill, down the hill, round the bend, look at the lake.

The monotony of the scenery and train's steady rhythm brought Emma's worries to the forefront. She felt utterly crushed under the burden of Elliot's secret. Alone in the parlor of the family's private Pullman railcar, she sat with her book unopened and her knitting untouched beside her. Her gaze was fixed on the endless trees that flew by the window. Mother was napping in the rear bedroom suite. Father had gone to the smoking car to find a card game and Maisie was busy unpacking and setting up the linens in the bedrooms.

Tears pooled heavily in Emma's big brown eyes, then brimmed over her thick lashes and ran in silver rivulets down her cheeks. She sniffed quietly as she searched her pocket for her handkerchief. She missed Mary. She missed Elliot. Feeling hopelessly lonely, she wept.

Having finished her tasks, Maisie hummed with happiness as she walked from the rear of the car. She was startled to come upon her young mistress in such distress.

"Miss Emma," she called softly. "Whatever is the matter?" Glancing about quickly to be sure they were alone, she sat next to Emma and put her arm around the girl's shoulder. "There, there, Emma, what is making you so upset?" She felt Emma's forehead as the girl squeaked in despair.

"Maisie, my life is in ruins! Absolute ruins! I have no one to turn to and I just don't know what to do."

"Now, now, Emma. It can't possibly be as bad as all that. Are you feeling ill?"

"No, I'm fine, that way. I would rather be ill than to feel like this. You get better from illness, but I don't think I will ever be better from my troubles. I have such a terrible dilemma, and I can't talk about it!"

"Why not?"

"Because it would betray a secret, a great big, very important secret; a secret that could destroy a person's life were it to be found out!" She looked up at Maisie with pink cheeks and teary eyes.

An uneasy feeling crept over Maisie, sending a tingling sensation up the back of her neck. Had Emma found her out? Had she been careless? Had she left a clue to her identity to be found by this sweet, innocent child? She suddenly felt dizzy.

"Is this a friend of yours, you speak of?" she whispered.

"No, not a friend. But, someone very dear to me."

"Not a friend?

"I'm sorry." Emma shook her head. "I can't say more. I might let slip what I know and then what? What might the consequences be?"

Maisie's blood ran cold. She had most certainly been found out. Her days in the employ of the Willows family were surely numbered. She needed time to regroup and plan a strategy to control the impending crisis. She peeked over Emma's shoulder to be sure that they were alone in the car. "Emma, would you like to have a cup of tea and a bit of a chat?"

Emma nodded, and Maisie jumped up, drying her sweaty palms on her apron.

"Maisie, I'm so sorry. I didn't mean to upset you."

"Upset me?" Maisie giggled. "What is there for me to be upset about? Listen. Let me get that cup of tea for you. And while we have some privacy, we'll find a way to ease the burden you are carrying." Her heart was pounding like a drum. How odd that the child just didn't blurt it out. Clearly she knew. She must have reasons for not speaking up. Then it dawned on her; perhaps there was a way to keep her job and find an ally in Emma at the same time. It was a great risk, but it might be the only way.

"I would like that, Maisie. I am so happy you came to

Ravenscraig. I think my life would be unbearable without you."

"You will always manage, with me or without me, Emma. Just remember that." Maisie headed toward the little kitchen at the rear of the car, tears now flooding her own eyes.

As she watched Maisie walk briskly away, Emma's brow wrinkled in confusion. What is she talking about? Is she planning to leave? Oh, dear God, not another blow! Not now. Please don't let Maisie quit her job!

Maisie was heartbroken. Her five years at Ravenscraig had been wonderful. She liked her work and the other staff members. She liked the sometimes quirky personalities of the family, and she especially liked the twinkling eyes of Mr. James, who admired her for being smart. He had been so quick to praise her work in his mother's sick room. She dropped her head in shame at the very thought of having deceived him. How sweet and caring he was. How she had wished that there was an opportunity for something more between the two of them, but of course that dream was worlds beyond her reach.

She winced at the thought of the young ladies he escorted to parties. Never mind. It's not as if he would ever think of her as anything more than a study partner. He probably knew nothing of her affection for him. How could he? There he stood, high on a mountain, a rich young man, and she a maid. And a Jewish one, at that. A great knot formed in her throat. This was no time to be silly, sentimental and lovesick. The game was up. Perhaps she could start over in Toronto or Vancouver, or even in New York. Perhaps she could find her own true love. She had overcome so many challenges throughout her life. This would be a new adventure.

She would have plenty of time to think about it, but the first order of business was to look after Emma. Balancing the tea tray, she closed the door of the kitchen and carefully locked it, thinking her calamity must have come from her carelessness. Emma must have seen the diary she wrote in Yiddish and had hidden in her room. Maybe it was Mr. Chadwick who found her out! How quickly one's world could come crashing down in flames.

Forlorn and pale, Emma had calmed herself enough to speak. She set her teacup down and placed her hands together. "I have had time to think and I believe that I shall just throw caution to the wind and tell you my entire tale of woe."

Maisie patted her arm. "Dear Emma," she said with warmth. "You may tell me anything you wish, but first, I must speak. When I am done, then, you can say anything you like."

"But, I really think it would help if I just told you straight out what is bothering me," Emma implored.

"I do understand and believe me, this is the correct way to start. Please, Emma. Let me have my say."

Emma was exhausted. She could muster no fight against the determined Maisie.

"What I'm going to tell you is not something I am ashamed of. However, I am ashamed and deeply sorry that I had to deceive you. I will ask you only to let me tell it all at one time, without interruption and then you can ask me any questions that you like. You have to agree to this."

Emma's brow furrowed in confusion.

Maisie took that as acceptance and plunged into her story. Unvarnished and truthful, her tale flowed from her heart. "I am a liar. I have lied to you and your family for many years. You see, my real name is Malka Zigman. I don't know how you discovered that I am Jewish, but it's true. When I first came to Ravenscraig I even lied about my age. I was fourteen. Just a few months older than you are now."

Utterly shocked, Emma sat spellbound as she listened to Maisie detail the facts of her life. She explained that she had been born in London and that her parents had died of typhoid. She added that she was immune to typhoid not because she had any special magic, but because she'd had the illness herself as a child and had almost died from it. She talked of her family in Winnipeg and told her how they had come out of Russia. She went on to her desire to be a doctor, and her hopes that one day she would be accepted at university to study medicine. The only thing she held back was the fact that she had been secretly studying with Emma's brother, James.

Emma sat silently, her eyes like saucers and color gradually taking over her pale cheeks until she looked like a china doll, with glistening eyes and pink cheeks against her dark hair. Finally a smile of relief appeared. Much to Maisie's surprise, Emma flew into her arms and hugged her hard.

"Emma, I didn't expect to see you smiling at the end of my story," said Maisie. "I am totally mystified. You don't hate me?"

"Maisie, I love you like an auntie, or the sister I don't have. If you can share that truth with me then I know I can trust you with anything. Maisie, how you have suffered." A frown creased her brow. "I am so ashamed and so very sorry that I have said things that I'm sure have hurt you. I know now that there were many times that I repeated nasty things that would have been insulting and painful to you. I will never again in my life say anything that would be hurtful to a Jewish person. I had no idea. Can you ever forgive me?"

Only then did Maisie realize that she had completely misread her predicament. "Of course I forgive you. You mean you didn't know I was Jewish until just now?"

"Not until this moment."

"Why didn't you stop me?"

"You said not to."

"*Oy!*"

"What does that mean? *Oy*. I like that."

"And I thought you were upset because you had found me out!"

"Maisie, your being Jewish has nothing to do with my problem. It doesn't matter to me one bit that you are Jewish. If anything, I admire you more. You took charge of your life. You made it what you wanted it to be. Not many people are strong enough to do that."

Maisie sat speechless, her mouth hanging open. She had blundered into her own demise.

"Maisie. Please, don't worry. I will not tell a soul about what you have told me. I promise. Nothing will change at Ravenscraig. My parents will never know."

Maisie refilled Emma's teacup and passed it to her. Her hands shook so hard the cup rattled in the saucer. "Thank you,

Emma. You are a remarkable young woman. And now that I've thrown myself overboard, why don't we deal with your real secret. Maybe I can help."

"I'm sure you can, Maisie. You will know what to do. You are the smartest and bravest person I ever met."

At this Emma spilled her story about Elliot's looming disaster in Palm Beach and his need to be shielded from their parents. Maisie immediately came up with a solution that Emma knew would work.

41
Palm Beach

February 2, 1905

Maisie stepped off the train, and felt as though she'd awoken in a magical land. As much as she had read about Florida, she was still amazed by the change in climate. Could it possibly have been only three weeks since they left the cruel bite of winter behind in Manitoba? She felt transported in time from the frozen streets of Winnipeg, entombed in winter white, to this lush, fragrant tropical nest of green, welcoming her with songbirds and the alluring sound of the ocean. It truly was a paradise with perfect weather. Just feeling the warmth of the sun on her face was enough to make things right with the world. Everywhere she looked, she was surrounded by green hedges and neatly clipped shrubbery dotted with brilliantly colored blossoms. Tall swaying palms reached up into the bright blue sky, as if waving hello. Maisie was instantly convinced that there was no finer place in the world to be. As she stood at the train station in Palm Beach she couldn't help but gawk at it all.

Mr. and Mrs. Willows had already left the station and gone on to Whitehall in a small wicker cart pulled by a man. It was a rickshaw and was apparently considered a charming part of the experience of visiting Palm Beach. Mr. Willows was delighted with the arrangement, as Maisie could plainly see. Mrs. Willows, on the other hand, seemed completely thrown off by the thought of a man working as a mule, but ultimately she relented and they were quickly on their way to the Flagler mansion, leaving Maisie to attend to the luggage with Sam, one of the Whitehall servants.

Sam was friendly, polite and well schooled in his duties. He stood well over six feet tall and had a booming voice and a brilliant smile. At first, Maisie couldn't take her eyes off him. He was the tallest man she'd ever met and the first Negro she had ever seen.

With the luggage all accounted for, two trunks for Mr. Willows and three trunks and two large traveling wardrobes, along with an assortment of smaller cases for Mrs. Willows, Sam made quick work of loading the wagon. Then he helped Maisie climb up onto the seat next to him. She had an endless supply of questions for her agreeable companion, and Sam happily helped with the names of plants and trees she had never imagined existed.

"That be a Royal Palm tree, up there. Tall and smooth like that. When we rounds this next bend in the road they is gonna be a great line of 'em takin' us right up to Whitehall. My, my, it is somethin' to behold, chile, the first time you sees it. Why doan y'all jes close your eyes, and Sam is gonna tell ya when to open 'em up when we is at the gate."

"Sam, I don't think I can close my eyes for one second. I don't want to miss one thing. I can't imagine that I am not dreaming," Maisie told him.

Sam laughed with gusto and started to whistle a tune. Suddenly they were upon the great house, and Maisie's first glimpse of Whitehall took her breath away.

"This is not a home, it's a palace!" she hooted, unable to contain her excitement. "I hope to remember every detail to recall later."

"Nah. Now doan you be doin' no worryin' bout it, Miss Maisie. Ah kin make sure y'all gits a pitchah of the place. They gots these special ones made up for the guests and Ah kin get one of 'em for y'all. They's called postcards." Sam delighted in her company. "They got so many diff'rint kinds a rooms in that house you cain't even think what else they might a missed."

"Have you seen every room at Whitehall?" Maisie knew she was being nosy but couldn't contain her curiosity. Ravenscraig was a grand residence, but Whitehall looked at least ten times its size.

"Not all, but mos' of 'em, yas, I have, mm-hmm." Sam nodded. "I gits to hep with the heavy work in gittin all of ev'rythin shined up for Mistuh Flagler in the month before he git down here at the start a January. Folks like Mistuh Flagler does lots a entertainin, a course. Right inside that front door is a big hall to be sho to impress ev'rybody who come in the house. You could fit a whole bunch a reg'lar houses in that hall, with the rooftops an' all not even comin up to the ceilin' in there. And the ceilin itself is something you cain't even 'magine. It's like the sky, but with angels and such all painted up in the clouds up there. You think you is lookin right in at heaven's gates, when you lookin up at it." He started to chuckle. Ah done fell flat on my face, tripped over my own feet, the first time Ah been in that room. Jes couldn't take muh eyes off a them angels."

Maisie laughed, hoping she would see the great hall ceiling herself.

"Tell me more about the other rooms, Sam."

"Lemme see. They also has a breakfast room, a sun room, a special fancy parlor for Mrs. Flagler, a music room, a billiards room where the gempmums has they smokin and chewin tabacca. And jes waits till you see the big ballroom. It's all gold and filled with mirruhs from one end t'other just like some fancy place over in Paris they say. Oh, yas, and it got great huge crystal chandeliers. Whasat place called?" He scratched his head. "Lemme think. Yeah, I got it. They say it's jes like Voors-eye, in France. Thas what they's sayin. There's nuf room to have everyone in town in that room for a dancin party all at one time. Ah's been in it muhself, cause they was short a folks for the Cakewalk, thas a special kinda dance we colored folks does for the fancy guests when Mistuh Flagler asks. Mostly it's down over at the Breakers, that hotel a his over thar, but once in a while he ask the servants to pick up they heels to entertain y'all.

Maisie was enchanted with the way Sam spoke and hoped to remember every word from the likable driver.

"Bein you is trav'lin with Mr. Flagler's guests," Sam went on, "you is gittin your place to sleep up on the third floor so to be convenient for your Mistuh and Missus in the case they needs y'all. Ya see, the Whitehall servants is kept runnin all day long in they own work and Miss Flagler, she like if her comp'ny brings his own servants, ya see. She wants em to have it easy to bring 'em so thas why you up on the third floor."

"Do all the servants stay in the house?"

"No, ma'am. Rest of us is in places nearby the house. Me,

Ah stay out in the barn with the fellas who is lookin after the garden and such."

The horses trotted along energetically in the warm sun, making their way up the magnificent drive. The three story house was as large as a grand hotel. It was brilliant white, adorned with enormous pillars lined majestically along the front. As they drew closer, they passed through an ornate iron gate. Marble statues were placed along the road to steps that led up to a fountain, and beyond that stretched the paved pathway to the porch and the front door. Black iron filigree delicately covered the massive doors of the main entrance. From a distance, they appeared covered in lace. Sam guided the horses into a turn along a side road that would take them along to the back of the house and the servants' entrance.

"Us is goin in the back way, course, and you ain't gonna see that front hall right off, but when ya do, ya'll be thinkin you somehow landed in what they call a museum. Wait'll ya see what kind of stuff they put in there. My, oh, my. It all rich folks stuff. Ain't got no use but to be looked at and to set folks to wonderin jes what they might standin there lookin at. They's clocks and tables and all manner uh stuff you find nowhere but mebbe castles. Thas what they say, anyway. Me, Ah nevuh been in no museum nor in any castle. This be the only castle I know." He laughed again.

"It must be something to live here. Do the Flaglers enjoy the summer weather?"

"Summuh?" Sam turned to her and snickered. "Watchu talkin bout? No white folks like these uns is stayin here in summuh. Jes farmers and us local folks. No suh, they ain't up for the heat in the summuh," he laughed boisterously. "Not this kinda folks. They be meltin their skin right offa they bones, Ah think." At this he laughed so hard he slapped his knee.

"Well if they don't stay in summer, how much time do they spend at Whitehall?"

"Miss Maisie, if you kin b'lieve it, this big ole house has folks in it for jes two months. Then theys all packed up an gone till nex' time. Thas it. House is empty but for two housekeepers who keeps a eye on it and make sho it don't get no dust on them old paintins and statues an' all."

"Two months?" Maisie was astonished. "They have all this money invested in a house they stay in for two months?" She wondered how many people could go to university to become doctors on the money invested in Whitehall.

"In Decembuh, long 'bout three weeks before Mistuh Flagler come down heah, the house manager and the chef gits in and gits it all set up with servants and food and all what you need to be comftubble if you is white folks that needs this much luggage to be happy." He thrust his thumb over his shoulder at the heavy load behind them.

"I can't believe it. Two months. You have to see how people live where I come from."

"An doan I knows it. Poor folks is poor and rich folks is rich. But, thas they way they do it down here, chile. Thas what they's callin the season. Two months. For all us who's workin here, most gits about three months or sometimes four months of workin time and bein' here to look after them and closin' her up after the Flaglers is on their way up north agin. Ah's lucky 'cause Ah gits to work in heppin with the gardens all through the summuh."

"Speaking of servants. Do you happen to know the chef?"

"Met him once. Chef La Chance. He seems a little high-strung, kinda like a young colt. But, Ah guess it's likely account a he bein' from France. He act a bit like he got some fancy airs, Ahguess, but he seem to be all right with everybody. They say he sho can cook."

Maisie carefully placed the pink organza dressing gown in the armoire and gently closed the door.

"Everything is in order, Mrs. Willows."

"Thank you, Maisie, I'm sure I will be able to find everything I need," Mrs. Willows dropped into a chair and let out a small sigh. "I do hope I brought enough clothing. I was counting on only three changes each day, but I think I underestimated my needs for afternoon excursions. Whatever does one wear to watch men wrestle with alligators? Perhaps

Rupert won't mind if I sit out that little gem of local lore." Mrs. Willows caught herself thinking out loud and drew a hand to her mouth. "Please, forgive me. I must be more tired than I thought, Maisie. I would just die for a cup of tea. Could you find that maid, what is her name? Luellen, is it?"

"I think she's helping Mrs. Wilcox get settled down the hall. I will be happy to go round to the kitchen and bring the tea for you, mum," Maisie said with perhaps a little too much enthusiasm. "Should I also bring refreshments for Mr. Willows?"

"Where on earth do you find all of this energy? I can barely keep my eyes open. I'm sure that Mr. Willows will not be lacking for refreshments. He's off with our host, discussing business, no doubt, but, yes, do please bring me a tray. Thank you, Maisie."

As Maisie found her way to the servants' stairs she noted the plush carpeting and rich paintings in the second floor hallway. Mr. Flagler had seen to every comfort imaginable, and his experience as a hotelier must have influenced his design choices for the mansion. Every guest room had its own ensuite bathroom. Whoever heard of such a thing?

She ran down the stairs to the kitchen at the rear of the house. Two kitchen maids were busy scrubbing vegetables and carving them into animal shapes while a third was pulling fresh bread from the oven. Maisie introduced herself and peeked over their shoulders to see if she could spot Mr. Elliot. He was nowhere in the kitchen. She asked if she could put a tea tray together for Mrs. Willows. A pretty young maid with dark auburn hair wiped her hands and welcomed Maisie with a big smile.

"I'm Clarisse. Let me put the tray together for your lady. Mostly we're accustomed to iced tea in the South. I'm from New Orleans, myself. But, I do know how to prepare hot tea," she said, anxious to show off her new training. "Chef says that the guests from the North always drink their tea hot, and I was taught to make it right."

"I understand that your chef is quite well regarded."

"He's dreamy," answered Clarisse with a glow. "But if you think you have a chance with him, you are mistaken. There is a line-up of girls hoping to catch his eye, and not all of them are staff members!"

"My goodness!"

"Do you think I might have a quick word with Chef La Chance, regarding the dietary needs of Mrs. Willows? She is recovering from a rather extended period of ... of exhaustion, and has asked that I might explain her needs to Chef La Chance." Her fingers crossed, Maisie hoped she didn't sound too clumsy.

"Well, certainly. Do put in good word for me with him, will you? He is in his office. Just a moment." She knocked on the door at the far end of the kitchen.

"He's very busy, but he will see you now for just a minute. Tell him how nicely I'm preparing a tray for your Mrs. Willows!" she whispered.

"I'm sure he will be delighted to hear that."

Elliot Willows was seated at a large table facing the window with his back to the door. Charts and pencils and a stack of cookbooks were neatly set before him. He was bent over his work as he spoke.

"*Oui. Une minute, s'il vous, plait!*" he said over his shoulder. *Excusez moi, mademoiselle.* Tell me, please, which guest it is that you are wishing to speak to me about."

"Mrs. Willows." She watched his back muscles tighten and his shoulders rise as if he might spring from the chair and fly through the window before him. But he didn't turn around.

"Did you mean to say Mrs. Willard? I have Mr. and Mrs. Willard on my list, but no one name Willow."

"Excuse me, no, it's Willows," she answered formally. "Willows with an s."

"I see," he said, still facing the table. "I am so sorry, I am so frightfully busy. Um, could you um, perhaps come back later?" As he spoke he shifted into a heavy French accent, and his voice deepened in what Maisie saw as a transparent attempt to disguise his identity. She fought not to laugh.

"Mister Elliot," she whispered urgently.

He wheeled around, with terror in his eyes. "Close the door," he whispered, his face white with fear. "Do I know you?"

"I'm, Maisie. I was hired at Ravenscraig shortly before you

left for your studies in Europe. I was pretty young then."

"Maisie! Yes. My God! Are you telling me my parents are at Whitehall?"

"They are. Just arrived. I have come to fetch tea for your mother and Clarisse is getting it ready."

"This will be the death of me!"

"No, it won't."

"Do you want money?"

"Of course not!"

"That's right!" Elliot brightened. "It occurs to me that we have something in common. If you keep my secret, I will repay you by keeping yours." He stood and stared down at her.

"My secret?" Maisie's mouth went dry. "May I sit?"

"Yes, I know all about your secret."

"What ... or when did she tell you?" How could Emma have deceived her?

"Great Scot! What are you talking about? He, not she!" Elliot was confused. Was she trying to throw him off his path? "I know all about your secret medical studies with James. I know how fond my brother is of you. He wrote and told me all about it. I could have you sacked in a minute if you breathe one word of my secret identity to my parents! They would be very unhappy, indeed, at the thought of a romance between James and a member of the staff at Ravenscraig!"

Maisie stared back. James? Fond of her?

"Now you listen to me," Elliot wagged a finger at her. "This job, this career, is the most important thing in the world to me, and as it appears we are both standing on the veritable precipice of ruin, I want to know exactly what your intentions are. Well, speak up!"

Maisie opened her mouth, but no words came out. She gasped.

Elliot's hysteria immediately abated as he saw how stricken she was. Clearly, she was more frightened for her own future than she was concerned about destroying his.

"Sherry?" Elliot's face loomed over hers.

"It's Maisie, not Sherry."

"I meant to drink. Here, take this. He shoved a glass into

her hands. "Take hold of yourself, Maisie. That tea tray will be ready in a minute. We don't have much time. All you need to know is that I will tell my parents about my life only when I am ready. If they learn now, I will be finished."

She downed the drink. "Don't worry. You can trust me. Emma asked me to help you."

She told him about her discussion with Emma and his sister's fervent desire to protect him. He was deeply touched. They made a pact to protect each other, for both immediately recognized a budding friendship. Greatly relieved, he fought down an urge to hug her as he wiped a tear from his eyes. She assured him that she'd keep a sharp eye out to keep him from running into his parents. The kitchen staff almost never came into contact with the guests; only the most extraordinary of circumstance would create such a meeting. They were certain they could keep their secrets.

"Maisie. Thank you," Elliot sighed with relief as she got up to leave. He opened the door for her. Mr. and Mrs. Willows would be given superlative treatment by the kitchen staff at Whitehall and the tea tray would be ready.

James.

James had confessed to his brother that he was fond of her. Maisie floated back up the stairs with the tray of tea and crumpets and knocked gently at the door.

42
The Jordan Report
February 19, 1905

Jim McGraw ran up the stairs and burst through the door of the composing room at the *Winnipeg Star*. Isaac glanced up as he typed steadily at the Linotype machine. "Ziggy!" Jim yelled over the clatter. "How much more time do you need? I've got something to show you."

"Hey, Jim, I'll be finished this page in half an hour."

"Well, hurry it up. You won't believe what I got my hands on."

"Free tickets for the fights?" Isaac grinned.

"Nah. Better than that!" Jim came in closer and patted his coat pocket. "I've got a copy of the Jordan report."

"So soon?" Isaac was astonished. "It won't even be presented to City Council until tomorrow. Where'd you get it?"

"That's none of your business. But it's the real McCoy, all right. Hurry up. I'll meet you at Mariaggi's."

"Give me fifteen minutes." Isaac began typing as fast as he could.

In their usual booth at the back of the hotel coffee shop, Jim was immersed in Dr. Jordan's report on typhoid as Isaac bounded in and flung his coat on the rack. "So? What does the Chicago doctor tell us about the water supply?"

"Hold your horses, cowboy," said Jim, still reading. "As you would expect, it seems the good professor is not particularly eager to offend anyone who hands him a pay envelope. He is awful damn careful with his criticism of City Hall. All we have in this paper is a pretty good summary of the various potential causes of the typhoid and a few obvious recommendations that aren't anything we haven't already heard from our local bacteria boys in the health department.

The one thing I can tell you is that folks are going to be screaming bloody murder about paying for this outside opinion."

Jim snorted as he tossed the report across the table at Isaac.

"What does he say about polluted drinking water?" Isaac asked as he scanned the report.

"Well, he's not as conclusive as the *Star's* mystery reporter. That was some pretty fine writing, my friend. And don't think you didn't get people talking about your theory. It's all over town. The numbers of new cases are way up, just like you figured they would be after the December fire. It's even in the report. Look here," he pointed to a chart. "See? In the first two weeks of January there were one hundred and twenty cases of typhoid reported. We haven't seen numbers that high since the end of last summer. I'd put money down that you are dead on with your theory."

"But what does Jordan say?" Isaac searched through the report impatiently. "Where does he talk about the drinking water?"

"Oh, for the love of Pete, you got even less patience than I do. For Gawd's sake, Ziggy, gimme the damn report. I'll find the section for you."

He flipped through the pages. "Here, get a load of this. Jordan writes, 'on two occasions in 1904, raw Assiniboine River water was turned into the city mains to boost the inadequate supply and meet emergencies caused by large fires.'"

"No kidding. He's got it!" exclaimed Isaac.

"Hold on, Ziggy. Then he puts in these tables, see, showing the number of new typhoid cases, which he says, 'reveal several interesting facts'. Then there's a lot of malarkey commentary before he finally gets to the point. Here read this part." Jim slid the report back across the table.

Isaac felt his spine tingle as he read aloud: "A striking increase of almost explosive character is shown in the next fortnight when the cases reported registered 120. It is a highly suspicious circumstance that the dates on which the Assiniboine water was pumped into the city mains, namely October 10th and December 28th, correspond with the dates of probable infection of the cases reported in the two periods referred to."

He stopped reading and looked up at Jim. "He's got the dates of the fires both wrong by a day, but he's confirming the cause of the typhoid outbreak was the drinking water!"

"No, he ain't doing no such thing. If you read this thing carefully you'll see that all that the professor is doing is saying it could be a factor. He also talks about sewers and the possible contamination of the milk supply. If you flip to the back you'll see his recommendations. He's real keen on getting rid of the outhouses and having sewer connections built to all the homes as soon as possible. Like none of us could figure that out ourselves." Jim snorted as he pulled the sheaf of papers closer and turned the page.

"Here's a good one. This one will melt that curly hair right off your little head, Ziggy. Read this."

Isaac looked at the line Jim was pointing to and again read out loud. "It is evident that it is not consonant with the public safety that any person ill with typhoid fever should be allowed to remain in a house without a sewer connection."

Isaac shook his head in disbelief. "So, anyone with typhoid should just move in with someone who has a sewer connection. Where does this man think these people will go?" He went to the last page again. "And what about the danger of pumping in dirty water from the Assiniboine? I don't see him addressing it at all in the recommendations."

"Oh, it's there, all right," Jim assured him. "You can bet your ass that I hunted through that fancy language to find that sucker. Take a look at the teeny, tiny little mention at the end of the fourth recommendation." He jabbed his finger at the copy.

"Water from the Assiniboine River should be used as little as possible," Isaac read. "What?"

"See, Ziggy? I think he's going out of his way to make sure everything is in nice, general terms. It's easy to condemn the outhouses because they're mostly in the North End, and the city's been hearing folks yammering about them for years. But Jordan can't actually condemn using the Assiniboine River water because our city fathers have probably done a real good job of letting him know the whole damn town would burn down, just like Chicago did in '71, if we can't use it to fight fires once in a while. Think about it. Professor Jordan is from Chicago, and I tell you, folks in that town still talk about the great fire as if it was last week."

Isaac was completely deflated. "So what was the point of having had Jordan do the report?"

"It's simple." Jim leaned on his forearms. "This is Canada. When you pay an outsider, especially a big shot American, to tell you something you already know, people take it more seriously. This makes the city look like it cares about its citizens and wants to do something about the sanitation problems. The soft recommendations leave all kinds of wiggle room for the city councilors to take their time before putting any real money into cleaning things up. You wait. Now that the water system is back to normal and coming from the artesian wells only, we've got no more rich folks suckin' up typhoid germs from the Assiniboine River. Typhoid goes back to being a problem in the immigrant neighborhoods and the story moves right off the front page."

"That's an incredibly cynical view, Jim." Isaac sighed.

"Yup. That's the way it is, Ziggy. Hey, but don't be totally down about it. There are going to be some good things to come out of this. I think the city council is actually going to do something about getting a new source of safe water for the city."

"You think the Jordan report will make that happen?"

"Nope." Jim slurped his coffee and signaled the waiter for a refill. "I think the report's small potatoes. I think the city is going to solve the water quality problem strictly because the upper class has been directly touched by the sanitation problems. I don't think they'll chance using the Assiniboine to fight fires a third time. You had a real influence in getting people thinking about water pollution, and you ought to be proud of yourself for sticking to your guns."

"And the North End will continue to be ignored while the city spends a load of money on the new water supply."

"Well, they've sure set the pattern for that, I would say."

"Maybe I should write about that and slip that story into the newspaper, too."

"Maybe not. They're onto you, Ziggy, and it's going to be a lot harder to get things into print on the sly."

"You sure?"

"That I am. I heard it from the copy chief. I also heard they aren't planning on reprimanding you if you stop doing it. But you gotta stop now. The boys in the front office aren't nuts about the criticism they've been getting from their buddies at City Hall. The only reason they haven't said anything to you is that they've sold more papers."

Isaac couldn't suppress a grin.

Jim folded the report and handed it across the table. "Here, I'm done with this. I'll be getting my 'official' copy tomorrow at City Hall. You read this through. And then you know what I'd do if I were you, Ziggy?"

"What?"

"Well, don't get your head all swelled up when I tell ya this, but you can actually write. You're good. I think you oughta go and write a story about how much suffering is really goin' on in the North End, how those greenhorns are starving because they're so poor, all the while battling typhoid, scarlet fever, diphtheria and all that, not to mention freezing to death. But don't write it for our paper. They'll never take you seriously. Write it for that new national magazine out of Toronto. You know the one: *The Dominion from Coast to Coast*. They've bought a couple of articles from me. I'll put in a good word for you."

"Well, I thank you, Jim. Maybe I'll try," Isaac shrugged.

Jim stood up to leave and looked down at Isaac who seemed to be sliding into defeat. He reached over and clipped the back of his head.

"Hey! What's that for?"

"That's for feeling sorry for yourself, like a girl. Stop it right now. This isn't something for you to *try*, this is something you really need to do, Isaac. This is why you belong in this business." Jim McGraw pulled his heavy coat up onto his solid frame and left his young friend to wrestle with his conscience.

Isaac sighed. Then he opened the report and read it through, carefully. True enough, there was some good information that had been gathered, and the recommendations would do no harm. But he found himself bitterly disappointed that the politely worded Jordan report was not the hard-hitting document he expected to see as a tool to fuel social change. There simply was no political will in Winnipeg to alleviate the suffering in the foreign quarter.

He rubbed his eyes, feeling hopeless. It was only then that it occurred to him that this was the first time that Jim had ever called him Isaac. He thought about their conversation on his long walk home; by the time he reached the house on Selkirk Avenue, he knew what he wanted to do.

Two weeks later, Isaac Zigman went to the post office and sent his story to Toronto.

43
Winnipeg's Shameful Secret
March 15, 1905

Rupert dug into his pocket for a handful of coins at the newsstand in Toronto's Union Station. He was thankful to be able to stretch his legs and take a breath of air before rejoining Beth on the train for the last leg of their journey home. Starved for Canadian news after two months out of the country, he had loaded up with three newspapers and two magazines.

"I'll also take that *Vanity Fair* for my wife," he told the newsie. "You don't happen to have a copy of the *Manitoba Free Press?*"

"Just a couple of old ones that came in last week on the train. You can have 'em for free. And if you're from Winnipeg you might wanna read this," he turned to the back of his magazine stand and pulled out a copy of *The Dominion, Coast to Coast*. "There's a humdinger of a tale about Winnipeg in this issue. Just out today."

"Well, yes, I'll take it, thank you." Rupert paid quickly and ran back to his private car, as the conductor shouted for straggling passengers. He handed his coat to Maisie, pleased to see Beth emerging from their private quarters to join him in the car's parlor.

"My, how lovely you look," he said admiringly. "I see that our Florida holiday has completely replenished both your beauty and good health. I am so delighted, my darling."

"It was truly grand, wasn't it, Rupert?" She reached for his hand. "It was so lovely to be around society people of that caliber. I will treasure our holiday forever, and I do hope that we will be back at Whitehall another time."

"I'm sure we will, darling. Everyone seemed quite enchanted with your charming ways. What did you enjoy most?"

"I think that fabulous costume party, the *Bal Poudre*, to

celebrate President Washington's birthday. What a fabulous evening."

"Really? I rather thought the alligator wrestling would have topped your list," he teased.

"Rupert! That vulgar little man and those hideous beasts! Darling, it was a sign of my deep and adoring affection for you that I even accompanied you to that…that pit!"

"Oh dear, and here I thought you might have wanted to take one home."

"Please!" She shuddered. "Actually the only thing I wished to take home from Palm Beach was the recipe for that incredible dessert that Chef La Chance made."

"The *Crêpes Suzette*?"

"I've never had anything quite so delicate. The amazing aromas of the Grand Marnier igniting the sweet orange juice. It makes me swoon to think about it. How impressed our friends would be if we could have something like that served in our home! The food at Whitehall was absolutely extraordinary in every way, and I'm so sorry that we couldn't persuade Chef La Chance to say hello to us in person. Rather rude, don't you think?"

"Well, Mrs. Flagler did explain that he was an *artiste*, and a bit temperamental. The French can be like that, you know. Perhaps remaining unseen was deliberate to add to his aura."

"Oh, I do hope we'll return to Palm Beach before long. Could we get a home there one day, Rupert? I would adore being there every year." Beth batted her eyes at her husband.

Maisie appeared, carrying a tray with a pot of tea and a plate of cucumber sandwiches.

"Excuse me, Mr. and Mrs. Willows, the dining car is reporting a delay, and I thought you might care for a bit of refreshment in the meantime."

"How thoughtful, Maisie. Thank you," answered Beth.

"I also have a telegram that was delivered to your attention, Mr. Willows, during the station stop in Toronto."

"A telegram, from whom?" asked Beth.

"It's from Alfred," said Rupert, with concern on his face. He tore it open, scanned it quickly and broke into a wide smile.

"It's wonderful news, Beth. There is to be a wedding at Ravenscraig!"

Maisie felt as though she'd been punched in the stomach. A wedding?

"Alfred is to be married to Lily Quartermain," Rupert announced. "Isn't that marvelous news?"

Beth clapped her hands with joy. "How wonderful! Such excitement after our holiday, Rupert. Lily is a fine young woman. Well educated and cultured. Her parents belong to all of the right clubs. Just the kind of wife Alfred needs."

"Yes, quite," responded Rupert. "A tad dull, perhaps, and a little timid, but I agree, he's made a good choice. Too bad James is so slow off the mark in getting involved in a social life. On the rare occasion he does go out, he picks the dreariest girls in the city to share his company. He seems much more interested in his medical studies than he does in romance. It's time he paid more attention to his future, don't you agree?"

"Now, Rupert, don't be marrying off all of my children in such a big hurry. James will be graduating this year, and he will find his happiness. You will see."

Much relieved that it was Alfred and not James announcing the upcoming nuptials, Maisie retreated to her place in the tiny kitchen of the Pullman car. She smiled to herself as the train clattered down the track, and she tidied up the workstation. Of course, it would be impossible to think of a life with James, but dreaming about it could do no harm.

In the parlor, Rupert had tired of discussing plans for the wedding and pulled out his reading glasses.

"I'm sure that you and Mrs. Butterfield will be quite capable of looking after all of these little details, and I will thank you to keep me out of the planning. Now if you would excuse me, my love, I'd like to catch up on the news."

"Did you find something worthwhile at the newsstand?"

"Plenty, including a society magazine you may like." He settled into his comfortable seat and opened *The Dominion, Coast to Coast*.

Maisie dozed as the train rocked along the tracks, happily thinking about telling her family all about her Florida adventures, and returning to her studies with James. It was the shouting that woke her up. Mr. Willows was in quite a state. She cracked the kitchen door open to better hear his ranting.

"How dare they print this rubbish? And here I thought *Coast to Coast* was a serious magazine, not a scandal sheet!" Rupert was on his feet, pacing.

"Rupert, dear!" Beth tried to calm him. "You frightened me out of my skin. What on earth are you reading?"

"Here, look at this. It's a dreadful expose on the foreign quarter of Winnipeg that has been written for the sole purpose of damning the actions of city council. It's written by a man named Isaac Zigman, a Hebrew, no doubt, who is out to destroy our image by unfairly painting a terrible picture of our fair city!"

The hair stood up on Maisie's neck. Isaac Zigman!

The Shameful Secret in the Gateway City
By Isaac Zigman

Winnipeg is hiding a dark secret from the world. While it clamors to be recognized as the fastest growing city in the Dominion, Winnipeg has turned its back on its most defenseless citizens—the impoverished slum dwellers, a great many of them children, in the foreign quarter, now known simply as the city's North End.

Sitting at the gateway to the North-West, isolated by geography a full five hundred miles from its closest large neighbor, Minneapolis, Minnesota, Winnipeg is home to theaters, opera, restaurants and hundreds, even thousands of citizens with the means to frequent these elegant establishments. The Manitoba capital boasts musical societies, art galleries, and piano stores, aplenty. There are rows of banks and real estate offices, as well as warehouses, fine department stores, and sewing factories. There are grain merchants, furriers, cloak makers, book publishers, bicycle shops, and motorcar sales offices. Doctors and dentists by the dozen are housed in fine tall buildings reaching six stories and more to the sky.

Winnipeg is also home to fine institutions of higher learning, filled with ambitious young men, and an increasing number of bright young women, all looking to the future. Even young girls, if they are from families of appropriate circumstances, may attend one of the finest girls' schools in the country, Winnipeg's Havergal College.

In short, it is a city with everything, except compassion for the under classes, whose daily suffering is equal to that in the world's worst slums. Vastly overcrowded, with the poorest shelter imaginable, the North End is tucked away out of sight and out of mind, lest the sensibilities of the upper classes be offended. Indeed, it would no doubt be a shock to many inhabitants of the Manitoba capital to know that such poverty exists in their midst.

Among those who live out of sight and out of mind, is Victor Gurevetsky, a child of the slums. This is his story.

Two hours before sunrise on a bitterly cold February morning, Victor takes his place in a line at the employment office on Winnipeg's Main Street. There are perhaps seventy men in front of him, and more quickly gather behind. They huddle together in the freezing weather, slapping their arms through patched coats to stay warm. In a variety of languages, they share stories about which company is hiring and how much is being paid. Is there a boxcar to unload? Wood to cut? Snow to be shoveled? Does anyone have need for a good blacksmith's helper?

Men skilled as tailors and machine workers fare better than the new immigrants who don't speak English, for they have little to offer beyond their strength and reliability.

After several hours, dejected and worried, Victor leaves the employment office without any work.

Victor is twelve years old, but since his father's recent death from consumption, he is burdened with the responsibility as sole provider for his family. Now, it is all up to Victor to feed and shelter his mother, his sisters, ages six and five, and his infant brother, who was born two months after his father was gathered by the grim reaper.

Consenting to allow this reporter to accompany him, Victor heads to the river to gather driftwood. Perhaps he could sell a few sticks and make a penny or two, he explains.

When her husband died, Mrs. Gurevetsky had no choice but

to move her children to the poorest section of the ghetto. It was all they could afford. It was here that Victor's baby brother, Sol, was born, with the help of a neighbor. He said it was so cold that his mother's hair froze to the wall in the shack during the birthing.

The slums of Winnipeg, generally known as the North End, are separated from downtown and the better neighborhoods by the train tracks and the sprawling railway yards. As Victor tells his story, we make our way from the river, back to Main Street, and head north across the tracks. Here we find a string of small shops frequented by the people of the foreign quarter.

There are fruit merchants and dry goods stores. Others are selling meat and sausages, with chickens hanging in windows and barrels of herring, sauerkraut and apples near the doorways. Shoppers haggle for bargains in the used clothing shops. Victor remarks that his sisters have a single coat to share. It is the same one they use as a blanket. He is trying to save money to buy a used coat for himself, but finds it hard to save. The money goes for food before clothing, he says.

The afternoon light is fading as we round the corner from Main Street and moved toward a clutter of wooden shacks on Dufferin.

The dismal shelters offer little comfort against the forty-below zero temperatures in this hard land. Tempers fray under the weight of hunger and poverty. Fingers, numb with cold, reach for shared scraps in a pot, while mothers watch to see that all of the children get a share of whatever there might be to eat.

Dirt is caked in lines along Victor's exposed wrists; his hands are reddened by the cold. With dark hollows under eyes too old for a boy so young, Victor explains that the hunger never goes away.

"Poverty in the old country and poverty in Winnipeg look and smell the same," he says. "You don't forget."

Acre after acre, the sights and smells of destitution have taken root here, strangling the ambitions of many of society's weaker members, citizens who have no one to fend for them.

The newspapers refer to the area as the foreign quarter, but "Mitzrayim", is what the Jewish residents call it. Strictly speaking, this is the Hebrew term for Egypt, but to those who call this area Mitzrayim, it describes the suffering of Jews still fighting to be free.

Here the shacks appear glued together for warmth against the bitter cold. Smoke wafts from a chimney here and there, and the dark, dirty sheds fade into shades of grey and black against the starkly beautiful blue of the fading prairie day. The neighborhood more closely resembles a heap of smoldering rubbish than a place for people to live.

The ugliness spreads well beyond this dreary corner, for thousands of families, transplanted from Eastern Europe are flooding into the North End. Those most fortunate occupy the more expensive tenements, hastily and poorly built by speculators. These property owners were quick to see that the steady stream of immigrants from Russia, Romania, Galicia, Bukovina, Poland, Germany, Hungary, and other countries would provide a rich return for landlords.

This prairie version of slum housing is a long, drab wooden structure, divided into narrow homes, each with its own door fronting onto a common porch. Often two, or even three, families will share the expenses of a two-room tenement. Some of the more imaginative landlords stack a second storey onto the first to get the most from their investment. Fire is a daily fear. Bedbugs are a year-round problem. Maggots, mosquitoes and flies are thankfully restricted to the summer months.

Cleanliness is a wish that goes unfulfilled in the struggle to survive. At best, a battered washbasin is filled with water that has to be carried in pails from a community pump two blocks away. Regular bathing is only for the rich.

The harshness of winter provides a bitter solace. It offers protection against the many diseases that flourish here in summer when flies and mosquitoes carry illness from one home to another. In summer, the small patches of yard, when they exist, are often not safe places for children to play, but rather breeding grounds for diseases like typhoid, diphtheria tuberculosis, smallpox, and scarlet fever. Human waste spills from the outhouses that stand too close to the back of the homes.

Inhabitants live in fear of the appearance of horse-drawn wagons that come to collect the dying folk, stricken with smallpox and other contagious, incurable diseases. For these hapless souls, the wagon means a one-way trip to a facility west of town on the edge of the prairie adjacent to Brookside Cemetery. It is the Pestilence House. From there, it is a conveniently shorter trip to the final resting place in a pauper's grave at Brookside.

Driven by the crowding, foul odors and constant arrival of new tenants, each year new shacks spring up next to the tenements as renters turn into squatters in homes they build themselves out of whatever they can find or steal. These shelters are hovels, some less than hovels. Most are barely more than lean-tos made of used crates and scrap yard cast offs, strung together by frozen clotheslines.

Desperation is always close at hand, ready at an instant to explode into violence. The wind moans through the rubble, occasionally punctuated by the solid smack of a fist landing on its mark. Wailing, crying. Death comes at night. Babies, too, come in the darkness, into a world steeped in the stench of wet woolen boot liners, dirty blankets and unwashed workers.

But, like a dying ember in the stove, so burns the promise of tomorrow in the ghetto; the defiant hope that spring will come. There are also signs of success as businesses take root, schools are built and children are educated. There is a pride and determination among the dwellers of the North End of Winnipeg as they are building the foundation for future generations, who will grow and prosper in the new country.

Victor says: "In Canada, the streets aren't paved with gold as they dreamed they were in the Old Country, but neither are they drenched in blood from the violent life they left behind."

Victor will go to the Main Street employment office again in the morning. He is there every morning. Every day he dreams of a future when he will own a business to support his family. A bakery, he says. A bakery on Dufferin Avenue, so that they will never again be hungry for bread.

Rupert continued to stew over the magazine article while Beth read the story. When she started to weep he couldn't stop himself from rolling his eyes and turned away.

"Oh, why can't you do anything about this, Rupert?" she whined.

He paused for a moment as inspiration charged through him. She was right. A brilliant opportunity was at hand.

He would wire Alfred to find this guttersnipe and hire him as an errand boy. Rupert paced as he calculated how much press he would generate from this act of generosity and grudgingly decided he would also have to throw in free rental accommodation for the wretched family to gain the attention of the *Manitoba Free Press*. It would be worth it. He'd have a good shot at making the front page.

44
Matters of the Heart
March 26, 1905

A joyous chorus of honking birds lifted Maisie's wilted spirits. The giant Canada Geese were filling the pre-dawn sky by the thousands, heralding the start of another spring. Thus awakened from her fitful, troubled sleep, Maisie threw open her attic window and stuck her head into the rush of freezing air. She took comfort in the sound of the geese as she sought to ease her painful matters of the heart. Perhaps the geese would help her answer James' question. She knew what she had to say. She just needed to find the words to face it. She blinked hard against the fresh tears.

She was barely able to make out the long strings of birds, stretching out in perfect "V" formations against the dark sky. The call of the geese was a sound like no other. To her, it was the sound of victory. Another migration behind them. Mating for life and driven only by instinct, these sturdy birds knew no barriers. They didn't question. They had no choices to make. They did what nature dictated, even nesting in ice and snow, if need be, to hatch their young.

Maisie closed her eyes and felt the chill of the air on her cheeks, the wind in her hair. She was soothed by her communion with nature. Her own family came to mind. How determined they had always been, together in strength and purpose. Had she gone astray? Had she forgotten how to be one with her own kind?

Within a few weeks there would be endless gaggles of bright yellow goslings to watch along the riverbanks, each little beating heart driven to fulfill its destiny.

Maisie pondered, for a time, the notion that each new bird arrives in the world knowing precisely what purpose it shall serve. To live an eternally uncomplicated life, uncluttered by the necessity to make decisions, put the geese in an enviable position, she mused. Oh, the benefits of being born with a plan firmly planted in your brain that would take all need for consideration out of your hands, out of your control. She sighed at the thought of the letter under her pillow. She took it out and smoothed it in the dark, caressing the pages until the early morning light became strong enough for her to see the words.

March 25, 1905

Dearest Maisie,

It has been so difficult for me to work with you since your return from Florida. I have come to a decision, and I hope you don't think me cowardly or unkind for putting my words on paper rather than taking the chance to speak to you in person. Forgive me if this seems a wholly inappropriate way to take what I desperately hope will be a new path for us.

As awkward as it is, given your position, and mine, I must confess my deep and abiding affection for you. I missed your company terribly when you traveled with my parents. Since your return, there are moments when I look at you and see that it may be true, and not just hopeful thinking on my part that you may care for me as I do for you.

I will say it straight out. It is my deepest wish that you will agree to be my wife. I have reconciled my understanding that the family, my father in particular, will put me out and perhaps never have anything to do with me, or us, ever again.

I do, however, believe, dear Maisie, that it is my destiny to be with you. To say goodbye to my family with the assurance that you will forever be by my side is worth the great price.

Please say that you will consider my request.

With all my love,

James

Maisie had found the letter under her door on her return the previous evening. It was shockingly wonderful and horrible all at the same time. As she read it, she felt her heart soar among the stars, but soon came the crushing realization that it was truly impossible. She had become a prisoner in her own lie.

Under the glaring light of truth, she saw the depths of her naiveté and recognized the terrible and unforgivable sin she had committed, not only in lying about who she was, but in leading this dear man to fall in love with her as she had most certainly fallen in love with him. What game did she think she was playing? All that she had thought of in recent years was that it was wonderfully romantic to think of James, and to encourage him to think of her. Now she saw how terribly unfair that was.

How had she come to live two lives? She was a goose masquerading as a canary, a goose that belonged with her own kind. She came from stable, reliable unchanging people who for thousands of years had clung solidly to their complex identity as Jews, even in the face of great oppression. Hers were a people burdened with reason, living largely through instinct. Such is the path of the Jews.

Dreaming of a life with James could have gone on forever. She had barely turned nineteen, and with James just twenty-two, she had blindly thought that she would have several years ahead of romantic daydreams around the unreachable young Mr. James, now Dr. Willows.

Now, in suddenly bringing her dreams into the open, and truly granting her wish for romance, she would set off a chain of events that would cause great pain and irrevocable harm to many relationships.

Her only possible course of action would be to set him free. She would have to tell him good-bye. She held herself and slumped achingly against the decision, believing her heart would surely break. Then she gathered herself and wrote the letter.

March 26, 1905

Dear Mr. James,

It is with great sadness and deepest regret that I must tell you that I cannot accept your proposal. Please do not ask me to explain any further than to tell you that I recognize this is an impossible situation with the potential of too much pain for you and also for your dear family. I shall greatly miss our friendship.

I do wish to stay on at Ravenscraig, but I will understand if you ask me to resign my post.

Sincerely,
Maisie Rosedale

45
Elliot's Return

May 21, 1905

The dew was barely off the lawn when Maisie stooped to gather the bundle of lilacs and breathed in their sweet scent. The entire perimeter of Ravenscraig was lined in the fragrant spring blooms and the early morning air was filled with their alluring aroma. Mrs. Willows had announced that as Alfred's fiancée, Lily Quartermain, would be joining them for Sunday dinner, they would be having a bit of a celebration of their engagement, and she had asked Maisie to fill every vase in the dining room with the pink and lavender blossoms.

Maisie was glad to be outdoors working with the flowers. In recent weeks, she took special care to notice and appreciate those things that she loved most, as a means of wrenching her aching heart free from thoughts of James.

He had not taken her letter well. He remained polite, but had immediately placed a distance between them. She had hardly spoken with him in weeks. He left the house a good deal, having increased his desire for social activities, it appeared. When at home, he stayed behind closed doors. The thought that he had so quickly severed their relationship stung. As much as it hurt, it was for the best, and she would move on with her life as James had. No one in the house asked for her resignation and she never offered it.

She had found a parting gift, or what she had assumed was a parting gift on her return to Ravenscraig the previous weekend. Stacked on the floor next to her door were fifteen medical textbooks.

> Dear Miss Rosedale,
>   I hope you find many years of pleasure from your studies.
> Please accept these books as a token of my gratitude for the many good things you have contributed to life in Ravenscraig.

With sincere good wishes for your future, I remain,

Yours truly,
James Willows

Though pained by the shift in their communication, and the loss of their study sessions, she was, in fact, relieved. As each day passed, her heartbreak had lessened. She worked to regain a sunny outlook and to focus on her dream of attending university. It was only right that James should stay with his own kind. Even so, she couldn't help but find it irksome that he appeared to be rather popular with the daughters of the captains of industry in Winnipeg. There was no shortage of young women vying for the attention of the quiet young doctor. He had joined the practice of Dr. Carruthers, and from all reports he was very well thought of.

It was also obvious that the twittering matrons who came to tea at Ravenscraig were competing for match-making opportunities. As a result, Maisie had had to steel herself against the frequent appearance of adoring young women seated next to James at the family dinner table. Tonight would be no exception. Well, be that as it may, there was nothing to do but shift her own attitude and take firm steps toward her own future. With pragmatism taking hold, she admonished herself, and forced her brain to accept that James had been a dream, a young girl's fantasy. Mr. James could go on and have all of the brainless beauties he desired. She would find her own romance one day. Someone of her own type, whatever that might end up being.

She buried her nose in the sweet-scented lilacs. Today was a new day. There were flowers to arrange and pastries to bake. Mrs. Willows had developed a special fondness for elaborate French desserts on her trip to Palm Beach and Mrs. Butterfield would be needing help with today's experimental creation.

Her arms full of flowers, Maisie stepped carefully along the path to the kitchen service door. The sun shone in her eyes as she rounded the corner. A man in a cap was waiting for her, and she assumed he was delivering something to the kitchen. But on Sunday? She ducked behind the flowers to shield her eyes from the sun. "Good morning," she called out.

"Please, allow me, Mademoiselle, to help you with those flowers."

"Mr. Elliot!" she gasped then quickly dropped her voice to a whisper, "I mean, good morning, Chef La Chance. What a wonderful surprise!"

"So good to see you, Maisie."

"But why are you coming in the servants' entrance?"

"Shh!" He put his fingers to his lips. "I'm so glad I saw you before I knocked on the kitchen door. I need your help with managing my surprise return."

With his engaging smile and the confidence of a champion, it was clear life had treated Elliot Willows well; he was returning to Ravenscraig in triumph. She was deeply pleased for his obvious success.

"Of course, I'll help you."

"You did me a great service in protecting me, Maisie. I will never forget your kindness and your trustworthiness."

Trust. She felt as though she'd been stabbed in the heart. If only he knew.

"Mr. Elliot, please. It was my pleasure to help. Where is your luggage?"

"I stayed at the Leland Hotel last night so that I could arrive in secret. I've asked Henry to go round and collect my things later."

"So no one in the house knows you are in Winnipeg?"

"That's right. I've come home on a special mission, Maisie. I told you I would share my secret with my parents when the time was right, and now is that time. I have so many opportunities in New York that I'm tired of the burden of carrying my secret life. I want to come clean with my family and see if I can bring them on side. You can't imagine how hard it is to live two lives."

"I can well appreciate how complicated it has been. I am so happy for you, Mr. Elliot." Maisie fought to keep her envy in check.

"Thank you. I have a plan and I do think it will be good fun in the end. I need you to find Mrs. Butterfield so I can speak to you both at the same time about the details of my scheme.

Please, do not tell anyone else that I am here."

"Of course, but Emma, I mean, Miss Emma, will be heartbroken to have to wait to see you," Maisie cautioned.

"She'll be fine," he insisted. "Trust me. Everything will work out splendidly. When you go inside, I'm going to slip in after you, and I'll hide in the pantry. I'll wait there for you to come back with Mrs. Butterfield."

Maisie was delighted. What an exciting day was in store.

Chadwick was deep into his sheaf of notes as he strode into the dining room to hand Maisie a ruler, barely glancing at her.

"Be sure your place settings are precisely balanced. It will be of utmost importance to Mrs. Willows that Miss Lily Quartermain is impressed by our dinner service tonight. She is very anxious to set the correct tone with Mr. Alfred's fiancée, and we mustn't disappoint. I am confident that Miss Quartermain is well accustomed to the ways of the proper houses in England, and our service at Ravenscraig mustn't be seen to be anything but of the very highest caliber."

"Yes, Mr. Chadwick."

Maisie placed the ruler next to a water goblet and nudged it over a tiny bit so that it would be placed exactly the right distance from a wine glass. She had spent two hours setting the table and decorating the dining room. Another hour to make the final adjustments to the table and she would be done.

"I see we have a guest by the name of Miss Hawkesford joining the family for dinner this evening," the butler read the neatly written notes. "Yes, Miss Priscilla Hawkesford, guest of Mr. James." His eyebrows went up with what Maisie read as disapproval. Whatever he knew of Miss Hawkesford, it was clear he was unimpressed by the name.

"Stop! Oh, stop the presses!" Mrs. Willows was laughing and calling from the hallway as she all but danced into the room. "Set another place, Mr. Chadwick! Oh, this is so terribly exciting!"

"Yes, Madam. Will Miss Emma also be having a guest join her?"

"No. I will have a guest and I cannot tell you who it is. Just make sure we have the table set for eight and not seven. This is a very special guest, indeed, Mr. Chadwick!" She flitted out of the room calling out to Mrs. Butterfield.

Chadwick turned to the table; before he could form a sentence he saw that eight places had already been set. He looked sternly at Maisie, who smiled back sweetly.

His jaw clenched. How was it possible that he would be the last to know of a surprise! He swiveled on his heel in a military about face and marched off.

Elliot held the flowers behind his back and knocked a little rhythm on Emma's door. At first there was no response. He tapped out the rhythm again. Then there was a quick pattern of knocks that harkened back to an old game Elliot had created with Emma when she was a toddler.

"Elliot?" She called from behind the door and a mere second later, the door flew open, and she launched herself into his arms. "I can't believe it is you. It has been so very long! Look how tall you are! My goodness, you're a grown man, Elliot!" Tears sprang into Emma's eyes as she regarded her brother before her.

"Emma, darling little sister, look at what a beauty you've become! You must come to Paris with me and allow me to show you the Champs Élysées and take you to the fine fashion houses!"

"When did you get here?" she demanded.

"Shh. We must be quiet. Just a few hours ago," he answered with his finger to his lips. "I've been cooking up a surprise for the family, you might say."

"I'll say you have. Who knows you are here?"

"Everyone, except Father."

"Oy."

"Oy?" He laughed heartily. "What is oy?"

"Oh, something I read in one of those novels Mother would never approve of. Oh, Elliot, you look just wonderful. How are you?"

"I am so happy, I could burst, Emma. Truly, I am."

"Shh!" she whispered. "Mr. Chadwick is probably hiding behind the curtains. Let's talk in the sun room." She closed the door, and they sat comfortably at the window seat overlooking the river.

"Emma, I can't tell you how tremendously gratifying it is to be doing the kind of work for which I am suited. People have been so kind to praise my creations."

"How did things go for you in Florida?" She asked, soaking up the pleasure of hearing his voice.

"Splendidly. Maisie was a terrific help. We had a wonderful chat about you. She absolutely adores you. She would do anything for you, you realize," Elliot said seriously, wanting his sister to appreciate the maid's devotion to the family.

"Elliot," Emma said, equally seriously. "Then you are not cross with me for having told Maisie the contents of your letter?"

"Under the circumstances, of course not! What choice did you have?" he pulled her into a hug. "Emma, the world is changing. I can't tell you how happy I am to have taken the path that I have. I will be announcing the details of my culinary career at dinner tonight."

"Elliot!"

"Don't worry. You'll see it will be fine. And if need be, I must tell you that I am fully prepared to face the wrath of our parents, Father in particular, as I really don't see how Mother will be that difficult."

"Mother will be fine with your news. She has developed a different perspective on things since her struggle with typhoid."

"Typhoid?" Elliot's face went pale. Emma clapped her hand over her mouth and stared back with wide eyes.

"Did you say typhoid?" He asked again.

"Yes," Emma nodded. "Elliot, Maisie saved her life. Mother insisted we keep the news from you because she didn't want you to worry."

The two settled into a deep conversation about their mother's triumph over her illness and then fell to catching up with the details of their lives, thoroughly happy to be together

388

again. All the while, downstairs in the kitchen, Mrs. Butterfield huffed and puffed, complaining loudly as she did her best to follow Elliot's detailed instructions for the dessert she was preparing.

"A toast." A beaming Rupert looked around the table. "A toast to my dear children and our lovely guests. Elliot, your mother and I couldn't be happier with your surprising us. Welcome home. And of course, a very special welcome this evening to our future daughter-in-law, Lily." He smiled at Beth as he raised his glass. "Having all of you join us at the dinner table tonight is a great joy for both of us. To the happiness of Alfred and Lily!"

An enthusiastic round of "Cheers" met his toast and the family fell into chatter as Mr. Chadwick and Lizzie efficiently served the dinner, while Maisie tended to the beverages.

Rupert was in exceptionally good humor.

"Lily, as you can see, one never knows what is happening next in this family. Elliot, it is truly wonderful to have you here, all the way from Paris. I want to hear all about your work at the Beaux Arts."

"I will be happy to tell you all about my life, Father, but it would be such a bore for everyone, especially Miss Quartermain and Miss Hawkesford, who might find all of this talk of business rather dull."

"Well, yes, quite," Rupert agreed with obvious reluctance. "Well, then, after dinner you can tell me all of your plans over brandy and cigars in the library. Ladies, you must excuse my impatience and boorish behavior. Elliot has shared with us virtually nothing of his work at the Beaux Arts, and we are very anxious, indeed, to welcome our own architect to Willows and Sons, aren't we Alfred?"

"We are, of course," Alfred smiled and looked to Lily. "You must pardon my distraction, Elliot. It is difficult to think of business when a beautiful woman has agreed to become one's wife. With the wedding just a month away, I'm afraid we've been rather preoccupied with our plans."

"I'm glad I'll be home for the wedding. It's obvious that

Miss Quartermain brings out the best in you," he teased. "Welcome to the family, Lily." Elliot raised his glass.

"Well, while all this happiness and good cheer is being launched, I'd like to make an announcement myself," said James with a shy smile.

"You've decided to drop your medical career and join us at Willows and Sons!" Rupert interrupted.

Everyone laughed as James shook his head. "No, but I must tell you that this family is expanding more quickly than you thought. He stood and raised his glass. "I'm proud to announce that I have asked Miss Priscilla Hawkesford if she would do me the honor of giving me her hand in marriage, and she has agreed."

Beth's eyes flashed. Applause swept the table, followed by polite words of congratulations.

"Oh, my, this has been a day of surprises and good news," Beth pulled her fan out and fluttered it over her rising bosom as her breath quickened.

Maisie felt faint. She avoided James' eyes and went about her duties while he discussed their plans. Not only were they marrying, they were moving away. Returning to the butler's pantry, Maisie grasped the edge of the service bar to steady herself. She didn't notice at first that Mr. Chadwick had come up behind her.

"Are you not well?" he asked sympathetically.

"No, not really. I may have caught a bit of a chill," she offered weakly.

The business between Mr. James and Maisie was something Chadwick did know about, as he had hidden within earshot of their study meetings for several months. As a result, he knew far more about scarlet fever than he ever intended, but he could also plainly see the deep and honest affection between the maid and the master's son. He felt quite disappointed for Maisie and even more disappointed that this source of amusement had suddenly disappeared. That being the case, he also admitted to himself that he felt generally restored by the revelation that he was in on a secret most of the household knew nothing about.

He was suddenly overcome with an urge to be kind. "Why

don't you go to your quarters, Maisie," he said gently. "Lizzie and I can take care of the dessert service." She looked intently at the butler, filled with gratitude. She suspected he knew of her affection for James and certain he didn't know a thing about Elliot's change of profession.

"Mr. Chadwick, may I have a word with you in the kitchen? Mr. Elliot has asked me to speak to you."

Ten minutes later, armed with information that Maisie had provided, Mr. Chadwick entered the dining room with renewed confidence and a gleeful determination to perform his part of the surprise with perfection. It was truly the most delicious of circumstances. A butler could wait decades to witness this kind of drama in a family.

He stood near the sideboard and arranged the coffee cups and the Russian samovar for the tea. Alfred had hit the punch line of a story and everyone was laughing and saying what a charming storyteller he was. At the precise moment before conversation resumed, Mr. Chadwick discreetly approached the table and spoke quietly to his employer.

"Would you care for dessert to be served now, Mr. Willows?"

"Who would like dessert?" Rupert called into the celebration with uncharacteristic playfulness. They all responded with enthusiasm.

"Cordials for the ladies, Mr. Chadwick," Rupert instructed, "and brandy for the gentlemen, if you please. We have much to celebrate at our dinner table this evening."

James attempted to smile. He had made his choice. Better to lead with your head over your heart. He was not meant to have a life with a housemaid, regardless of his deep feelings for her. Perhaps it was best for all that Maisie had refused him. His heart would heal, and he would have Priscilla to run his social calendar. It was a fine idea. Priscilla came from the right kind of family, and, though a bit high-strung, she would be no embarrassment as he built his new medical practice. The offer to establish his practice in Kenora, on the Lake of the Woods, a hundred and thirty miles east of Winnipeg, had come at a perfect time. Priscilla would probably be happy to be leaving the rigors of the Winnipeg social life she had said so often that she disliked.

Meanwhile, Chadwick was tingling with anticipation. What a shocking story Maisie had told him! She had gone over all of the instructions very carefully, and he was certain he could accomplish what was needed. As he brought the serving cart close to the table he looked at Mr. Elliot, who with an almost imperceptible nod acknowledged it was time to ignite the dessert. The cart came alive with flames as the alcohol burnt off to the sounds of the ooohs and ahhhs of those present. Beth almost wept for joy as she brought her hands to her face and shook her head.

"Oh, it's just as though we're in Palm Beach again! Just look at that magnificent creation. Rupert, how on earth did you arrange this? Did Chef La Chance come himself to prepare this dish?"

She laughed in utter delight as Rupert tried to make sense of the presentation of the exquisite dish, duplicating exactly that which had so impressed them in Palm Beach. Only Maisie could have arranged this, and she wasn't even in the room. He looked to Chadwick.

Chadwick smiled and bowed very formally to acknowledge their appreciation of the spectacle.

"Mr. Chadwick," Rupert laughed. "This is stupendous! Who is responsible for this magnificent surprise?"

"Thank you, sir," Chadwick savored the moment and responded with utmost formality. "But I can only suggest that you look to your left for the answer. May I present Chef Louis La Chance, of Paris and New York and most recently of Palm Beach."

"Elliot!" cried Beth in admiration.

A collective gasp went through the room, and the brandy and cordial glasses were hastily refilled.

Rupert switched to scotch. Stunned by the revelation, he said nothing for a time, receding into his thoughts, happy to give the spotlight to his wife. Beth took command of the table with her ebullient patter, expressing how utterly delighted and thrilled she was with Elliot's announcement.

The shock gradually abated. Rupert was deeply disappointed

but saw no benefit in turning the event into a confrontation. Elliot had never been his favorite child, so why bother fighting it? The boy had always been a little odd, in Rupert's view.

There was a time, years earlier, when Rupert had even questioned how it was possible that he could be the father of such a child. His speculation had prompted a terribly ugly scene with Beth, who was so deeply angered and hurt at the suggestion that she had been unfaithful that she almost ended their marriage. Secretly, Rupert was so uncomfortable with Elliot's manner, he would have been relieved to learn that someone other than himself had sired the boy.

Now, sitting at the table, listening to Elliot explain how to make the perfect *flambé* was almost more than he could bear, but bear it he would. He would make the best of it for the sake of family peace and for Beth, who deserved her happiness. Willows and Son, it would be. *C'est la vie.*

As he sipped at his glass and watched the easy and joyful chatter around his dinner table, it occurred to him that, Elliot aside, he'd done all right for himself. He was among the wealthiest businessmen in Winnipeg, he had power and respect, and here Alfred was marrying into the highly respected Quartermain family. He pondered his good fortune and a new opportunity entered his mind. Elliot could prove useful, after all.

Flagler's anointing of Elliot as a sought-after chef had created a golden path for Rupert to develop future business contacts in New York. Elliot was going to be famous, thanks to Henry Flagler. Rupert would profit from being Elliot's father and supporter. Perhaps there could be a restaurant in their future.

There are worse things a man could have to deal with than a son who was a celebrated chef. That boot-faced Priscilla as a daughter-in-law was a prime example.

Maisie had a difficult week as she worked her mind around the complete severing of her relationship with James. By the time she went up to Selkirk Avenue the following weekend, she had regained her determination to set her own future. It was late on

Friday night by the time Maisie and Ziporah made their way up to their room and huddled together like little girls to share their secrets.

"Are you sure you are all right, Maisie?" Ziporah looked into her cousin's pale face with worried concern.

"Yes, I assure you that I will be fine. This is truly for the best, Ziporah. James and I could never have a life together. It would cost us so many relationships. What would be the point of going forward with all that pain? It was really a fantasy. A romantic daydream. I let get out of hand because, well, because I let it happen."

"I understand, Maisie," Ziporah hugged her. "But, fantasy or not, I also know you loved him."

"I hope he's happy," Maisie said softly.

"You don't like his choice, do you?"

"Oh, as if it were to me to decide what's best for him." Maisie flipped her handkerchief and dabbed at her eyes.

"I know, but you really don't like her, do you?"

"It sounds so nasty to be tearing her apart, Ziporah, but, yes, I think he could have waited for a better candidate. Betsy Campbell wasn't so bad, and I liked Molly Peterson quite a bit. She smiled a lot and seemed to be more, well, more caring. This one, this Priscilla Hawkesford," she tossed her head in imitation of Priscilla's haughty look, "is a woman of airs, I think you would say. She carries her nose in the air, as if there is an unpleasant smell in the room, and she was quite visibly upset at the dinner table when James mentioned that they would be moving to Kenora so he could open a practice there.

"He said he rather thought she enjoyed the Lake of the Woods, and she remarked, 'Yes, for holiday and tennis and boating, but it's quite another thing to think of actually living there year-round.' Then she said she thought he had been joking about it when he first told her about it. Miss Hawkesford seemed to think that they were going to have a home in that new Crescentwood neighborhood here in Winnipeg. It's all the rage, the new 'best neighborhood' among their set. Mr. Alfred and his bride will be building their new home on Wellington Crescent.

"I could see that James was quite displeased, as she prattled on about her poor impression of moving away from Winnipeg. She quickly pulled back, though, when she saw he was upset, patting his arm and insisting that wherever he wanted to go she would be happy. It was right then that Mr. Chadwick came to me and thankfully allowed me to be excused from the rest of the dinner service."

"So, he's serious about moving there?"

"Quite serious, it seems," Maisie said thoughtfully.

"He probably wants to distance himself from you."

"Maybe. I must admit I will be quite happy if he moves. It will make it easier for me to continue at Ravenscraig.

"I admire your generosity of spirit, Maisie. It's hard to get over a heartache like this."

"There's nothing to admire, I'm afraid, Ziporah. Simply put, I'm a fraud and an opportunist," Maisie declared. "I'm also selfish, as I suppose it could be said that I used James to learn about medicine. I do hope that one day I will be able to atone for my sins by becoming a good doctor. A doctor with a real degree and real office. It's what I dream of."

"I think you're 'the amazing Maisie', and that you are too hard on yourself. You didn't use him. You helped him and he helped you. That's very different."

"Thanks, Ziporah. I so appreciate you sticking up for me. What would I do without you and our wonderful family? And of course I want to spend as much time as possible with Baba and Zaida before they leave for Palestine next month. I've asked for a little holiday time so we can visit more. Just look at the two of them. Baba and Zaida let nothing get in the way of their plans, even after all of the years they had to be apart. If there ever was an example of brute determination in our family, those two are it."

"Yes, it's quite astonishing when you think about it, moving thousands of miles away, across the world in fact, to live in Jerusalem. Isaac is writing about it, so we'll have their story for our future children to read."

"You see, Ziporah? The Zigmans are unsinkable." Maisie picked up a photo of her grandparents. Look at everything this family has come through. Look how bright the future is. A romance that was not meant for me is not going to defeat me." She smiled. "Perhaps now, I too, will have a chance at happiness. Maybe I will meet my new love at your wedding to Max in a few weeks. There is a good deal to look forward to this summer.

"Now, we've spent quite enough time talking about my troubles. I want to hear every detail about your plans and the apartment you two will be taking on Main Street. Tell all about your handsome tailor and your dreams, Ziporah."

The two talked late into the night, and when the time came for Maisie to return to Ravenscraig the next day, she did so with a solid resolve to put her past behind her, to live up to the example of her grandparents. The future was hers to determine. All she needed was to stay focused and work harder.

46
Red Lights on Annabella Street
March 2, 1909

Henry tugged his scarf tighter against the brisk March air as he headed toward the stable, his footsteps crunching in the damp snow. His frustration fed the growl in his stomach. He had had quite enough of that motorcar, yes sir, and it would have to wait one more day before he would take another run at getting it going. Why on earth His Nibs wanted to have it out while the streets were still full of snow, he could not imagine, but he would get that metal beast running or die trying.

But not today. Mr. Willows had sent word that he wanted to speak with him, and he needed to clean up and get over to the main house. No doubt the discussion would be about the Packard. With more and more cars coming into use in Winnipeg, how much longer would he even have employment as a coachman? Muttering to himself, he framed his reasons for not being able to fix the dratted vehicle.

He needed to be among the horses to take in their heady, humid smell, and feel the comfort of their deep and honest purpose; to hear their rich throaty greetings and to be warmed by their affectionate nudging for the expected carrots in his pocket. Horses bring out the best in a man. On God's good earth, there is no greater truth. That infernal motorcar, on the other hand, is nothing but an oversized toy with lots of trouble. Not much use in these parts, that's for certain. Too bloody cold to ride in during winter, and too unreliable against the hot weather of summer. And the spring! Now, there's a rare treat. Another few weeks and it will be too muddy to take it out. Mr. Willows was in such a state last year when he got stuck outside the Eaton's store. Only a team of horses could free the metal beast from the prairie gumbo called Portage Avenue. Now that was a sight. His Nibs in full rant with mud and sludge soaked up to his knees, veins bulging out of his neck and his beloved Packard firmly in the grip of the muck, stuck there as if chained to hell itself. All of this nonsense and extra work just to be a show-off to his rich friends.

"Ha! That infernal machine was lucky not to have been sold on the spot!" Henry sputtered as he slammed the tack room door against the cold and yanked off his scarf.

"Are you having a tough time of it, Henry?" Rupert was sitting at the worktable next to the neatly racked saddles on the wall. His legs were elegantly crossed as he glanced through a copy of *The New Yorker*.

"No, sir. Evening, sir." Astounded to see Mr. Willows, Henry quickly removed his hat. It was the first time he had ever seen his employer in the tack room. "I mean, yes, perhaps I'm a bit frustrated today, sir, but that Packard will be purring like a kitten by tomorrow, or my name isn't Henry the Eighth, sir." Henry always resorted to his old joke when nervous and this time with a good result.

"Are you really the eighth born in your family, Henry, or have you just been having your fun with me all these years?" Rupert laughed out loud. At first, Henry was uncertain as to whether to be wary or charmed by Mr. Willows' magnanimous bearing.

"You are very kind, sir." A little deference was always safe ground with his master. "The car will be in good running order tomorrow, Mr. Willows."

"Yes, yes, Henry. But it's not the car that I wish to speak to you about. If the wretched thing is being uncooperative, we'll have Maw's Garage send someone around tomorrow to have a go at it. I am here to ask a favor."

Henry's heart stopped. This could mean anything from his having to travel down to Chicago to pick up a package, to having to shine a pair of boots. He felt his mouth go dry.

Rupert saw the fear and enjoyed it a moment longer than necessary. "Oh, please, not to worry, old chap. Let me explain. Please, do sit."

Sit? Old chap? Maybe Henry did have reason to worry.

"You do know who C.P. Walker is?" Rupert asked, and Henry of course knew the famous man, but stayed quiet. "He owns the Walker Theatre," Rupert continued. "I ran into him at the club today, and he asked me for help. You see, he has this big show coming in from New York this month, and he needs some help with horses."

"To get him to the theater, sir?" Henry asked respectfully.

"No, no!" Rupert laughed out loud and slapped his knee as Henry felt his face turn red. "He needs help with horses on stage." Rupert was pleased with Henry's discomfort. He, too, had had a similar foolish moment with C.P. early in the afternoon and wanted to take the sting away with his sport with Henry.

"I am afraid I am not following, sir. What kind of theatrical play needs horses on the stage?" Henry asked.

"It's called Ben-Hur. It is a spectacular success on Broadway and the Walker Theatre is presenting the show this month. You really should read a newspaper now and again, Henry."

"Yes, of course, sir." Henry felt his ears on fire. He had been so distracted with his new romance with Lizzie, that he'd forgotten that Ben-Hur was coming to Winnipeg.

"Well, let me see what I remember of the story." Rupert tapped his fingers on the worktable. "It's set in biblical times and is apparently about a Jew, who comes to know Jesus and ultimately embraces Christianity. Somewhere along the way there is a horse race. The Jew is Ben-Hur. He has an enemy. Oh, what the devil is his name?"

"Messala, sir. He's a Roman. It's uh, not a horse race, but a chariot race," Henry risked adding to the conversation.

"My dear man!" Stunned, Rupert couldn't hide that he was also impressed. He arched his eyebrows and stared at Henry. "However do you know this?"

"I've read the book, Mr. Willows. Very exciting, I must say, that chariot race." Feeling he might have gone too far, Henry cast his eyes down in embarrassment.

"Yes, well ... yes, indeed." Rupert was caught off guard. "There's a book you say?"

"Yes, sir. It's by a retired Civil War general by the name of Lew Wallace."

"Well," Rupert pushed on, anxious to reclaim his authority,

"Walker needs a couple of good horsemen to help backstage with the horses for that chariot scene. There are to be twelve horses and three chariots in that scene. The horses are all traveling with the show and are highly trained, I'm told. Oh, and there is also a bloody camel along. It's not pleased with Canada's cold weather and Mr. Walker wants to cheer it up. I told him there was no better man in Winnipeg than you for the task."

"Oh, my. Well, thank you, sir. Thank you very much." On the face of it, the assignment sounded tremendously exciting. "It will be my honor to help your friend."

"Very well. I will make the arrangements." With that Rupert was off, whistling down the path to the house, leaving Henry to sort out what had just happened.

What had he allowed himself to get into? Twelve horses on stage. And a cranky camel to boot. Lord be thunderin' Jaysus!

"Rupert!" Beth was clearly agitated as she came upon Rupert in the rear entrance hall near the riverside garden. "I've been looking all over for you."

"I was out chatting with Henry about *Ben-Hur*. What is it, darling? You are all flushed. Are you not well?" Rupert put an arm around her and guided her down the hall to the library.

"Oh, Rupert the most dreadful circumstances are seizing our city, and I am afraid to go out even for a shopping trip."

"What happened, Beth?"

"I was accosted by a man who thought I was one of those women, one of those sporting women!"

"Did he hurt you? Did you call the police?" Rupert took her arm.

"No, no, he didn't touch me. He just ambled over and asked me if I kept my place nearby. He showed me a two-dollar bill! I was horrified and let out a shriek. Ruby Smithering was nearby, and her chauffeur quickly appeared to rescue me. The man apologized and slipped away into the crowd. Oh, Rupert, what is becoming of our city if a lady can't be left unmolested entering a restaurant?"

Rupert stroked her hair. "You're sure you are all right,

then?"

"I am, Rupert dear, but really, it is high time the city did something about this…this problem. You see those harlots everywhere. They exhibit not one iota of shame in parading about among the better classes to seek their customers. It's absolutely scandalous."

"Beth, darling, I can assure you that complaints like yours are coming in with sufficient volume that very soon there will be a solution to this."

"Why not now, Rupert? I insist that as a member of the police commission and my husband that you do something. I'm not one to ask favors of this sort. But I don't think my nerves can take it any more!"

"Beth, please do calm down. You must know that we are well aware of the problem, and a number of remedies are under consideration. You just need to trust me that there will soon be a solution. There now, dearest, give me a hug, and let me dry your tears."

She fell into his embrace and was calmed by his solicitous murmurings. "Better now, darling?"

She smiled back at him. "Yes, thank you, dear, I'm much better now. Do you have time for a game of anagrams or dominoes? Shall I call for refreshments?"

"I'm so terribly sorry, Beth dear, I would love to have a game with you, but Percival Wright is on his way here to meet with me. Could we play later?"

She sighed and then remembered her parcels. "Well, in that case, I'll go put away my shopping. I found two new dresses I think you might like." She tapped his nose with a delicate finger.

"I will look forward to you showing them to me later." He smiled at her as she rose to leave. "Darling," he whispered naughtily in her ear, "I should think the bloke would have offered you at least a tenner."

"Rupert!" She slapped him playfully on the shoulder and minced prettily toward the door, glancing back with a wink before she left.

In the hallway outside, Chadwick stepped a few paces back from the door so as not to be caught eavesdropping. With the silver calling card tray in his hand, he straightened into his most formal posture and moved forward as Mrs. Willows emerged laughing from the room. Barely acknowledging him, she flew by to attend to her new dresses.

"Mr. Wright has arrived, Mr. Willows."

"Yes, of course, Chadwick, my favorite real estate man. Do bring him in directly and please serve the scotch I hold in special reserve."

How unusual, Mr. Chadwick thought. In the fourteen years that he had been in Mr. Willows' employ, this was the first time he had ever been instructed to bring anyone in immediately to a meeting with the alderman. Mr. Willows had always required his guests to wait in order to maintain his image of being a man with great demands on his time. The butler was greatly intrigued.

Within minutes, host and guest were seated comfortably, their whiskey poured over ice in Baccarat crystal glasses that Wright had properly and enthusiastically admired. Rupert was pleased to inform him that he had brought them home from Austria, a new stop in their most recent travels abroad. As this was a meeting of unusual importance, Rupert had chosen to move away from his desk and sit with his guest in the heavy leather club chairs that he reserved for his more intimate discussions.

"I see that you have made quite a showpiece of this library, Rupert," Percival Wright nodded in admiration. "You have made exquisite choices in your new acquisitions."

"You are very kind, Percival." Rupert held a box of cigars out to his guest. "It has been many years since we first stood in this library, and I wrote you a check for Ravenscraig." He smiled at the thought.

"It has, indeed, Rupert. A lot has happened since then. We've signed a great many contracts since that day."

"True enough. I must say that it has been a fruitful relationship that has developed into a most valued friendship. I thank you, Percival, for your unfailing discretion and your loyalty in all of these years we have been doing business together." He raised his glass.

"It has been my pleasure, I assure you." His hands were

suddenly clammy at the unusual comment. Rupert had never spoken to him this way before, and it made Percival very nervous. "I take it that there must be something on your mind to have called me to your home instead of the office."

"Yes, quite," said Rupert. "I have a rather interesting proposition for you, and the subject matter is such that I could not risk meeting you at the office and chancing having the conversation overheard. Here's the thing. You know I still have my seat on the police commission, don't you? Well, the commission is under a great deal of pressure to do something about the, well, to put it plainly, the very obvious presence of the sporting women conducting business all over the city."

"I see," Wright's bushy eyebrows reached up over his glasses. He was not only relieved, he was tantalized. Rupert wanted to talk about whores! "I must say, I've seen a number of stories on the topic recently in the newspapers," he offered. "Some of the writers would have you believe there is a brothel on every city block."

"That's certainly the perception. It all started when the city shut down the Thomas Street brothels five years ago." Rupert shook his head. "Idiots. They should have left well enough alone. So now, my good man, the police commission has developed a plan to go back to the old order of things."

"Is that so? So, we are talking about setting up a new red light district?" This was astonishing news.

"Correct."

"I take it there will be no proposal to legalize their business activity."

"None whatsoever."

Percival felt his bald spot heating up, as if bared to the summer sun. He shook his head. "I must say, it sounds a little risky. I daresay members of city council will be drawn and quartered if the council votes to do this."

"There won't be any need for a vote of that type."

"Why not?" Percival was confused.

"We'll simply instruct the police chief to handle the problem in the best way he sees fit."

"Prostitution is a violation of the criminal code." Wright hit the obvious flaw in the plan.

"It is. No one is ever going to stop prostitution. We owe it to the citizens to manage the problem in the best way possible. In the coming weeks there is going to be a meeting of the police commission. We are going to instruct Chief McRae to have a talk with Minnie Woods. You know who she is, don't you?"

"Madame Minnie. Indeed, a well respected leader in her profession."

"Right you are. Hear, hear." Rupert clinked glasses with the realtor. "McRae will meet with Minnie, and together they'll work to gather the girls into the new segregated district. This is where you come in."

"Me?"

"Yes. Don't look so surprised, Wright. I was asked if I knew a real estate professional who could quietly help facilitate the transactions needed to establish the new district. Naturally I thought of you."

Wright felt a prickly sensation run up the back of his neck as he considered what his wife, Mildred, would think of this. She had recently become active in the Women's Christian Temperance Union. No, she wouldn't go for this at all. Percival shook his head. "Well, my goodness, Rupert. Thank you for thinking of me, but I don't think this is my cup of tea."

"Don't be so quick to say no, Wright." Rupert sat back and crossed his legs. "The real estate agent will make a good deal of money on this. It might as well be you."

"You don't say?" Wright's head was reeling as he worked to keep up with the full scope of the unfolding scheme.

"Minnie has told me that she has already spotted an area she believes will be suitable to the purpose. It's in Point Douglas. She likes Annabella and McFarlane Streets. Do you know them?"

Wright squinted as he tried to recall the layout of Point Douglas. "If I am not mistaken, Annabella looks out onto a steam plant, and McFarlane is the next street over, on the east side. They're just a couple of blocks long. The river wraps around them and isolates the neighborhood. I would say the majority of people don't even know where it is."

"That's correct. How far is Annabella Street from the

railway station?"

"A five minute walk."

"And how long by streetcar from downtown?"

Percival suddenly saw the scheme in sharp focus. "Perhaps eight or ten minutes, and it's a short walk, really, from more than a dozen hotels and maybe forty or more saloons and gambling halls. Far enough away to be out of sight and close enough to be very convenient. It's brilliant."

Rupert smugly sipped his scotch.

"So, here is what I have in mind for you, Percival. I wish to anonymously purchase as many of the homes on these two streets as possible before the police commission gives the order to set up the district. Of course, I need to maintain my distance. I will put up the money to buy the houses and you will put them in your name with separate documents that show me as an investor. I will own ninety percent of each of the properties. You will own ten percent for your part in facilitating the arrangements. I'll pay top dollar, so it shouldn't be difficult to encourage some of the homeowners to sell. Then, Millie and the police chief will direct the ladies to see you for the purchase of their new homes. Naturally, as soon as word gets out among the girls about the new segregated area, the interest in the properties will drive the prices up, and we will sell or rent the houses at what I expect will be a significant profit."

"Well, it does sound like it has possibilities." Wright plucked a pencil from his pocket and started scribbling notes. "How many properties are we talking about?"

"At least thirty, possibly up to fifty."

Percival stopped writing. He was going to be rich.

Rupert continued. "Of course, several of the lots are vacant, and some have little more than shacks on them now. Where it suits, we will put up some kind of housing that we think will be appropriate. Many of the madams will have five or six girls working with them, so we will design some nice two and three story homes that will be to their liking. Many will want to accommodate card rooms or social parlors with access from the back lane."

"Social parlors?"

"Of course. The big money in brothels is in selling booze, Percival. You will learn a lot in your meeting with Minnie, I'm sure."

Wright whistled. "This could be very profitable, indeed, Rupert."

"It will make you wealthy, Percival. But there is so much more to it than that. Think of the good turn we'll be doing for the ladies, my friend. Left to carry on their business in this way, their profits will increase, their safety will be improved under the watchful eye of the police, and their need to market their services openly on the streets downtown disappears. Everyone benefits, you see. Most of all, the city will appear to have gotten rid of the problem of the social evil of prostitution. It's wonderful don't you think?" Rupert asked, congratulating himself on his brilliance.

"Well, it's quite amazing, I do think." Percival patted the sweat off of his bald head with his handkerchief. "When, precisely, do you think this will happen?"

"We need to act immediately to secure the properties. Things will happen very quickly. By July the brothel district will be well established in Point Douglas."

"And the police will protect it?" asked Wright.

"Perhaps I have overstated that. Yes, in a matter of speaking. It will be to McRae to work out the details. His instructions will be to contain the problem."

"See no evil, hear no evil?"

"That's a fair assessment of the policy, yes."

Greed won out. Percival was ensnared in the prospect of becoming a wealthy man. Even Mildred would see the value in this noble work, if he ever had to explain it to her.

"Thank you for giving me this opportunity, Rupert, to be a part of making things right in the great city of Winnipeg," Percival said with reverence.

With business now concluded, Rupert settled in for a social visit with his friend. "Tell me about how things are coming with the sale of homes in Crescentwood. Charles Enderton, the developer, is a pretty decent fellow, but I can hardly believe the tremendous amount of money he has riding on this area. Do you think this is going to be as grand as Armstrong's Point?"

The two fell to discussing the finer points of Enderton's grand scheme and the massive homes going up on the south side of the Assiniboine River. Chadwick, sitting quietly in his secret eavesdropping place, lost interest.

Moving about silently, he replaced the piece of wall behind the silk wall covering that separated the hall closet from the library. He stood and straightened his jacket. He had a telephone call to make. His sister lived on Annabella Street and Chadwick was a part owner of the house. There was no reason that he and his sister should not profit from the inevitable.

47
Courting Emma
March 11, 1909

Emma leaned back into the cushions and pushed her needlepoint to the side. Life was positively delicious, and her mind was full of thoughts of her fabulous evening at the theater. It would have been enough just to have seen *Ben-Hur*, a "thunderous spectacle unequalled by any other entertainment ever seen in Winnipeg" as the newspaper put it, but to have seen it sitting next to Charles Fortune had been an unexpected pleasure. How could she have known that he would be so different from the awkward gangly boy she knew as a child?

It was all her father's doing, of course, for he had engineered it. He always had plenty to say about the young men who paid attention to her and always tried to steer her into the direction of suitors from families he approved of. The Fortunes were top of Father's list.

She closed her eyes and recalled Charles' gentle laugh. Tall, broad shouldered, and known to be an outstanding hockey player, he was strikingly superior to all of the other young men who had come to call on her. What a pity that he was studying so far away at Bishop's College in Quebec. Charles was quiet and thoughtful. There was none of the false bravado so typical of the boys she knew.

She would have plenty to discuss with her friend, Mary Doogie, when she saw her at dinner. So deep was she in her daydream that she let out a whoop when she heard the knock at the door.

It was Mr. Chadwick carrying a letter for her on his silver tray; the first of many that Emma was to exchange with Charles Fortune over the next three years.

March 11, 1909

Dear Miss Willows,

It was a most delightful occurrence that I found myself seated next to you at the Walker Theatre last evening. I can scarcely believe we are the same two people who played together as children those many years ago.

Seeing how much you enjoyed the performance, I hope you don't think me too forward for including a small gift with this correspondence. It is a theatre program that was signed by Conway Tearle as a remembrance for you of his outstanding performance as Ben-Hur.

I am very sincerely,
Charles A. Fortune

March 11, 1909

Dear Mr. Fortune,

How very kind you are to have sent the delightful souvenir program. Thanking you for your thought of me, I am
Cordially yours,
Emma Willows

March 13, 1909

Dear Miss Willows,

If you have no previous engagement for this evening, I would be very glad to come up to visit you for a short while. Would half-past eight o'clock be suitable?
Sincerely yours,
Charles A. Fortune

March 13, 1909

Dear Mr. Fortune,

No, I do not have any other engagement, and I shall be glad to have a visit from you. My father would prefer nine o'clock, as he is otherwise occupied earlier in the evening.
Very cordially,
Emma Willows

March 18, 1909

Dear Miss Willows,

I received a message this morning from Mrs. Doogie inviting me up to visit this evening for an "at home" in honor of Mr. Wainswright from Toronto. She asks that I go by Ravenscraig for you, which I take as a most welcome request as it proves that you have informed Mrs. Doogie you wish to go and suggests you would consider allowing me to escort you. So, if it be agreeable, I will come by for you at eight o'clock.

Sincerely yours,

Charles A. Fortune

March 18, 1909

Dear Mr. Fortune,

Emma was not home this morning when the note arrived from Mrs. Doogie and as yet has not returned. In her absence, I accepted Mrs. Doogie's invitation on her behalf. I now also accept your escort for her, as I know of no previous engagement.

Very truly yours,

Elizabeth Biggleswade Willows

March 19, 1909

Dear Miss Willows,

It is with some sadness that I will be on my way to the train station this afternoon, embarking on my journey back to school in Quebec. I have so enjoyed the short break in Winnipeg and the opportunity to have visited with so many people whose company I enjoy.

I am sending a book I liked very well with the hope that you may also enjoy it. It is *The Sky Pilot*, by Ralph Connor. I read it on the train on my ride home this month.

Lennoxville now seems a terribly long way from Winnipeg. I shall look forward to returning to the prairies at the end of the semester in seven weeks time.

If you see fit to let me hear from you sometimes, I shall certainly appreciate it. I am enclosing my address at Bishop's School.

Sincerely yours,

Charles A. Fortune

March 19, 1909

Dear Mr. Fortune,

You must have secret knowledge that the book I have been reading was boring me to tears. I was ever so pleased when your man dropped your parcel for me at Ravenscraig this morning. I do wish you a safe and comfortable train ride.

I shall very much enjoy the relief your book will surely provide from the dreary tale I can now put aside. My mother is very keen on the writings of Ralph Connor, and I hope that you don't mind if there is a delay in my returning the volume, as she would like to read it as well.

Mother is very impressed with the fact that one of the best selling authors in the world lives in Winnipeg and is pastor of our church. Sometimes I never know if I should address him as Reverend Gordon or Mr. Connor. I wonder if Mrs. Gordon also calls herself Mrs. Connor. I must ask her sometime.

Oh, my. Do I sound cheeky and spoiled?

I hope this letter finds its way to you in Lennoxville, Mr. Fortune, as I did not want to chance having our driver, Henry, miss you at the train station to get it to you there.

Sincerely,

Emma Willows

May 1, 1909

Dear Miss Emma,

It is always a special day when a letter from you is waiting for me after class. I daresay that you have helped the weeks to pass quickly for me here at Bishop's with your letters and cards. Your letter of today is such a relief from the constant studying for the upcoming examinations next week. Do wish me luck!

I rather suspect that you are becoming quite accomplished in your musical abilities. My goodness, to take on cello lessons along with the piano is quite ambitious indeed. I can imagine how lovely it must be to hear you play and look forward to being part of your audience. That is, of course, if I might be so fortunate as to be invited to listen.

I shall be arriving in Winnipeg on the 20th of May. I am anticipating a very productive and interesting summer working in my father's firm, renewing my acquaintances, and catching up on the news in Winnipeg.

Speaking of news, I was most intrigued to learn from your letter that Mary Doogie is planning to go on to university in the fall. How novel. I rather thought she was an old-fashioned girl, and I'm surprised her father approves of her advanced education, let alone that she will be going to New York. You poor girl, I'm sure you will miss her terribly.

Sincerely,

C.A. Fortune

May 21, 1909

Dear Miss Emma,

It is so wonderful to be back in Winnipeg. The train ride was forever long, but I am ever so glad to be reunited with my family and to enjoy Cook's wonderful delicacies.

I do feel rather put out because I did not receive any letter from you since before my examinations, and I expect that I must have missed one between leaving Lennoxville and arriving at home.

If it suits you, and you have no previous engagement, I should very much like to come up for a visit at Ravenscraig this evening for a short while.

Yours truly,

Charles Fortune

May 21, 1909

Dear Mr. Fortune,

I am happy to hear that you have arrived safely. I am sorry to tell you that I have a previous engagement this evening.

Very cordially yours,

Emma Willows

May 22, 1909

Dear Miss Willows,

If it would please you to ride with me, and if the weather is agreeable, I would be very glad to come round to pick you up for church on Sunday morning.

Yours very sincerely,

C.A. Fortune

May 23, 1909

Dear Mr. Fortune,

Thank you for the invitation, but I have already accepted a ride with Mr. Wilton for the church service this Sunday.

I do hope you will be attending the picnic and softball game in celebration of Queen Victoria's birthday. It would be a shame to miss such a pleasant event.

It might profit you to know that I will be providing a picnic basket for the auction to benefit the Victorian Order of Nurses. I very much hope that a certain "C.F." will see fit to bid for the opportunity to lunch with me under the trees at City Park

Very cordially yours,
Emma Willows

May 26, 1909

Dear Mr. Fortune,

It was extremely generous of you to pay such a very large sum for my little picnic basket. I have received several letters from the committee members expressing their gratitude for the unexpected windfall that came from your financial gift, and each has expressed her desire that I pass along the sincere and deep appreciation the committee feels for your support. The Victorian Order of Nurses is a most deserving recipient of the funds that have been raised for the very good work they do in our city.

I only wish that the contents of my meager basket were worthy of the exceptional price you paid, and it is my hope that I did not bore you to tears with my enthusiasm for the university classes I will be taking in the fall.

I remain just a bit put out that my father will not allow me to go to school in the United States, as I thought Vasser would be an ideal school for me, but I shall make the best of the opportunities presented me at the University of Manitoba.

Very cordially yours,
Emma Willows

May 27, 1909

Dear Mr. Fortune,

Emma sends her regrets that she is unable to accept your invitation, as she has a previous engagement.

Very cordially yours,
Elizabeth Biggleswade Willows

June 28, 1909

Dear Mr. Fortune,

I am returning the book you gave me at the picnic, and I do hope you have not been inconvenienced by my having kept it this long. It was terribly rude of me, and I should have returned it to you long ago. The novel was greatly interesting to both my mother and to me.

In appreciation, I am sending you one of my favorite volumes. I do hope you like it. It is a novel by Mary Johnston called: *To Have and to Hold: A Tale of Providence and Perseverance in Colonial Jamestown.* I expect you must be terribly busy at work. I hope you do find time, now and then, to enjoy our glorious weather.

It seems a very long time since the picnic in May when I last saw you.

Cordially yours,
Emma Willows

July 7, 1909

Dear Miss Willows,

Pleases forgive my bad manners in the delay in thanking you for your thoughtful letter and the book.

You are a very sweet and intriguing girl, and I must confess that I am at a bit of a loss to know if you welcome my attentions or not.

Your choice of a book to send to me is most interesting. I have read *To Have and to Hold* before and shall enjoy re-reading my favorite parts. I hope you do not consider me brash with my questions, but I must ask: am I to assume that you may be wishing for me to understand something deeper in having sent me a story about a man's deep love for his wife and the challenges he faces in that regard? Am I to hope that in your heart there might be found a glimmer of an interest that we may one day be sweethearts? Dare I think that possible?

In truth, I have really no choice but to dare it, as I am literally tormented. I think of you every day from the first moment that I open my eyes and then all the way around the clock to the last fleeting images in my dreams before I awaken again.

There are very many pretty girls in Winnipeg. There is only one who has captured my notice. Or might it be more correct for me to phrase it that her fleeting notice of me has utterly captivated me?

I therefore feel I must take a chance and bare my sentiments to you, in the interest of complete and honest disclosure and at the great risk that what you read might cause you to sever our friendship, leaving me to never again receive another of your letters and worse, to never again gaze upon your lovely face.

My dear Miss Emma, nothing would give me greater happiness than if you were to allow me to court you in a proper and well-intentioned manner. If you could find it in your heart to think well enough of me to give me this honor, I shall make every effort to gain insight so that I may appreciate your point of view when it differs from mine.

Please understand that for me, some modern ideas are quite difficult to accept, and I will need time to learn to adjust my thinking. I must also say, with honesty and humility, that I make no promise that I am of adequate character to make certain adjustments you may think necessary. The idea of higher education for women is just not something that I have thought a great deal about and I suppose it must be said, at great risk of offending you further, that I fail to see much value in it. Women do not work after they are married, so what is the point in studying and working so hard to earn a university degree?

That said, I clearly see your passion for formal education. It is quite obvious that you possess a quick and able mind and a great facility for learning anything and everything that catches your attention. You put forth very solid reasons for your intentions, and it is obvious you have done much research toward your desire to go on to the university. I suppose it might be said that I am dumbfounded by this side of your character. At the same time, I am thrilled by your intensity and your knowledge of who you are and the woman you wish to be. There is no other girl like you in the world.

I do agree with you that Reverend Gordon's wife stands as a fine example of a woman of great accomplishment in her having earned a Bachelor of Arts degree. I also see Mrs. Gordon as very feminine and traditional and in no way seeking to cast her education about as any type of battering instrument to put her husband down. She is of great reputation and has never been seen or thought to detract from her duties as a wife and mother, and indeed, a committee chairwoman in the many good works she does related to her husbands parish at St. Stephen's.

You can perhaps start to see, dear Emma, how all of this can be confusing to a man raised with strong traditions as I have been. You must realize that as the last to be born after my brother and four sisters, I have had a great many people bearing down on me with their views and notions concerning how I am expected to conduct myself. We are very accustomed to doing things a certain way in the Fortune family. My father is a terribly strong influence on us, and I don't ever wish to disappoint him.

That doesn't make the Fortune way any better than the approach taken by the Willows family, it just means that it is different, and I hope that you will allow me time to learn about these modern ways of yours without expecting that I might be able to just abandon everything that I know to be true in my view of myself, and the honorable man I wish to be.

I expect to be a gentleman first and always; a man who will forever put his wife above all else and do everything in his power to love, protect and cherish his wife and his children with every breath of his being. If that is an offensive or limiting view of the person with whom you wish to be associated, when you one day choose a husband, then it is best that we know now that our lives are destined for different paths.

Dearest Emma, I do so much wish to see you, even knowing it may be for the very last time.

If it suits you, and if you have no previous engagement, I would be glad to come up to Ravenscraig for a short while on Sunday evening.

I have missed you so.

Yours very truly,

Charles A. Fortune

July 8, 1909

Dear Mr. Fortune,

My parents and I would be very pleased if you would accept an invitation to dine with us at Ravenscraig on Sunday evening next.

Mother suggests that as the weather is so fine, perhaps I could give you a tour of her lovely riverside garden in advance. I think you shall be delighted to see what you will find there. The Garden Club has awarded Mother first place for her roses.

Would half-past four o'clock suit you?

Yours very truly,

Emma Willows

July 8, 1909

Dear Miss Emma,

I am very glad to accept your invitation to dine with your family, and I shall be very pleased to enjoy your tour of the garden.

Sincerely yours,

C.A. Fortune

48
The Rottenest City in the Dominion
November 21, 1910

Rupert puffed away at the remnants of his cigar as he paced about the library, working to control his anger at the contents of the letter.

A prickly sensation traveled through the nerves on the back of his neck as he looked at his watch. He ripped the cigar stub from his mouth and smashed it repeatedly into the ashtray as if attacking a cockroach. Where on earth was that bloody lawyer? It had been almost an hour since he had called his office. As if on cue, there was a knock at the door and Chadwick appeared with a bespectacled man in tow.

"Mr. Grenville Doddsworth is here to see you, Mr. Willows."

"Thank you," Rupert waved the butler from the room. "We are not to be disturbed, Chadwick."

"Very good, sir."

Doddsworth had never seen Rupert in such a state.

"My God, man, you look terrible. I apologize for not getting here sooner, but I was in court. My secretary told me nothing beyond the fact that you said it was urgent. I take it this is the matter with the Russian."

"The Russian?"

"The demand for more money, from your, well, Mr. Volinsky. He wants an increase to seventy-five dollars a month. You never responded to my question about what you wanted to do about it."

"Send him the bloody money and get him off my back!" Rupurt shouted as he flew to his feet. "I have much bigger problems, Grenville. I am on the precipice of facing utter ruin to my reputation. It's the bloody inquiry into vice. I need you to get me out of testifying before the Royal Commission."

"The Vice Inquiry?"

"That's what I said," Rupert answered, thrusting forward a folded paper.

The puzzled lawyer took the letter from Rupert.

The letter was a summons commanding Rupert Willows, Esq. to present himself before the *Manitoba Royal Commission Inquiry into Vice in the City of Winnipeg*. He was to appear as a witness and was being called to testify two days hence, on November 23, 1910.

"This could wind up being a full-blown scandal, Grenville. I could be ousted from City Council."

"Why exactly have you been called, Rupert?" Doddsworth's brow wrinkled as he looked over his glasses.

"Because I own the mortgages on thirty-seven of the houses in the Red Light District."

"Oh. I see."

"I thought I had it properly masked, but apparently some overly ambitious clerk followed the paper trail right to my bank account. Now that this Reverend Shearer fellow out of Toronto has pushed the City of Winnipeg into staging this mockery, this lynching trial, I will be ruined." Rupert was on his feet pacing again.

"Rupert, forgive me, but I don't follow every story on harlots in the city. What has this Reverend Shearer got to do with it? Who is he?"

Rupert put his glasses on and snatched up a sheet of paper from his desk.

"He is the General Secretary for the Moral and Social Reform Council of Canada," he read, "and solely responsible for the inquiry having been called. It seems that the good reverend was touring the wild and woolly West looking to shine a light upon the social evil he claims to have found in great abundance. Upon returning to Toronto, he spoke to a number of newspapers and declared Winnipeg to be 'the rottenest city in the Dominion'. The papers ate it up, and now we are embroiled in full battle aimed at destroying the image of our fair city."

"On what is he basing this charge?"

"Exactly the point! On what, indeed? Well, for starters, he says the City Council has approved of the existence of a segregated area for the brothels, and further that the women are paying for protection to live and conduct their business there."

"And you're saying there is no truth to that? Everyone in Winnipeg knows about the existence of the Point Douglas brothels. My God, Rupert, Annabella Street has become a veritable tourist attraction on Sunday afternoons."

"It's not a truth anyone needs to expose, Doddsworth! Establishing the segregated district in Point Douglas has been of enormous benefit to the citizenry in getting the sporting women off the streets and out of view. This is a quiet and workable arrangement. It's too complicated for an oafish boor like Shearer to understand, and all he wants is to create trouble so he can make a big name for himself."

"What about the fact that the city was involved in organizing the district?"

"That's not exactly true. Instructions were given to the police chief to deal with the prostitutes who were scattered in brothels all over town. He went to work, and by summer of 1909 the complaints about the social evil were considerably lessened. That, Doddsworth, is the whole story."

"How is it that you came to own the properties?"

"I bought the houses as a silent partner with my real estate agent, a very capable man by the name of Percival Wright."

"Yes, I know him."

"It was strictly a business opportunity. Once it was decided to have a segregated district, I quietly furnished the money to secure the properties, and Wright handled the transactions to sell the homes to the ladies. Some of the keepers chose to rent. In some cases, where the buyers were short of money, we offered financing to allow them to buy their homes on Annabella and McFarlane Streets."

"What level of profit did you see?"

"Do you have to know?"

"If I am to be of help, Rupert, I have to know everything that will be asked of you if you testify. How much profit?"

"On average?"

"Sure."

"Well, I bought most for between two thousand and

twenty-five hundred dollars, and we sold the houses for between eight and twelve thousand dollars."

"Nice."

"Oh, for God's sake, Doddsworth! There's nothing illegal about making a profit. And the truth of the matter is that we did think it was rather nice for these women business owners. They came off the streets, everyone knows where to find them, and there is the added benefit of the cops keeping an eye out, which makes it safer for them."

"So, they are also paying for protection then. Is that it?"

"They are certainly not paying me for anything but the mortgages or their rent."

"But you are on the police commission."

"What has that to do with anything?"

"People will expect you will have knowledge of whatever protection has been promised. What can you tell me about it?"

Rupert shot out of his seat and began pacing again.

"They have a variety of arrangements, I am sure. My involvement ends with the financial concerns for their properties."

"So you've said."

"As to the rest, Doddsworth, you would have to discuss the matter with Police Chief McRae."

Doddsworth read the document through and shook his head. "This does have the makings of a major scandal, Rupert. You could get hurt."

Rupert exploded. "What do you think I've been saying? Now, let me tell you something, Doddsworth. If I do get hurt, it will only be because my lawyer is not smart enough to help me finesse my liability."

"That's a low blow, Rupert."

"Forgive me. I am rather rattled, as I am sure you can appreciate."

"When does the inquiry start?"

"Tomorrow."

"Tomorrow? That's awfully fast."

"City Council dealt with the request this afternoon. A resolution was passed, and the Lieutenant Governor of Manitoba has ordered it to start tomorrow."

"That's very fast, Rupert. It would be very helpful to learn who has been asked to testify."

"I've seen the list."

"Oh?"

"Someone in the court owed me a favor," Rupert winked. "It includes the chief of police, of course, the mayor, some of the commissioners, a few residents in the area, and a good long list of the prostitutes."

"And how long will the inquiry last?"

"Thankfully, not long. It's scheduled to run just two or three days."

"Excellent."

"Excellent? What are you talking about? I could be ruined."

Rupert, calm yourself. It appears to me that with the extremely quick response in launching the inquiry, the city is looking to face the charges and discredit their accuser as quickly as possible."

"Well, that could be true. Yes, I would say that calling Winnipeg the 'Rottenest City' was like poking a smoldering stick directly in the eye of City Council. The council would have voted to start the inquiry the very day of the resolution, had it been possible. Everyone is very embarrassed and angry."

"Exactly my point," said Doddsworth. "Rupert, they might not even have time to hear you. If my hunch is correct, no one is going to put a businessman on the stand ahead of a long list of prostitutes. If I've learned anything about Winnipeg in the time I have lived here, it is that there is a great appreciation for theater. From what you are telling me, this inquiry is shaping up to be the best show in town, and there appears to be no time to ruin the production with boring details like the ownership of the properties. Leave it to me, Rupert."

Rupert peered at Doddsworth as he processed his words, and then a smile broke across his face, like sunshine breaking through cloud cover.

"Now I know why I pay you so handsomely. Thank you, Doddsworth."

Doddsworth's assessment of the inquiry's theatrical appeal proved correct. Despite cold and snowy weather, he and Rupert had to push their way through the throng that had gathered on Main Street in front of City Hall to get to their seats as it began.

Men in top hats carrying walking sticks stood next to scruffy boys in worn out shoes and patched jackets as the crowd grew in anticipation of the arrival of the witnesses.

Once inside, there was standing room only in the City Council chambers as the proceedings began under the direction of the Honorable Hugh Amos Robson, chief justice of His Majesty's Court of King's Bench. Some well-heeled audience members had paid people to hold places in line for them. Rich and poor, all wanted to hear what the prostitutes had to say. Just to have a chance to see them in person was titillating. The hearing had the potential to escalate from theatre to circus.

"Oyez! Oyez! Oyez! All rise!" the court clerk cried out as Chief Justice Robson, tall, broad, and imposing in his black robes, swept into the room and took his place. With a scowling glare beneath his curly white wig, he grabbed the gavel off his desk and pounded it heavily against the rumble of chatter in the room.

"Quiet! This court is now in session. Anyone who cannot behave will be removed from the courtroom, forthwith!" the chief justice shouted over the noise and settled into a long preamble stating the purpose of the inquiry as people jockeyed for space and pushed against the rails of the oak balustrade to catch every word.

The judge held the large document out at arms length and read with a booming voice. "Whereas, according to reports contained in the press, allegations of graft have been made against the police authorities in the City of Winnipeg, and it is stated that houses of prostitution pay for police protection, and whereas Reverend Shearer has been quoted in articles published in Toronto newspapers saying, quoted here "that these dives sell liquor twenty-four hours a day, seven days a week, and as the price of being permitted so to do, each house pays four hundred dollars," end of quote.

"And whereas Reverend Shearer further states that the district could be shut down in twenty-four hours if there was the political will to do so, we commence this inquiry on November 22nd, 1910 A.D."

He smashed the gavel down again, and the crowd hushed with anticipation. Next on the agenda was another long reading of the order passed by Winnipeg City Council that initiated the calling of the Commission of Inquiry.

While Commissioner Robson droned on through one "whereas" after another in reading the resolution, Rupert read through the witness list for the day and whispered to Doddsworth.

"I thought you said McRae would be saved for last. He's testifying today."

"This is better," answered Doddsworth, looking very important, in his starched white collar against his black courtroom robes. "This way he eats up the time. By the time they get to the prostitutes and then the mayor and Magistrate Daly, they are going to have to start dismissing people from the witness list."

"Who's this J.B. Coyne fellow?"

"He's a talented young lawyer who will be acting on behalf of the Moral and Social Reform Committee. He will be questioning Chief McRae."

"Do we need to worry about him?"

"Not at all. Coyne is here with James Aikins, of the law firm you might know as Aikins, Robson, Fullerton and Coyne."

"Did you say Robson? The commissioner?" This was startling news to Rupert.

"The same." Doddsworth polished his glasses as he whispered, "The name of the firm has actually changed since Robson was recently named a judge. But the thing of it is, all of these men know each other, and I believe it is fair to say they all want to see Winnipeg's reputation saved.

"I don't think we can expect to see anything come of this inquiry that will put Winnipeg into a difficult light over the long term. In fact, Reverend Shearer may end up facing charges of defamation by the time we're done here."

"Quiet!"

The gavel sounded again, and Justice Robson ordered two boys and a man removed from the courtroom for creating a disturbance. At this, the crowd finally quieted and testimony began with the swearing in of Police Chief John McRae and the introduction of Mr. James B. Coyne, who would examine the witness.

After establishing that the chief had been in his job over twenty years and was very familiar with the pertinent issues, the crowd was finally rewarded with the entertainment they sought to find at the hearing.

Mr. Coyne walked purposefully about in front of the witness stand as he asked his questions. Chief McRae's demeanor was polite and confident in the early questioning.

"What motivated the women to settle on Annabella and McFarlane Streets?" the lawyer asked.

"They understood they were going back to the old order of things," the chief answered.

"That they would be undisturbed?"

"No, because they were not undisturbed when they were on Thomas Street," McRae explained. "They were going back to the old order of things. They would be apprehended when there would be sufficient cause to justify it."

"What do you mean 'sufficient cause'?" Coyne looked at his notes.

McRae sat back in the chair and considered his words. "Oh, disorderly houses, thefts, robberies, the admission of persons who should not be there and traffic in virtue."

"That would leave them open to conviction?"

"Trafficking in any young persons, thefts, drunkenness and robberies. That was the old order of things and that would subject them to conviction."

"What did you know of the proceedings for the establishment of the colony? We will call it a colony in distinction to area." Coyne faced the judge's bench.

Rupert felt his heart start to pound, and his eyes slid to Doddsworth who motioned to him to stay quiet.

"I got a telephone call from Minnie Woods," the police

chief answered. "She was well known to police and to the other ladies of the profession from her previous prominence on Thomas Street and had a role in selecting the new area for the colony, as you say. She had picked the area and told me she had a man who was acting on her behalf to help secure the properties."

"Do you know the name of this man?"

"Percival Wright. He is a real estate man," answered McRae. "Mr. Coyne, at this point I would also like to state clearly to the commission that despite what has appeared in some newspaper accounts, Mr. Wright is not my brother-in-law. I do not have any connection financially to this man, and I have not profited in any way from the sale of the houses."

A murmur went up from the crowd. The rumors had been widely circulated, and everyone had an opinion on whether the police chief had been making money from the brothel district.

"After the real estate man became involved, then what happened, Chief McRae?"

"Minnie understood that they were going back to the old order of things, and she was asked to talk to the other girls about it." McRae answered. "Then she got in touch with the real estate man, and by summer there were many properties all set up, as was the implied intent of the police commission."

"Did you talk to other women?"

"No, I sent them to Minnie Woods to get their information."

Rupert felt his heart leap and cupped his hand over his mouth as he turned to Doddsworth.

"He dropped it. He's not going to pursue the question of profit and ownership."

"So far, so good, Rupert," Doddsworth nodded.

Mr. Coyne strutted about the witness stand and consulted his notes before he approached the police chief with a new line of questioning. "I suppose the object of the department was that, when the segregated area had been decided upon, they would drive anybody of that description from the rest of the town to that area?"

McRae nodded his head in agreement. "It was intended to

bring about the change of conditions to remove the evil that had spread throughout the city into one area."

"Did you collect the names of the men who were customers of the brothels?" Coyne asked.

This sparked another eruption from the crowd, and the commissioner had to silence the courtroom before McRae could answer. "We tried it, and it didn't work. There had been an order in place from the police commission, but typically when officers were posted at the houses to ask the names of the men, what they got in answer was 'some very prominent names', or answers like 'none of your business', or fictitious names, names of well-known businessmen. Finally there was a very brutal attack on a constable because he looked into a hack, a taxi. Since then we don't ask the names. I don't know of any right which I have to ask men under those circumstances."

"Chief McRae, how do you mean you don't know of any right you would have to ask the men, these customers of the brothels, their names?"

McRae paused, searching for the right way to explain himself. "Here is what happened. On that previous occasion I just spoke about, at a house we had picketed, we had instructions to collect the names. That was done. What led to the rescinding of the order is that one special constable was brutally assaulted there when he looked inside the hack to identify the brothel customer. The person committing the assault was committed for trial. The judge and jury acquitted him, and the judge said the police had no right to ask people their names."

The questions continued for two solid hours. Near the end of the afternoon, the tireless young James Coyne appeared as composed as he had from his first question. The chief of police, however, was starting to wear at the edges.

Coyne consulted his papers and turned again to the witness box. "Chief McRae, Reverend Shearer claims that the fifty-three houses of ill fame which exist on Annabella and McFarlane Streets could be closed within twenty-four hours. Is that charge true?"

Chief McRae grimaced and rubbed his hand on his jaw. "Well, I don't know what is meant by that. If it means the district could be closed within twenty-four hours if they would sell out, it might be so. I don't know who would buy them. They might be closed out by arrangement, but I doubt it very much."

"But if it means that you, the chief of police with your force could close them out in that brief space of time, could that be done?"

The lawyer's tone had escalated, and the police chief finally ran out of patience at what he saw as an insinuation that he was not capable of doing his job. "It is a physical impossibility!" The popular chief railed. "The women plead not guilty, and all the police can do is to submit the evidence to the court. The women are penalized if the evidence is accepted. I know of no law which permits me to dynamite, cremate, or eject immoral women!"

The crowd erupted into laughter and spontaneous cheers in support of the shouting police chief. The entertainment was everything the spectators had wanted it to be.

The commissioner called for a recess and announced that the testimony would continue the next day. The throngs rushed for the door, and Rupert beamed at Doddsworth.

"They went right by the question of property ownership. I might get out of this after all."

"It's looking good, Rupert." Doddsworth shook his client's hand.

The inquiry continued with onlookers packed to the chamber walls. Rupert was never called to testify. When it was over, the newspapers had a field day, printing the testimony from the prostitutes who were made to tell stories in great detail of how they had come to be prostitutes, how many visitors they received, and how much money they made. They also explained on the witness stand their understanding that if they followed certain rules such as keeping the music low and staying out of downtown, that they would be left alone to conduct their business. With the newspaper stories on the brothel district, ever-increasing crowds took up sightseeing in the red light district, leaving the prostitutes to cope with thick Sunday crowds of citizens looking to catch a glimpse of a fallen woman on

428

Annabella and McFarlane Streets. The women didn't mind so much, for it also brought an increase of business.

In time, to a large extent, things were returned to the old order of things, and the final report from Commissioner Robson, presented in early 1911, left no doubt that while the charges were serious, there was little evidence to support them. While acknowledging that the brothel district existed, and in fact had grown, in the end Justice Robson emphatically concluded that the conditions were not brought about by the corruption of any police authority and that the occupants of the brothel houses did not pay for police protection.

So ended the hoopla over the harlots and so, too, ended any fear Rupert had that a brothel scandal would destroy his life.

Little did he realize that the whisper campaign that would ultimately ensnare him, would be far more damaging.

But that was not yet on the horizon.

49

Charles and Emma

August 15, 1911

My darling girl,

I think of you all the time and am aching for the day when you will rest in my arms and know the bliss of our permanent union as husband and wife.

I dread getting on the train to return to Quebec next week. I think of our long conversation during our buggy ride yesterday and have played your words over and over in my mind.

Yes, we are young and there is a long life ahead of us, but I think it important to shape that life according to the values that I possess and that I wish to live by my whole life.

You are quite right to say that I care deeply about how people think of me and that my position in society is truly important to me. I don't understand how you might object to that. Of course I believe that having you as my wife would enhance my reputation and my standing in society. How could it not? Who would not be a very proud man to be married to you, dear heart? But please understand that this sentiment is not motivated by thoughts of who your father or mine might be. It is because you are a sweet, beautiful and, I must say, brilliant young woman from a strong and respected family. Moreover, you are someone who makes everyone around her feel their hearts lighten and a smile come to their lips through the simple act of being in your presence. You are what every intelligent and caring man could ever desire.

As for me, I do accept that I have some weaknesses like anyone might have, but I can honestly tell you this: I know that my habits are industrious, moral, and faithful. When I say I will do something I try my hardest to see it through. I don't involve myself in business that is not mine. I do like things of quality but will have no debts. To be an honorable man is of greatest importance in what I expect of myself. It is my great desire to stay in this world for a long time, and I expect that will be so, but when the day comes that I shall leave it, I would like people to say, "A good man has gone, one who did no harm and who did his best to do right."

This is the man I am, dearest Emma. I am pledging my life to you, to love and protect you through every day of the rest of my life.

To finally come to that day when we are each other's completely, forever and always in marital union, sends deep contentment through my soul. I am tormented with missing you every moment that we are not together.

I know how strongly you feel about wanting to be a teacher and I wish to be supportive, but I am afraid that I am still having a great deal of difficulty with the idea. As I am not yet your husband, I have no right to prevent you from taking on this teaching position. I do wish that you will receive all of the satisfaction that you expect from the experience.

In the meantime, I will have completed my studies by Christmastime, and I think it would be ever so wonderful if we were to have a January wedding. What do you say, darling? You will be able to teach this fall for a few months, to have your goal met, and then I shall happily place you in a very pretty house to move to your next career as homemaker and wife.

I can promise you that I will be the sweetest and most devoted and adoring husband a girl could ever wish to have. I will cherish your every smile and every touch and will live to provide every comfort and happiness that is in my power to give you.

I cannot tell you how disappointed I am that you will not allow me to set a wedding date and go to your father to ask permission for your hand. It will make it so much easier to be able to return to Lennoxville for the fall semester, knowing that I will return home to our wedding, my life with you, and my job in my father's business. Life will be ideal for us both.

Please do reconsider my request, my cherished sweetheart.

Forever with love,

Your devoted Charles

August 16, 1911

My sweet Charles,

Darling, you are so dear and wonderful, it brings tears to my eyes to think of you being away for so long. I shall miss you so very much. I don't wish for you to be tormented, but please, you must understand how terribly important it is to me that in just a few weeks I will begin my duties as a schoolteacher. I want to hear the little children call me "Miss Willows" and join them in their delight in discovering how to read and to do sums. That I will have a chance to be part of their journey to learn these skills and to better their lives with education fills me with a sense of purpose and a deep desire for the fulfillment that will come with my work.

Charles, my dearest friend, please know how much I love you and want to be married to you. It is really a matter of finding the ideal time.

Surely you can understand now that I did find it somewhat of a surprise to read in your letter that you believe that my "goal" will have been met by having had the opportunity to teach for a few months. My goals are conflicting, my love, and I see it as most unfair that I cannot be both a teacher and a wife.

Please know that I adore you and am thrilled at the thought that I will one day be your wife. Nothing will make me happier than to be the love you treasure, to make a home with you forever and always, and to welcome our children when we are blessed to have them. But once I am married, I will be released from any teaching position I might have, and I do so want to work. It is terribly unfair that married women are not allowed to teach, but obviously that is not going to change any time soon.

We had agreed that we would wait until after my 21st birthday. Please, let's stay with that agreement, dearest Charles. June 9, 1912 isn't all that far away, is it? It is less than a year, and we will have our entire lives together. Will you wait for me, my love? Adoring you now and always,

Sincerely yours,
Emma

September 16, 1911

Dearest Emma,

I received your letter this afternoon and tore it open the minute I was alone in the dormitory. I must admit that I am greatly disappointed by your reply.

Well, I do have my studies to occupy my time and my thoughts. I will try very hard to become accustomed to these "modern" ways of yours, dearest. Be patient with me. This is quite a challenge for me, as I do tend to be very old school about these things.

I agree, that under the circumstances, it is best to postpone our plans for marriage. I should think that for the time being we might also suspend any further discussions about it, as it is just too painful for me to think that your job as a teacher is more important than your desire to be married to me.

Your faithful friend,
Charles

November 2, 1911

Dearest Emma,

I am greatly impressed by your stories of success in the classroom. Your students are truly very fortunate to have someone as dedicated and caring as you to guide them. What a different world you have entered! I am very pleased for your happiness despite the great loneliness that I so often feel. How I wish we could be together.

My days are endless, it seems, with studying for examinations and completing assignments. The last few weeks have seemed to be an endurance trial. As to your question about my social appointments on weekends, I have been much too busy to avail myself of the invitations for visits with my classmates whose families are near.

I do miss you, so very much. Won't you please think of coming to visit your Grandmama in Montreal so that I may see you there? That is a visit I would take time to enjoy!

Adoring you, always,
Charles

December 1, 1911

Darling Emma,

How long it has been since I have seen your beautiful face. Thank you so much for the photograph. I will place it near to my lamp so that I can see you smiling at me as I work at my desk. Yes, of course, I do understand that you cannot get away from your responsibilities at school. I suppose it was a wish even more than a hope that you would come.

As to your question about my arrival at Christmas, I am sure that you have heard the news by now. Unfortunately, it will be some months before I will see you again. My father telephoned this morning with news of a "graduation present" for me. Father is quite insistent that I travel with the family on the Grand Tour. It is to be a celebration, in honor of my achievements at Bishop's.

It would have been unthinkable to tell him that I would much rather have been back in Winnipeg, spending time with my dear sweetheart, taking you to church and concerts and basking in the glow of your company. Perhaps even discussing our future. But, then again, I promised you that I would not bring up such things.

My father has booked passage out of New York in late January and, of course, it makes no sense for me to travel from Quebec all the way home to Winnipeg to just turn around and head for New York. He, my mother, and three of my sisters, Ethel, Mabel and Alice will be traveling. He really wanted all six of us children to be on this trip, but because both Robert and Clara are married and settled into their own lives, it is not practical. So, the Fortune family will be a total of six, instead of eight on the tour.

Oh, Emma, I must ask. Will you miss me?

Thinking of you always,

Charles

50

Tickets for the Titanic

December 1, 1911

Chadwick tingled with excitement. The master was in a state and the mistress had been summoned. His duties completed, the butler checked to be sure he wasn't being watched, then disappeared into his hiding place so he could listen in on their conversation in the library.

"Rupert, dear, whatever is the matter?" Beth searched her husband's face. "Are you not well?"

"I'm in perfect health, Beth. Please, just sit." Rupert stiffened his back and paced around the room. "I had lunch with Mark Fortune, today, and do you know what I learned?" Anger chilled his words. Beth opened her mouth to reply, but before she could speak he pounced on her. "It seems our daughter has taken up with that group of old bats fighting for the women's right to vote. Did you know about this?"

"Rupert, my goodness. Of course, I knew. They aren't 'old bats', they are a dynamic group of women, journalists and writers, mostly. I think Emma is in good company."

"So, I appear to be the last to know. I had to learn this from Mark Fortune, a business associate, and the father of our daughter's suitor!" He glared at her, letting the words hang in the air.

"What did Mr. Fortune have to say about it?" she asked, finally, to break the dreadful silence.

"Only that he knows about it. The man is much too polite to be openly critical, but I assure you that we will not be seeing any of his daughters involved in such unladylike activity."

"Oh, come now, Rupert. It's committee work, no different than raising money for the children's hospital."

"Beth, you are wrong. This is a dangerous idea. There is no need for women to have the vote. A great many influential people are against it, and it will do nothing to further Emma's standing in society. I wouldn't be surprised if young Charles would be very distressed, indeed, if he were to learn of Emma's participation in this."

"I should think that he already does know about it. She writes to him every week," Beth said calmly, hoping to quiet her husband's anger. "And Rupert, dear, I can't imagine that there is anything that Emma could do or say that would put him off. He's mad for her. You've seen how he looks at her."

"Charles is an old fashioned fellow who has expectations of a life with a traditional woman. You know he is not happy with this teaching job of hers," Rupert countered.

"Mark told you that? That his son is disapproving of Emma's work as a teacher?"

"Beth, let me spell it out for you, my dear. It is Mark who disapproves. Don't you see? Our Emma, bull-headed as she is, is about to lose her grasp on one of the most promising and wealthy young men in town. Other girls are perfectly content to think of marriage and children, but not our Emma. It's not enough that Charles is besotted with her. Oh, no. This darling daughter of ours must show the world what great talents she has, how totally important she is to the small children in her care in a classroom. And now, to dedicate herself to the suffrage movement! She is on the verge of destroying her entire life and all of my plans for our family being joined to the Fortunes. She should have married Charles by now. As her mother, Beth, it is high time you told her that she is behaving like a perfect idiot!"

"Rupert!" Beth was aghast. "You called her an idiot!"

"She is an idiot! An idiot who will be called a spinster in another five years," he shouted. "And does she care for one second how this might affect me? How good it would be for my future to have the Fortune and Willows families related by marriage? All that property Fortune bought up on Portage Avenue is skyrocketing in value. He is a man of wealth and great influence. His opinion is sought on everything that moves in Winnipeg. And his son, Charles, poised to take over his father's empire, has had his tongue dragging in the dirt behind our Emma all these years, anxious to marry her. What does she do about it? She keeps him at arm's length, frittering away her opportunity with this nonsense about being a modern woman!"

"Rupert, please, don't worry. She's just twenty years old."

"Yes, Beth. She's twenty years old." Rupert worked to contain his frustration. "And you watch. Mark is going to persuade his son to move on to other young women who are more traditional. Girls who understand a woman's place is in the home."

"Oh, Rupert, do calm down, dear. That's utter nonsense. Charles will be home at Christmas, and I am sure that just seeing him will light a fire in her heart and she will agree to stop teaching at the end of this school year. That's just a few more months to wait. They will be married in summer and all will be fine. Trust her to make her own way, Rupert."

Rupert sat opposite Beth and took a deep breath. "No, Beth, Charles will not be home at Christmas. He won't be home until spring because he is going on the Grand Tour. Mark is making it a family celebration in honor of Charles' graduation from Bishop's College."

"Oh, dear." Beth's eyes flew open. She had witnessed romance being sparked on more than few occasions while traveling abroad. "Oh my, Rupert!" Beth seized on the realization. "Why didn't you tell me this first? You think Charles might actually become interested in someone else, don't you?"

"And with the encouragement of his father. I do, indeed. Fortune has booked travel at the end of January out of New York for his whole family, as I understand. In fact, he confided in me that one of his daughters has taken up with a musician Mark doesn't care for. He told me he is taking her on the tour with hopes she will forget about him. It is my guess that he is doing the exact same thing with Charles."

"But, the Fortunes do seem so fond of Emma," Beth said. "It doesn't make sense."

"They do like her. She's a delightful girl, but I think Mark invited me to lunch to give me a bit of a warning. He doesn't like her behavior, and he wants me to know. He also wanted me to know that as they are sailing out of New York, Charles will meet the family there, as there is no point in his coming all the way west for Christmas."

"Emma must know about this. Why hasn't she said anything?"

"She doesn't know. Not yet anyway. Mark only just made the arrangements. He told me he telephoned Charles and told him all about it this morning before we had lunch."

"She'll be dreadfully disappointed. What are we going to do?"

"Beth, first you have to get her to quit teaching."

"Quit teaching? Oh, my, Rupert, no. I cannot and will not ask her to do that. And even if you forced me to do it, what could I say to her? That she should run out on the Grand Tour to chase after Charles?"

Rupert stopped and stared at Beth as the obvious solution came into focus. "Yes," he said quietly. "Beth you are brilliant."

"I am?"

"Yes, you are." Rupert jumped to his feet and thrust his fist into the air in victory. "She should go on the Grand Tour."

"Nonsense. A young lady does not travel alone, and it would be wholly inappropriate for her to travel with the Fortunes."

"She'll travel with us," Rupert stated.

"Please, dear. We're leaving for Palm Beach right after Christmas. I made all the arrangements."

"Cancel them. I am feeling a strong urge to see the pyramids and perhaps the Holy Lands. We're going on the Grand Tour!"

"Rupert! This is ridiculous. There is absolutely no time to arrange it, and besides, this is a matter of love, and it is for Emma and Charles to work out. There is no place for us to get involved in this."

"Beth, you are wrong. This has nothing to do with love. This is business. Now, don't worry. I will take care of everything."

"Rupert, you have me frightened that poor Emma will have her heart broken. Oh, this is just terrible." Tears ran down her cheeks.

The plan instantly took shape in Rupert's mind, and he needed Beth on side. It was essential that she support his decision to travel overseas and he had much work to do to put

438

his scheme in motion. As soon as he could tear himself away he would need to talk to his lawyer. The man had proven himself indispensable in sticky circumstances requiring the utmost discretion.

Rupert swept to the side of his weeping wife. "There, there, pet." He stroked her hair and tenderly wiped her tears away. "I do believe that Emma and Charles are meant to be together. I didn't mean to spout off about my business concerns. That was terribly bad form, and I do hope that you will forgive me. Will you, my darling?"

He drew closer and ran a finger gently across her brow and started to hum to her, coaxing a smile and a sigh from Beth. She was so easy to handle, he thought, as he moved the hair back from her ear and brushed his lips gently against her cheek.

"Now, don't you worry about a thing, my sweet, li'l darlin'." Rupert dropped his voice and played his words with the slight southern accent of his youth. "You have some shopping to do, sugar, and I know there are some special little boutiques in Montreal that will be only to happy to look after my dear lady and her needs for the Grand Tour, and our daughter, too, of course. Perhaps Emma will choose to come with us on her own. Let's wait and see what happens. How would that be?"

The color rose in Beth cheeks. With his eyes on hers, he raised the back of her hand to his lips and kissed it, slowly, sensually. The heat of his gaze was almost too much. She thought she might faint, but held her wits. Such delicious moments like this were rare and not to be wasted. He turned her hand to kiss her palm and drew back. He looked at her as if it were for the first time, and as if she were the most beautiful woman he had ever seen. His smile widened, revealing those perfect teeth and heartbreaking dimples. Her heart started to race and her ribs strained against her tight bodice. He brought her hand to his lips again, timing his kisses to her quickening breath. She moved closer, mesmerized under his power as he tilted her chin up toward his full lips.

"Perhaps we should lock the door?" she whispered.

The crash in the hallway spoiled everything. Rupert was on his feet and out of the library before Chadwick could pick himself up off of the hallway floor.

Bloody hell. Chadwick was furious at his clumsiness. For all of his interest in snooping about, he was a man of a somewhat prudish nature, and had no stomach for the more intimate moments at Ravenscraig. Realizing that the atmosphere in the library was heating up beyond his comfort, he had made a hasty retreat from his hiding place and in so doing, his feet became entangled, causing him to fall against the closet door to be spilled out into the hallway in a most awkward and embarrassing fashion.

"Chadwick!" Rupert shouted, fearing his man had had a heart attack. "Someone send for the doctor!"

"No, please, sir! I'm quite all right, I assure you. I just stumbled as I was stowing a box away." Chadwick scrambled to his feet and pressed the closet door shut. He straightened his jacket and smoothed his hair before turning smartly on his heel to find half of the staff staring at him with their eyes popped open. He was mortified. Like a row of wretched little meerkats, they stood next to his employer. Then, as if the moment was lacking in intensity, he caught sight of the mistress, hustling full tilt toward the gathering, her bosom jouncing like jelly. Had a more dreadful moment ever occurred in any butler's life?

Rupert took charge. The staff members were quickly sent on their way, and Chadwick was folded back into his dignity with the task of pouring brandy for Mr. and Mrs. Willows in the library. The butler considered the sweat pouring down his back and prayed to be blessed with amnesia as he carefully shut the door and returned to his quarters.

Beth, an expert at dismissing unpleasant occurrences, was already planning her holiday.

"Well, dear, I'm off to see which items in my Palm Beach wardrobe will be of use on our travels abroad." Beth beamed at her amazing husband as she rose from her chair. All would be right in due time. Rupert would see to it, and she needn't worry for another minute.

Rupert made a quick phone call and left the house. There was still the matter of Emma's employment to contend with, and his lawyer, Doddsworth, was the ideal man to help him make the necessary arrangements.

At dinner that evening, Emma was crushed at the news that Charles would not be coming home for Christmas, but instead be traveling with his parents until springtime. She wept in her father's arms and then spent the weekend crying in her room, wondering if she had made a mistake in taking on the teaching job.

Three days later, Emma was fired from teaching. The principal called her into the office and produced a letter from one of the school's most important benefactors. The man had explained he was deeply worried about the fact that Miss Willows was discussing such political issues as women's suffrage in the classroom. He declared that unless she was dismissed, he would be compelled to withdraw his financial support for the school.

Pale and numbed by shock and humiliation, Emma sat before her untouched dinner.

"Father, I never once talked about voting rights in the classroom. I don't know where this complaint came from, but it's unfounded," Tears slid down Emma's face as she talked about losing her job.

"It's appalling that you would be dismissed in this way," Rupert fumed. "I will have Grenville Doddsworth look into the matter and urge a full investigation of the circumstances. No daughter of mine is going to be treated in this frightful and unfair manner!"

Emma shook her head. "Oh, what's the use? I am ruined as a teacher. What a terrible winter this turned out to be. Now Charles is finished with school, and I am finished as teacher. You're going away, and I will be rattling about in this big house with nothing to do everyday."

Rupert nodded at Beth, who smiled and took her daughter's hand. "Emma, dear, how about a trip to Montreal?" Beth paused as Emma's eyes, filled with self-pity, came up to meet hers. "Oh, darling, it just breaks my heart to see you this way. Do come to Montreal. You can shop with me and visit Grandmama, and …"

"And Charles can come to visit me from Lennoxville so I

can see him before he goes on tour ..." Emma perked up. "Oh, I do miss him so. I've made such a mess of things, haven't I?"

Rupert was enormously pleased with himself. It couldn't have gone better if he had scripted it.

"Then you will go on to Palm Beach from there, I expect," Emma said. "Daddy, do you think I might come along? I know Elliot will be there, and I think it would be so wonderful to see him."

"Actually, there's been a change in plans," Rupert replied. "Your mother and I have a gift for you, to cheer you up, Emma." Rupert went to a side table and produced a large envelope. He asked Emma to open it and out tumbled a bundle of brochures, maps, and a neatly outlined list of tour destinations.

"We are going on the Grand Tour, my dear. But for a few exceptions, it is largely the tour that Mark Fortune and his family are taking."

Beth beamed, and Emma caught her breath. "Oh, Daddy, you are the dearest father a girl could have!" Emma threw her arms around Rupert's neck and danced him about the room as she pealed with laughter. "Oh, please, tell me all of the details. Where are we going?"

"Allow me," Beth said as she reached for the itinerary and her spectacles. "Well, from Montreal we'll go on to New York where we will be boarding the *Franconia* and head for Trieste, the main seaport in the Austro-Hungarian Empire. We will be making a number of stops along the way to see places like Algiers, Monaco, and Athens. We'll find our way to Egypt where we'll spend some time exploring ancient history and see the pyramids. And we'll be staying at the fabulous Shepheard's Hotel in Cairo. Very fashionable." Beth smiled over her reading glasses. "Wait until you see how exquisite Cairo is. The city is overrun with barons and dukes on holiday. You'll adore it. Then on to Haifa and Jerusalem. If we aren't completely worn out by then, there will be the European part of our holiday. We'll travel through Italy and then on to Paris. From there over to London and by the end of April will be heading for New York and home on the *Mauretania*."

"It sounds very exciting," Emma said. "Will Maisie come, too?" she asked with her fingers crossed.

"Of course she will. I wouldn't think of traveling that far without her."

"Before you two start working up your lists of wardrobe needs, I do have one more surprise for my girls," Rupert said as he slid a second envelope across the table for Emma to open. Inside were gold trimmed cards with each of their names on them.

"A present,' Rupert said, unable to suppress his glee. "Tickets for the *Titanic*. The maiden voyage is scheduled for April 10th. She sails from Southampton to New York. The first class accommodations are second to none, I'm told."

"The *Titanic!*" Beth was clearly impressed. "The world's most luxurious ship. Well, won't we be traveling in style? But, Rupert, they are still building it. Are you certain it will be ready?"

"Yes. I was talking with Hudson Allison about it. Do you remember him from when he worked in Winnipeg some years ago? He's done very well for himself in Montreal, and he wrote me that the White Star Line is now firm on the launch date. He is traveling abroad with his family and said he intends to be on the *Titanic* at the end of their trip. I expect there will be a number of families from Winnipeg and Montreal that we will know on the voyage."

"Including the Fortune family?" Emma asked.

"Well, not at this point, I'm afraid. Mark Fortune has a particular affinity for the *Mauritania,* and that is what he has booked for their return voyage, but we'll see if I can persuade him to change his mind, shall we?"

Emma smiled her approval.

"The maiden voyage, you say?" Beth asked with a frown. "Are you certain that is a good idea, Rupert?"

"Whatever do you mean?"

"Well, will the crew have enough time to get to know the ship? Can you be sure the passengers will be well accommodated? Perhaps Mr. Fortune is right in booking the *Mauritania.*"

"Beth, dear, you are not to worry for one minute about this.

It will be an historic event to be on the Titanic. I daresay it will be one of the biggest stories of the century. All the papers will be interviewing all of the passengers. It will be wonderful. And," he teased, "if the crew is not up to the task, I assure you, I'll bring your caviar to you myself, my darling," he teased.

"Oh, Rupert, of course you will, but what about the newness of the ship. Do you think it will safe?"

"Please, my love. Haven't you heard? The ship is unsinkable. It's the *Titanic*. The name alone should tell you everything you need to know."

51
Jerusalem
March 4, 1912

Rupert proved right in his assessment that time together with Charles would inspire Emma to shift her concerns from women's rights to romance. His daughter was clearly enjoying the holiday abroad and so too, it appeared, was her ardent sweetheart. Rupert felt smugly triumphant as he quietly watched Charles manage Emma. The two were a terrific match, and Rupert saw tremendous potential in the couple. They were the kind of people who could found a dynasty. Rupert was greatly pleased that his sought after connection to the Fortune family was alive and well.

Emma was quite surprised at how quickly her classroom troubles and thoughts of voting rights had faded into the background. Charles proved to be an enthusiastic and engaging travel companion. Not once did he discuss marriage. At first she felt it was because he was being sensitive to her having lost her job. Then she worried that she had offended him in talking about the suffrage movement. As time went on, she longed to hear his flowery words of affection, but he only smiled.

Full of life and keenly interested in learning everything he could from every person they met on the tour, Charles impressed her greatly. He was not the shy young man she had first come to know years before. Seeing him in earnest discussion with the guide while visiting the pyramids at Giza, impeccably dressed, and quietly confident, she came to see him in a new light. She realized that she had perhaps been taking him for granted. He expressed great interest in her opinions and openly praised her knowledge and interest in the historical sites they explored. But, all the while, he kept her at a bit of a distance. It was true that they were almost constantly in the company of their families and the dozen or so others on their tour, but not once had he even tried to steal a kiss.

It went on this way for weeks. Emma began to worry that he had changed his mind and was no longer interested in marrying her. She began to flirt with him. She longed to be swept away, to feel his strong arms around her and to melt beneath his kisses. Charles smiled but held her back.

It was in the rose garden at the Shepheard's Hotel in Cairo that Emma's dreams finally came true. On bended knee, he told her he would be utterly devoted to her for the rest of his life. He had chosen the date for their wedding and asked for her hand. Emma, pink-cheeked and with glistening eyes, was very ready to agree, and enjoyed a girlish delight in saying yes. He kissed her sweetly, and she thought she would swoon. It was every bit of romance she ever could have wished to have.

Cairo had suddenly taken on a brand new magic, and Emma couldn't wait to share her excitement as she dashed through the hotel hallways to Maisie's room.

"Just one moment, please," the maid called through the door. "I'll be right with you, Mrs. Willows."

"Maisie, it's Emma, I have the most wonderful news!"

Maisie opened the door, smoothing her apron, and Emma all but ran her over as she rushed in and shut the door behind her.

"My goodness, Emma, what is it?" Maisie asked, reaching out to steady herself on a chair.

"Charles and I are going to be married."

"Emma! This is so right for you." Maisie grabbed her in a hug. "He is such a wonderful, caring man. I wish you both a lifetime of happiness. When is the wedding?"

"In June. Right after my twenty-first birthday. We had a long talk about it in the garden after breakfast today, and when I agreed, I thought he was going shout out loud. It was so much fun, Maisie. Then he pressed a little package into my hand, and in it was this beautiful locket."

Maisie smiled as she admired the round silver locket with the amethyst embedded in the center. "Oh, my, this is lovely. It's so delicate."

"His picture is inside and on the back he has engraved: *Emma, my love, When this you see, Think of me. Charles.*"

446

"What did your parents say? I presume he has spoken to your father."

"Not yet. It's a secret for now. Charles wants to speak to him in London before we sail for home."

"Why is he waiting?"

"Because Mr. Fortune wishes to go on to Italy from here with his family, and we'll be going on to the Holy Land. I'll be aching the entire time we are apart, I'm sure. But the time will pass quickly, and soon we'll be on our way to London where we will rejoin, not just the Fortunes, but all our other friends from Winnipeg. Father is already organizing a farewell dinner. It makes sense to save the surprise. It's so utterly romantic. I can hardly believe it."

"It will be wonderful," Maisie whispered hoarsely, fighting for calm. "I have no doubt that you will have a beautiful wedding, and the two of you will make a very happy life together."

Emma sat and looked at Maisie, suddenly aware of the distress that lingered on her friend's face.

"Why, Maisie, look at you. You've been crying."

"Oh, it's nothing really."

"I'm sure I can guess part of it. We'll be in Jerusalem next week. I know you've been overwrought with concern about this part of the trip. Can't you tell me why, Maisie?" Emma pressed. "You just haven't been yourself in recent days, and I know you well enough to know something is bothering you. Are you not feeling well?"

"Quite well," answered Maisie as her eyes welled with tears.

"Maisie, please tell me. We've been keeping each other's secrets for years and I've just told you about, Charles."

Maisie sighed heavily and nodded her head. "It's my grandparents. Emma, they live in Jerusalem."

"They do?" Emma was astonished. "Why on earth haven't you told me?"

"Emma, I have so many secrets in my life that sometimes I don't feel that I can keep track of them. Imagine what a burden they would become if I shared all of my complications with you. I could never do that. You've become such a dear friend to me, protecting my identity all this time."

"Well, of course, you know I would never betray you, Maisie. It would be an outright impossibility." She reached for Maisie's hands and looked into her sad eyes. "There must be a way to manage this. We've come all this way, you must be able to visit your grandparents."

She jumped to her feet and wheeled toward the window, tapping her chin with her finger.

"Maisie, I have an idea that I think could work. Mother has been going on about wanting to travel to Bethlehem. It's very important to her, and father is trying to arrange for a guide to take us there. Now, if I were to take ill, you would have to stay with me in Jerusalem at the hotel. And then, while they are touring Bethlehem, we could go together and find your grandparents, and no one would know because you would be required to be my chaperone and of course, being the fussy miss that I am, you would have to agree to take me anyplace I wished."

Maisie thought carefully. "Do you really think we can risk it?"

"Certainly, we can. We must, Maisie. We are going to be right there in Jerusalem. So, you and I will find a proper guide to get us to your grandparents' home. We'll find them and you will have a visit and it will be our secret."

Looking at Emma, Maisie saw nothing but compassion and warmth as she waited for her answer.

"Emma, I can't tell you how much this means to me. Thank you!"

The days flew by, and all too soon, the Jerusalem segment of the trip was behind them, leaving Maisie filled with a new understanding of the life of her grandparents. Exhausted but filled with contentment as they embarked on their journey to London, she pulled out her writing paper to send a long overdue letter to Winnipeg.

March 18, 1912

Dear Uncle Zev, Tanta Hannah and all my cousins,

I am writing to you with a heart full of joy in having seen Baba and Zaida at their home in Jerusalem. I must tell you first that they look well and are deeply happy with their life. I am indebted to Miss Willows who was able to arrange the surprise visit in complete secrecy from her family. Everything went very smoothly and it was the most beautiful moment of the entire journey for me.

Baba and Zaida live in a small apartment in what is known as the Jewish Quarter. They have made friends among the neighbors and have made a good life centered on Zaida's work at the synagogue and his continued support for the Zionist movement in Canada. His eyes light up with excitement as he speaks of his daily studies with the other scholars. For Zaida, it is clear that the spiritual connection he has to this ancient land is a great source of strength and contentment. He is truly fulfilled and looks years younger than his age. He says he feels he is home in a way he never felt anywhere else.

Baba, too, has become accustomed to her very different life here and proudly showed me how she has adapted her cooking to take advantage of the fresh fruits and vegetables in the market place. She made a beautiful lunch for Miss Emma and me to enjoy with them.

I would say they live humbly but are lacking nothing they consider important. They miss Mrs. Weidman, of blessed memory, who is interned on the Mount of Olives. Mr. Weidman continues on well enough and has a new wife who looks after him with great kindness.

Baba and Zaida are also staying in touch with other families who have come from Winnipeg and Montreal to live in Jerusalem. There are quite a number of people from Canada here.

Several of these families live in communal farm communities known as kibbutzim. It is a very different way of life. They all work very hard here, but there is joy in their commitment. Everyone says it is a relief not to deal with the bitter Canadian winters.

Jerusalem is really the most amazing city you can imagine. To walk on paths that are thousands of years old and imagine who may have been in the very spot where I stood looking up at the old stone walls of the city is a very humbling experience. The walls are light in color, almost white, actually, and appear washed in gold.

Beautiful bursts of green plants have affixed themselves to the walls, high off the ground, somehow managing to grow in nothing but the mortar between the stones. It is astonishing. To me it is like the Jewish people who have also planted themselves in the most inhospitable grounds to flourish wherever God has taken them. It is quite beyond description.

Everywhere, the stone buildings rise above the pathways. Children run through the streets with their games, and women call out to peddlers who make their rounds.

Jerusalem is filled with colorful sights and sounds one cannot hear anywhere else in the world, I believe. It is a city filled with people and animals, and such a blend of cultures and beliefs. The air is light and warm, like summer in Winnipeg, with a clear blue sky, hot in the day and cool at night. There are few signs of wealth and modern convenience. Here you see people herding goats and riding camels and donkeys.

In every market and bazaar the vendors reach out to touch and tug at the passersby, desperate to sell their wares. The foods, and especially the fruits, are exotic and strange, but ever so appealing, as are the sounds of the jangling instruments and spirited drum beats of the Arab children playing their instruments in the streets.

I have been so fortunate to see so many wondrous sights, like the pyramids and the Sphinx in Egypt, the ruins of Athens in Greece, and finally, Jerusalem. I understand now why Zaida has worked his whole life toward this goal of living in this sacred place. It sings to you and wakes up something that sleeps inside the soul, Zaida says. I think he's right. It makes me weep just to think of it. It makes me feel different about who I am. But, I will save that to talk about when I am sitting at your table, drinking tea and enjoying Tanta Hannah's delicious honey cake. How I miss all of you!

It has been incredibly interesting to see so much and to have these wonderful experiences, but I will be very happy to be home in Winnipeg again. We are now making our way to Paris and then London where the Willows family will relax for a few days in preparation for the voyage to New York and then the long train ride to Winnipeg.

Tanta Hannah, I know you always worry about travel, especially when it involves the ocean. You must know that you should not worry. Everyone has been talking about the Titanic being an unsinkable ship. So, you see, I will be home safe and full of stories in your house in just a short few weeks.

Love,
Maisie

52
London Farewell

April, 7, 1912

London's elegant Metropole Hotel was filled to capacity and humming with activity as the staff and management scrambled to keep up with the needs of their guests. All of London seemed alive with *Titanic* fever. After years of work and preparation, the great luxury liner was finally ready to sail out of the port of Southampton, and the entire population of England seemed to be crowded into the capital city to take part in the festive events to mark the occasion.

Only one person seemed immune to the fever. Preoccupied with her own future as a bride, Emma stood outside her parents' suite and listened carefully at the door. How long had he been in there? Surely there could be no reason why her father would object to Charles' desire to marry her. What on earth was taking so long? She paced up and down the hallway, counting her steps.

Finally the door opened and her father appeared with a broad smile and a champagne glass in his hand. "Emma, darling, do come along. You don't wish to keep your fiancé waiting do you? There is a celebration to be had!"

She hooted with laughter as she picked up her skirts and ran like a child all the way down the hall.

Beth felt as important as the Queen of England as Rupert, beaming with pride, offered his arm. How handsome he looked in his top hat and tails as they rode from the Metropole to their dinner engagement at the nearby Carlton Hotel. Rupert had arranged the farewell dinner and invited all of their friends who were traveling on the *Titanic*. That this had also turned into an engagement celebration was like fireworks at the end of a parade.

How quickly the years had passed. Here Emma, dear sweet

little Emma, was to be married, and the last of her children would be leaving the nest. Well, her daughter had made a good choice in Charles Fortune. He truly would be a wonderful husband for Emma. He would protect and love her, and he was set for a good future in his father's real estate development company. They would stay in Winnipeg, and Beth would have the pleasure of having her daughter nearby. Rupert was right. The year 1912 would long be remembered.

The dining room at the Carlton was resplendent in lush decorations in recognition of Easter Sunday. A joyful display of jonquils and brightly colored Easter eggs greeted them as they were ushered to the large table in the center of the room. In all, there would be close to twenty in their party. Rupert's guests included their Montreal friends, Hudson Allison and his wife, and several new people they had befriended in their travels, in addition to the Fortune family and the Winnipeg bachelors known as the three musketeers, John Borebank, John McAffrey, and Thomson Beattie.

As Rupert and Beth approached the table, a single man rose and greeted them, grandly sweeping into a deep bow. Beth was amused by the extravagant and showy behavior of Americans, and she stifled a giggle as the man kissed her hand. She recognized him as the fellow who was so smitten with Alice Fortune. If only she was better with remembering names! She smiled brightly and looked to Rupert to fill in the blank.

"William! You are the first here. How very good of you to join us this evening." Rupert pumped his hand and turned to Beth. "Mr. Sloper was kind enough to accept my invitation at the last minute."

"We are charmed to have you join us, Mr. Sloper," Beth said.

"Good evening, Mrs. Willows. I thank you both so much for inviting me."

Rupert's eyes twinkled with mischief as he nodded in acknowledgment. "One more opportunity to gaze upon the loveliness of Miss Alice Fortune, I suppose?"

"Indeed, you are correct, sir." Sloper saw no reason to shield his motives. "But I shall have even more time to enjoy her company. You see, Mr. Willows, Alice told me that you had persuaded Mr. Fortune to change ships for the crossing home and that they will be joining you on the *Titanic*. Alice suggested I might do the same. Of course, I heartily agreed and was fortunate to have secured rather nice accommodations, even on such short notice."

"I'm delighted to hear it, Sloper."

"Well, it does seem it would be a pity to miss the maiden voyage of the greatest and most luxurious ship on Earth."

"I'll be expecting you to join me for a card game or two on the voyage home," Rupert said. "It will give me a chance to win back some of the money you took from me in Paris. Ah, here comes the lovely bride-to-be with her intended."

"Bride, you say?" Sloper reached to kiss Emma's hand. "Well done, Mr. Fortune. May you have many sweet years of marital bliss ahead. Congratulations to you both!"

As the guests found their way to Rupert's table, there were enthusiastic greetings and many compliments for the beautifully dressed women. To great amusement, William Sloper liberally showered each of the ladies with air-kissed greetings in the manner of the French and set an animated and warm tone for the evening of celebration.

Rupert was thrilled with the chance to play host to such a well-heeled gathering. He presided grandly, making great show of welcoming the Fortunes in his toast to the future bride and groom and in praising Mark and Mary Fortune for having raised such wonderful and interesting children. The wine flowed, the service was second to none, and the party was charged with an easy and enjoyable liveliness. There was a good deal of merriment in the eyes of the revelers as the servers presented an exquisitely prepared menu of eight courses, ending with a very rich chocolate cake along with banana mouse, whipped cream, and a dazzling array of confections. Rupert could not have been happier.

In time, the diners fell to discussing the highlights of their vacations and the very exciting business of being among the first passengers on the *Titanic*.

"Mr. Sloper, are you quite sure that you haven't been

frightened off after my experience with the soothsayer in Cairo?" Alice Fortune's eyes danced as she teased the love-struck man beside her.

"Nothing could keep me from your side, dear Miss Fortune," he said, pretending to swoon and prompting a giggle from the women. "Besides, if that man knew so much about the future, why on Earth is he still poor? If he had any ability at all, do you not think he would have used his talents to pick the winner in a horse race or two to wrench himself out of his poverty?"

"You should be on Broadway as an entertainer!" John Borebank laughed.

"Whatever are you talking about?" Beth asked over the laughter. "What man?"

Alice raised her eyebrows and fluttered her fan mysteriously as she gained the full attention of the table. "While we were in Cairo, I happened to go out on the veranda one afternoon to rest and enjoy a cup of tea. Mr. Sloper came along shortly and agreed to join me. Just as he was sitting down, this little man popped up in front of me and looked deeply into my eyes. He reminded me a bit of one of those organ grinder monkeys because he moved so rapidly and played his hands with tiny movements. Then he asked if he might take a look at my palm." She delicately turned her hand to the crowd in demonstration. "I found it rather amusing, so I agreed. He took it in both of his hands. He had such a gentle touch, like feathers holding my hand, but just for a fleeting moment. He practically reeled backward, and I laughed out loud, as I thought he was being dramatic for the purpose of securing a good size gratuity from Mr. Sloper."

"Did he say anything?" Beth could hardly wait to hear. She had long been fascinated with card readers.

"He said he could see that I would be 'floating about on the sea in an open boat'. I could only laugh. Mr. Sloper gave him a few coins and the man disappeared into the crowd."

"Were those the actual words?" Rupert was enthralled.

Alice's eyes slipped to her mother. It was clear Mary Fortune was greatly displeased with the story and was shifting uncomfortably in her seat. The young woman immediately sought to move on to something else.

"Oh, I don't remember, exactly." She tossed her hand to dismiss the interest. "That really was all there was to it."

But William Sloper missed the cue and barreled on. "He told Alice that she would be in danger every time she traveled on the sea. He said she would lose everything but her life." He finished with a nod for dramatic emphasis.

"Good heavens," said Beth, clutching her fan to her breast. "And you are not alarmed?"

"Perhaps I would be had my father not changed our tickets from the *Mauritania* to the *Titanic*," Alice replied. "But, no, I can say that I am perfectly at ease."

"Sounds ominous," said Hudson Allison, polishing his spectacles.

"Nonsense. Utter rubbish, I say," Rupert put in. "There are too many good things happening in the world and particularly among the people at this table. There is simply no room for anything ominous. It would be simply impossible to have anything untoward happen on the world's safest ship. You did well, too, Mr. Sloper, in changing your tickets. Let's raise our glasses to the *Titanic!*"

"Hear, hear," the gentlemen responded, clinking glasses as the ladies smiled.

Emma looked at Charles and saw a fleeting moment of emotion. Fear, perhaps? He forced a smile, and whatever she had seen in his eyes was gone as quickly as it had appeared. How sensitive he was to be touched by his sister's story of the soothsayer.

Emma squeezed his hand and smiled warmly as she looked into his eyes. In the glowing light of the candles on the table they appeared to be the color of the ocean against his sandy curls. What lovely children they would have! How proud she would be to be his wife. She ached to be home and preparing for her wedding. Her heart overflowed with happiness at the thought that there would be thousands of moments just like this, holding hands with her darling husband as they built their future together.

53
The Titanic
April 10, 1912

Rupert found the *Titanic* to be everything it promised to be. He was greatly impressed with the fine attention to detail exhibited in the luxurious appointments afforded the first class passengers. They were told the ship was carrying twenty-two hundred people with both passengers and crew and, as such, was at only two-thirds of its capacity. Rupert saw this as an advantage, as it meant that their steward would have extra time to look after his family with two empty cabins in his section.

The designers had done a marvelous job, in Rupert's opinion, in creating a breathtakingly beautiful and comfortable ship. In the days prior to sailing out of Southampton, he had read everything he could find about her. All the facts and figures concerning the mammoth vessel fascinated him, and upon boarding, he was as excited as a boy in candy shop. He took his time examining everything from the choice of the electric lights to the very fine craftsmanship of the spectacular grand staircase placed so beautifully beneath the bowled glass ceiling.

He also appreciated the very careful manner in which the designer had ensured, with discreetly placed locked gates, that the passengers traveling first class would never once have to come into contact with the under classes. Truly, if you hadn't seen them at the dock, you'd never know that such people existed on the ship. One never saw, heard or smelled them. It was perfect.

Everywhere he turned, Rupert found new aspects of the *Titanic* to admire. The first class dining saloon was comfortably and brightly decorated, the gymnasium had the latest equipment for exercise, the Palm Court Café was delightful in a manner that reminded him of the refined tastes of Palm Beach, and the covered promenade adjacent to their suite allowed for the full benefit of enjoying the sea air, while being protected from the wind. It was magnificent in every way. Well, perhaps not in every way.

There was the matter of the lifeboats. He thought they cluttered up the boat deck unnecessarily and spoiled the clean lines of the ship. The *Titanic* exceeded the standards of the day with twenty boats when it would have been allowed to sail with just sixteen. That there were not enough boats to carry even half of the passengers and crew, should the ship be at capacity, troubled Rupert not at all. Why should it? With all he'd read, he was convinced the ship would have to be struck by a meteor before it would founder.

Immediately upon boarding in Southampton, while the ladies saw to their unpacking, Rupert took several hours to explore the vessel. With a keen eye for detail he walked from one end to the other and then through it all again, twice more. It amused him that he was able to offer assistance to a lost crewmember and point him correctly on his way. Like the majority of seamen on the ship, the young steward had been too busy at his post to become familiar with the ship's layout. Everything was new and every person working on the ship was new to it.

In the first two days at sea, Rupert was careful to take the time to write down clever descriptive passages of what he saw and experienced so that he would be well prepared with his comments for the newspapermen in New York. He expected the harbor to be thick with reporters who would want interviews with the first disembarking passengers from the ship, and he intended to appear in as many newspapers as possible.

Although the ship was spectacular in every setting, Rupert had no difficulty in naming the first class smoking lounge as his favorite location. Set just behind the dining saloon, it was ever so inviting with its richly dark and plush interior, ornamented in beautifully wrought stained glass. The elaborate fireplace, the long, handsomely lighted bar, and the deep and heavy chairs made one feel as if there were no finer accommodation for a gentleman in any private club, the world over. The pleasurable scent of Cuban cigars wafting over expensive brandy proved the perfect complement to the affluent sounds of the robust and cultured voices that murmured forth. Add to that the soft interjections of clicking poker chips, and Rupert was sent to the top of the world. It was the sound of wealthy men at leisure, a sound he cherished above all others, though he had practiced saying that the sound of the orchestra was truly his favorite, should he ever be asked.

Sunday dinner on the ship had been spectacular. His daughter was walking on air, and his wife was delighted she would finally have in-laws in the family that she felt of equal social status to her own. Now with dinner behind them and Beth and Emma safely in the care of his daughter's besotted fiancé, there was nothing to interfere with Rupert's pleasure in preparing for an evening of poker.

Alone in his stateroom he enjoyed a quiet moment as he took his time readying himself for his visit to the smoking room. Tonight, he would take a run at the professional gamblers.

He opened his closet with all of the anticipation of a matador dressing to star in a bullfight. His preparations required the use of his special garment, a custom-designed money vest that he wore beneath his formal evening attire. An experience with a clever pickpocket had resulted in Rupert's designing the pocketed vest some years before.

He opened the safe and pulled out the wads of bills, carefully counting and stacking each one before slipping them cleanly into the six side-loading pockets on his vest. In addition, near his waist there were two top loading pockets that buttoned closed, so that he could carry chips or other valuables, if need be. Over the vest he wore a special evening shirt that was split on the sides to allow discreet access to his money by simply reaching under his coat.

It was a pity that Captain Smith appeared so intent on getting them into New York a day earlier than scheduled. Rupert would have been quite happy to have added an extra day or two to the voyage. He had enjoyed a rather good run at poker in the first three nights of the passage. He had won a little more than he had lost, but mostly he had accomplished his desire to attract the attention of the cardsharps on board. He had spotted two who were certainly professionals: Harry Homer and George Bradley, both posing as first class millionaires and getting away with it, as far as Rupert could see. The thrill of probable victory in the evening ahead set his skin on fire as he readied himself.

Rupert had a secret. He had trained himself to cheat at cards. About a dozen years earlier Rupert had received a fateful call from Minnie Woods who was having a spot of trouble at her house. One of her customers from Toronto, a man of great reputation, was in need of help to avoid appearing before the magistrate. Rupert settled the matter with a single phone call, and the gentleman was only too happy to express his gratitude with a series of private lessons to explain the technique of "flashing" to Rupert. A good flasher sees the cards he deals out to the other players. Having it explained was one thing, but learning to do it well without being detected was another. Rupert took it as a personal challenge and in time he had mastered the technique.

As it turned out, he was better at flashing than some of the professional gamblers he had encountered on this particular voyage. His game of choice was five-card stud. Flashing cards with cardsharps at the table was especially titillating.

Both Homer and Bradley had noticed him in the smoking room. Each had invited him to play and he had politely refused, claiming discomfort with their rich stakes. In truth, Rupert had needed time to watch them. The two generally worked separate tables. Tonight he would accept their invitation and work to get both into the same game.

As he patted down the money-vest, his confidence grew. He was about to close the safe when his eyes fell on Beth's diamond necklace, with the matching bracelet and earrings neatly placed next to it. He looked for the emeralds and realized Beth had chosen to wear them today. As she never opened the safe, he knew she would just wear the jewels to bed, as was her custom until she could hand them directly to him. Looking at the diamonds, a thought crept into his mind. What if the two thousand dollars he carried wasn't enough? He scooped up the diamond pieces and placed them securely in one of the chip pockets on the money garment, carefully buttoning it closed. Then he noticed the tiny box in the back. Oh, yes, the little diamond earrings that Charles had bought for Emma. He glanced at them, thinking how charming it was that this earnest young man had so proudly presented this bit of sparkle to Rupert's little girl. How endearing. No doubt, in time, Charles would be able to afford to graduate to the heavier gems that Rupert and other men of his ilk bestowed upon their wives. He chuckled to himself. He would take Emma's tiny diamonds for luck.

He felt very pleased with himself as he spun the dial to lock the empty safe and then stood to check his debonair image in the mirror. Those cardsharps had no idea what was coming.

Charles Hays eyed his cards and bit down on his cigar. The railway tycoon was off his game. He didn't much care for five-card stud. He cared even less for losing. He had joined the table as the fifth man and quickly saw all were more than casual poker players. He suspected that two of the fellows, Harry Homer and George Bradley, were professionals. Homer had a good stash of winnings tonight, but Bradley was hurting. There were two men from Winnipeg at the table. Thomson Beattie was a gentleman through and through, but this Willows fellow was hard to peg. A friendly enough chap, but there was something about his game over the last hour and half that he found just wasn't sitting well.

Hays watched carefully as Willows dealt the final cards in the hand and the bets were made. Three of the five players had folded. Hays was left with strong cards and Willows staring him down.

"All in," said Rupert, and without hesitation shoved all of his chips toward the pot.

Hays, sitting with three tens, took his time while he speculated whether Rupert had just bought the flush when the fourth heart, the jack, hit the table. Hays figured he had and wasn't going to throw his remaining two hundred into the pot to find out. "I'm out," he said, tossing his cards face up onto the table.

"Trips? Thank you, so very much," Rupert said politely, as he reached forward to gather in the chips. "All I had was a little pair of jacks."

"Damn it to hell!" Hays shook his fist in the air then smacked his hand down hard on the table. "Naturally a damned heart had to come up. I was sure you had that flush, Willows. You bluffed me out and just had to rub it in, did you? Well, gentlemen, this is too rich for me. Time for me to turn in."

"So, we'll see you in Winnipeg, you say, Charles?" Thomson Beattie asked.

"Yes. I'll be there in a couple of months to get the plans in the works for the construction of the new railway hotel. It will be called the Hotel Fort Garry, and I promise you it will be the finest in the city."

"When are you opening the Ottawa Hotel? What's the name again?" Beattie inquired.

"The Chateau Laurier. The grand opening is on the twenty-sixth of this month. That's why I chose to come home on the *Titanic*. Do stop in to see it on your way out west, gentlemen," he nodded to the two men from Winnipeg. "I'll make sure your names are on the guest list." Hays stood up and bowed courteously, reaching to shake hands with his fellow card players. "Mr. Homer, Mr. Bradley. I wish you good luck this evening. It has been a pleasure, but I really must say goodnight."

Homer's eyes moved to Bradley as he picked up the cards and addressed the mysteriously talented Mr. Willows.

"I daresay, Willows, this is rather a good bit of luck I see you are having this evening," Homer said warmly. "Do you care for another game? Perhaps you would be so kind as to give us a chance to get back some of our money, old chap? How about you, Beattie?"

Thomson Beattie hesitated as he pulled out his watch and saw that it was twenty minutes before midnight.

"Well, perhaps just one more hand. Good heavens, there goes my drink. Did you feel that bump?" He jumped back from the table so that his evening clothes wouldn't be soiled.

"That wasn't a bump, that was your heart sinking in your chest," laughed Bradley. "I see there has been a change in your luck and not for the better in the last hour or so, Mr. Beattie."

"Well, I do think I felt something," Beattie said as his eye caught a disturbance across the room. "See. Look over there. I'm not the only one with a spilled beverage. That fellow over there appears quite out of sorts. I think we hit something."

"Hit something? In the middle of the ocean, you say? Perhaps a whale?" Bradley snorted and slapped his knee, while Homer shuffled the cards.

"Well, perhaps an iceberg, my good man. We're in the North Atlantic." Beattie wasn't at all impressed with Homer and Bradley the way Rupert seemed to be, and was reluctant to continue. "As fast as we are traveling, I'd say we're not far off Newfoundland and this water is known to have icebergs this time of the year."

"So, even if it was an iceberg, what harm could come to this ship? It's built to withstand that sort of thing," Harry Homer interjected.

Rupert was annoyed by the interruption and anxious to get back to the game.

"There, now. Let's ask the steward." He waved to the closest one. "I say, is there some sort of trouble?"

"No sir, not a bit that I've been told about." The skinny steward wore a jacket too large for his small frame and bobbed slightly, like a wooden puppet on strings, as he cleaned up the spilled drink. His hollow eyes went from one to the next at the table. "It seems everything is perfectly fine and you are not to be alarmed. Would you gentlemen care for another drink?"

Beattie was rattled by the activity. "Not for me, thank you. As a matter of fact, I think its time for me to cash in my chips," he said. "I will bid you goodnight and shall return to my cabin to lick my wounds. Perhaps we'll meet for another game tomorrow. Gentlemen," he nodded politely and left.

With three left at the table Rupert smiled calmly, holding the deck. "Well, shall we play?"

Homer shrugged with indifference and Bradley slapped his money down the table. "You bet your Canadian ass, Mr. Willows."

"Dealer's choice?" Rupert smiled at them.

"Let her rip." Bradley reached for his brandy.

Rupert gradually became aware that the room had started to

empty. Then he was startled to see a man rush in, wearing a lifebelt. He was even more surprised when he recognized him as Charles Fortune.

"Please excuse me for interrupting, Mr. Willows," Charles said.

"So, are we sinking then?" Rupert couldn't suppress his laughter at the sight of Charles in the lifebelt. "Forgive me. This is Charles Fortune, my daughter's fiancé. Mr. Bradley and Mr. Homer."

"Good evening, gentlemen." Charles' cheeks colored with embarrassment as he calmly stated his business. "It's a precaution, Mr. Willows, but they are asking people to put on their life belts. Father has gone to look after my mother and sisters. I don't wish to overstep, sir, but I must say, I think it prudent to follow suit. They are calling for the women and children to get into the lifeboats, sir."

"The lifeboats? Good heavens." Rupert thought the idea ridiculous. "The *Titanic* will never sink, but if you think it prudent, as you say, perhaps you would do me a great favor and see to Emma and my wife. Use your best judgment, as I know you will, and I am certain that they will be in very good hands. I'll finish up here and join you on deck. Tell Mrs. Willows that I will be right along, but that she is to follow your instructions until I arrive."

"Of course, Mr. Willows," answered Charles, as he ran out of the room.

"Are we still playing, gentlemen?" Rupert asked.

"Sure. They won't let the men into the boats yet anyway, and I can't see how we all won't be more comfortable here than freezing our tails off while we float about in tiny boats only to be returned to the *Titanic* in few hours."

"I agree completely. I think they're rushing this lifeboat business," said Harry Homer. "You must realize that in the very worst case, this ship will float about for nine or ten hours, even if it's crippled. There's plenty of time for ships in the area to come to our rescue should this prove to be of any concern at all. Willows, it's your deal."

Rupert was enjoying himself mightily despite the distraction of the lifeboat activity. He had lost just enough to go in for the kill against the cocky cardsharps, who had proved to be genuinely charming company throughout the evening.

He knew the time was short, and he had just this last chance as dealer to hit the big win. The cards were dealt and the betting was aggressive.

Everything changed in the next instant. A rocket blast split the night and a shriek went up from the boat deck outside the smoking room.

"Rockets! That means we are sinking!" Homer went white and reached for his chips.

With almost two thousand dollars in the pot, Rupert maintained a steely determination to continue, and reached for Homer's arm to stop him.

"Excuse me. We haven't finished the hand."

"Are you mad, Willows?" Bradley's eyes shot at him. "The ship is going down!"

Rupert quickly dealt the last card and dropped a nine onto Bradley's up cards. Knowing his three kings were the strongest hand, he egged his opponents on. At his turn to bet he pushed his chips forward, "All in."

Homer folded, and Bradley, nervous to get moving but smelling a bluff, tossed his chips into the biggest pot of the night.

With great flourish Rupert flipped over his hole card. "Ha! Can you do better than my three kings?"

"Bastard!" Bradley yelled. Homer jumped out of his seat, and Rupert shouted out loud, as if he had just scored the winning goal in a rugby match.

"Goodnight, Rupert. I hope you choke on that pot. And I don't mind telling you that you are a bad cheat!" Bradley barely got the words out before he was on his way.

"Thank you, gentlemen. It was a pleasure!" Rupert called after them, cheerily, as they darted from the room. He put his hands on the abandoned cards and as he moved to sweep in Bradley's hand, it suddenly registered. He was looking at aces and eights. A shiver went up his back. The dead man's hand. These were the identical cards, right down to the nine of diamonds, that made up Bill Hickok's hand when he was shot and killed in a saloon in South Dakota.

There was shouting out on deck and Rupert glanced out the window to see a growing crowd was moving toward the lifeboats.

"Mr. Willows. Where is your lifebelt? You must go put it on, sir." Standing next to Rupert was the sunken-eyed steward who, in Rupert's imagination, now appeared, eerily, as a ghost. Rupert ran from the room and bounded down the hallway in search of his heavy buffalo coat and his lifebelt.

Emma sat on her bed with her blanket pulled up under her chin and refused to move. Maisie was in no mood to argue.

"Well, you will please excuse me, then, while I get my things together?" The maid grabbed a pillowslip and efficiently began gathering up her most precious belongings, tucking the parcel firmly inside her coat.

"Oh, goodness, Maisie," Emma answered. "Do you really think it necessary to be changing out of our night clothes? Everyone knows this is just a false alarm. It is utterly impossible that the *Titanic* would sink, even if it did bump into an iceberg or something. I mean, really, look at the size of this ship. I don't believe for one second that we are in any danger."

Maisie swiveled to look at her. "Emma, please, just do as Mr. Charles has asked. We really must hurry. I will attend to your mother. Your lifebelt is here, and your heavy coat is on the chair. Please, remember your extra stockings and your gloves. Wear the warmest shoes you have."

"Maisie, you're frightening me."

There was a pounding at the door and an urgent plea.

"Emma, it's Charles, are you ready? It's time to go on deck."

Maisie opened the door and squeezed past the young man.

"Miss Emma's things are all ready and on the chair, there, Mr. Fortune. I'll be right along with Mrs. Willows."

"Charles, really, what is this all about?" Emma protested. "Do you think the ship is in danger? And where is my father?"

"He's instructed me to see that you and your mother get up to the boat deck and he will meet us there. My father has already taken my mother and sisters up, and it would please me greatly if you would just hurry along and do as I say. Here, let me help you with the lifebelt."

"Charles, I don't see any reason for alarm. I spoke to the steward, and he said there was nothing to be bothered about. Why do you look so worried?"

Charles tugged at the straps of the lifebelt and gave it a thorough inspection as he helped Emma put it on. "I have a cautious nature, my sweet, and I have you and your mother to care for until your father joins you on deck. Those are his instructions. Now, I must insist we move along."

Simultaneously feeling the sting of the reproof and the comfort of the manliness of her fiancé, Emma fell in behind her mother and dutifully followed Charles, with Maisie bringing up the rear.

In the hallway they saw a few passengers emerging in nightclothes with coats pulled carelessly over their shoulders, wandering aimlessly about and speculating about the nature of the trouble. Few had put on life belts and with no sense of urgency anywhere around them, Emma felt like a child overdressed for winter when spring had arrived. She was about to protest again, but seeing the serious expression on Charles' face, she held her tongue and followed him to the port side of the boat deck. They came upon Officer Lightoller leading some men in stripping the covers off a lifeboat and readying it for lowering. A few other first class women had made their way up to the largely empty deck and all stood casually by. Some were with their husbands; others said the men were stopped from coming up to the boat deck.

"That explains why we haven't seen your father," Beth suggested. While Emma chatted with Charles, she reached into her pocket searching for something she couldn't seem to find. Maisie, ever attentive since the bout with typhoid, knew what her mistress was looking for and discreetly moved closer to whisper to her.

"I refilled your two flasks and put them in your inside

pocket, Mrs. Willows."

"Thank you, Maisie. The brandy might help against the cold."

The small group idly watched the boats being readied with no more concern than if they had been watching a street sweeper at work. None had ever really looked at a lifeboat before, let alone been in one, and there was more curiosity than worry among the onlookers.

"Excuse me, sir!" A tall heavyset woman with absurdly small feet and an enormous feathered hat barged passed Maisie. "I said, excuse me, sir!" She was wearing a fur coat trimmed in fox about the collar. The dead animal's glass eyes stared out next to the darting eyes of a shivering little Chihuahua, wrapped in its own tiny mink coat and tucked under the woman's fat neck. She shouted over the dog's ears to get the attention of Mr. Lightoller.

"I take it these are all reserved for the first class, are they?" Her light blue eyes snapped with impatience, and her jowls shook as she flipped a gloved hand in the direction of the boats on the forward deck. Mr. Lightoller turned away, and it wasn't clear to Maisie whether he had deliberately avoided the question. But as she looked around, it was plain to see that there were only first class passengers on the deck. Her heart leaped as she remembered that the ship was segregated and there were gates in place to separate the classes. When were they going to allow the others up to the boats? Had they even been told they should come up?

Activity intensified with shouting from the crewmen. Long ropes were dropped into place and the davits swung the lifeboat out over the water. As it swayed and settled, a crewman cried out, "Lifeboat number four is ready, sir!

Mr. Lightoller waved his arms, "Women and children only! Come quickly, ladies. Step lively and get on board."

The fat lady yelled back with obvious disdain for the arrangements. "No, thank you, Mr. Lightoller." The feathers jumped in her bonnet as she jerked her chin forward. "I really don't think I can manage that ghastly leap from the deck out onto that boat, sir. I will wait for another lifeboat. Where is Captain Smith? I wish to speak to him."

Her pronouncement set off a ripple of commentary and speculation among the passengers gathered on the deck. "That is very far, indeed," suggested one of the men as he eyed the lifeboat. "Perhaps there is a gangplank or bridge to assist in the transfer to the boats. I daresay, Mr. Lightoller, I should think this will be a bit of hazard."

The group hesitated, and Mr. Lightoller threw his hands up, turning his attention to ordering a group of seamen to get the next boat ready.

"Charles, do you think it's safe?" Emma's eyes went wide as she clutched his arm.

"It is perfectly safe. It's nothing more than a short step, and you must get into the boat as quickly as possible," he insisted. "I will help you, and there will be seamen on board to be sure that everything is done properly."

While Charles comforted Emma and her mother, Maisie broke from the group and moved closer to the deckhands to see if she could hear something useful.

"It's seventy feet to the water, sir," she overheard the urgent voice of one of the older seamen. "I don't think it wise to fill the boats up completely. What if the davits don't hold and we drop the boat? The women will all die whilst we're tryin' to save them, sir!"

Maisie went white with fear and moved away before she heard what Mr. Lightoller would have to say in response. She stepped toward the edge of the ship and leaned out over the rail to look over the side of the ship. A cry caught in her throat when she realized how far it was down to the black shiny sea. It was like standing on top of a skyscraper.

She pulled back and thoughts of home and her Aunt Hannah's fear of traveling on the water gripped her. She could see her breath in the air and her nose was already cold. The temperature had plummeted since the afternoon. Being in the water would mean death in minutes. She pulled her collar up tightly and tried to stop her teeth from chattering. Whether her shaking was from fear or the cold she couldn't tell, but she knew she had to get hold of her emotions and compose herself before rejoining the others. Her life depended on it.

She thought of her grandfather and his wise ways. She heard his words in her mind. When things get bad, think of something that makes you thankful. It seemed like a ridiculous notion, but she needed to have something to hang on to. It instantly came to her that they all had their winter coats on and there was no wind. There was not even a hint of a breeze in the midnight air and the sea appeared as flat as a midsummer lake. At least they would not be set adrift in a rolling ocean. The optimism revived her. Perhaps they wouldn't have to leave the *Titanic* at all. Maybe this was just a precaution, and they would soon all be allowed to go back to bed.

An ear splitting sound shattered her composure. Rockets! An incongruous shower of sparkling streams of light, so immediately recognized as a sign of celebration, instead was announcing with certainty that the ship would founder. It was a desperate cry out for help to nearby ships. In an instant everyone on board knew this horrid truth and the question was simply, when would it sink? Panic rose as passengers were suddenly motivated to get into the boats. A roaring blast of steam erupted from the bowels of the ship, rendering conversation impossible.

Mr. Lightoller shouted as loud as he could over the chaos as he returned to the task of trying to organize the passengers for the troublesome boat number four.

"Ladies, please go down the stairs to 'A' deck, the promenade deck! It will be easier and safer to get in to the boats from the windows on the deck below!" Maisie rushed back so as not to be separated from Emma and Mrs. Willows, and Charles led them down the stairs.

"Hey, what's this? The windows are shut!" the seaman yelled as the party crammed forward on the promenade deck. "Everyone, go back up to the boat deck!"

"Is there anyone in charge who knows what is going on?" shouted a frustrated woman.

"Where is Rupert? Why hasn't he come for us?" Beth cried out.

"Mrs. Willows, we need to go back up to the boat deck," Charles urged. "Mr. Willows is probably up there. He may be having trouble finding you."

On returning on the boat deck, a shout came up from the deck below that the windows had been opened. Mr. Lightoller apologized as he sent the nervous troupe for lifeboat four down a second time. Finally they were able to step through the windows and seat themselves in the boat.

"Charles, I am so frightened. Please come with us." Emma's eyes filled with tears and she refused to loosen her grip on his arm.

"You'll be fine, Emma, dear. I must go get an extra coat for my mother. I will find your father and let him know you are safe. Emma, just know that I love you and I will be waiting for you when this is all over. You are my life and my own true love."

She kissed him hurriedly and felt the strength of his arms around her as he helped her gently into the lifeboat. She obediently took her place between her mother and Maisie. She gripped the locket he had given her. Charles waved and blew her a kiss. Then he was gone.

Another rocket exploded overhead and lit up the sky. Beth lost her nerve and started to sob. A familiar young woman, slight and fragile in appearance approached the boat clinging to her husband. Emma recognized her as Mrs. Astor, the eighteen-year-old wife of the recently divorced Mr. Jacob Astor.

"Please, commander, my wife is having a baby in just a few months and in her delicate condition I really do think it best if I accompany her and help with the other ladies," Mr. Astor begged.

"I'm sorry, Mr. Astor. Women and children only, under orders from the captain." Mr. Lightoller would not bend.

Right behind the famous millionaire, a lanky boy threw a leg over the rail and jumped in. Lightoller caught him by the collar. "Women and children only! Step out, please!"

"He's only thirteen! A child!" A woman was crying. "Please, Mr. Lightoller, this boy is a child. Please, let me have my son! Please, sir, he's just a boy!" The tears streamed down her cheeks as she grabbed for him, and the commander waved that he would allow him to go.

Emma watched as Mr. Astor kissed his leather gloves and tossed them down into the lap of his terrified wife. Fresh pain cut through Emma, as the young woman crushed the gloves to her face and wept.

Suddenly the ship lurched sharply to port and women shrieked in fear that they would be dropped into the sea as the lifeboat swung out an additional foot and a half from the ship.

"Everyone over to starboard! All passengers, quickly now! Everyone get over to the starboard side!" An officer was shouting nearby, and people panicked and ran.

"They're trying to stop the list of the ship with the weight of the passengers," Mr. Perkis, the commander of the lifeboat explained.

At this point, the lifeboat was about half filled with just over thirty passengers, almost all of them women. The boat was left to dangle precariously in the davits, too far from the ship to allow passengers to jump in. Throngs of people were now streaming onto the promenade deck, fighting for a place in a lifeboat.

"Get a deck chair!" a crewman was shouting. "We need something to use as a bridge to get people into the boat!"

The rockets exploded again and, with another jerk, the list to port slipped farther, and the lifeboat jumped like a toy being yanked on a string. It was a living, screaming nightmare with time racing and standing still all at once. Beth fainted, and Emma held onto her mother for dear life as Maisie kept a close eye on the creaking davits. Would they hold?

Below deck, Rupert heaved the heavy buffalo coat over his evening clothes and struggled with his life belt, finally deciding to carry it. He emerged on the boat deck in time to see the two cardsharps neatly make their way toward the boats. My God. They're getting off!

Suddenly he was struck by the awful realization that the *Titanic* was actually going to sink. To this point he had been more concerned about the expected wrath of Beth for his not being there to escort her to the boats than he was of any potential danger. It was in this moment of stunned paralysis that Charles Fortune came upon him.

"Mr. Willows, don't worry. I put your family off on boat number four on the port side. Maisie is with Emma and Mrs.

Willows."

"Thank you, Charles." Rupert quickly recovered his senses and his manners. "And your mother and sisters?"

"They are all together and are well away from *Titanic*, I should think. There's my father over there." He pointed to Mark Fortune who was helping the crew get the women settled in the boats. There was a masculine calmness about the young man as his eyes gripped Rupert. He showed nothing but a placid resignation and stalwart acceptance of his role as a gentleman. In a simple and poignant move, Charles reached out and firmly shook his hand.

"Good-luck, Mr. Willows," he said, as he left to join his father.

Rupert had no time to feel shame in the presence of a man whom he recognized as far superior to himself. He struggled into his life belt knowing that he had to get off the ship.

A crowd had gathered around a group of seamen working to free the last of the lifeboats, the collapsible ones, from their storage. Water had filled the lower decks. Off somewhere nearby, shots were fired. Rupert jumped. He wasn't sure if it the shots were directed in the air or to kill a would-be stowaway in a lifeboat. With his heart racing, he slipped along through the frenzied crowd and made his way starboard aft, following the path of the gamblers. Three large lifeboats were being readied for lowering amidst much shouting and confusion. With the final weak remnants of civility now destroyed by the undeniable truth that they were facing the specter of a violent and painful end to their lives, passengers were scrambling over each other to get on board the remaining lifeboats.

Rupert pulled his coat closed against the freezing air. More shots were fired. He shoved his hands into his gloves. He would get onto a boat one way or another, even if he had to leap over heads and risk being shot in the process. Death by shooting would be preferable to death by drowning or hypothermia. He glanced out at lifeboat number nine being lowered and George Bradley caught his eye with a sneering smile and a wave.

"So long, Willows! I see that last hand was a costly one for you!" he shouted.

Rupert pushed his way toward lifeboat thirteen where he recognized Dr. George Dodge hesitating near a group of women that was tumbling into the boat. Children were being grabbed up and tossed on board with little more regard than if they had been sacks of flour and with no worry for whether they had the waiting arms of mothers to receive them.

Into this erupting hysteria came Rupert, striding importantly up behind Dr. Dodge. Without a second of hesitation Rupert brought his arms forward and solidly pushed the doctor through the people in front of him and into the boat.

"Get in, Doctor!" he yelled as the two dropped over the rail of the ship and into the boat with more people clambering in behind them.

"Lower away! Lower away!" The commander yelled and signaled to the men operating the falls so as to be understood over the shrieking of the passengers and the groaning of the foundering ship.

The bow was sinking ever more quickly into the water and the slope of the deck made for difficult footing. People started falling and hurtling into walls and railings, crying out in agony, as legs and arms were broken and families were separated. With the last of the regular lifeboats now filled and being lowered, a thrashing, violent frenzy took hold of the passengers still on the deck. Their only remaining hope was the flimsy collapsible boats yet to be freed by the crewmen. Some men started throwing deck chairs into the water to be used as rafts, and then people quickly followed, dropping like dolls from the deck into the black sea, buoyed by the life belts and screaming against the shockingly cold water; others silenced instantly as their necks broke against the force of the life belts hitting the water.

Rupert braced himself as lifeboat thirteen began to lurch its way down to the sea. The lights on the ship flickered but kept burning. His heart was beating so hard he felt as if it would rip apart in his chest. He could feel the Grim Reaper looming over them, swatting at the dangling lifeboats and preparing to swallow the *Titanic*.

He forced his mind to seize upon the single thought that all they needed was to make it safely to the water. Just a few more moments, and they would be rowing away from the sinking vessel. He would survive.

The untested lifeboat, heavily loaded with the full capacity of sixty-five people, strained against the ropes in the shuddering davits for the endlessly long drop. Twenty feet down from the boat deck, a wild scream of desperation was heard from above. Rupert looked up to see a flailing man flying down toward them, aiming for the descending lifeboat. But the jumper had misjudged his target and to Rupert's utter horror, the scream was abruptly ended when the man's head struck the gunwale in a sickening crack, smashing open his skull. The lifeless body dropped down to the water as a bloody spray of brain tissue and bone chips splattered onto Rupert and the woman next to him. The woman stifled her scream but couldn't stop the vomit that spewed into Rupert's lap.

Rupert, reeling from the gruesome act and the horrid hot smell on his coat, instantly felt his own bile rising against death closing in on him. He clenched against the fear and did something he had never done before. He prayed. He prayed that the quivering metal arms of the davits would not snap before they reached the water. He prayed that he would survive. The lifeboat pitched and wrenched its way downward, in a staggering display of inadequacy. All the while, the woeful strains of the violins of the orchestra on deck played bravely in the macabre scene. The music wafted eerily into the terror, and Rupert's prayers suddenly crystallized into one clear request. If death did come, please let it be swift.

Rupert bargained with his Maker. He offered that he would be a better person if only he could live through this. He pledged to stop putting himself in front of others. The davits throbbed and the ropes creaked. The passengers shrieked again as the falls in the stern of the lifeboat slipped, tipping the boat toward the sea, before it was caught hard by the men on deck spending out the controlling ropes. His prayers for his survival ran silently and incoherently through his mind, and as the boat splashed softly into the smooth water, it suddenly occurred to Rupert that Beth and Emma were also in peril and hastily added his request for their protection.

On settling in the sea, there was barely a moment for the occupants to breathe their relief before a greater worry needed their attention. Their lifeboat was caught in the ropes, which would not release to allow the craft to float clear of the ship. There was just enough rope to have allowed the lifeboat to get stuck directly under the rapidly descending lifeboat fifteen. A harrowing cry of warning went up from the endangered boat thirteen as the passengers raised their hands against the bottom of the upper boat. They could feel the vibrating craft in their fingertips as it abruptly slowed and paused for five heart-pounding seconds. It was enough. With not a moment to spare, a crewman worked his knife through the ropes on thirteen, cutting the lifeboat free to slide out safely away from the one above.

Unbeknownst to Rupert as they struggled to find the oars and pull away from *Titanic,* boat number four was still not in the water. It had proved to be an exasperating challenge for the deck crew, and Mr. Lightoller was running out of time.

"Have they forgotten to lower us away?" The demanding woman with the dog screeched to commander Perkis. "What on earth is happening? We'll be dragged under with the ship!"

"We don't have enough men on board to row the boat!" Perkis answered back and a horrified Emma cried out in desperation, searching to see if she could spot Charles to be the needed man, but he was nowhere in sight.

Their attention went to the cries of a hysterical woman who was being pushed onto the deck chair bridge. Screaming at the top of her voice she landed hard in the boat and in so doing, she knocked the wind out of Beth. The woman cried as though she was dying, but it was in a language none of them could understand. None but Maisie. The woman was babbling frantically in Yiddish. She had been separated from her baby.

For a fleeting moment, Maisie's heart stopped as her devastating options flashed through her conscience. She could stay silent and save herself or speak up and save the child. There was no choice. There was only instinct.

She grabbed the woman by the shoulders and shook her hard to stop the screaming. Then she asked her urgent questions in Yiddish. Emma's hand flew to her mouth and Beth squeaked out a pitiful cry.

It was the fat lady with the barking Chihuahua that spoke first. "My God, they've allowed a Jewess on this boat! This maid is a Jew!" she squealed. "And this steerage class woman is a Jew also. They must be removed! I want to see the Captain. This is unacceptable. I won't have it!"

At this moment the boat began to lower, and the frantic Jewish woman shrieked again. Two crewmen from the deck were scrambling down the ropes into the boat. The woman continued to cry incoherently as if she had lost her mind, and Maisie gripped her and shouted her questions again. Dazed, the woman finally gave the needed information. Beth looked on in speechless amazement at the scene and Maisie yelled as loudly as she could up to the boat deck.

"Stop lowering! Where is the baby in the red bonnet? Someone took her baby from her when she climbed the rope ladder up from the dining room. She is missing her baby!"

Miraculously, the baby with the red bonnet appeared as a man shoved his way through the crowd and dropped the tiny child fifteen feet into the boat. Maisie dived into the lap of the fat woman to safely catch the wailing toddler, at the same time knocking the woman's feathered hat over the side of the boat. With the baby now safe, the Jewish mother turned to Maisie, her face soaked with tears and twisted in emotion and offered her thanks and a blessing in Hebrew.

The fat woman, bruised in the blow of the landing child began to cry out. "They are all Jews! They must be removed! I won't stand for it!"

This was Beth's breaking point. She calmly handed her brandy flask to Emma, then turned to the woman and slapped her fleshy jaw with all of her might. "Shut up, you stupid old bat, or I'll take that little mutt away from you and push you overboard!"

The shocked woman yelped in pain and grabbed her face. "I think you broke my face!" Then seeing Beth's raised fist threatening to plow her again, she shrank back and whimpered.

The boat descended rapidly. Beth took a hearty swig from the returned flask before she turned to Maisie. "My dear God, Maisie! When did you learn to speak Jewish?"

Suddenly the boat splashed heavily into the water, soaking some of the passengers, and sending up a shout from Mr. Perkis, the commander of the lifeboat, to take up the oars. The task of releasing the oars and getting them into the water proved clumsy and awkward as the women struggled over their bulky life belts in the dark night. Maisie was finally able to get an oar in the water. Emma's eyes were as wide as saucers. She started to cry. Stiffened with fright and desperate for Charles' safety, she felt her entire world was crumbling.

Though the boat was only two-thirds filled, it seemed dreadfully crowded as the women shifted for space. Some, clad in nightclothes and hastily grabbed blankets, expressed their misery at the several inches of water that had settled in around their feet.

There were no more lifeboats for the screaming passengers left on the *Titanic*. A deck chair flew toward the boat from overhead and was deflected by one of the men. The chairs were quickly followed by more bodies splashing into the water around them, one after another. Most were beating their arms against the water, but many were frighteningly still.

Maisie's heart pounded as she spotted two men making their way toward their lifeboat, swimming hard. She shook Emma out of her daze and yelled sternly at her.

"Hang on tightly to this oar!

From the other end of the boat, commander Perkis also saw the men in the water. "We're taking these men aboard!" He yelled over the cries from the water. "Move into the center and sit on the floor of the boat to make room."

Maisie and another woman near the gunwale reached over and helped the men drag themselves into the boat. Perkis ordered them to row as hard as they could to pull away from the ship so as to avoid being sucked under when she sank.

Suddenly the moment arrived. The bow dipped beneath the sea, and the stern of the great ship wrenched upward into the air, revealing her propellers. Up it climbed toward the sky, then for a gruesome single moment it paused, hovering motionlessly. Then there was a roaring, shrieking sound of metal on metal. The people in the lifeboats covered their ears, and some covered their eyes as *Titanic* split in two, then slipped away to the bottom of the ocean.

Shivering and wet, but alive in the bone-numbing cold, the shocked survivors frantically worked the oars. Three more men were hauled into lifeboat number four from the freezing ocean. The trial proved too great for two of them, and they died shortly after, their anguished death-filled faces urging Maisie to push Emma and Beth to keep rowing, to keep moving to stay warm.

Eventually the screams from the water quieted, and within the hour there was only silence and the quiet slapping of the water against the boats as the wind came up late in the night. A handful of boats with a few hundred survivors were all that remained of the unsinkable *Titanic*.

More than twice as many had perished. The hours dragged on. The survivors took turns with the oars. Some sang. Some prayed. Some gave up fighting the cold and died. Finally, the terrible night came to an end as a blood red dawn broke over the ocean to reveal the piteous sight of the boats floating about the ice field with massive icebergs rising out of the water near them. The sight provoked fresh pain and more tears in the boats heavy with the aching hearts of widows and orphans. It was in the early dawn that a cry of hope and relief sang out at the sight of the long awaited rescue ship on the horizon. The *Carpathia* had come for them.

"Row harder!" the fat woman yelled, and Beth strained against the oar with tears streaming down her cheeks. Other than the few in the lifeboats, it seemed the men were all lost. She was heartbroken for her daughter, but Emma's life with Charles had just begun. She was young and beautiful, and she would have another chance with another man. Beth found herself overwhelmed with her own feelings of grief and sadness. Whatever would she do without Rupert? They had been together for close to forty years. Both strong and healthy still, she had never imagined life without him. They had raised four children and together had enjoyed building their place in society and their home at Ravenscraig. What joy could there be in remaining alive when your life was gone? She was crushed under the fear of what would become of her. Thank goodness she had grown sons to help her. Compared to some of these women, she was very lucky. She knew she was blessed.

Taking the sorry and sodden group of survivors off the lifeboat and onto *Carpathia* was an arduous affair that required the use of slings for those too weak to climb up on the rope ladder. Maisie went before Emma, and together they half dragged Beth onto the deck with the help of the crewmen. Standing with stiffened muscles benumbed by cold, they welcomed the blankets given them as they searched the deck in hope of finding the faces they were desperate to see. Could they hope? Emma turned and saw him first as he emerged from the crowd, moving briskly toward them.

"Father!" she cried as he wrapped his arms around her and Beth together.

"It's a miracle, Rupert! Oh, thank God you are alive!" Beth sobbed with relief.

"What about Charles, Father? Is he here, too?" Emma clutched his sleeve and cried.

"Not yet, dear one," he said softly, pulling her firmly into his embrace. "The boats are not all in yet. We must wait to see. Mary Fortune and the three girls are safe. The doctor is seeing them now."

One by one, the lifeboats came to the side of the rescue ship. Seven hundred five people were taken on board. Emma searched the faces and looked out desperately at the ocean to see if yet another boat would come. It was a terrible blow when the captain announced they were set to leave for New York.

A horrible hurting hush descended upon the deck with the awful knowledge there were no more survivors, no more lifeboats floating about in the ice field. Emma wilted into Rupert's arms and cried hard.

"I never had time to say good-bye to Charles," she choked through her tears. "He said: 'Just know that I love you and I will be waiting for you when this is all over,' and then he was gone."

Beth cried with her and stroked her hair to comfort her. Rupert suddenly remembered something and pulled away from Emma, as he reached for a hidden pocket.

"I have something for you." He brought out the tiny jewel box and opened it. Emma gasped when she saw it held the little diamond earrings that Charles had given her. She took the box and her knees began to buckle as the tears flowed down her face. Rupert reached his arms around her and helped her to sit down. Then he went again into his pocket and showed Beth the diamond pieces that he had stuffed into his money-vest. Beth was astonished. It was all clear to her now.

"Rupert, darling. That's why we didn't see you on the deck! You went to retrieve our jewelry. Why did you take such a chance, Rupert?"

"I didn't know what to think. I knew Charles was with you," he answered simply, feeling too much of a cad to be honest.

The hush on deck slowly gave way to weeping and then disbelief. Only one third of the people on board *Titanic* had found their way to safety. Yet, the human spirit proved hard to suppress in this time of utter anguish and despair. Immediately, faint hope flickered anew and caught fire as speculation swept through the crowd. Perhaps other vessels in the area had picked up their men, and they would be reunited in New York.

Maisie searched for assurance that this might be so, but could find no encouragement in the grim faces of *Carpathia's* crewmembers.

Emma, dazed and exhausted, clutched the jewel box in her hand, and seemed unable to respond to questions.

It would be fifteen days before Emma would speak another word. Pitiful and small in that moment on the deck of *Carpathia*, she sought solace in the comfort of her mother's arms, rocking gently in her grief, healing her heart, one beat at a time.

The ship turned and headed for New York, threading its way back through the ice field. The wireless operators on the *Carpathia* sent a steady stream of messages to the loved ones ashore. Among the messages was a telegram Rupert sent to his sons in Winnipeg. "Family fine Stop Chas and Mr. F. lost RJW."

54
New York Assignment
April 14, 1912

I t was almost midnight, and Isaac was not pleased with having to work an overnight shift. He had law school tests to write the next day, and when the overnight Linotype man called the paper to say that he was suffering from a bad cold, Isaac was asked to stay and fill in.

Though his primary job at the paper was as a writer, he truly enjoyed the simplicity and the feel of the Linotype machine, so he continued to take shifts in the composing room when the paper was short-handed. Isaac had become the fastest Linotype operator on the floor and took great pride in learning shortcuts to make the machine run even faster.

He loved the smell of the molten lead and the feel of the clinking, whirring equipment in his hands. His fingers tapped fluidly over the keyboard and the Linotype machine sang out with musical efficiency as the front page for the morning edition neared completion. Soon he would be able to go home.

With just a few more weeks of study before he would write the bar exams, Isaac was torn. He was driven to achieve and was recognized as a top student, much admired by both his peers and professors for his persuasive and insightful arguments. He had no doubt he would pass the bar. Yet, he remained undecided as to whether he would have a career as a newspaperman or a lawyer.

He loved everything about the newspaper and had steadily increased the number of articles he was writing for magazines. Working thirty to forty hours a week and carrying a full load at school made for an arduous schedule, but Isaac enjoyed the fact that he had paid for his own education. His savings were growing, and he had a few dollars to spend, just for fun. The problem was that with his workload, there was not much time for fun.

It wasn't that he minded the work, but he did mind the toll it took on his social life. Ellen dated him for six months before she gave up, and Bessie, who was prettier and even more fun than Ellen, seemed to be a good sport, at first, about Isaac's last minute cancelations, to go out on a story or to study. But it didn't take long before she made it clear that she wasn't happy about having to miss Saturday night dances because her beau had to work. It hurt when she broke off their romance. It hurt more when Ziporah told him Bessie was getting married to one of the Guberman brothers. Well, he'd come this far with his delayed education, and he was almost at the finish line. Then, whether as a lawyer or a newspaperman, he would make time for girls.

The clatter of the Linotype machine took on a subtle change, and Isaac stopped to investigate. While he set to work on the mechanical problem, his mind went to thoughts of his ideal girl. Surely there was a nice young lady somewhere who would like him well enough to want to marry him.

He reached over to adjust one of the machine's small conveyor belts as his imagination soared. She would be kind and not too quick to complain. She would certainly be pretty. She would be loving and patient with children. He would take very good care of her and she would adore him. She would be his treasure. His *tchotchkelah*.

With the machine now humming to perfection, Isaac stretched to loosen his muscles and then sat down and reached for the next piece of copy. One day. All good things happen in time. Like his Zaida said, the most important thing you had to have in life was patience.

In the meantime, there was always a good story just around the corner. It helped that his good friend, Jim McGraw, had recently been promoted to night news editor. Jim always plucked the juicy stories out of the pile for Isaac to go after.

For his part, McGraw could never understand why a talented reporter like Isaac Zigman was killing himself in law school. And, even worse, why he would want to bother hunching over a noisy, miserable Linotype machine for hours at a time when he could be out on a story. In answer to his questions about all this, what he got back from Isaac was a sack full of poetry on the many virtues of the composing machine. Jim just figured that Isaac was a special kind of eccentric, but it was fine by him if it made him happy. The kid sure could work. There was nothing about the newspaper business that Isaac didn't have a talent for, Jim believed.

He opened the story idea file to see what he could assign to Isaac for the next night and got into the details of a murder in the Red Light district. This would be right up Isaac's alley.

Suddenly, all hell broke loose as Eddy, the copy boy, flew into his office waving a tape from the news ticker. "Mr. McGraw! The *Titanic* has struck an iceberg! It's being reported out of Montreal." Eddy almost landed on Jim's desk as he handed him the message.

"What?" Jim read the ticker tape and seconds later was shouting orders in the newsroom.

Isaac had just one more section to complete on the page when Jim burst into the room. "Ziggy! Stop what you are doing! We've got a new front page. The *Titanic* has struck an iceberg, and they've put out a call for help."

Isaac's blood ran cold and his heart stopped beating. Maisie!

"No!" Isaac shouted as though stricken with pain.

"Ziggy, are you all right?"

"My cousin is on that ship."

"Is she from Winnipeg? What's her name?"

Isaac caught himself. Everyone knew that he was Jewish, and it didn't matter at the paper, but revealing Maisie's truth could ruin her.

"Isaac, what's her name?"

He chose to answer with a half-truth. "Her name is Malka Zigman. She's from London. She's on her way to Winnipeg."

"I'm so sorry, Isaac. I'll check for her name when they start sending lists out. But just be prepared, the White Star Line isn't going to be in a big hurry to get the names out for anyone but the first class passengers."

"Are you sure it was struck?"

"I'm not sure of anything. We're getting bits and pieces in over the wire, and the boys upstairs are hammering the story together now. The wire says sometime just before midnight the

Titanic struck an iceberg a few hundred miles off Newfoundland. Even in mid April, the north Atlantic is full of ice, so it could be true. The message also said there were a number of ships in the area and that they were rushing to its aid. The closest port will be Halifax."

"Hey, Boss!" Eddy dashed into the composing room in search of Jim. "There's a new message, Mr. McGraw," he said thrusting wire copy to the editor.

"Good God! It says the *Titanic* is sinking by the head and they are putting the women off in lifeboats." He turned to the copy boy. "The first thing we have to do is get a list of names of Winnipeg folks on that ship. There might be a mention in one of the society news columns somewhere in a recent issue. Go!" he yelled at the copy boy.

"Alderman Willows is on *Titanic* with his wife and daughter and a maid." Isaac said, worry etched on his face.

"You sure?"

"Yes, I'm sure. The maid's name is Maisie Rosedale. Also Mark Fortune is on it with his family. There are five or six of them, I think."

"Good God. I know Robert Fortune, the oldest son. He curls at the Granite Club. I'll call him on the telephone. Do you know the alderman's son Alfred? And there's another son who moved to Ontario. The doctor. I can't remember his name."

"James," said Isaac. "Dr. James Willows. He lives on the Lake of the Woods."

"Do you know them?"

"No, I don't know them, but I have a home telephone number for Rupert Willows."

"Well, you hot dog. You're always full of surprises."

"Want me to call?"

Jim stopped for a moment. There at least two prominent Winnipeg families on the *Titanic*. Always after the story, he made an instant decision on how the *Star* would beat the *Manitoba Free Press*.

"No. Just give me the number, and I'll do it. Isaac, I want you to go to Halifax for the *Star*.

"Halifax?" Isaac's heart raced.

"It's the closest port. We need a good reporter out there to talk to the survivors, if there are any. The train east is pulling out in one hour. Get your stuff and meet me at the station. I'll look after your ticket and bring you some cash."

"What about the front page?"

"Screw it. We'll bring in Jack from shipping to take over here. Get a move on."

"Yes, sir!"

The train was not crowded, and Isaac was thankful. He paced up and down the aisle restlessly until the first stop that would be long enough for him to telephone the paper for fresh news on the disaster. The most recent update he had was encouraging, and he was hoping to hear confirmation that it was true. The owner of the *Titanic*, the White Star Line, had issued a statement saying that all of the passengers had been taken off by several ships that had arrived at the scene. It also said that the crippled ship would be towed to Halifax for repair. When the train finally chugged to a stop hours later, Isaac leaped out of the car and found a phone. Then he spent an agonizing amount of time waiting for a long distance connection.

"All aboard! All aboard!" The conductor shouted as Isaac finally got his telephone call through.

"Hello, hello, Jim!" He shouted into the phone "It's Isaac. Can you hear me?"

"Yes!" Jim's voice came faintly through the wire.

"They're calling us. The train is about to leave. Tell me quickly." He heard garble in return. "Say again! I can't hear!"

"I said it sank, Isaac! The *Titanic* is lost!"

"Any survivors?" Isaac shouted past the knot in his throat.

"Yes, a few hundred people were picked up by the *Carpathia*. They confirmed they are going to Halifax."

"Last call! All aboard!" The conductor bellowed and Isaac saw him getting ready to close the door.

"I've got to go. I'll call you from Toronto!"

He counted the hours down until the arrival in Toronto. He'd be able to pick up a newspaper, and more importantly, he would be able to call Jim again at the *Star* to see if they had anything new on the disaster.

As the train headed out of the station, Isaac worried about how the news would hit his family, especially his mother. She adored Maisie as if she were one of her own.

When Isaac got off the train in Toronto, the station was in a frenzy as newsboys hawked their papers and shouted out the headlines.

"Titanic sinks! Eighteen hundred souls are feared lost!"

He snatched up a paper and tossed a coin into the newsboy's hand as he made his way to the telephones. It was beyond belief. People were weeping at the shock. Others screamed with relief at seeing a name on the survivor list. James had read through the copy twice, but the list that was printed had barely a hundred names; almost all were identified as first class passengers. He headed for the telephones with his head in the paper. So engrossed was he in his reading, that he bumped into a man and almost knocked him off of his feet.

"Oh, I beg your pardon! I wasn't paying attention," he said to the bespectacled man.

"Not at all. I think we're all in a daze." The man looked as if he had not slept in a week.

"I wish they were faster in putting out names of survivors," Isaac said.

"So do I. Your family was on the *Titanic?*"

Isaac nodded. "My cousin. And you?"

"My parents, my sister and their maid."

"I'm so terribly sorry."

"I've heard nothing of them." The man was close to choking with emotion. "At this rate I probably won't know anything until I get to Halifax. When I got on the train in Kenora, I had heard they were all being transported to safety."

Isaac reached out to shake his hand. "I'm from Winnipeg. My name is Isaac Zigman. I'm a reporter with the *Winnipeg Star* and I'll let you know what I learn when I get through to the paper."

"I'm James Willows. Please go ahead of me, Mr. Zigman."

"You're the alderman's son." Isaac's heart started to pound, and he fought down the urge tell this distraught man about his cousin.

"Yes. If you could please ask about my parents and Emma Willows, my sister, and their maid, Maisie Rosedale, I would be grateful."

Isaac was all business. He soon learned that *Carpathia* had been redirected to New York. The two men made a wild dash and succeeded in making the connection they needed, catching their breath as they settled into their seats. There was an outside chance that they would be in New York in time to meet the ship.

The information they were able to get was terribly inadequate. Isaac and James were hardened to the idea that they needed to expect the worst while hoping for the best. It appeared they would learn nothing of the safety of their loved ones until the *Carpathia* docked.

When the two got off the train in New York, they learned that it would be several hours before the *Carpathia* would arrive in port. They also learned from a telephone call to Jim McGraw that Alfred Willows had reserved rooms for them at the Belmont Hotel. They checked into the hotel, and James was finally able to get a telephone connection through to his brother at home in Winnipeg.

"A wire? From Father!" James shouted and lit up with hope as he motioned to Isaac to come closer. "I didn't hear that, read it again!" Isaac watched as darkness came over his face. "Could you write this down, Isaac? I have someone else here with family from Winnipeg, Alfred. "Family fine Stop Chas. and Mr. F. lost. RJW." Dear God, Alfred! Charles and Mr. Fortune missing! There is no mention of Maisie? Alfred, are you there, Alfred? Hello, hello, Alfred?" James slowly put the telephone down, and slid into a chair, dropping his head into his hands. "I lost the connection."

Isaac's eyes flew open. No mention of Maisie? Family fine. Did that include his cousin? He was dying to ask, but could hardly show his interest without revealing her identity. The waiting for news was nothing short of torture.

"James, I'm going to the dock. I know the arrival is hours off yet, but I have a story to do, and there might be something to

488

learn."

"Would you mind, Isaac? That is, could I come with you?" James was on his feet with his hat in his hand. "I'll go mad waiting."

"It's pouring rain."

"So? I don't see you worrying about it."

"Sure, James," Isaac admired his companion's pluck. "I'd like you to come. Here, give me your hat," Isaac said.

James looked puzzled, then immediately understood as Isaac pulled out a spare card marked "Press" and stuck it in James's hat band. "You are now unofficially working for the *Winnipeg Star*. This way, we won't get separated."

On the way, the two made a stop at the offices of the White Star Line. Lists had been posted in the windows and they joined the mob in front of the office and carefully scanned the names. Isaac was quick to pretend to be examining the bottom of the list to see Zigman. But not only was there no Zigman on the list, neither was there mention of Willows, Fortune or Rosedale. Of course knowing that Mr. Willows had sent the message from the *Carpathia* gave them comfort that they had been rescued, but had not yet been added to the list.

A shout went up from the crowd as a new list was posted in the window. James fought his way through the group and emerged with a look of relief. "Oh, thank God! My parents and my sister are on the list. Also, Alice Fortune, but there is no Zigman mentioned, as yet. I'm sorry."

"Rosedale?" Isaac asked and James cast his eyes down and shook his head.

"No. No mention."

"Well, then, let's get over to the pier. It's number fifty-four."

Pandemonium was the only way to describe what they found at the pier. Thousands of people had assembled, crowding their way to edge of the dock. Police set up lines to hold the onlookers back. The City of New York was trying to help the survivors' families to get to the waiting area where they would be reunited with their loved ones, but was instead beleaguered with members of the press who appeared thick as bees swarming the waterfront. The press was everywhere. Several had jumped onto a fishing trawler and headed out to meet the tugboats bringing in the *Carpathia*.

Luck was on their side, and James and Isaac ended up standing in an ideal location. The rescue ship came in, and the first class passengers were whisked off. Within minutes, James spotted his father talking to a reporter and in the next instant he was reunited with his family.

"Are you all right?" James rushed to embrace his parents and then to wrap his arms around the pathetic figure that was his sister. So small and sad was Emma that she seemed to barely recognize him, and the thought immediately occurred to James that she was literally dying of a broken heart. He hugged and consoled her in her silence and eased back as his mother enveloped Emma to shield her from the newspapermen. James searched the faces in the crowd.

"Mother, where is Maisie? Is she safe?" James asked.

"She's here with us. Yes, yes, she's fine."

On the other side of the gangway, Isaac too, was anxiously searching for the assurance that Maisie was safe. Finally, he spotted her and waved. She looked on in amazement before it registered that it truly was her cousin coming to meet her, and she cried for joy.

"Isaac, Isaac!" She had expected there would be no one for her, and here was her cousin Isaac, all the way from Winnipeg! She started making her way through the throng toward him, when James spotted her. He was about to wave his hand and call out to her, but to his astonishment, Isaac was shouting her name and pulling her close into his arms, both of them laughing and crying with relief. James felt as if he had been struck by a thunderbolt. Maisie had a beau! How could this be possible? Maisie and Isaac? Look at them crying and hugging. He couldn't bear it but it was impossible to tear his eyes away from them.

"Isaac, I've never been so happy to see anyone in my life." Maisie hugged her cousin again with all of her might.

"Maisie, James Willows is here, too and he's frantic to find you."

"James?"

Isaac craned to see over the crowd and found James looking back at him. He waved madly at the doctor and shouted out for him to come.

James felt his heart was breaking but he had to see her, to know with certainty that she was alive. He pushed his way through the crowd, and there she was with tears streaming down her face, clutching the knot of her kerchief under her chin.

"Maisie is my cousin," Isaac said, "also known as Malka Zigman. I couldn't tell you before. Maisie will explain it all to you, in time."

"Cousin? Maisie is your cousin?" James looked stunned. His emotions scrambled, he searched for the truth in her face.

"Dr. Willows!" She stood and stared at him, then her shame overcame her. "Yes. I'm a fraud. Your father never would have hired a Jewish maid," she said softly.

"Maisie, dear Maisie. The only thing that matters is that you are here. It's a miracle."

55

Letter to Mary

Belmont Hotel
New York City
April 19, 1912

Dear Mary,

So heavy is my heart that when I open my mouth to speak, I cannot form a word. It is so hard to think. I must tell you that truly, from one minute to the next, I don't know whether to feel the relief of being spared or the utter anguish of being crushed beneath the pain of loss.

Every day, I keep hoping to hear that Charles and his father were found, but it is not to be. The horrible truth is that only those of us who made it to the lifeboats will be counted as survivors. The others have all perished. There were so many people and so few boats. I am horror struck at the memory of it.

I am ashamed to tell you I put up a terrible fuss because I did not want to get into the lifeboat. Charles was very insistent. We had but a quick glance and hug before I was on board. So much is a blur, now.

The sea was calm and we were ordered to row hard to get away from the ship. I searched the darkness to find Charles, calling out to him. Just minutes later the Titanic gave itself to the sea. Mary, I could not take my eyes from the dreadful spectacle.

The lights were extinguished one deck at a time as the back of the ship rose up from the water, showing the great propellers as it climbed up and up toward the sky. In absolute terror we watched and heard as people were falling, hitting the railings and walls and then there was the roaring sound of the boilers and metal twisting apart. It was utterly shocking when the ship broke apart and slipped away, leaving the sea awash with the litter of death; deckchairs and carnage intermingled with those buoyed by the life belts, the dead bumping up against the living. It seemed impossible that the ship was gone.

What remained formed something of a horrible funeral wreath, to mark the very place where the Titanic plunged into the sea. Then we could hear only the death cries of those in the freezing water. There were hundreds of them, fighting to stay alive, screaming out in the night, beseeching those in the boats to come back for them. I am haunted by the sounds. I imagined Charles swimming hard to get to a boat, and ours, just half-filled, had so much room to take on survivors. I screamed out his name until I had no voice left at all. I pray to God that he didn't suffer.

I fear you won't be able to read through the smudges in this letter as my falling tears ruin the page. I just cannot stop weeping. I am so bewildered. Poor Mrs. Fortune. She is prostrate with grief at the loss of both her husband and her youngest child. She is anxious to return with her daughters to the family in Winnipeg and believes that once home they will have the will to move forward. I am so ashamed of my weakness. Moving forward is the last I can think of at this time. My darling Charles is never to hold me again. I am wracked with the pain of his loss.

Tomorrow we will board the train for our journey home. It brings me great comfort to know that you are there, dearest Mary.

Your loving friend,

Emma

56
Homeward Bound
April 22, 1912

The journalists had descended on New York and were relentless in their pursuit of survivors, dogging every move of the heartsick widows and orphaned children. The newspapers had a particularly strong appetite for the wealthy passengers, but were also interested in the stories about destitute immigrant families who had traveled in steerage on the ship. Three quarters of the women on board survived, but only one in five men made it to the lifeboats. Their husbands lost, many of the women were left stranded in a new country with no money. Molly Brown, one of the first class survivors, immediately stepped in to champion their cause and started fundraising.

Rupert, ever quick to recognize opportunity, had overheard Mrs. Brown arranging to meet with a group of reporters in his hotel. Within the hour, the newsmen gathered and the room assigned to them instantly filled with onlookers.

Rupert slipped into the crowd and found a place to stand near the front. Molly Brown proved to be a passionate speaker and great motivator. She told the story of the harrowing night and the dreadful hours in the lifeboats while they awaited rescue. She talked at length about the women survivors, and the pitiable state of their lives, following the tragic loss of more than thirteen hundred men. As the reporters scribbled and the camera lights popped and flashed, she made her plea for money to help the women get home to Europe. Rupert smiled to himself as he reached into his money vest and pulled out a hundred dollars. Mrs. Brown tied a baby's bonnet to a basket and held it out to the crowd. Rupert stepped forward, but the hotel manager beat him to the front of the room.

"I have two hundred dollars for you," the manager said with great dignity, and Mrs. Brown shook her head, feeling pride in humanity. The camera lights flashed again and the reporters rushed to learn how to spell the manager's name.

Others came forward, with tens and twenties, and the occasional fifty dollar bill to drop into the basket. Rupert was angry with himself for not having moved faster. He watched the scene and considered how best to win the attention he was after. He hated to part with the money, but it was, after all, gambling winnings. He reached back into his money vest and eased his way through the throng.

When she finally turned to him, he bowed and said in a clear and cultured voice, "Mrs. Brown, as a fellow survivor and one who has been greatly blessed to have been rescued with my both my wife and daughter, I humbly wish you Godspeed in your quest to help these unfortunate people. Please accept my gift of a thousand dollars."

A rumble of approval rolled through the room as the reporters crowded in to learn more about the gentleman survivor with the very generous donation.

While Rupert gave interviews, James was busy making the arrangements to slip the Willows family out of New York.

The train ride from New York to Winnipeg seemed endless. They all wanted to be home to put the disaster behind them. Maisie, ever professional, tended to the Willows family in the private rail car. The mood was deeply subdued as each receded into personal thoughts of their ordeal. Even Rupert found little to say. Emma, pale and weak with grief, remained incapable of conversation. Beth hardly allowed her daughter out of her sight and sat quietly with her, offering her biscuits and tea. There was little that Emma would accept beyond the comfort of her mother's company.

Maisie, sitting alone in the small kitchen of the private rail car, had plenty of time to contemplate the imminent changes in her life. She prepared herself to be fired. Nothing had been said as yet, but she considered the termination of her employment to be inevitable. Her secret exposed, she expected that Mr. Willows had sent word ahead to Mr. Chadwick to prepare to rid Ravenscraig of the Jewess. She was convinced she would return to find her belongings packed and ready at the door along with her final pay packet. Well, so be it. She had spent almost twelve years with the Willows family, and it was high time she turned her attention to her future.

She wished that Isaac would have been able to be on the same train with her for the ride home, but the newspaper had asked him to stay in New York. The American government had ordered an inquiry into the *Titanic* sinking, and Isaac was assigned to cover it.

Maisie put her mind on her future. The time had come for her to apply for university. She had saved enough money to pay for two years of school, and she was sure that if she ran short of funding, she could borrow money from her Uncle Zev. In fact, she knew he would insist on paying for her education if she would allow him.

If she wasn't accepted, she would try for nursing college and work her way up through whatever opportunities she could find for herself. She seized upon the plan and started imagining her life after Ravenscraig. She was twenty-six years old. It was also time she started paying more attention to the young men Ziporah had been inviting over to the Zigman home to meet her. Bless her heart. Ziporah's solid marriage to Max had fueled intensity in her quest to find a proper husband for Maisie.

Driven by her fierce independence, Maisie's immediate concern was steady employment. She would have a few months to work before the fall semester started, so she started listing the places that she thought might hire her. She would be unlikely to find work as a servant in the upper class homes once the gossips picked up the news of her firing. She considered working as a telephone operator, or in a factory. The factory would probably pay better, she thought, and started writing down names of businesses.

The train was just about to pull into Union Station in Toronto, where there would be a two-hour stop. Maisie decided she would stretch her legs and treat herself to coffee and cake. She was alive and well, and it was important to count her blessings. Having come through the terror of that awful night, she knew that anything was possible. Anything could be achieved as long as there was breath in her body and belief in her soul.

"Maisie! Wait!"

She heard her name being called out over the noise of the station and saw James emerge from the crowd. He was striding briskly toward her.

"May I speak with you, Maisie? It's a matter of some importance, and I would like a private word with you."

Dread filled her. She hadn't counted on having to hear the news of her termination before their return to Winnipeg.

James guided her over to a café next to the station and ordered lunch. She answered his polite questions about the details of their travels, both of them carefully avoiding any discussion about *Titanic*.

The waiter arrived with dessert as James checked his watch. He had much to discuss. With pie and coffee before them, he looked up and smiled at Maisie. She smiled warily back at him. He saw her as a woman of remarkable resilience. The color had returned to her cheeks, and she seemed to have put some distance between herself and the horrible night of the shipwreck.

"I enjoyed getting to know your cousin, Isaac," James said. "He is terrifically smart in the way he goes after information and was very helpful in getting us to the right place when the *Carpathia* came in."

"I couldn't believe he was there," she said in agreement. "I'm sorry he couldn't be traveling home with us, but I'm sure he counts himself very fortunate to be writing about the inquiry. I'm happy none of us was delayed by being called to testify."

James took a deep breath. "Maisie, I told you that I have something important I wish to tell you." The serious look on his face took the steam out of her.

"Oh," she said, bracing herself for the announcement.

"I can't imagine the strength you must possess in order to be as level headed and as capable as you are. There is a certain quality of indestructibility to your character, Maisie."

She shook her head with a quiet laugh. "Well, you don't know me very well." She worked the napkin in her fingers.

"But, you know that's not true, Maisie. I do know you very well. I watched you throughout my mother's illness, and I saw the strength and instinct you have. I was overcome with fear, but you managed to ease me out of it. You always find a way to move forward. From your example I learned that when all of the options before you are horrible, choose the one that is least horrible and get on with it. That's what you did with my mother's care and I will never forget that, Maisie. You taught me to be a better doctor."

Maisie was stunned. She opened her mouth to respond but he put a hand up to stop her.

"Maisie, let me say this, please. I also know that through these recent days, my life has been shaken to the very core. I don't wish to sound trite or affected, in the aftermath of the terror that you have been through, but this colossal disaster has changed all of us forever. And I have to say I have come to the humbling realization that I need to live better, to do things that have meaning. Life is not to be squandered, and I see now that I have been stuck in a kind of life-sapping muck of my own choosing for just too long.

"I've decided to move my practice to Winnipeg. This is what I wanted to speak to you about."

Maisie was completely floored. "Your practice? I thought you asked me to lunch to sack me."

"To sack you? What on Earth are you saying?"

"It's obvious that will happen. Now that everyone knows that I am Jewish, I am most certainly going to be fired from Ravenscraig. I thought you were sent to deliver the message."

James tightened with irritation. "Maisie, dear God. Listen to me. I am not here to 'sack' you. Furthermore, no one 'sends' me to do anything. I have no idea what my father intends to do at Ravenscraig, and frankly, I don't care."

Maisie was instantly flustered. "Oh, dear. Please forgive me. I do have a way of putting my foot in my mouth."

"Maisie, I want to set up my medical practice on Selkirk Avenue, right in the heart of the foreign quarter."

Maisie stopped and caught her breath. "Why, Dr. Willows, this is wonderful news! There is such great need."

Heartened by her reaction, he continued on. "Here's the thing of it. I need another doctor to work with me who understands the area. The problems, the particular kind of medical care that is of greatest need. I need someone who is trusted by the people who live there."

"Well, I think that might be a bit difficult to find. Are you looking for me to suggest candidates? I really don't ..."

"No, no. I know the candidate," James answered. "It's a question of convincing her to do it."

"Her? You are going to ask Dr. Mary Crawford to join your practice?" Maisie was truly impressed that he would hire a woman.

"No," he said slowly.

"Dr. Amelia Yeomans?"

"No, this doctor's name would be Maisie."

"Me?" Maisie laughed out loud, completely caught off guard. "Well, I don't know what to say. But perhaps we could start with the fact that I am not licensed, and that I would need to go to university to become qualified."

"Yes, but you will be a doctor as soon as you have finished medical school. Maisie, please, listen to me. You were born to be a doctor. I would be deeply honored if you would allow me to pay for your education. I would also like to introduce you to the dean of the medical school. I do believe that I can make a strong case for your acceptance, based on your knowledge and experience."

Maisie's mind flew to the possibilities of her future. "Well, my heavens, this is nothing I ever would have dreamed to hear today, Dr. Willows. Do you really think there is a chance I would be accepted?"

"I do. I think it safe to say that fate has brought you an unusual opening. The whole world is talking about the *Titanic*. It's crass, but at the very least, the medical school would probably like to brag about having a *Titanic* survivor among its students. I realize that sounds absolutely dreadful, but I know these people."

"And the matter of my Jewish heritage, Dr. Willows?"

"It depends who is serving on the acceptance committee," he answered. "I have some sway with a few of the members. The school has allowed a few Jewish men into the faculty of medicine. I can tell you honestly that every single one of them is an outstanding student."

"Dr. Willows …"

"Please, Maisie. It would please me greatly if you called me James."

Her cheeks flamed and her heart skipped a beat. "Very well, James," she answered shyly. "I really must ask, and I don't wish to offend but, what about you? Does it not cause you concern that I am Jewish?"

He stopped and stared at her. A flurry of emotions ran through him as he considered for a moment what his father would have to say. Finally he spoke.

"Maisie, this is a complicated business. I don't share my father's prejudice. But I do admit that I have a lot to learn and, indeed, a great deal to think about. I would hope you would help me learn about the customs of your people. But, no, I can tell you, honestly, that it does not concern me that you are Jewish. As a medical practitioner in the North End, it would be a decided advantage. You speak the language. You understand the culture. You know the medical needs of this population. This is what I know, what I see. I can think of no person I would rather work alongside than you."

Maisie could find no words to express what she was feeling. She was reeling from his openness and quite stunned by his words. She looked into his eyes and nodded.

"This is so wonderful of you. I really am speechless."

James smiled and continued. "Maisie, this next request is most important to me. I would like to meet your family. I would like to make a proper introduction to the people you hold dear, so that I may proceed as a gentleman and fully state my intentions."

"Oh, I'm sure they would be pleased to meet you, and they will be very happy to have me working with you. This, I can assure you."

He stopped and regarded the amazing woman before him. He ached to reach out to touch her, but felt it best to be cautious. He chose his words carefully.

"There is more to it than that. I have a confession to make.

I think of you a great deal. Not just as one professional to another but in a way that makes my heart pound when I see you."

"Oh, dear!" She drew back, feeling the crushing awkwardness of his words.

"Yes, I know it is shocking, and you have already turned me down some years ago."

"But you are married!" Maisie stammered. "I am afraid I can't do what you ask."

Now, it was James who was embarrassed. "Oh, my. You don't know my news! Priscilla divorced me shortly after Christmas. She's already remarried and moved to Chicago. Apparently there was a lot going on in her life that I didn't know about."

"Divorced?" She worked to absorb his words.

"Yes. Our marriage failed, largely because of me. Priscilla and I really had nothing in common, and it was a mistake for us to have married in the first place. I deserved to have her leave me, and I wish her happiness. I was embarrassed and didn't tell anyone in the family until I saw my parents in New York. I'm such an idiot to have assumed you knew. Oh, dear God. I am babbling."

Maisie's cheeks felt hot. She hoped that if this were a dream that she would stay asleep long enough to enjoy it for at least a few minutes more.

James watched her expression and regained his composure. He took both of her hands in his. "What I am asking is if you would allow me to court you properly, Miss Maisie Rosedale. I would like to earn your trust, and if it is at all possible, your affection. I think it only right that I meet your family and discuss the matter with your Uncle Zev. You don't have to answer this minute, but you will think about it, won't you?"

Maisie's eyes filled with tears. She hesitated, but formed his name carefully before she spoke. "James," she smiled. "I don't have to think. I already know. I feel as if my life is beginning all over again. I say, yes, and thank you. My Uncle Zev will find you very impressive, as do I."

57
After the Titanic
April 20, 1913

Everything in Rupert's complicated life came to be divided into just two time periods: before the *Titanic* and after the *Titanic*.

On returning home, due to the immediate public fascination with the tragedy, and outpouring of sympathy for the victims, it seemed that Rupert's survivor status was going to rocket him to international celebrity.

Stunned by grief and perhaps by guilt, the majority of the seven hundred survivors seemed extremely reluctant to speak about their experiences. Rupert, however, played his experience to his advantage and very carefully placed his story among those listeners he thought would be most inclined to see him as something of a hero.

Generally, he told his tale only to very small audiences. Never would he consider accepting an invitation to address a formal gathering, no matter how tempting, for fear of being seen to be vulgar, or worse, seeking glory. No. It was far more effective to let the gossips broadcast his tale through the community in hushed tones over cups of tea and glasses of sherry.

In his discreet talks, Rupert told an incredible story that never failed to keep his audience enthralled. He explained how he had helped Captain Smith and the crew to load women and children into the lifeboats, working furiously to get as many passengers to safety as possible. With the boats all gone, and the bow dipped into the sea, he described how he had scrambled to grab onto the exterior rail on the fantail deck.

"The rail I was clinging to was at the back of the ship, at the extreme end of the after deck. The deck was pulled straight up from the water against the weight of the front of the ship. It shuddered and shrieked in the most terrifying manner as it lurched skyward to an upright position, absolutely perpendicular to the water surface, all the while dragged by the weight of the bow section, which was fighting to break the ship apart.

"There I was, dangling from the rail like a ragdoll as the leviathan stopped and hung motionless for an unworldly moment, when it finally came to rest at its peak, before plunging violently into the black ocean below, with me, now desperately fastened to the rail, clinging for dear life as I rode the wreckage down to the sea."

Rupert would pause at this moment to enjoy the gasp he could expect to hear and would wait until someone spoke to urge him on with his story. He would then tell how he jumped free at the very second before he would have been dragged under the waves to the bottom of the ocean.

"The breath went out of me as I hit that freezing water, and I was instantly submerged by the weight of my buffalo coat soaking up water. I struggled madly to rid myself of the coat so that I could swim to the surface and was left to beat wildly against the water. I swam with all of my might until I was finally able to lift myself into a lifeboat with barely my shirt left to protect me against the cold."

He survived, he told his audience, by rowing non-stop through the night to keep warm, not even feeling the blisters on his hands in the numbing cold of the frigid air.

Rupert would tell the story quietly and deliberately. In parts, he slowed the telling of it to appear reluctant, stopping to pull out his handkerchief. He would touch it to his lips and cough softly into it while his listeners would shake their heads and hope with fervor that he would have more to tell.

Very occasionally, and only if there were women present, he would speak of how he encouraged the others in his lifeboat to sing to keep their spirits up and he would start to sing in a low voice. Usually he liked to sing *Danny Boy* and watch the women weep into their handkerchiefs as his voice strengthened into the phrase "the pipes, the pipes are calling." Only once did he attempt to sing *Amazing Grace* in one of his *Titanic* talks. He caught sight of Mrs. Anderson rolling her eyes as she turned away, and he never sang it again. *Danny Boy* always evoked the correct response.

Inevitably, Rupert would wind up his talk with an analysis of the numbers of the survivors, always including how greatly fortunate it was that three-quarters of the women and more than half of the children were saved. Then he would say how lucky he was that he did not perish, as eighty percent of the men on board the ship had been lost.

"Only seven hundred survivors," he would shake his head again. He was amazed, he would tell them, as he wondered aloud what purpose he was destined to serve for having been spared.

It was an exceptionally powerful performance, and for a time Rupert enjoyed the feeling of being greatly popular.

This golden moment, however, was brief. Three weeks to be exact. When Rupert's dazzling light of fame went out, it went not slowly, as the gradual dimming of the long summer evening on the prairie, but instantly, as the tiny flame on a match extinguished with a puff of breath.

It turned out to be a bit of good reporting in the *Winnipeg Star* that toppled Rupert from his pedestal. Because the paper had a reporter in New York at the American Congressional Inquiry into the Titanic Disaster, many stories were published about the passengers enroute to Manitoba. One such story appeared about the Willows family, accompanied by a photograph of Rupert standing tall with a scarf at his neck and warmly clad in his hat and buffalo coat as he was being helped off of a lifeboat at the side of the *Carpathia*.

Things started to change immediately after the story was published. The invitations to share his story still trickled in, but they were no longer from the right kind of people. A whisper campaign took hold and started to destroy his reputation. He still went to the Manitoba Club, but in the coming months, he lost his seat on City Council, and new business proved hard to attract. The upper class had abandoned him.

By the first anniversary of the sinking, Rupert had lost his power and magnetism. The world had moved on, and no one seemed interested in his opinion any longer.

The final blow came on April 20th, 1913. James and Maisie had come to lunch at Ravenscraig, and James announced that he would be marrying Maisie on the third Sunday in June. Beth was delighted. Rupert remained silent. It was a short visit that ended with excuses from the young couple that they needed to get along to their next stop with their happy news.

Rupert retreated alone to his library and mulled over the matter in silence. He felt that he had reached the crushing end to everything he had tried so hard to achieve in his life. He had never approved of their courtship and was aghast that his son would so belligerently disobey his order to drop the girl. He felt that his whole life was in a shambles, and he didn't like it one bit. He wanted the old way back and despaired that it might never return. He had to take a stand. He summoned Beth for a private discussion, having resolved to attempt to stop the upcoming marriage. Perhaps if he just stated his position, it would slow down all of these awful changes.

She eyed Rupert warily as he began explaining. "I'm sorry, Beth, I can't accept this. I will do anything for you, my love, but this is simply improper, and I cannot give my blessing to James marrying Maisie."

"I am afraid I really can't comprehend your objections, Rupert," Beth responded with starch in her tone. "It is wholly unfair of you to not give them your approval. Let's not even consider the fact that he's a grown man who has already been married and truly doesn't care whether he gets your approval or not. He's going to marry the woman he loves. All that you are going to do is tear this family apart with your attitude."

"Beth, listen to me. Be reasonable. She's Jewish. James is studying with a rabbi with the intention he will also be a Jew, which means you will be the grandmother to Jewish grandchildren! Does none of this concern you?"

"No, Rupert, it doesn't," Beth slammed her hand down as she rose to her feet. "What harm have the Jews ever done me? All my life I have hated Jews. I don't really don't know why I have, but I have. I never thought about it but I can tell you that I am ashamed, Rupert. Deeply ashamed. Perhaps I have been spared death in the disaster to come to this understanding that I really need to question my attitudes."

Rupert put his hand up to stop her but she railed on. "Do

the Jews not believe in one God and is that one God not the same who hears my prayers? I ask you, am I better than a Jew simply because I am not a Jew?"

Beth stared hard at her husband, waiting for an answer.

Rupert sat silently and kept his eyes on the floor, his hands clasped over his crossed legs, his foot bouncing in the air at twice the pace of his rapid heartbeat. "I will be cast out of society," he said pitiably, completely flummoxed by the fact that his wife was capable of such a rant.

"Rupert, stop it! Has it not already occurred to you that the glory days are gone?"

As apt as Beth was to jump to anger in the aftermath of the shipwreck, the effect of the tragedy seemed to have an opposite affect on Rupert. The shouting seemed to have gone out of his character. He seemed distracted and analytical, his swagger gone and his confidence knocked flat. What remained, though, was his determination to regain his position in society.

"Beth, please, come sit." He patted the place next to him on the settee. "I want to explain my feelings to you."

She regarded him cautiously before accepting his invitation. He took her hand and shifted so he could face her and spoke calmly.

"As to the issue of having a Jew in the family, it's not as easy for me, Beth. Quite apart from the fact that it is just not done among people of our standing, you have to understand that I have always had very strong feelings about the Jews. I must say, truly, that I never for a second would have considered hiring Maisie all those years ago, if I had known."

"And how lucky for all of us, Rupert that we didn't know and that we were blessed to have this wonderful girl come into our lives," Beth jumped to her feet and started pacing again.

"Rupert, she has saved my life twice. What more demonstration do you need that she is worthy to be our daughter? I tell you as plainly as I can say it, I do accept Maisie, and I will welcome her into the family whether you attend the wedding or not. I think you should be ashamed of yourself. We were spared death on the *Titanic*, and you are worried about your son's choice of a bride. Really, Rupert. I do hope there will be little Jewish grandchildren to bring us joy in whatever else God has planned for our future. I love Maisie, and I will be proud to call her my daughter."

"Beth, I don't wish for this to sound ridiculous, but the truth is I do admire you. You are far more accepting than I believe I can ever be. I know you think of me as capable of being dishonest, and I admit that even to myself at times. But I cannot extend that dishonesty as far as pretending to accept a Jew into the family."

There was no fight in his tone, nothing more than a calm explanation. "You go to the wedding," he said. "I will do the best I can. I will withdraw my objections to the marriage, but I will not offer my blessings."

Beth turned for the door. "Suit yourself, Rupert."

58
Shabbat

April 17, 1914

Hannah was rushing to get everything ready for Shabbat dinner. It was a special night. Not just because welcoming the Sabbath always made it a special night in the Zigman home, and not just because all of the family and especially the grandchildren would be there. But tonight was special because Isaac was bringing home a date.

At twenty-eight, he was getting a little long in the tooth she thought. Getting married was not such a bad idea. Not that he had actually said anything about getting married, but just to bring someone home meant he thought the family should have a look. He said only that she was someone special. He wouldn't even give her name.

It was always the women that suffer from mystery, Hannah reflected. A woman's mind never lets go of mystery. It's easier to be a man. A man can rest his brain when he stops working. He can think of nothing and be happy because he is thinking of nothing. Just look at her Zev. It would be something if he even remembered that Isaac said he would be bringing a girl to the house.

As for the mystery girl, all that Isaac said was that she was a nurse, a pretty nurse he met when he worked on a story at the hospital. Tonight the table would be set with the good linens and would be extended to stretch from the dining room all the way into the front sitting room. The pretty nurse would eat from Hannah's gold rimmed plates, special for Shabbat. Plates that Zev gave to her as a gift when they opened the new delicatessan. Eighteen people worked in the expanded restaurant, and life was finally easier for the Zigman family.

As always, when Hannah bustled about cooking and making ready the house for Shabbat she considered the many blessings she had. They were blessed because first of all they had their health and their beautiful children. They were blessed also because they had good fortune in business and a comfortable life. Zev didn't have to work so hard now and had time to enjoy other things. Fishing he liked. In the winter, yet. Imagine to make a hole in the ice to go fishing. She shrugged. But he likes it, she thought, shaking her head at the idea. She thought of her warm fur coat and her big sheepskin boots in the basement closet. A gift from Ziporah and Max for her birthday. Now that is how to get through the winter in Winnipeg.

Hannah finished setting the table and counted the places one more time to be sure that she had the right number. With the smell of chicken soup on the stove and brisket in the oven she was filled with contentment. She turned to the big china cabinet in the dining room and reached for the long silver Shabbat candlesticks. They were her mother's candlesticks, the same ones she frantically searched for in the bundles when they had left that dark night long ago. As was her habit, every time she placed them on the table, she whispered a prayer of thanks that her family was safe and happy. With all of the beautiful things they had added to their home, nothing was more precious among her treasures than this pair of candlesticks.

She and her Zev had enjoyed many years of happiness. They had much to be proud of in their children and grandchildren. Ziporah was a wonderful businesswoman, making a great success of the Selkirk Avenue Delicatessen. She was loving and kind and adored by her Max, the tailor and their three smart children. Isaac was a big shot of some kind now with the newspaper. A lawyer he could have been, but he chose, instead, to be with the newspaper. Her hardworking Aaron had his clothing store, and Mendel, now also studying to be a businessman and working with Aaron in the clothing business.

And Maisie. What could she say about Maisie and her husband? The two doctors who were adored by everyone. They were the poorest of her children and the richest at the same time. They turned away no one in need.

The sound of the crying baby, waking from his nap, wrenched her from her thoughts and she rushed to pick up her new grandson. "Irving Willows! It is an opera singer you will be!

Shush now, my *tchochkelah* and let Baba sing to you. Or should I tell you a story before everyone comes to the house? Everything is ready in the kitchen. Let me sit with you my sweet baby boy and sing with you. Lots of stories you will hear at the dinner table. Singing we should start now. Will you sing with Baba?"

She fussed in her accustomed way, changing him and playing and finally sitting in her rocking chair next to the stove, with Irving on her lap.

Hannah sang her favorite lullaby, a song her mother had sung to her when she was little and that she had sung to all of her children.

Tum bala, tum bala, tum balalaika,
tum bala, tum bala, tum balalaika,
tum balalaika, shpil balalaika,
tum balalaika, freylekh zol zain!

The baby reached for her face and gurgled away. Hannah sighed with happiness. They had made it. They were truly alrightniks in the new country.

59
First Class Gentleman

April 19, 1914

By the spring of 1914, Rupert's life had dramatically changed. He still had a business and his family and Ravenscraig, but it was clear that never again would he regain his social standing in Winnipeg.

Rupert's fabricated story of his heroism on the *Titanic* may have hastened the ruin of his reputation, but it was not, strictly speaking, the cause of it. As time passed after the disaster, international public opinion on the male survivors of the *Titanic* had begun to shift against the men who had found their way into the lifeboats—particularly the fifty or so gentlemen of first class. Plainly put, the very fact that they had not gone down with the ship was seen as bad form.

Of course, no one of good breeding would ever say such a thing out loud. Quiet, private commentary was far more appropriate and, indeed, more devastating as the gossips imagined how it was possible that a gentleman would not have given his place to save a woman or a child.

By the second anniversary of the sinking, the newspapers had reported two suicides among the surviving men, and Rupert had the distinct impression there were those at the Manitoba Club who were wondering why he had not yet become the third.

This is how it came to be that Rupert's status as a *Titanic* survivor ultimately killed all of the joy in his life. Beth, for her part, did what she could to jolly him out of his doldrums, but he was just not the same man. After the unpleasant fuss Rupert had made over James marrying Maisie, she found herself wondering what she was fighting to save. It was just too difficult, and there was too little to be gained.

Beth turned her attentions to Emma, who had found emotional healing in having returned to teaching and in her recent passion: the fight to win voting rights for women. Emma was a tireless campaigner, greatly inspired by the leadership of Nellie McClung. Beth slowly came to see the value of the arguments of the suffragists and ultimately pledged her support. Unbeknownst to her practically estranged husband, Beth Biggleswade Willows was helping to finance the movement.

Rupert missed her when Beth stopped paying attention to him but was at a complete loss as to how to improve their relationship. He gave up. Nothing in his life was fun anymore, and Rupert came to realize that his life would never again be as splendid as it once had been. The glory days were truly a thing of the past.

In their place were small pleasures that had grown into matters of great significance in his desire to find comfort in life. Chief among them was his Sunday bath. It had come to be viewed by everyone in the household as a ritual of the highest order. His bath was never rushed. It was an inviolable private time the master of Ravenscraig required above all else. Naturally, he was extremely finicky about the preparations, all of which were entrusted to his faithful man, Chadwick.

Rupert's Sunday bath on April 19, 1914 was no exception.

Chadwick took great pride in his work. Impeccably dressed in his black butler's uniform, he stood next to the tub with a towel over his left arm and a thermometer in his right hand. The clock in the hall struck two, and the butler immediately plunged the thermometer into the water. It was one degree too cool, and he turned the hot water on full force while keeping a sharp eye on the climbing temperature.

By the summer after the *Titanic* disaster, the construction crews in Ravenscraig had completed elaborate renovations Rupert had designed for his personal quarters. The center of his posh apartment was the original ornate bathroom of the master bedroom. This he left completely intact.

The work crews also built a splendid adjoining suite for Mrs. Willows. There was a connecting door between the two bedrooms that had yet to be unlocked. Rupert was not surprised, but he was disappointed.

The butler bowed and slipped quietly from the bathroom. Rupert eased himself into the tub and slid slowly into the steaming water. He breathed deeply and felt the comfort of buoyant bliss, the silky warmth soaking away his tensions as the water lapped lightly against the porcelain-clad sides of the great iron tub. For sixty minutes he would luxuriate, having instructed the household that he was not be disturbed for anything less than a raging fire.

On this particular afternoon, he mulled over the contents of the letter he had received, hand delivered in the morning. He had opened it in the privacy of his library and on reading it, had struck a match and watched the letter burn in his ashtray. He then summoned Chadwick to send an immediate reply stating that he would see the author of the letter at his office on Main Street at ten o'clock that very evening.

The note was from Rupert's father. Ira Volinsky was on his way back to Toronto, apparently having had a bad experience in San Francisco. He wanted money. The man had turned greedy. He stated plainly that only a lot of money would keep him from disclosing the proof he carried of Rupert's true identity as Reuben Volinsky.

Rupert slid deeper into the tub, and his thoughts turned to Dr. McDonnelly. In less than six months it would be the twentieth anniversary of the death of the man who had built Ravenscraig. Poor Dr. McDonnelly, slipping and striking his head on the same bathtub that provided so much pleasure to Rupert Willows. What a terrible end to a fruitful and productive life.

Rupert picked up the handgun he had purchased in Deadwood Gulch and spun the chamber. He kissed the barrel. He caressed it slowly under his nose and breathed in deeply. The steam of the bath rose around him as he brought the pistol to his open lips and touched his tongue to its rounded smoothness. The taste was unexpectedly pleasant.

Rupert's funeral was a solemn and understated affair. Few beyond family chose to attend. Interestingly, Ginger Snooks, the scavenger who was known to run in every civic election was called upon to be a pallbearer. All of the instructions for Rupert's funeral had been neatly spelled out in his will.

His requirements were clear and very specific, as had been everything in Rupert's life. Grenville Doddsworth, his long trusted lawyer and confidant, spoke eloquently and movingly about the loss of his friend and the great contribution that Rupert Willows had made to the City of Winnipeg. Rupert's children were shocked and resolute in their pain-filled silence, their attentions focused entirely on their grief-wracked mother.

Beth was inconsolable. It was the day before the funeral that she had found the love letter Rupert had written to her. He had tucked it into her sewing basket. By the date on the letter, she knew it had been there for several days before he died, and it tore her apart that she had not seen it in time to speak with him about its contents.

Shivering in misery, she sagged against the supporting arms of her sons as she made her way to the graveside ceremony. Beneath her black cloak, the sweet last letter from her Rupert rode lovingly between her breasts.

April 15, 1914

Dearest Beth,

On this very sad anniversary of the tragedy, I feel overwhelmed with a need to tell you how I wish that I had the power to change your feelings for me. I have made a terrible mess of things, and I have only myself to blame.

I miss you terribly. I miss your laugh and the way you used to come to me with your little worries. How easy it was for us, so long ago, pet, when you reached your hand for mine and said you would always love me, no matter what.

I don't know how it all went so wrong, and I am deeply sorry that it did. Know that I cherish you and that if you can find it in your heart to forgive my having pushed you away, as I truly have in these times of darkness, then it would forever be my salvation. I wish to try again.

Would you consider, my darling, the opportunity to travel with me? Might we again go to Europe? This time I would love to take you to Scotland, the birthplace of my dear long departed mother and I should like also to have us visit Ravenscraig Castle, for which our home is named.

Would you come with me, darling Beth? Will you give me one more chance to show you how much I love you?

With deepest affection,

Forever yours,

Rupert

How Beth wished that she had known he was planning to romance her again, to rebuild the life they had known as newlyweds. How was it possible she did not get to her sewing basket in all of those days! The poor darling man. It was all there in his letter and never apparent in his speech. She was bereft with grief.

That the tragedy of his murder should come at the moment when they might have come together was more than she could bear.

The following day, the *Winnipeg Star* published a front page story on the tragic death of Rupert Willows.

Rupert Willows Murdered Last Night
Former Alderman Gunned Down in Office
Body Burned Beyond Recognition
Building Explosion and
Fire cause $80,000 Damage

Winnipeg, April 20, 1914—Police are investigating the murder on Sunday night of longstaning City Councilor Rupert Willows at his office building on Main Street. He is believed to have been shot to death, at close range, prior to an explosion and fire at the office premises.

Shortly before eleven o'clock last night, an explosion ripped through the Main street office of Willows and Sons, igniting a raging conflagration that would quickly overtake the building just north of Bannatyne. Three fire crews worked for more than two hours to bring the fire under control and succeeded in stopping the fire from spreading to the adjacent buildings.

At dawn, police investigators picked through the rubble of the destroyed Willows building and came upon the gruesome discovery of a badly burned body. The police report that the body has been identified as that of Mr. Willows. The medical examiner has declared that the cause of death appears to have resulted from gunshot wounds. Five bullets were found in the chest of the victim, with four having been fired at close range.

Gold Watch Helps Identify Victim

In order to spare the family further suffering, the body was identified with the help of lawyer, Mr. Grenville Doddsworth, KC, who for many years acted as legal counsel and was a close friend of the deceased. Although the body was terribly burned, Mr. Doddsworth was able to positively identify the victim as Mr. Willows by the measured height of the body and more importantly, by the presence of a gold watch that was found clutched in the right hand of the dead man. The watch was inscribed on the back with the words: "To my darling husband on our wedding day, forever in love, Beth."

Robber Suspected to Have Murdered Mr. Willows

Mr. Doddsworth speculated to reporters that a robber may have startled Mr. Willows who was working late in his office on Sunday evening. Mr. Willows was a collector of art and fine goods. Police agree that there is much evidence to point to this being a case of a hold-up that turned deadly and are almost certain that is so.

The cause of the explosion is unknown at this time. Police have made no arrests in the case and appear to not have any leads at this time.

Insurance Will Cover Costs
of Damages and Provide for the Widow

Mr. Doddsworth confirmed that the insurance on the destroyed Willows Block is at a maximum level but that it is too early to know if the family will wish to rebuild the office building. Mr. Alfred Willows, the only son of the deceased who is active in the business, has disclosed to Mr. Doddsworth that he is considering relocating the company to Toronto.

There is also a very large insurance policy to see to the needs of the widow, Mrs. Elizabeth Biggleswade Willows. According to Mr. Doddsworth, she plans to stay in her home, Ravenscraig Hall, for the time being.

The late Mr. Rupert Willows survived the sinking of the Titanic along with his wife and daughter.

60

Letter to Doddsworth

The Carlton Hotel
58 La Croisette
Cannes, France
May 20th, 1914

Mr. G. W. R. Doddsworth
Lindsay Building
228 Notre Dame Avenue
Winnipeg, Manitoba,
Canada

Dear Grenville,

We are enjoying the most delightful weather on the French Riviera and I must say that I am feeling fit and rested as I become accustomed to my new surroundings. I have decided that I will be stopping here at the Carlton Hotel in Cannes for several weeks.

Thank you, Doddsworth, for your discretion and your professionalism. I very much appreciate all of your help in having finessed my new arrangements and identification papers. Your work is, as always, first rate.

You will find an enclosure in this letter with all of the banking information you will require for the new account that has been established for you in Switzerland.

I did receive your letter, and I thank you so much for the news articles on my demise. I do feel somewhat badly that more people did not attend my funeral, but so be it. I'm dreadfully unhappy that Beth took it so hard, but it is rather for the best that things concluded as they did. She was so annoyed and displeased with me by the end of it. She has plenty of money to keep her comfortable and to fund her wretched causes. I know things will work out fine for her. I'm sure all of this dreary business concerning voting rights for women will fill her days. It's so unattractive and unfeminine, wouldn't you agree? Despite my disappointment in the matter, it does appear to be a most powerful movement, and I daresay that the Manitoba women will be the first suffragists on the continent to have their precious voting rights. So be it. I am bloody tired of hearing about it.

I am rather sorry, though, that I will never again see Ravenscraig Hall. We did have our good times there over all those years, I must say. However, I do intend to visit Ravenscraig Castle in Scotland next month. I have always been curious about the ancient place and I understand it is located in a charming little village on the coast.

I am also happy to report that despite all that is behind me, I do feel intensely alive and ready for adventure. I am considering two transatlantic cruises to test my card playing abilities but I expect to be back in France by late fall.

Grenville, we have had a great many positive dealings over the many years we have known each other, and I expect the future will be the same. I sincerely hope that you will want to accept my invitation to visit with me here. I do miss listening to you prattle on about Winnipeg politics.

Let's have a bit of fun, shall we?

I will expect to be the owner of a stunning little villa called Palmerose in Les Issambres by late summer. It is up on the hillside and affords a spectacular view of the coastline villages wrapped around the sea. I will be able to sit in my front garden and watch the sailing vessels arriving at Saint-Tropez. It is also a short ride to Cannes and conveniently within reach of the gambling casinos of Monte Carlo. I'm certain you would find it amusing to visit.

The gambling is splendid, the dining exquisite and the women are ever so enchanting.

Very sincerely,
Reginald J. Wilkesbury

Sandi Krawchenko Altner is the winner of the 2012 Carol Shields Winnipeg Book Award for her first novel, *Ravenscraig*. She enjoyed a distinguished career in television and radio news in Canada before she chose to follow her passion for writing fiction. Sandi was born and raised in Winnipeg, and is very proud of her roots. Her family descended from the first group of Ukrainian speaking pioneers who settled in Manitoba in 1896. A Jew by choice, Sandi celebrated conversion in 2005. She and her husband have two daughters and two happy dogs. Sandi lives, writes, and blogs in Florida.

Follow her posts at www.altnersandi.com.

fiction
Altner, Sandi Krawchenko
Ravenscraig 3

Made in the USA
Lexington, KY
30 May 2013